BOOKS BY CATRIN RUSSELL

The Light of Darkness

The Power of Conviction
The Path of Salvation
The Resurgence of Light
Nefarious Echos - July 2021
Book 5 - September 2021
Book 6 - November 2021

* * *

The Light of Darkness Prequels

Righteous Dawn
The Redeemed

To everyone who stays by my side, hears my constant rambling over characters and their lives, I thank you, from the bottom of my heart. I could never do this without you, my dearest friends and family ♥

THE RESURGENCE OF LIGHT

THE LIGHT OF DARKNESS, BOOK THREE

CATRIN RUSSELL

The final approval for this literary material is granted by the author.

First Edition

Print ISBN: 978-1-949382-70-9

This is a work of fiction. Names, characters, businesses, places, events and incidents are either the products of the author's imagination or used in a fictitious manner. Any resemblance to actual persons, living or dead, or actual events is purely coincidental.

PUBLISHED BY FALLBRANDT PRESS

www.FallbrandtPress.com

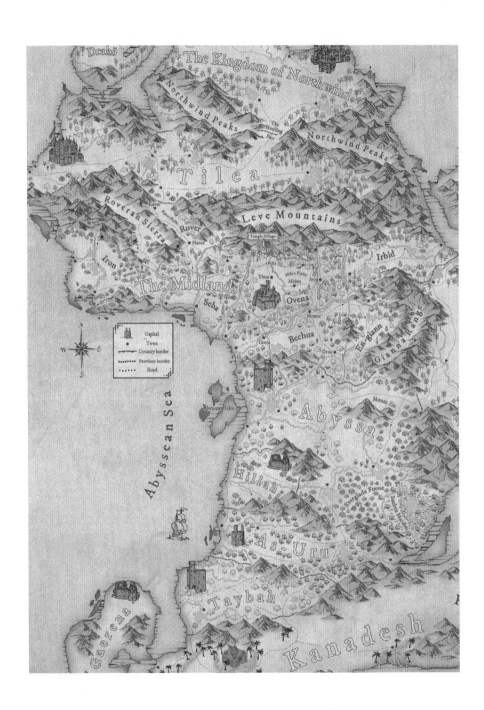

PROLOGUE

The first rays of the sun shone across the sky as the young demon climbed the ladder. He reached the landing above, putting his hand on an iron door handle. With a cleansing breath, he entered a small hut built around a soaring tree.

"I am back, aunt Corliss." He traversed the room, then sat down beside the bed, clutching the woman's hand. She stirred.

She smiled wearily, her eyes barely open as she looked at him. Reaching up, she touched his face, the skin bruised and his left eye badly swollen. "What happened?" she asked. "You have not gotten yourself into trouble again, have you?"

"Oh, no," he said. "Nothing like that." Bending down, he brought up a small basket containing a loaf of bread and some cheese.

"Lee," his aunt sighed. "Don't tell me you have stolen it."

"Of course not, aunt Corliss," he answered. "I... I have learned my lesson. I was given it as payment for helping in the tannery shop." He proceeded to break the bread in half, then grabbed a knife from his belt, slicing the cheese. He helped his aunt get seated before handing her the food.

Corliss released a breath. "I have no appetite today, dear nephew. I am sorry." She gazed down at the bread, a tremor shooting through her under-nourished hands.

Softly, he urged her. "Save it for later, aunt Corliss. Maybe you will feel a bit better then."

"Perhaps," she said.

They sat in silence as the young boy ate the other half of the loaf, the hunger causing him to barely chew the food before swallowing it. He grabbed a small pitcher of water, forced to drink to ease the bread down his throat.

"Have you heard any more of the village?" Corliss asked.

"What about it?"

"Are people to return?"

Lee stood, walking over to the nearby window. He gently tugged at the curtain, looking outside. There was a thick pillar of smoke in the distance, but it was eerily quiet, not a soul roaming the streets. "None has returned, as of yet, aunt Corliss," he replied. "But I am led to believe it should not be long."

She silently nodded. "And... *the Prime*?"

The boy shivered as she mentioned him. "It was a horrible sight," he admitted. "But now, he seems to be... in one's right mind."

1

A WORLD OF DARKNESS

L ilith yawned tiredly. She had yet to retire for the night, and the sun was now rising in the east. With the soft morning light reflected across the Atua river, the serenity of nature was a stark contrast to her immediate surroundings. She watched as another body was carried past her, merely pointing down towards the water.

The shaman had a large funeral pyre burning, only south along the waterways. Corpse after corpse was brought there, thrown over the flames as he performed their last rites. Demon or human made little difference – they all needed to be sent into the afterlife.

Before her, lay the beheaded High Priest, his remains still bathed in his own blood. The body was yet to be removed, but Lilith had not decided what to do with it. His head had been wrapped up in a cloth, placed beside his left shoulder.

She righted her dress, her cold hands white, grasping at the fabric. She had so far counted thirty demons, and nearly fifty priests, slain at her son's feral onslaught.

Ever since the priestess had returned him, they had both slumbered. It had been over twelve hours, and she had yet to see Samael. The demon usually only slept very little, so this was highly unusual, but she knew the feat of slaughtering this amount of people must have severely depleted his strength.

Another body was brought forward, a young woman wearing priestly robes. She looked to be in her late teens, her body slim and her hair dark blond. There were four long gashes along her back, and the woman's belt hung loose, slashed, dragging across the ground. A leather pouch was attached to it, as well as a long row of throwing knives.

"Bring her to the funeral pyre," the Matriarch ordered. She felt the cool air seeping through the layers of her dress, and she brushed her hands across her arms in hopes of staying warm.

Arax soundlessly approached her. "My lady," he said. "Perhaps you should have some rest? I can take over if you wish."

Her tight expression showed she was not fully committed to his suggestion. She rubbed at her eyes, straining as she blinked. "You might be right," she eventually huffed. With her vision momentarily blurred, she saw a towering silhouette round the corner of her house. A black cloak fluttered as he strode across the courtyard.

✶ ✶

Dressed in a layered sleeping gown, the Matriarch was seated on her bed. She tweaked an eyebrow, resting her back against the padded headboard, and scrutinised Samael as he stood before her. The curtains were drawn across the windows, and flames roared in the open fireplace.

"Anaya is yet to awaken?" she asked.

"Yes."

She quietly nodded. "Arax will deal with the rest of the corpses," she continued. "There are not many left, but there is the issue with the High Priest's body. I am yet to decide what to do with it."

Samael was uncomfortable thinking about the man, averting his eyes at the subject.

"My son," Lilith said, leaning forward. She attempted to gain his attention, but he would only glance at her. "You have no blame in this."

The demon cursed. "But I killed all those people!" he flashed.

"No!" she pressed, her tone severe. "You most certainly did *not*. It was all the High Priest's doing. You had no part in it."

4

"It was by *my* hand. I was the one who tore into all those around me, even my own wife!"

The Matriarch offered him an encouraging smile. "You did not do it by your own malicious intent. It was out of your control."

"It matters not in the eyes of our subjects. If they struggled to look at me before, they are completely incapable of it now. They all withdraw as I near." He forced out a breath. "How am I meant to earn their respect if they fear me? One cannot lead by intimidation."

"It is true as you say, but their apprehension of you will lessen in time. Especially as you assume your role as a father for the next Scion Prime. They will see your compassion, Samael."

Forcing a laugh, his arms slacked. "At the moment, that is but a fantasy."

There was a sudden knock at the door, interrupting their conversation.

"Enter," Lilith said.

Arax came through the opening, closing the door behind him. "All the dead have been recovered and placed upon the funeral pyre, my lady."

"Good," she said. "And the body count?"

The manservant rolled out a parchment and held it up in front of him. "Fifty-three priests and thirty-seven panthers," he read. "A total of ninety slain, my lady."

Samael clutched the hair on the top of his head. "I knew it was bad, but I did not expect that," he huffed, the sharpness of his tone tinged with unconcealed anguish.

"The High Priest has been placed in a casket, for the time being, my lady."

"Very well. You are dismissed."

Arax bowed deeply, then left the room.

Lilith peered at her son. "I repeat – you are not to blame. Had Anaya not been able to bring you back, many more would have been killed, yourself included."

"That offers little consolation, mother."

"I can imagine so, yet it does not make it any less true. I would suggest speaking to your Consort about it when she wakes. Perhaps she can give you a bit more peace of mind." She watched him intently, the mention of his wife immediately relaxing his demeanour.

"Yes, maybe so," he admitted in defeat. "I will go check on her soon."

Pulling a knee up, the Matriarch repositioned herself against the headboard. "Speaking of the dead, however," she said. "I am surprised the Priesthood left all of theirs behind."

"I assume they did not want to risk being in my presence after my… feral state."

"Mm, perhaps," she said. "I suppose they had no way of knowing you were back to your senses."

"They do not seem to know much about us demons in general, mother," he said. "I doubt we shall see them any time soon."

"Indeed, the Priesthood is no more. I can only imagine their village now." Bringing her hands together, she paused momentarily. "Tell me, what happened as you turned feral?"

The Prime flinched at the question. "What do you mean?"

"Samael, surely you must realise the importance of this. You are the first to ever re-emerge from such a condition – to return from the dead and eternal damnation. *You have visited hell.* So tell, me; as the feral engulfed you, what did you experience?"

Samael's expression turned grim. "Darkness… only darkness."

"And when Anaya brought you back?"

His eyes flitted as he tried to remember, seeing the scene play out in his head. It had all been as if in a dream, blurry and muted. "Her Light," he eventually said. "I saw her Light. The grip of the feral loosened and I broke free. I ran towards her Light… and her song."

"You ran?"

"Yes. The feral… it-it is everything that the shamans have told us about – warned us about. It is a world completely shrouded in Darkness." He licked his lips, envisioning it, his mouth dry. "You see nothing, hear nothing… you cannot utter a word. As I… lost myself to it, I wasn't even able to move. It was like the feral had me shackled, and Anaya's Light shattered the bonds."

"I see," Lilith said. "She is truly something else, this priestess."

Samael grinned. "Indeed, she is."

Adena and the rest of the surviving priests had reached the edge of the forest. Satisfied they were not followed by panther demons, they gathered at the outskirts of the Midya plains. The female officer believed it to be highly unlikely they were pursued, considering the outcome of the battle, but one could never be too careful. Sentries were stationed as the rest began setting up a makeshift camp.

"Leo," she ordered, turning to the man. "Group everyone up according to the amount of healing they require. We shall obviously start with those most gravely wounded."

"Certainly," he said, quickly heading off to begin the task.

Adena ran a hand across her black hair, gazing up at the skies. The heavens were bright blue, the sun now reaching just above the trees. There was not a cloud in sight, the last of the snow slowly melting away in the warmth.

Clutching her sword in her hands, she brought the blade up before her. It was stained with blood, the liquid drying on the cold metal. She thought back, reciting Ekelon's words in her head: "*On the day of my death, my life shall trickle away as my blood flows along the ground. It will slowly pool underneath the one destined to usher the Priesthood into the brightest of futures.*"

Looking down at herself, Adena watched the bloodied hem. The claret was light in colour, not dark as demonic blood. She knew what it meant, having stood in the High Priest's flowing crimson. But how would she achieve it? The Priesthood had been decimated, and if Anaya was right, then their village would be no more.

Adena attempted to push the thoughts out of her mind, but it was challenging. She had been the only one to follow each of the High Priest's commands, no matter how gruesome. Did that mean she was to continue his work? It made no sense, as the Priesthood had been more than just erroneous in their quest for eradicating demons, so what was the Goddess planning?

Looking around her, Adena's heart sank as men and women slumped to the ground, many of which burst into tears. They attempted to console one another, speaking words of calm, but most questioned the Goddess much like herself.

In all her years with the Priesthood, she had only heard of the Goddess ever communicating directly with the High Priest himself. He was the sole person to ever have received her blessings first-hand, so what did his death truly mean? Were they now forsaken beyond question, by their one and only saviour?

"We have only a few healers available, Adena," Leo said on his return, pulling her out of her anxious thoughts. "But everyone has been told to lend a hand, no matter their proficiency within the arts."

"Good," she replied. "I shall join you shortly."

The remnants of the Priesthood would need to come together and stand firm against all adversities, no matter from where they came, or if their trust in the Goddess faltered. First, they would need to recuperate, then travel west. They needed to find any additional survivors.

Ninety dead. It was hard to even consider having killed ninety innocent people, only due to one man's foolishness. His mother had claimed it had all been out of his control but had it really been so? For the High Priest to turn Samael feral, he needed to be within range, and the demon had most certainly placed himself in his path. It had been the plan all along, only realised because of Samael's overconfidence in his own abilities.

And even if it were true, that he was not to blame, this still did not lessen the burden on his conscience.

It was the second time now that his audacity had set him in harm's way. Adding insult to injury, it had not only risked his own life, but also that of everyone around him, including his own family.

Samael cursed, agitation building within him. His mists started seeping out as he left the Matriarch's house, prompting him to stop on the porch. Looking down, he noticed the fog rolling over the steps beneath him. It felt strange, almost as if his demonic aura was yet again new to him.

The effects of Anaya's enchantment were most likely ebbing out, giving way for his demonic nature as it resurfaced. It was seething within him, waiting to burst out whenever given a chance.

Gritting his teeth, Samael descended the steps. He would need to speak with the priestess and find a way to control it. He felt unsure of what would happen, should he need to assume his demonic form.

The silence had been deafening; the Darkness blinding. With his metamorphosis involuntarily taking place, the experience had shaken Samael to the core. Lost between time and space, he had felt his existence slipping between his fingers. The dread he had seen in Anaya's expression, as he was enveloped in mists, had terrified him.

To then return, to survive the feral, and instead, believe her gone... It had broken him.

For Samael, the two evils seemed interconnected. To be lost to the feral was equal to that of losing the woman he loved. Neither would allow him a peaceful existence, let alone a future worth surviving for. Either would condemn him to reside solely within a world of Darkness.

2

ALLEGIANCE

L eaving a trail of mist in his wake, Samael traversed the courtyard. Demons around him lowered their heads, some even backing away as he neared, clearly frightened of his presence.

Coming around the corner of the Matriarch's house, he followed the path towards his hut. Reaching the slope, he immediately halted, noticing Anaya emerging from their home.

Wearing a white gown, she pushed her hair back behind her shoulders before moving on. She looked up, meeting the demon's gaze. She instantly grabbed hold of her skirt, freeing her feet as she hurried for him. Tears flowed down on her cheeks as she ran into his embrace, Samael circling her waist and lifting her away from the ground.

He felt her tremble while sobbing against his shoulder. Gently caressing her, his hand tenderly brushed across her chestnut hair. He kissed her on the forehead, then stood silently, merely holding her, allowing her time to calm down.

"Samael," she sniffled, clutching on to his dark mantle.

"I am here, Anaya," he said.

Merely nodding, she kept her face buried within the fur of his cloak.

"Where is Aaron?"

"Asleep," she told him. "I just needed to find you."

Samael carefully lowered her to her feet. "I was merely visiting with my mother. I am not to leave you alone."

The priestess clutched his hand, then noticed the mists slowly trickling down his legs. "What is going on?" she asked.

Firmly returning her grasp, the demon looked at her. "Honestly, I do not know. I need your help."

"Come down for me," Anaya said, watching as he knelt before her. She placed her hands on either side of his face, chanting; Light shone around her hands as she delved into his mind.

Within a moment, the priestess frowned. Samael's inner spirit felt unaccustomed and strange. It was not broken, no pieces needing to be replaced. Instead, it seemed fractured, long cracks expanding out everywhere she looked. Reaching out to touch them, she was shocked to find black liquid oozing from the fissures. It stung her fingers, forcing the priestess to pull back. Releasing Samael, she locked her eyes on his.

"What is amiss?" he asked, seeing her troubled expression.

"I… I am not sure," she said. "It might be what remains of the potion, but something is building up inside you. I will need some time to figure out how to deal with it. I would suggest you stay away from assuming your demonic form for the time being."

"I wasn't exactly planning on it anyway," he muttered. "Trust me when I say, I have never been as reluctant to take on the form as I am now." He rose, gazing down at the priestess. "But I would still like to stay in your presence."

Anaya cocked her head. "Are you concerned?"

"Yes. This is as far as I can dampen my aura." The fog still rolled out around them, spreading along the nearby ground.

Bending down, the priestess felt the mists, swirling them with her hand. "It is your regular aura, so at least it has not been distorted. It is only your feral state not quite contained still."

Samael forced a laugh. "*Only?*"

"It is not as bad as it sounds," she said. "As long as you stay in your human form, it will not be released."

"Fine. I trust you."

She allowed their fingers to interlock. "Let us fetch Aaron and sit down for a meal. I will need to eat if I am to gain enough strength to help you."

"You are right," he said. "I will come with you."

Adena's head spun, and she was forced to sit. She had no power left to stand as she finished healing the wounded. Some were still in need of additional help, but at least none were actively bleeding any longer. It was past noon, and the sun was high in the sky, offering a comfortable heat in the cold air.

With very few horses available, the priests would have to leave on foot. Most had not eaten since the previous day, and it would be close to a two-day march back to the Temple village, were they to stop along the way. The amount of wounded meant they would be lucky if they only needed to halt once.

Leo came to her side. "What are your next orders, Adena?"

Lying back on the wet ground, she merely shrugged. "I have none," she admitted. "I only wish to rest for a while."

"That is understandable, yet we need to decide what to do. Should we head west?"

"It is our only option. I know Anaya said the village was under attack, but even so, it is our best bet."

"Aye," Leo said, surveying the expanses of the Midya plains. His eyes narrowed as he noticed a faint shadow over the horizon. It was moving towards them, the mass reminiscent of a large group of people. "Adena, look."

The female officer seated herself again, peering in the direction of where Leo was pointing. The oncoming crew seemed to consist of both men and women, some mounted on horses, and others travelling on foot. Adena immediately rose. "Do you… think it might be the rest?"

"Perhaps," he said. He turned towards a nearby campfire, around which sat several priests. "Perry, have all able-bodied ready their arms, in case they are hostile."

"Yes, sir." The archer removed himself from the blaze, the rest standing up, clutching their weapons.

As the distant group closed in, Adena recognised Edric on his massive stallion, his arms curled around Vixen who sat before him. Next to them, walked a burly man with blond hair, wearing heavy armour. "Kaedin!" she called, running to meet them.

"Hail, Adena," the former Knight greeted her. "How do you fare?"

"I was about to ask you the same." She scrutinised the meagre party in front of her. "Where are the rest?" There was a moment of silence before she heard sobbing in the back.

"With Edric's group we are thirty-two," Kaedin said. "And that is all." He took a glimpse across her shoulder. "And you do not look to be much more."

"No, I'm afraid not," she said. "Come, let's get you all settled, and we shall speak of... what transpired."

✴ ✴

"Ekelon is dead?" Edric asked.

"Yes," Adena grimly stated. "I am not sure why he did not remove himself from the Prime's path. Perhaps he got complacent in his own abilities... or this was the outcome he had hoped for, considering he most likely assumed the Prime would eliminate the whole tribe."

"And the Priesthood." Kaedin cursed, then spat on the ground. "Damned man went mad! But Anaya managed to thwart the demon's rampage?"

"She did, but we ran before the dust even settled. We were not going to stick around and wait for the panthers to have their revenge. The Prime killed almost as many of them as it did us."

Leaning onto his legs, Kaedin viewed those around him. The Senior Priests were all gathered, as well as Vixen, Lenda and Eden. He fixed his gaze on the young healer. "Tell me, did you all orchestrate Anaya's disappearance?"

Her eyes darted, to both Edric and Vixen. An abrupt peep left her mouth, but there was no answer.

"You might as well be truthful," he continued. "We are not to flog anyone any longer."

Edric met his gaze. "We did indeed rescue Anaya. We all know Ekelon would have killed her, as well as her son."

"But what about the demonic influence?" Adena stressed. "Why would she even have fallen in love with a demon, to begin with?"

Lenda shook her head. "If anyone was being influenced, it was the Prime. You should have seen him as they reunited. He seemed to have been in shambles without her. He had no influence on her, the way we were led to believe."

"I must say I am not surprised," Adena sighed. "The way the panthers held back. They could have easily overrun us, but they allowed us to leave."

"What about Anaya then?" Lenda asked. "Was she alright?"

The female officer rubbed at her temple, looking at the young girl. "I cannot say for certain," she said. "Last I saw her... she lay unmoving on the Prime."

Standing up, the healer's features tightened. "I need to see her," she proclaimed.

Eden instantly grabbed hold of her dress. "No, Lenda. We can't go there."

Pulling herself free, she glared at the man. "She is my best friend! If she is injured, and I have a chance to save her, then I will!" Lifting the hem of her skirt, she bolted off toward the woods. Her husband grabbed his spear, sprinting into a fast pursuit.

Edric cursed. "You four stay here." Retrieving the arrows out of Leo's quiver, he placed them into his own, then whistled for his horse.

"Humans!"

The word echoed outside the Matriarch's home. Grabbing his cloak, Samael flicked it across his shoulders, then headed for the door. Anaya and Lilith hurried after him, stopping on the front porch. Guards quickly fanned out around them.

"Stay your attack," the Matriarch ordered. "I wish to hear them."

A large horse came up the hill, the rider clutching a readied bow. Beneath him walked another man, also armed, and a young girl.

"Put down your weapons!" Lilith demanded. "If you wish to live!"

With a growing smile, Anaya instantly recognised the small group. She descended the steps, taking off running across the courtyard.

Racing after her, Samael reached out and grabbed her. His mists swirled around them as her feet came off the ground.

"Let me go, Samael!" she said, squirming to free herself.

Baring his fangs, he growled. "I do not trust them!"

"They *saved* me! Now, let me go!"

An arrow hissed passed the demon's head, the rider's bow left empty. Edric reached across to his quiver, then placed another shaft on his finger. "Do as she says, or I will shoot you!" he threatened.

Smoke immediately billowed around the couple, a menacing rumble bursting from Samael.

"I do not need your help, Edric!" Anaya snapped. "Now, stand down!" She pushed an elbow into her husband's stomach, the demon finally releasing her. Turning around, she locked eyes with him. "You need to be able to trust my judgement, Samael." She could see him tense, but he said nothing. Reaching up, she placed a soft hand on his cheek.

With the mists receding, he averted his gaze.

The priestess barely had time to turn before Lenda darted into her embrace.

"Oh, I thought you might have been injured, dearest sister," the healer said. "I came as soon as I heard what had happened."

Stepping back, Anaya retained a grip over the girl's shoulders. "What about the rest? And Vixen? Did you all make it?"

Her lower lip trembled, the young healer's eyes welling up. "Kaedin managed to amass enough priests to free us, Vixen included, but most perished as the demons attacked."

"How… how many are left?"

Edric dismounted, walking up to them. "Currently, we have sixty-nine survivors in total. Kaedin, Adena and Leo are camped with them along the Midya plains. Well… at least sitting around some fires. We have literally nothing left."

Panthers gathered around them as the Matriarch approached. "Are you representatives from the Priesthood?" she inquired.

The male officer glanced at Anaya, but she merely ushered him on. "I, eh… I am." He cleared his throat. "I am Senior Priest Edric Ramsey."

"Good. I would like to speak with you." Lilith turned on her heel, striding across the courtyard. Without so much as looking back, she repeated her request. "What are you waiting for? Come inside."

Samael stared at her. "You can't be serious!" he snarled, but the woman had already entered her house. With his mists increasing, he felt a touch to his hand.

"Let us go inside and see what she wants," Anaya said. "These people are no threat." She turned to the priests. "Just leave your weapons outside."

✶ ✶

A servant sat crouched in front of the fireplace, adding logs to the dying flames. It was already warm in the entrance hall, but the Matriarch had called for it to be done, nonetheless. As tiny embers rose with the smoke, the attendant left, curtsying as she hurried past Lilith. The woman sat on her daybed, with her arms folded over her chest. Arax stood behind her, and Samael and Anaya to her right. The walls were lined with her guards.

"What is your purpose in coming here, priests?" she asked.

Edric felt a drop of sweat trickle down his neck. "We... came to see Anaya."

The Matriarch lowered her head, studying him. "What business have you with the *Scion Prime Consort*?"

Unsure what she even meant by the name, Edric quickly looked at the priestess. "We request an audience with her."

"I see." With a hand on her daybed, she turned to Anaya. "The request is granted, as long as you allow it."

"I do," she replied but immediately heard a low gnarl behind her. Mists swirled around her feet, so she reached back, clutching hold of Samael's hand. He instantly quieted down with the contact.

"Very well," Lilith said, rolling her hand to gesture Edric into speaking. "We have not all day, priest. Get on with it."

"We only wished to know of Anaya's wellbeing," he said.

"She is in good health, as you can see." Pressing her lips flat, the Matriarch paused for a moment. "Now, tell me what is left of the Priesthood, or I shall not allow you safe passage out of this village."

Hooves clapped in the distance, gaining Kaedin's attention. He squinted, attempting to discern the source. As the grey horse flashed between the trees, it could not be misinterpreted. Edric was returning.

The stallion sharply halted before the other officers; patches of grass sent flicking with the manoeuvre. Edric's expression was wild, staring at them.

"What on earth is going on?" Vixen asked, straining to push herself up onto her elbows. She had laid down beside the fire, wrapped in a blanket and given water and food from the little provisions the Priesthood had available. "You look as if you have seen a ghost."

"Gather everyone," he said. "We need to hurry back to the panther tribe. The Matriarch has offered us refuge."

Adena rose, her breath catching. She began to mentally run through the situation, struck by disbelief. "There is no way she would do that without ulterior motives. What does she want in return?"

"You are right," he admitted. "But I believe they are in our own interest, should we wish to divert from the path paved by Ekelon."

"What if it's a trap?" she questioned.

Edric glared at her. "You honestly believe Anaya would allow us to walk straight into a trap? She warned us of the attack on our village!"

Adena expelled a breath. "You might be right, and it is probably our only chance. Either way, we are a day's march away from anything. We won't make it long without supplies."

Kaedin heaved himself onto his feet. "Better get going then," he said. "We don't have much to lose."

Samael stood before his mother, his expression overcome with incredulity. "You are to *what*?"

"To offer them refuge," she repeated. "It plays perfectly into my hand."

"After all they have done? Coming here, attacking us? Turning me *feral*? Attempting to *murder* Anaya and our son? *Killing* my father? Have you lost your senses?"

"I have not," she calmly stated. "The one who caused all that is dead. We both know the High Priest was the sole ruler within the Priesthood. With him eliminated, I see a chance to influence their powers. Powers which we have now seen first-hand." Her eyes momentarily shifted to Anaya.

"You mean to return a demon from a feral state?" she asked.

"Indeed. And not only a demon. A *Prime* at that. With the Priesthood on our side, we can truly make an impact on demonkind, as well as on humans. This is a chance I am not to pass up, only due to old grudges."

With the continued trickle of Samael's mists, he stood silent.

"Good. Now, Samael, I would have you prepare the area west of my house. It will be more favourable with the lesser incline. The Priesthood will not turn this offer down. Anaya stays in the courtyard and awaits their arrival. Bring the male officer back, as well as the one highest ranking. The others can focus on setting up camp, and I shall call for a conference with all of them later tonight."

The streets inside the panther village were covered in blood, but there were no corpses in sight. Smoke billowed to the east, and demons stood watching as the surviving priests quietly passed by. They led whatever horses they had, Vixen riding on Edric's stallion, heading towards the Matriarch's house.

Reaching the courtyard, the officers found Anaya standing alone. She was at the top of the front steps of the grand home, offering them a warm smile as they approached. "Welcome to the Fahd village," she said. "We are to offer you refuge on the order of the Matriarch of the Panther Tribe."

Edric instantly came forward, finally able to embrace her. He held her tightly, planting a kiss to her forehead. Stepping back, he allowed for Kaedin to greet her.

"You look well, lass," he said. "Gladdens me to see you in good spirits."

Anaya nodded, exchanging a brief hug with the man, then looked past them, at Adena and Leo. "The Matriarch wishes to see Edric and the highest-ranking, which would be you, Adena."

The woman stared at her, unable to utter a word. Her conscience clawed at her, knowing all she had caused.

Descending the steps, the priestess joined hands with her. "It will all be alright, Adena."

Droplets rolled down the woman's face as she held her gaze. "I am so sorry, Anaya. How am I ever meant to repent for my sins?"

Gently brushing the tears away, Anaya merely smiled at her. "The Goddess shall see your resolve, sister. She knows, and She is forgiving. You stood in the blood of our High Priest, and as such, you stand to lead the Priesthood into the most honourable of futures." Anaya paused, regarding those around her. "Kaedin and Leo, you lead the priests to the field west of here, where you will be supplied with tents and other essentials. Make campfires ready for food within the hour. Adena and Edric, you follow me."

3

A NEW YEAR

The sun was setting, yet the area outside the Matriarch's grand house was alive with people. Several fires were burning, and the grounds were swamped with humans and demons alike.

Standing in one of her spare bedrooms, Lilith inspected the makeshift camp through one of the windows. "Who is the man in armour?" she asked.

"That is Senior Priest Kaedin Reed, my lady," Anaya said. "He is the only one to ever wear that type of gear. He was originally a Royal Knight."

"Interesting. Master Reed may very well prove a great benefit as we move forward. And the others?"

"Next to him, the man with ginger hair, is Senior Priest Leo Blythe. Adena and Edric you have already met. The rest are mainly fully trained priests, a handful of Junior rank, then a few disciples."

"I see. And this is all that is left of the Priesthood?" Receiving no answer, the Matriarch turned, finding the priestess quietly crying. "Oh, Anaya," she whispered, swiftly embracing her.

She sobbed on Lilith's shoulder, desperately holding on to her.

"There, there, child. I am truly sorry for everything, and that we were unable to see a different ending to all of this. The High Priest was much deluded."

Attempting to calm herself, Anaya nodded, then took a deep breath. "The Priesthood has been all... I have ever known. Ekelon was like... a father to me."

Lilith held her hand in both of hers. "I know it is but a small comfort knowing that we now have a chance at a new beginning."

"A new beginning?"

"Yes. As the one prophesied as *the Salvation,* you are destined to *'rejuvenate the thousand-year divide'.* I am keen to believe it is meant to involve the Priesthood, hence why I offer them sanctuary. We shall not forsake them, Anaya. I promise you this."

Wiping her tears away, the priestess smiled. "You have no idea how happy I am to hear it, my lady. Although, I do believe you will have to explain this prophecy more in-depth. I am yet to understand it myself."

Lilith patted the back of her hand. "Do not worry. We will have plenty of time to go through silly old religious texts and traditions, but for now, we need to focus on the task at hand. We shall invite the officers for a meeting after dinner and discuss how to proceed."

"Is it fine if I also invite a friend and her husband? I would like for them to know what is going on, considering they were the main instigators of my release."

"I assume you mean the young girl and the man with the spear. That is fine. They will all be told the meeting is private, so it makes little difference." Walking up to the bed, the Matriarch felt the mattress, pressing it down. "It should do. I shall have Master Ramsey stay here with his mate. I am not to have a woman with child stay outside in the cold."

Anaya's grin widened. "They shall be elated to be offered such accommodations, my lady."

Tents had been erected across the field, the encampment forming a tiny settlement in the Matriarch's gardens. It was a generous area, allowing the priests to allocate space for both gatherings and combat practice. Moving aside the front overlap to his shelter, Kaedin entered his temporary home. He began to finally remove his armour, loosening the straps between the metal plates. As it all laid piled up in a corner, he pulled his trousers down, rubbing at his exposed leg. A wide bruise was visible on his thigh, yet he breathed a sigh of relief, having worn the heavy equipment for much longer than usual. He had already placed his sword and shield away from the entrance of his tent since the priests were currently not allowed to be armed. It was understandable, considering all that had happened, and their indisputable career of demon-hunting.

Kaedin felt intrigued by the proposal of the leader of the panther demons, but he reserved judgement until their meeting had been held. Either way, this was the Priesthood's only chance at survival. The man did not worry about his own future, as he could always return to serve under the King. Instead, it was all those who had joined the Priesthood after him, the trained priests, he felt concerned for. Most of them had nothing outside the Temple village. No home, no family, and no trade to support themselves with.

The Priesthood had fast become a place for redemption, where those who had nothing and were nothing, could finally make something out of their lives. Most would, therefore, be very grateful for the Goddess' gifts and Her forgiveness, which thankfully still rang true amongst those left alive after their encounter with the Prime. Kaedin had heard only some words of doubt in and around the camp, but the main question was how the officers would proceed if the remaining priests were willing to stay within a revived congregation.

Rubbing his chin, Kaedin contemplated the options. Either they would stay and give the Priesthood a second chance, or they would leave, disbanding it for good.

"Kaedin." The call was heard from outside. He recognised the voice as Adena's.

"I will be with you shortly," he answered. Without any clothing to change into, his grey woollen trousers and his white shirt would have to suffice, despite the top suffering from a rip along the neckline, and bloodstains over most of the chest and back. It was a disgrace to be dressed in this manner, meeting with those who were most likely regarded as nobles amongst demons. He grabbed a cloth he had been supplied, rubbing it over his face and hands, removing as much dirt as he could. It wouldn't get any better than this. Standing up, he exited the tent.

"We have been summoned," Adena said. "It is for the officers, as well as Lenda, Eden and Anna."

Kaedin smirked. "Probably by Anaya's request. We shall not keep them waiting."

✶✶

The door briskly opened to the Matriarch's dining room. Arax emerged, motioning for those behind him to enter as he settled down behind Lilith. She was seated at the end of the table, with Anaya and Samael along the far side. They were silent as the members of the Priesthood trailed through. First Adena, Kaedin and Leo, followed by Edric and Vixen, then Lenda and Eden.

"Welcome; have a seat," Lilith instructed, regarding each of them attentively as they immediately complied. "I have summoned all of you to go over the plans for your organisation."

Adena audibly sighed. "Is there anything to even plan for?" she asked. "Everything is lost. And to add insult to injury, we have been terribly ill-advised, myself more than most."

With intense focus, Lilith fixed her gaze on the woman. "First of all, I am the Matriarch and should be referred to as such. I have been lenient enough about this since you arrived, but I will be so no longer. I am royalty amongst demons, so you'd better show respect. Second, there is no such thing as everything being lost. You have over sixty strong out there. Your village may have been ruined, but that is only material damage."

Her face red, the female officer sunk in her chair. "My deepest apologies, your Highness," she said. "And you are right."

"Of course, I am. Now, I would like for you all to decide amongst yourselves who is to lead the Priesthood going forward. As I do not know anyone, except Anaya, I do not feel competent enough for the task."

"That would be you, Adena," Kaedin said. "Being the highest-ranking officer."

"Yes, but…" She scraped a hand over her face. "To be honest, I feel lost right now."

He offered her a comforting smile. "Do not worry. We all feel the same. It will get better in time."

Adena nodded, then locked eyes with the Matriarch. "I suppose I will be the leader, your Highness."

"Excellent. Then who are to be the officers?"

"That would be me, my lady," Kaedin said, then looked at Edric.

"Yes, that goes for me as well," he replied.

"And me," Leo proclaimed.

Lilith clasped her hands on the table. "Good. We might need additional officers as we move forward, but it will do for now."

"What about Anaya?" Edric inquired.

"She will be unavailable. She is to be tutored for leading the Panther tribe."

Everyone around the table seemed confused at the statement. They looked at each other but said nothing.

"Samael, whom you have all come to know, is the heir of the throne." The Matriarch leaned forward, a content expression spreading on her face as she looked at the couple. "As married, she will be staying here with us, as well as their son."

Lenda's eyes widened. "You have married?" she exclaimed.

Anaya blushed, grasping Samael's hand. "Yes," she said.

"But when?" the young healer asked.

"The eve of the Winter Solstice."

Kaedin chuckled. "I won't be asking you how married life's treating you then."

Snarling, Samael glared at him, the building rumble sending the man into instant silence.

Kaedin held his hand up in surrender. "No offence, sir. I am only attempting some banter," he explained.

The demon was about to speak when Anaya tugged at his hand.

"It is alright," she said. "He means well, my love."

Crossing his arms, Samael leaned back. "Fine," he mumbled.

Lilith smiled, watching them. "They have indeed married, and a fierce couple they have become. I am very pleased with the union, despite the unconventional choice of mate for my son." Pressing a finger down on the table, her features hardened. "I will make it clear to all those gathered here, that I intend for them to inherit the Patriarchy of the Panther tribe, thus making Anaya the next Matriarch. Or *Queen*, if you will. She is free to attend conferences with yourselves, but she cannot be presumed to take on sole responsibility for designated areas within the Priesthood."

Adena acknowledged her words but remained silent.

"Now," the Matriarch continued. "There will have to be obvious changes within the Priesthood, where I wish for a collaboration to be initiated between humans and demons. It will be the first of its kind, and as such it will most likely be a steep learning curve, and slow going to entice other demons to join, but we shall manage in due time." She paused, awaiting any questions from the visitors but continued as they all remained quiet. "I plan for us panthers to be the first to form an allegiance with the Priesthood. It is still a work in progress, but I intend for it to include sharing intelligence and resources, as well as functioning as a peacemaker between our individual races. You will thus continue to persecute those who do not abide by the laws of society, only now including both humans and demons alike."

"We are to act as law enforcement, my lady?" Kaedin asked.

"In a way, yes. It is only a suggestion, as of yet. We will need to request an audience with your King in order to come to an agreement." Lilith peered at him intently. "It is also of utmost importance that we have full insight into the Priesthood's experiments and development when it comes to the usage of your Light. Anaya's ability to push back the feral within my own son has piqued my interest in your magic."

"Not to be rude, but what do you offer in return, my lady?" the former Knight countered.

The Matriarch grinned. "First, refuge. Second, to retake your village. And third, that which I have already mentioned: unity, of intelligence and resources."

The man looked at the other Senior Priests. "Should we take a vote? I am inclined to accept their offer."

"I am for," Edric agreed.

"And I," Leo said.

Adena watched them in silence, then returned her attention to the Matriarch. "I also agree to your terms, your Highness."

"Splendid. I shall have all the information drawn up in writing. For now, I suggest you get comfortable in your tents, for it might take a while before we can clear your village, as we do not want to start by adding demons to our list of enemies. The new year is to be celebrated in the coming week, after which we will meet again to see to our progress." She turned towards Arax. "As soon as the villagers return, I want the council to be summoned. All demons must be aware of their refuge and acknowledge that they should be treated as equals."

The manservant bowed deeply. "As you wish, my lady."

The week that followed brought fair weather. The temperatures allowed for the remaining snow to melt, but the grounds across the panther settlement were still wet.

As the demons returned, the Matriarch met with the village council. They reluctantly accepted her change of heart towards humans, receiving orders of treating them as any other inhabitant. Lilith had spoken of the same reasons as with Samael; the priestess ability to thwart the feral, and how this might affect demonkind in the future.

However, the priests mainly kept to themselves, attempting to be as self-sufficient as possible. Edric and a few others were often out hunting or fishing to provide food.

Benjamin had worked tirelessly to produce clothing for the humans, after directives from Anaya. She knew they would never ask, so she had gone ahead on her own. Once delivered, it was gratefully received, the garments quickly handed out amongst everyone in their camp.

Vixen's contractions had lessened as she was given bed rest, with Lenda often checking on her. The baby was fine, and the heartbeat strong. They only hoped for it to remain within the womb for the rest of the parturiency.

Arax slowly traversed the human campsite. He could feel the stares, most likely the same as what the humans experienced whenever they stepped outside their designated area. He approached Adena's tent. The front canvas was tied to the side, the female officer visible within. "Excuse me, ma'am," he said. "The Matriarch is summoning you and your officers for a brief meeting."

"Very well. We will attend within a moment. You may leave."

The man bowed, then walked back across the encampment.

Adena hurried around the camp, the gathered officers soon striding towards the Matriarch's house.

"What is this about?" Kaedin inquired.

"I do not know," she admitted. "But her servant seemed in good spirits, so hopefully it is only a routine conference."

Walking inside, they found Edric already present.

"Welcome, Senior Priests," Lilith said as they soon stood in a line before her. She turned towards Arax. "Make sure no one enters as it is a private meeting."

"Yes, my lady." The manservant ushered a maid out as he left, closing the door behind him.

"How fare the survivors of the Priesthood?" she asked the four officers.

"As well as could be expected, your Highness," Adena replied. "We still lack much of our supplies, but we will make do with what we have."

"Mm. I see you have received fresh clothing at least." She especially eyed Kaedin. "You look much more presentable when not covered in blood," she told him.

"Aye, my lady," he answered. "I apologise for my previous appearance."

"It matters not," she said. "Now, to the reason I summoned you. I am to host a party in celebrations of the New Year tomorrow evening. Should our... *mutual understanding* persist, it shall be the day used to honour our alliance. Therefore, I am obviously to invite all of you to attend. I understand that you might not have the appropriate attire, but your presence would be of benefit, nonetheless."

"We would be honoured, your Highness," Adena said, lowering her head.

"Yes, well. We must move forward at a steady pace to show we are serious in our intentions." The Matriarch paused for a moment. "For our next meeting, I would require a drawn structure of the Priesthood – you have a renewed one, I assume? And as for the name, you are to keep it, yes?"

Adena winced at the question, blinking through an empty stare. Her mouth opened, yet no time was given for answers.

"The foundations for it would have to change to equal it; I suppose," Lilith went on. "Perhaps, moving towards a more democratic organisation?" Again, the Matriarch's speech allowed for neither replies nor arguments. "I would suggest a new ranking system, as well as creating a joint council between humans and demons. A proposal for this would be best served next week."

Clutching her own hands, Adena wrung them red. She had a feeling this was the outcome of the partnership with the demons, but it all felt overwhelmingly soon. The Matriarch's suggestions were sound, however, and they were most definitely worth pursuing.

Adena moistened her lips. It was time to step up. She could not leave her Priesthood without the guidance of a dependable leader, especially not in a time such as this. "Yes, my lady," she eventually replied.

Lilith nodded, then steepled her hands on her lap. "Do any of you have any questions?"

The female officer took a deep breath, readying herself to ask what had been on her mind ever since they returned to the panther village. "What... happened to our fallen?"

The Matriarch's expression softened. "They were all given their last rites and placed upon a funeral pyre, their ashes spread in the winter breeze. All except your High Priest."

Everyone stood silently, watching her, waiting for her to continue.

"He has been buried in an unmarked grave, to be devoured by the earth. The Spirits shall dissolve his flesh, and his soul will be locked away, thus, never to be released through to the afterlife."

Adena noticeably swallowed but kept quiet. Lilith's words of damnation were not unlike those of the Priesthood, where one's only chance to reach the Goddess was through cremation and the subsequent release of one's soul. To be buried in such a shameful manner was a certain way to never achieve salvation. Ekelon would be doomed to an eternity in the darkness of Hell.

"The man caused enough problems in this world, to be given a chance to wreak havoc upon the next. If there are no more questions, you are all dismissed."

The Senior Priests all bowed in reverence, then turned to leave the building.

"Master Reed," Lilith unexpectedly added, halting Kaedin. "Allow me a moment with yourself."

"Aye, my lady," he said, returning to stand before her. "What can I do for you?"

"I am merely curious," she said. "Tell me why you chose not to kill demons within settlements."

The man's brow lowered; he was unsure of the purpose of her inquiry.

Undeterred, she pressed him. "Answer the question, Master Reed."

"It is simple, your Highness. No matter the adversary, I am not to punish civilians merely for being associated with them. Culling entire generations has never been a successful strategy when conquering an enemy; it is morally appalling to even entertain the thought. The choice was also a matter of conscience. I told the High Priest then, as I tell you now, that I would not – under any circumstance – bloody my sword on innocent women and children."

Lilith's lips briefly curled in the hint of a smile. "Very good. You may leave."

With his raven hair flowing down his shoulders, Samael slumped to the bed. He looked at Anaya, enjoying the sight of her beauty. She was dressed in a long viridian gown, her skirt flaring out along the floor.

Turning around, the priestess met his gaze. He was wearing a pair of black leather trousers and a matching shirt. "You look nice," she said.

Samael looked down, dispirited, watching as his mists trickled over the side of the bed.

"I will perform another session before we leave," she continued. "Perhaps it will reduce them for the evening."

Samael quietly nodded as she neared. With her hands flanking his face, he closed his eyes.

Anaya began her enchantment, Light instantly enveloping the couple. She saw the cracks within his mind, and the black liquid seeping out from them. She had managed to stem and heal several, but many more remained. For each crevice to fuse, vast amounts of her spiritual powers were consumed. She slowly worked her way down, evaporating the fluid.

She performed her treatments daily, often ending up sleeping until midmorning to recover from the strenuous spellcasting. Taking care of Aaron, as well as studying the ways of demonkind, was straining on her body. Fatigue was slowly building, yet she had to stay strong.

A dull whirr sounded from the demon. He cursed, opening his eyes. "It is as if I have no control over my own body anymore."

"I like that sound though," Anaya said. "It soothes me."

"Good at least one of us enjoys it," he tonelessly stated.

"Better than nothing, I suppose. Now, let me concentrate. I am soon finished with this one." With a final push, the taint was cleared, and another crack sealed. The priestess staggered, the demon instantly embracing her.

"Perhaps, we should stay in for the night," he said.

Nestling into his lap, she leaned her head against his chest. "No, we need to be seen, but I shan't be long. Aaron will not allow it anyway."

They looked at their son, the sleeping baby lying in his crib.

"As long as you are alright. I am not to have you pass out from exhaustion."

"I will be fine," she said, then pinched hold of his shirt, moving the fabric. There were no traces of his demonic mist coming through. "And you shall be aura-free for the evening."

Samael smirked. "Yes. Thank you, but I will still stay with you."

✸ ✸

The bonfire was lit in the courtyard, the entire space packed with people. A large feast had been prepared, free for all to have their fill from. Demons and humans were still mainly separate, grouping up on either side of the cobbled surface. Tables had been placed around the edges of the courtyard, and a live band was playing in the background.

The Matriarch's home was designated for those of higher birth, as well as the officers within the Priesthood. Lilith was seated on her daybed, cradling a glass of red wine. She seemed pleased as her son and his Consort entered the room. "Good you could join us," she said. "I would suggest you make yourself acquainted with the priests, Samael."

The Prime had yet to spend any time with them, so far only staying in

Anaya's company. He gave his mother a dissatisfied look but refrained from speaking.

"There will be enough time for that," the priestess said. "Since we intend for a lengthy collaboration with them."

"Very true, my dear," the Matriarch granted.

"Anaya!" Edric called, having spotted her. He was sitting alongside the other Senior Priests, at a table further down the room. "Come, have a seat."

The priestess bowed before Lilith. "Excuse me, my lady."

The older woman merely motioned her off with her hand, then took another sip of wine.

Walking across to the priests, Samael was close behind Anaya, stopping just short of her as they arrived at the table.

"A bit of a stalker you've got there," Kaedin pointed out.

Samael's already vexed expression grew further agitated.

"There are reasons for that, brother. I am yet to take on a manservant of my own, and Samael is obligated to act as my protection until such a time." The priestess knew it was not the complete truth, but it was more than enough as a reason for her husband's closeness. Sitting down, she was instantly served a glass of wine.

"Why don't you sit down?" the male officer continued, looking at the demon.

"I am fine standing."

Kaedin shrugged. "Then, by all means."

Anaya leaned towards the former Knight. "With Samael being the *Scion Prime*, you are quite rude to him," she whispered. "Remember he has the same social standing as a Prince."

Kaedin immediately rose. "Terribly sorry, your Highness," he said. "Allow us time to get used to the titles and standings within your social system. Should we stand in your presence?"

"Your apology is accepted," Samael replied. "And no, there is no need. I may come off as unapproachable, but I am not a monster."

"Never thought you were," Kaedin said, sitting back down. "For you to court someone like Anaya, you must be both caring and courageous. The union in itself speaks volumes of your character. You need not explain yourself."

A grin spread across the demon's face with the compliment. "Thank you," he said, then felt the priestess clutch his hand.

"He is indeed what you say he is," she concurred. "Since we have now all been introduced, we might as well enjoy the evening together."

4

NINE-FINGERS

Rain. Blasted rain. As if the darkness wasn't enough, then nature was to force the cold and wet upon him. Trekking along the muddy road, the man looked down at his black outfit. Had it not been for his thick cloak, his clothing would have been further soaked.

The wind picked up, the downpour whipping against his face. Pulling his hood further down, he strode on. The town was close, lights shining in the distance.

Reaching the outskirts of the settlement, the man surveyed the nearby buildings. The rain was becoming heavier, so he needed to get inside. A few houses down the street, he saw a structure resembling a tavern, with a metal sign hanging from the exterior wall. It read *The Salty Merchant Inn*. Kicking the muck off his boots at the door, he stepped inside. Along his calves, rows of buckles chimed as he traversed the room.

A blaze flickered in a large open fireplace along the far wall, and tables and chairs were placed in rows throughout the room. Many were occupied, the room buzzing with drunken stupor.

Pulling his hood back, the tall man stopped in front of an empty counter. Slamming his fist on the wooden worktop, he forcefully cleared his throat.

"I'll be right out!" a man's voice called from a room at the back. Within moments, an older man came through. He was short, his belly protruding underneath a stained linen shirt. He had an apron around his waist, scratching his bald head as he stepped forward. "Welcome, to the Salty Merchant Inn, good sir."

"Give me something edible. And a pint of good mead."

"That'll be three copper, sir."

Dropping the coins on the counter, the man walked away in silence. He sat down at an empty table, the sheathed longsword on his back bashing against the backrest. Adjusting the baldric across his chest, he shifted its position for comfort. He went on to unclasping his cloak, throwing it back across the chair, then rubbed at his neck. Holding his hand up in front of him, he noticed fresh blood coating his fingers. Luckily, the wound wasn't deep, but it would be another scar to add to the collection.

"Here you go, sir," the innkeeper said, setting down a plate of cooked eggs and bacon, as well as a couple of boiled potatoes. "You looked like you needed a good meal, so the extra is on the house. Just spread the good word."

"I will, thank you." He grabbed the fork and ate in silence. The mead was poor but good enough for the occasion. Sitting back in his seat, he silently listened to the background noise around him. The hammering of rain on the roof seemed to have finally dampened.

"A game of hazard, stranger?" someone asked, causing the swordsman to turn.

It was a middle-aged man who had addressed him, sitting together with several of his friends. They were throwing two dice, betting on various numbers to be rolled.

"Why not?" the swordsman replied, his voice gruff and low-pitched, spinning his chair around. His robust build made those around him flinch, not expecting him to be so large.

One pressed his arm into a neighbour. "Let the stranger have a go. You've lost enough, Bill."

Being handed the dice, the newcomer moved them around in his hand. "Seven."

A hum of bets was spoken around him, then the man flicked the bone cubes over the table. They counted seven.

"He rolled the main."

Two of the men cursed, having wagered against him.

"Nine," the swordsman stated.

The bets got louder this time, discussions held. The dice were thrown, landing with nine visible markings on the top.

"Blast!" someone swore.

The man smirked, scratching his bearded chin. "Nine again."

A pint was tipped out over the floor, men cramped around the table. The dice landed on eleven.

"He throws out."

"I know!" a man snarled, flinging his coins over the table. "Sard him and his luck!" He stood, slamming his hand on the wooden piece of furniture.

Rising to meet him, the newcomer clutched the hilt of his sword but left it in its scabbard. "You better not make a move, if you wish to keep your head."

"Oy!" the innkeeper shouted. "No fighting in here! Take it outside if you have a disagreement."

The two men glared at each other, the first finally settling down, but their eye contact lingered.

"I pass the turn," the swordsman declared.

✶ ✶

Hefting his pouch, the man seemed satisfied with his winnings. He grabbed his belongings and headed for the door. It was pitch dark outside, close to midnight by now. The rain had let up, but it was still spitting. Swinging his cloak over his shoulders, he walked further up the road. It was going to take him a few hours to reach the camp, but at least he was no longer cold and hungry.

Hearing a noise behind him, the man ducked, an arrow hissing past. Spinning on his heel, he saw a man mounted on a large horse. It was the one from earlier, who had lost a substantial number of coins while gambling, most of which the cloaked man now carried in his satchel.

The attacker nocked another arrow, drew, and quickly released it.

In a single swipe of his hand, the newcomer had his sword unsheathed, batting the shaft aside, then charged. Slashing across his opponent's leg, he severed the limb, blood instantly spraying. Reaching up, he grabbed hold of his shirt, pulling the now screaming man down to the ground. The horse whipped its head at the sudden upheaval, rearing back from the men.

"No, please! Spare me!" the archer cried, whimpering miserably as he attempted to crawl away in the mud.

"You didn't listen." Replacing his grip on the weapon, the swordsman swung down, the head rolling clear of the body. Clutching some of the man's shirt, he cut a piece of the fabric off and used it to wipe his blade. Sheathing the cleaned sword, he then walked up to the frightened horse and grabbed the reins. He hushed, running a hand over its muzzle, soothing the mount. It was a black gelding, steam billowing from its nostrils.

The broad hooves soon seized to move, and the animal's head came down against him. Satisfied it was calm, the swordsman walked around and placed a foot into one of the stirrups. Vaulting into the saddle, he touched heels to it, the beast setting into a sprint.

✶ ✶

With the travel much faster on horseback, the man arrived back at the encampment within the hour. Tethering the horse to a hitching fence, he walked through the grounds. The rain had still not let up completely, so it was empty of people, everyone most likely in their individual tents.

A front flap opened to one of the shelters, a tall, heavy-set man coming into view. "Gus!" he exclaimed, his dark blue eyes gleaming. "You made it!"

"Not thanks to you," the swordsman snapped. "You left me, you bastard!"

"Only because I knew you'd be fine on your own," he replied. A grin quickly spread. "And I was right."

Gus snorted. "I began to think you'd gone senile in your old days, forgetting I was even there."

The older man laughed. "That'd be something, wouldn't it? I bet you'd tell me if I were to lose my wits."

"I'd just kill you, Cyrus."

"Or that." The man yawned, stretching. "I'll go get some shut-eye. We'll speak more tomorrow. You want me to send the wench over to your tent? I've finished already."

Gus' eyes narrowed. "You know I don't want your leftovers, Dog."

"Oh, but when we've got such nice company in our camp," Cyrus said. "Why not enjoy it?"

"I'll pay for the pleasure in the next town if I feel like it. Goodnight."

The sun was rising, the morning rays breaking through leafless trees. The sky still had some clouds drifting across it, but the rain had ceased.

"Get up, you shiftless mongrels!" Cyrus called out across camp, grunting and groaning immediately heard from within the tents. He strode over to a ring of stones, charcoal gathered within. Building a fire, he sat down on a log next to it.

Men began appearing, several more flames soon roaring across the encampment.

"Where's Gus?" he asked, looking at everyone around him.

"Let me piss in peace, damn it!" the man snarled from within the trees.

Cyrus chuckled. "Always a happy camper, you are."

Retying his trousers and fastening the belt, Gus approached the older man.

"Ey! Nine-fingers, you're back!" said a youth sitting at the campfire. He was slim, with a slender face and dark hair. His blue eyes peered at him as he approached. "Knew you'd make it."

Gus spat on the ground. "Horseshit, Jason. None of you bloody batted an eyelid as I went off that cliff."

"We ain't divided up your gear yet though. That must count for something," the man replied, offering a sly smile.

There was a sudden whimper behind them, prompting the men to turn around. A woman was pushed out from a tent, only wrapped in a blanket. She was darker skinned, her black curly hair reaching below her shoulders. She glanced at the man behind her but remained silent as she stalked away.

"Oh, so you were the one to take her, Landon," Cyrus said as the man joined them.

He was tall but slim, his fair hair gathered at the nape. "Indeed. Very warm… and comfortable," he said, smirking.

"I bet."

Gus reached out towards the fire, yet he could not help but inspect his left hand, and the stump which was all that remained of his ring finger.

"At least we got ya before they cut the rest of 'em off," Jason exulted.

The larger man merely glared at him but said nothing.

"No talking about our mess-ups now, men," Cyrus told them. "We completed our mission yesterday, the success bringing quite the fortune."

"So you say," Gus said. "But where to now?"

"Not quite sure. I was inclined to head north. Since we just came from the south."

"North?"

"Well, not *that* much north. We won't be visiting with your ancestors," Cyrus chuckled, nudging him.

Slapping his hand away, Gus stared at him.

"Eat something. Maybe you'll be more affable." The older man grabbed a loaf of bread, breaking it across his knee, then handed one end to the man. "I was thinking maybe Bechua or Irbid."

"What 'bout east? Like Hammath," Jason suggested.

"Not east again," Landon sighed.

"No, not east," Cyrus agreed.

"Rover then?" another man asked. He, too, was tall, but lean, with brown hair and dark eyes.

"No use, Davis. The Tilean army has already retreated. They would have little use for us. No, I believe Bechua is a good start."

A female emerged from a tent. She looked to be in her upper thirties, quite short, but with a muscular physique. She had long blond hair and brown eyes. Dressed in leather garments, she had a sword strapped to her side. "Good morning," she said, then halted as she saw Gus. "Nine-fingers!" she exclaimed.

"Surprise," he muttered.

"Hey, whose horse is this?" a man called in the distance. He was well over six feet tall and burly, with a bald head. He was standing next to the large black gelding Gus had brought the previous night.

"Mine," Gus replied.

"It'd suit me!"

"I'm sure it would. Now get your hands off it, Fargo. I won it in a bet. Well, kind of."

The big man laughed, gesturing a surrender with his arms out. "Alright, alright," he conceded, then joined the others around the fire.

"It feels a bit strange," Cyrus said. "To not have an ongoing assignment. Long since that happened."

Jason snickered. "Always need for *the Unn*."

"Shut up. You know I hate that name."

"Better than *the Unnamed*," Gus said. "But I suppose anything is better than that."

"We don't have a name!" Cyrus barked. "I hate names in general."

"Stranger approaching!" someone bellowed from the edge of the camp, prompting everyone to immediately stand.

Gus drew his sword, striding across the encampment with Cyrus.

A short and wiry man sat mounted on a brown mare. He had halted along the path leading up to the encampment. "I wish to speak with whoever is in charge," he proclaimed.

"I am in charge," Cyrus said, stepping forward.

"My master would like to… employ *the Unn*. He will pay handsomely for your… services."

The old man swore. "We will never get rid of that name now, will we?"

5

MISTS

The sky was bright, its soft shade of blue spread above the landscape. With the sun warming her back, Adena walked across the grassy plain, her white dress flowing in the breeze. Reaching out, she caressed the crimson poppies around her, the whole field coated in the soft blooms. Unsure of why she was there, she merely continued her stroll. The sea of flowers seemed endless, no trees or mountains visible in any direction.

Where was she?

She suddenly heard laughter and singing, the voices high-pitched and cheerful.

Turning around, Adena faced the sun. The warm rays were glaring, forcing her to shield her eyes with her hand. The voices sounded like children, but the Senior Priest could only make out faint silhouettes in the distance. They jumped and danced, joining hands in a large circle.

As Adena came closer to the children, the skies darkened above her. She threw a glance at the heavens; grey clouds were quickly gathering, the sound of thunder rolling out. As she looked back towards the children, they stood silently, staring at her. Standing in a single line, their eyes traced her as she neared. There were boys and girls of all ages, dressed in simple linen clothing.

Adena looked at each of them, their expressions flat and emotionless. A disconcerting feeling spread through her, an icy shiver rippling down her spine.

Who were they? Why did she recognise them?

A flash of lightning forked across the heavens, the skies opening up above them. As the rain poured, Adena felt the drops tap on her skin. She flinched as one touched her face, the liquid warm. Holding her arms out in front of her, she saw them starting to get stained red with blood. Within moments, her dress was drenched in crimson, and the children panicked, screaming with anguish. They desperately cried, yet they would not move or attempt to comfort each other.

The wind picked up as they wailed, like the souls of the dead howling across the blood-covered landscape.

The claret drops created piercing crystals, ruthlessly tearing through the children. Flesh and bone ripped and crumbled with every hit. One by one, the children slumped to the ground, their battered bodies dissolving into the undergrowth.

The poppies shifted to black around them, the sun no longer visible through the menacing clouds.

Adena felt despair building inside her. She hurried forward to grab one of the young girls, but no matter how far she ran, they were never within reach. It was as if she couldn't move from her spot, forced to watch as they all perished in her presence.

Dark mists swirled around her, her skin blackening as the torrential rain flooded the plains. Waist deep in the crimson, she saw her own reflection on the red surface.

A monster. She was a monster.

Samael ran his tongue over his teeth, his mouth dry from his early morning sleep. He had crept into bed as the priestess slept but now found himself alone as he awakened. He threw the covers aside, his body naked underneath. His long hair touched the mattress as he swung his legs over the edge, then stood. Looking down, he could see the mists slowly emanating from his skin. They were still faint, with most of them evaporating before even reaching the floor, but he knew they would soon increase.

Finished getting dressed, he threw his cloak around his shoulders and pushed his feet into his boots, then left the hut. He needed to find Anaya.

She wouldn't be far away, most likely in her room inside his mother's house. The priestess had made it into her study, so plenty of bookshelves had been brought in. Spending most of her time reading there, she often sat overlooking the courtyard. Since Samael and Anaya had yet to create a marital home, which traditionally would have already been arranged ahead of their wedding, they solved it by splitting their accommodations between their own hut and parts of Lilith's living quarters.

Coming through the entrance hall, Samael halted in front of his mother.

"Slept well, son?" she asked, seated on her daybed.

"Yes."

"Good. There will be lunch served soon, so I would suggest for you and Anaya to attend."

"We will," he said, then motioned to leave.

"Wait, Samael."

He looked at the Matriarch, waiting for her to continue.

"What is going on with you lately? I can see your mists, and your aura is much more active. Are you really that upset with what is happening with the Priesthood?"

His shoulders dropped. "No, mother. I am not agitated if that is what you think."

"I agree that you do not sound it, but certainly look it with those mists of yours."

"Indeed, but it is… a delicate matter."

Angling out from her seat, Lilith frowned. "Do tell."

Samael rubbed at his temple, then left his hand resting on his head. "The High Priest's potion is still in effect."

Her eyebrows shot up. "Really?"

"Yes. Anaya is… working on it."

"I thought you stayed unusually close to her."

The demon nodded. "I do not wish for my feral state to return. As such, I cannot transform at this moment."

"I would have thought not," Lilith said. "Very well, it is as it is. We can only hope your Consort is able to remove the taint."

"She will. It only takes time and a lot of effort on her part."

"Is that why she sleeps more than usual?"

"Yes."

The Matriarch tapped a finger to her lip. "I see. Do you wish to be relieved of your duties?"

"No," Samael replied. "But I cannot do anything which would require taking on my demonic form."

"I understand. Anaya is upstairs, as always. You may go to her."

✶ ✶

Stopping at Anaya's door, Samael tensed, his mists swirling around his feet. His demonic aura was intensifying quickly. He cursed, clenching his fists. It was becoming increasingly annoying, his emotions only worsening his condition.

"Come in, Samael," he heard from within.

With a heavy exhale, he pushed the door open.

"I could sense you even as you walked across the courtyard," the priestess told him. "Sit down on the bed, and we shall begin today's session."

Silently traversing the room, the demon did as she asked.

As Anaya began to scan him, she met his gaze. "I can see why," she said.

"What?"

"One of the rifts has opened. It is not one previously sealed, however, so we will continue as before. I will only need to put a little bit more effort into this one." Initiating her chant, Anaya's hands immediately flashed with Light. "It might... hurt."

Samael flinched as she began, the treatment much more vigorous. He closed his eyes, snapping his jaw shut as the pain shot through him.

Clearing the contagion within his mind, the priestess worked her way across. The tar-like substance slowly burnt away with her enchantment, allowing for the crack to gradually diminish. She had to energetically

43

advance this time, forcefully reciting her words as she worked her way across the crevice.

A growl sounded, the demon baring his fangs. His eyes were dark as he stared at her, then his mists whooshed around them.

"Samael, *focus!*"

"**ANAYA!**"

She shivered as his distorted voice reverberated within the room. It was as if the remaining corruption from the High Priest's concoction was consciously digging into him, desperate not to be dissolved.

The demon's hand lashed out, clutching hold of her wrist. His claws extended as the grip tightened. Time was of the essence, as he moved towards the feral.

We don't want to die!

"You are already dead," Anaya whispered, unsure of where the voice came from. She knew her words rang true, but how? Light enveloped the priestess' body, her eyes shining brightly as she made a final push. She screamed, feeling Samael's claws digging into her skin.

The demon fell back on the bed, his mists finally receding. The rupture was healed, but what had she encountered?

Leaning forward, Anaya felt Samael's wrist. His pulse was slow but steady, and his breathing deep. He was in good health, only unconscious. She briefly smiled, then slipped into darkness.

✷ ✷

Edric sat up in bed, startled by what sounded like a scream. He placed a parchment on the bedside table, then nudged Vixen. The woman was sleeping beside him, merely rolling over with the touch.

"Did you hear that?" he asked.

"Hear what?" she mumbled, pulling the cover over her shoulder.

The man cursed, heading for the door. Coming out into the hallway, the Matriarch strode past in high speed. Her manservant was close behind, along with several of her guard. She wasted no time in knocking on the priestess' door, immediately entering the room.

Edric came in behind her, finding Samael and Anaya unmoving on the bed. He joined Lilith, hurrying forward. Performing a brief scan, he met her gaze. "They are only unconscious, my lady."

"I assume you heard the screaming?" the Matriarch asked.

"I did. I won't pretend to know what has occurred, however. I shall leave that to you, your Highness. Call on me, should you need any further assistance." The officer bowed, then exited the room.

"Smart man," she said, then looked at Arax and her guards. "Remove yourselves. I will watch over them."

It was noon as Kaedin strode through the camp. Walking past one of the tents, he pulled at a corner string, then pressed the anchor peg down with his foot. Not all the priests were used to such a lengthy stay in canvas shelters, so many neglected to make sure their homes would remain standing.

If the Priesthood were to be revived, then plenty of changes would have to be brought into effect, including the way they prepared their recruits. If the priests could not even stay camped for more than a couple of weeks, training schedules definitely had to be revised.

Kaedin stopped and talked to many of the inhabitants, gathering information on everyone's status, and making sure they had received their supplies. More clothing had been prepared, most of the priests now in possession of at least two sets. They attempted to be as self-sufficient as possible, but it was a struggle to obtain enough food. Meat and fish, they procured themselves, but they needed the Matriarch's charity for bread, oats and vegetables.

The officer was surprised at the fact that none of the priests had left. He had believed most would abandon the cause as it took this most sudden turn, but they did not. Despite the apprehension of the Goddess' possible abandonment of the Priesthood, through the death of their High Priest, most agreed that it had been his madness alone which brought them down the bloodied path of needless slaughter. Others were less sure of why they stayed, many expressing concerns of having nowhere else to go, but either way, they remained loyal to the Priesthood.

Kaedin would not abandon them. He may have sworn an oath in front of a zealot out for vengeance, but it had been done in the name of the

Goddess, and he refused to let Her Light be tarnished. The Matriarch's suggested future for them intrigued him, and it was worth exploring. The Goddess would renew her presence, he was sure of that.

Knocking on a tent post of Adena's temporary home, the man took a step back. "You in there, Adena?" he asked.

"I am. I will be right out."

A few minutes passed as he waited, listening to some dull shuffling from within the tent.

Pushing the front canvas open, Adena popped her head outside. "I apologise about that. I had to get changed." The woman looked beyond weary, dark rings formed under her eyes, but she offered a smile.

Kaedin blinked, surprised at her appearance. "I… have been discussing our ranking system with Leo and Edric. Both are fine with whatever we decide, so I thought we should sit down and talk about it."

"Certainly, brother."

They strolled along the outskirts of the campsite, sitting down at a dwindling flame overlooking the Atua river. The fire had probably been lit for lunch but was left to die out by itself.

"I have drawn up a suggestion I would like to show you. It should correspond to the democratic vision the Matriarch currently holds for us. *Disciples* will remain, the next rank being *Priest*, removing the current need for *Junior Priest*. I would suggest having a higher rank of priest, but without the duties of an officer. Said person would act as the one in charge when out in the field and be called a *Sergeant Priest*, or *Sergeant* for short."

Adena nodded as she listened to the man.

"The Senior Priest rank is to be divided up into two, the lower of which shall oversee training of recruits, and the higher ranking having larger managerial roles. They would be called *Lieutenant Priest* and *General Priest*, respectively. You would receive the title of *Cardinal*, with general responsibility for preachings, and acting as head of whatever council we are to form with the demons." He gave her the parchment to read.

"And these are the names you suggest for each title?"

"Aye."

She skimmed the document again. "It is well made. I have no objections."

"Good. I shall speak to those listed. They will obviously have to accept the positions. Rick and Eli are the only ones I have already informed." Kaedin looked at his senior officer, expecting a reply, but none came. Instead, she had adopted a blank stare, her gaze stranded on the charred pieces of wood in front of them. "Adena?"

A visible tremor shot through her, then she shook her head. "I'm sorry, Kaedin. I was lost in thought."

"I could tell. Is something amiss?"

"Oh, no. I am merely tired. Living outdoors has never been a favourite of mine."

The man chuckled. "None of mine either, believe it or not. A warm bed is preferred. Hopefully, it won't be long until we can return to the village. I pray something remains of it."

"Indeed." Adena rose, straightening her clothing. "I will see to speaking with Perry about his position as Lieutenant, then Maya if she has any suggestions for additional healers."

"We agree then. I shall send word to the Matriarch and inform her as soon as she accepts the request for an audience."

Anaya moaned, straining to open her eyes. She felt as if she had been whacked in the head with a hammer, her vision blurred and head spinning. A gentle touch outlined the priestess' side, then she felt someone clutch her hand. "Samael?" she asked, seeing his dark silhouette above her.

His gathered hair spilt over his shoulder as he angled across her. "I am here," he said.

Lilith leaned over, meeting the priestess' gaze as it cleared. "You have been sleeping for the best part of three hours. I am taking it you used a lot of your spiritual powers on Samael?"

Nodding, Anaya pressed her fingers to her temple as she accepted the demon's assistance to sit. "How did you know?" she asked the Matriarch.

"He told me. It is not as if I haven't noticed his persistent aura, so I questioned him about it."

"I see." The young woman looked at her husband. "We need to speak about… what I saw."

Letting out a breath, the demon ran the heel of his hand along his thigh.

"I have a feeling I already know. The Darkness wasn't as... empty, as it has been."

"Yes. Something lingers within the corruption... something that should have already passed over to the afterlife. What did you see?"

"I cannot say. The forms were dark, merging with the surroundings, but they were large creatures."

She pondered his answer for a moment. "Perhaps, they are spirits connected to Ekelon and his experiments... if they were absorbed into his rage potion as he... created it."

"Spirits?" the Matriarch questioned.

"I mean lost souls, my lady. I heard... voices saying they did not wish to die, but I have a feeling they already have, only that they do not know it."

"Could it be whatever demons he may have used in his experiments?" Samael suggested.

"It may very well be, which makes it incredibly hard to know what we might be facing since he... used quite an extensive amount of them."

Lilith gave her a sidelong glance, but her head remained still. "I am aware of his atrocious experiments, Benjamin giving us more than enough intelligence on the topic. Any of the live subjects would have been especially susceptible to attaching themselves to their remains, if not properly brought into the afterlife."

"Which would be every single one he ever laid his hands on. They all..." The priestess fell silent, imagining it. It was only weeks since she stood shackled to the cavern wall herself. Her eyes welled as she placed a hand over her mouth.

Folding his arm around her, the demon pulled her close, kissing her hair. "Do not concern yourself with his choices, Anaya. You had no part in it."

Tears began rolling down her cheeks. "But I did," she said. "I could have said something. I could have *done* something. I *knew* it was wrong!"

"You would only have been punished ahead of time, my dear," Lilith said. "My son is right." Sitting down on a chair beside the bed, she peered at the couple. "Tell me honestly, Anaya. Is Samael going to survive this?"

He instantly locked eyes with the priestess, anxious for her answer.

Anaya merely smiled. "I am certain we can fight it, even if it is bound to offer us resistance." She reached out to touch his face. "We shall see how the next session turns out, but if the spirits' opposing powers are to further increase, we might need to rethink our strategy."

"Why is it worsening?" he asked.

"I am not entirely sure, but I initially avoided the larger fissures, expecting there would be a need for stronger enchantments as we progressed. I am now beginning to think these rifts contain more powerful foes, and my spells seem to stir them. Which could be what happened now. As soon as the previous healing faded, the… *blight* came boiling to the surface very quickly, no?"

"It did."

"Mm, I figured as much." Placing her hands upon him, the priestess chanted, with Light instantly shimmering around them.

"Do not overexert yourself," the demon swiftly said.

"I am merely scanning." Silent for a while, she closed her eyes. She could see his mind, the cracks still running across it, but the liquid was gone, for now. "It seems fine at the moment."

"Yes, but do not leave me again." The apprehension in his eyes could not be ignored. "I cannot trust myself to keep it contained."

6

UNDEAD

Another week had passed, offering decent weather. There had been a minor snowfall, but the white blanket barely formed before it once more melted away.

It was early morning as Anaya came walking down the stairs into the Matriarch's entrance hall. She halted on the bottom step, noticing the older woman's resolute stare.

"My dear, do join me," Lilith said.

"As you wish, my lady."

The Matriarch huffed. "You know there is no need for such formalities. I am your mother-in-law."

Anaya smiled humbly. "I know. I only wish to be correct still."

"Very well. Do tell me of your progress with Samael. He is of little help when it comes to admitting to anything related to his health. And everything else, for that matter."

"I am less than surprised," the priestess said. "But the last few sessions have been uneventful. I have focused on less powerful rifts, so there has been no additional push towards the feral."

"Good. But I assume there will be?"

"Most likely, yes. I am to attempt a more potent one tonight, as I feel rested today."

Lilith nodded. "You are welcome to remain here, should you wish."

"We will probably stay in the hut but thank you. We should be fine."

"If you say so. Speaking of which, where is Samael now?"

"Only outside, my lady. He stays within range for me to read his aura."

"It is good to hear you have solved the issue for now." The Matriarch paused, taking a moment to look about the room. The two of them were alone. "As formerly part of the Priesthood, I would like to ask something of you."

"Yes, my lady?"

"You might want to sit down," Lilith urged her, gesturing towards a nearby chair.

Anaya quickly retrieved it and sat down before her. "What is the matter? Is it something serious?"

"Oh, no," the Matriarch assured her. "I am merely curious, and one can never be in possession of too much knowledge." She grinned, flashing her pearly row of teeth. "In all honesty, demons – not unlike humans – are taught very sparingly about the other race. For us to join together, I need to understand your religion better, and the foundations on which you base your principles and way of life."

"Ah, of course," Anaya said, nodding. "Where would you have me start?"

"The beginning," Lilith decided. "Your story of creation – why is the Goddess supreme?"

The priestess sat pondering the question for a moment, as it was seldom spoken of within the Priesthood. They were all told the story as children, but they rarely discussed it as adults. "The one exact origin of the Goddess exists in various adaptations, but the scholars all agree she was created in order to save all living creatures from the Darkness by fighting it and locking it away."

"The Darkness? Meaning demons?"

"Not exactly. The world was created by a number of ancient spirits. It was initially veiled in Darkness, and the spirits living across the earth joined together, forming the Goddess of Holy Light. Thus, all great powers combined, and all life could prosper in the absence of Darkness."

Lilith frowned. "How does that make demons the enemy? I have never understood this. It makes little sense."

Anaya rubbed at her neck. "In retrospect, I can only agree," she said. "I suppose it is due to the belief that *hell* is a place of Darkness, situated somewhere deep in the earth, the ruler of which is an entity not entirely different from the demonic mists that demons create. The evil being is faceless, genderless, and formless. However, despite the Darkness being locked away by the Goddess, it can still work its magic through the evil of others. Some scholars even claim that demons were originally humans lost to the Darkness through sinful deeds, such as greed and lust, and that the Goddess was forced to fight against them as she brought her Light into the world."

"Oh, how we have sinned," Lilith grimly chuckled. "And so, these terrible characteristics of the fallen humans that you just mentioned – lust and greed – are what regulates your way of life? Like some sort of code to live by?"

"Yes, for one is believed to be damned to an eternity in Darkness – to lose one's inner Light and be sent to hell – if acting upon the human sins, such as greed, lust, pride or envy," the priestess explained. "Ekelon firmly believed that demons had once lost their Light – and thus all their human qualities – due to sin. According to him, his direct blessing from the Goddess, as he once asked for Her powers to thwart the Darkness, was proof of this. Demons were spawns of Darkness, the servants of Hell if you will, working diligently to undo the Goddess' work and to bring the world back into complete Darkness. By eradicating demons, Ekelon stood to finish the Goddess' work." She paused, rubbing at her neck. "So to us humans, living a devout life is the only way to secure a place with the Goddess in the afterlife; for our souls to reach Her paradise... and *salvation*."

The Matriarch listened carefully, nodding. "And the afterlife? What is that to you?"

"A place of eternal Light," Anaya answered. "It is the home of the Goddess Herself, where one will forever be cradled by Her comfort and love. Some believe you can even see it in the heavens – the sun."

"Mm, I can see some similarities with our own beliefs, such as your mention of ancient spirits, and even your mention of Darkness as *hell*. It is all very interesting, and it brings the *feral* to mind, but we will have to discuss that at a different time." Lilith brought out a quill and ink container, as well as a piece of parchment on which she quickly scribbled a few notes. "Now, tell me about the officers. I need to know their background, strengths and weaknesses, and so on. Kaedin will be granted an audience with me this evening, so I would like to be well-informed before the meeting. I will bring forward my own suggestions as to dividing areas of responsibility, depending on what you will disclose to me."

Only two months away from her due date, Vixen was fast becoming tired of her bed rest. With her blond hair pulled back into a high ponytail, she sat up on the bed. "Is there no way to birth the child a bit ahead of time?" she asked Lenda.

The young healer laughed. "I am afraid not, dear sister. And either way, it is much too early now. We still do not want to risk inducing labour."

The Commander flashed a stare at Edric. "This is your fault."

He jerked back. "*Mine*? You're the one who hoped to become with child!"

"Yes, but you… you *allowed* it! It takes two, you know!"

He placed a hand to his head. "What was I meant to do? I wanted a family, and you offered it!"

Lenda cleared her throat, gaining their attention. "Goodness, you two. It is a little late to discuss this now." She looked at Vixen. "You are free to move around, as long as you do not suffer from any contractions. Any sign of them, however, then you have to hurry back to your bed! It was the same for Anaya, so you might as well get used to it."

Avoiding eye contact, the Commander crossed her arms. "Fine."

Edric sat down on the bed, his hand resting on her leg.

Vixen instantly glared at him, yet she couldn't help but soften her expression as he smiled at her. "Oh, alright, then. Come here!" She held her arms out, inviting him into an embrace. Ending it with a smooth kiss, they glanced at Lenda.

Her face red, the girl pressed her lips flat. "I will leave now. Fetch me, if you need me."

Dipping her quill pen into the ink container, Lilith continued to write on the small parchment beside her on the daybed. "Commander Anna Ramsey is of interest," she told Anaya. "She might prove useful in the future, should the King agree to relieve her of her duties within the army."

Coming down the stairs, Lenda placed her hands over her ears, holding her head low as she attempted to speed past.

"Healer!" the Matriarch called, instantly halting the girl.

"Y-yes, your Highness?" she asked. She faced her but was unable to meet her gaze.

"The conversation with Anaya is of no consequence if you were to hear it. She only speaks of knowledge already known within the Priesthood. You may leave in peace."

"Thank you, my lady." Lenda bowed, then offered a tight smile to the priestess.

"Wait for me outside, dear sister," Anaya said.

"I will," she replied. Coming out on the porch, Lenda barely made it far enough for the door to close before she suddenly froze. Her legs felt weighted down, and shivers spread through her limbs as she began to physically shake. Turning her head, she saw Samael sitting on the far end of the decking, leaning against the wall. His mists slowly rolled out underneath him.

Within moments, Anaya appeared. Not expecting the girl to be so close to the door, she bumped into her, sending her falling forwards. "Lenda!" she cried, clutching hold of her skirt.

The healer flailed her arms, swaying, barely managing to maintain her balance.

"I am so sorry!" the priestess whined.

Having finally regained her footing, Lenda brushed at her skirt. "No trouble. Nothing came of it. You only helped snap me out of my terror, so thank you."

Anaya had a glimpse at Samael, the demon returning a flat look. He had made no effort to come to their aid. "Ah," she said. "I should have told you."

Lenda let off a nervous laugh. "Yes, well... What was it that you wanted?"

"For us to spend some time together," Anaya said.

"I would be delighted, sister. Perhaps we can go on a stroll? Like we used to."

"Of course. Let us bring some baskets, and we can collect any herbs we may find. Hopefully, they have not all perished in the recent snow."

✶✶

The morning sun brightened the cold woods, the thick undergrowth shifting in green and brown. Anaya and Lenda sauntered along, breaking into song like they so often had done before. The priestess clapped, and the healer whistled. Reaching an opening, they soon found a small bush of thyme and began harvesting the shrubs.

Thyme was very often used in cooking, but also served well as a medicine when pressed into oil, both as an anti-inflammatory and to relieve constricted airways.

With their song ebbing out, Anaya faced her young friend. "How is everything at camp?"

Lenda cut a small section of the greenery. "From my point of view, things are well. Everyone has recovered from their injuries, despite only Maya and I being available... as full-time healers." Her movements slowed to a halt as she slipped into silence, her thoughts centring on all those lost along with the Temple village.

"We do not know what happened to the rest," Anaya said. "Padma and the others might still have made it."

The young girl shook her head. "Not the way the demons overrun the village, sister. There will be no survivors."

In dire need of a change of subject, Anaya cleared her throat. "How are the rest of your duties working out?"

"You mean medicinal and herbal?"

"Yes."

Lenda cut another couple of twigs off, placing them in her basket. "Good, considering the demon running the herbalist shop is, in a way, forced to work with me. She is nice, at least to my face, and she is very knowledgeable."

Looking around, Anaya spotted a perennial herb. Called *Midland rosemary*, it was also one often used in cooking, yet served well for treating persistent headaches and digestive ailments. "That is pleasing to hear," the priestess said, walking across to the small bush. Bending down, she carefully began cutting the stems. "I am sorry we are unable to spend more time together, but I need to prepare for my duties as Matriarch. I am meant to assume the role sometime late summer... so I have a lot to learn."

"You need not worry, sister. I completely understand. Perhaps, we shall be forced to *schedule* our dates in the future."

The girls laughed.

"Indeed, that might be for the best." Standing back up, Anaya returned to Lenda's side. "How are things with Eden and yourself?"

"Very well, thank you. He is as loving as always. It is only hectic, so we have little free time." Lenda smiled, thinking of him. "What about you and Samael?"

Turning around, the priestess nodded towards a nearby tree. The demon sat perched on a branch, one of his legs swinging over the edge. "We are doing just fine. But he has to follow me around, I'm afraid, so no privacy for us just yet."

Lenda giggled. "Maybe it is best not to speak too much of our husbands then."

"You might be right," Anaya said, softly holding Samael's gaze. "Even if we would only offer them compliments."

"Speaking of you becoming the Matriarch," the young girl inquired. "What does the role entail? Is it the same as being a Queen?"

"Not quite, as a Queen very often doesn't have formal power, unlike a Matriarch. Samael and I will be considered equals but given separate duties. Simply put, he will oversee our tribe's defences and the everyday running of our village. He will also be the executioner for sentenced criminals, for as long as we do not have a separate Prime. Surprisingly enough, his third, and most important, duty is to care for the family and make sure our offspring receives a proper education. I, on the other hand, will be focusing on organisation and collaboration, both within the tribe and towards other demon tribes. I am also to preside over crime investigations and act as a judge when adequate evidence has been brought forward. This is the typical setup – if the Patriarch is a Prime. Otherwise, the roles are simply reversed."

Lenda's eyes widened. "My Goddess! That is a lot of work. No wonder you spend so many hours studying."

Cleaning the needles on a branch of rosemary, Anaya replaced it in her basket. "It is, but..." She looked across at Samael again, the demon still watching her. "He is worth every second of it."

In the encroaching darkness, Kaedin was summoned to the Matriarch's entrance hall. They had spoken for some time, as he presented his suggestions for the Priesthood.

"As a whole, I like what you have done, Master Reed. However, there is a slight change I would prefer you to make."

He remained silent, only slightly shifting his stance.

"Mistress Adena Barton should indeed remain highest in command, her duties being that of continuing your preachings of the Light, even if I do not agree with your Goddess being a supreme entity. Be that as it may, she should also be the head of this Congress you are suggesting. Someone will have to run it, consolidating humans and demons. She may have gravely sinned against demonkind, but she is well equipped for this assignment." She paused, but the man still said nothing. "If Master Edric Ramsey is to oversee the training for recruits and Master Leo Blythe act as the general manager for your settlement, then it is *you* that I want."

Kaedin's features hardened. "*Want*, your Highness?"

"You already said you would be responsible for intelligence and strategy, which excellently plays into my hand. As Matriarch, I am receiving vast quantities of such, through my scouts and servants. I offer to exchange our information, to enhance both of our standings amongst human- and demonkind alike."

"I understand that you wish a collaboration with the Priesthood," Kaedin said. "But this sounds much closer than that, should we even share scouts. Are you sure your tribe would accept something such as this, my lady?"

Lilith leaned forward in her seat. "Stand on one leg, Master Reed."

His eyes narrowed for a moment, but he decided to oblige, lifting his left foot off the floor.

"You see, you are one to follow orders, yet not without first weighing your options. You are also one to tell it as it is. Adena followed blindly, but *you*... You stood up to your High Priest, yet you did not leave. Most likely because you sought a way to save the Priesthood, not just removing yourself from their ranks. It speaks of great character. Loyal, but self-sufficient. Those characteristics are perfect for the role. If we are to truly work together, our decisions need to be based on the same knowledge, and as such, we need to draw conclusions from the same sources." She leaned back again, watching him. "At ease, Master Reed."

Setting his foot back down on the floor, Kaedin rubbed at his bearded chin. "If I accept, how do we go about working in this manner?"

"We should have weekly meetings. Until such time as you have your own set of established scouts, I will lend you a few of my own. They are very efficient. I am even to supply you one of my best. Benjamin."

"Benjamin?"

"Yes. The same man who has created that shirt you are currently wearing."

With an open expression, Kaedin raised an eyebrow. "Benjamin is here?"

"Why, yes. He was my scout inside your base of operations."

"He is a demon?"

"Indeed, he is. His ability to dampen his aura is unlike any other. He can lower it to the point of your defensive systems not triggering. Not even the High Priest managed to snuff him out."

Kaedin laughed. "My word. I have noticed yours, as well as your son's, ability to reduce it, but I had no idea it was manageable to such a degree."

"Benjamin is merely of low birth, but it matters not when demons are sent for scouting. Strength is not needed in such assignments."

"True, my lady, but why have we not heard about this until now?"

"You have not asked, Master Reed. I am not to tell you things on a whim. You need to inquire in order to attain information." She moistened her lips. "And I expect you to do so, from now on."

He nodded. "Aye, my lady."

"So, you accept?"

"I do."

"Then you may go and inform your fellow officers. I am still working on reclaiming your village, seeking out those responsible for the attack. We might have to retake it by force, but I am inclined to await their response first, giving the squatting demons the option to leave voluntarily."

"As you wish, my lady." Kaedin showed reverence, then left the building.

Crossing her legs, Lilith sat in stillness for a moment. "You can come out now, Arax."

The man slipped out of the shadows under the staircase, placing himself in front of her. "Are you sure about this, my lady?"

"Which part?"

"Making Kaedin such a close… confidant."

"I am," she replied.

"But a *human*, my lady? To know all of our secrets?"

She released a curt breath. "May I remind you; my son is now legally married to one? And besides, we are meant to work together from here on out. Should they betray us… we will just kill them."

Samael sat down on the bed, rumbling out a breath. His mists billowed out around him, rapidly increasing. Clenching his jaw, he attempted to dampen them, but to no avail. He cursed, slamming his fist on the bed frame. His aura instantly flared, causing him to lurch back up on his feet.

Coming through the door, Anaya gasped. She had been gone for only minutes as she left Aaron with his grandmother, returning to a mist-filled room. "What in the world, Samael," she said, flicking her hand in front of her as she moved through the mists. Barely able to see where he was, she chanted, evaporating them with her Light.

The demon breathed heavily, standing with his hand against the wall. Turning to look at the priestess, his eyes were wild, and his lips drawn over his fangs. The mists whirled out as he growled.

"Focus, my love!" the priestess cried, hurrying forward.

"I AM TRYING!"

She planted a soft hand on him, standing firm against the raging aura. "You need to sit down," she said. "Another rift must have opened."

Samael laboriously lowered himself before the priestess, pushing his knee onto the floor.

Grabbing hold of his head, Anaya began chanting. She immediately found the source for his outburst, black liquid gushing out of a crevice. Her eyes widened, seeing it. Samael was indeed fighting the corruption, and she had never seen it this violent before.

She suddenly felt her inner self becoming drenched in the tainted tar. Her spirit forcibly separated from her body as she was pulled into the depths of the demon's mind.

★ ★

Anaya found herself overcome by darkness, demonic mists enclosing on her like a tornado. As it finally settled, Samael was nowhere in sight, and she, unable to even voice his name. Her surroundings reminded her of the night sky, only lacking a sea of stars. The absence of light was disturbing, causing an unnatural shudder to crawl under her skin. There was a swirl among the blackness, the space around her slowly taking the shape of a vast cavern.

Silhouettes of people emerged, solidifying against the cold stone backdrop. The priestess could count seven of them, all sitting in a small circle on the cave floor. Muffled sounds were echoing, but they gradually became both louder and increasingly clear. The gathered people were speaking to one another, some animated as an argument ensued.

"We have discussed this long enough," a female said, attempting to ease the situation. "I would suggest we retire for now."

"But what if the Priesthood arrives, my lady?" another female stressed. "Those who survived the last attack would have spread the word of us being killers."

A man cursed. "Why not leave now? We can make do on the run, Prime."

"It is of no use. We have too many young," she replied wearily. She brushed her black hair back behind her ears, then rubbed at her eyes.

"They have all gone through their *evolution*, my lady," the first female added. "They will be fine."

"They are right, my love," another man said, placing his hand on hers. "There is no-"

The Prime's mouth fell open as she gasped, watching him slump before her. The tip of a sparkling arrow protruded from his forehead, and another two demons laid dead behind him. She shrieked as her mists exploded out around her, her bones snapping through her transformation. Ducking underneath another wave of arrows, she charged the assailants.

Enchantments of Light quickly filled the cave, revealing an enormous black spider. More shafts rained down, slamming into its head and abdomen. The Prime screeched with rage, bearing down on one of the priests. With her poison instantly spreading through him, she flung him aside, then attacked another.

A female priest was shouting orders, her short raven hair more than enough evidence for Anaya. It was Adena.

The remaining spiders soon perished, leaving the Prime alone as she fought to defend herself.

Reaching out, Anaya could do nothing. It was as if she wasn't even there, unable to touch those around her or make a single sound. She recognised all the priests' faces, Edric and Vixen among them.

The gargantuan spider cried out, flailing her legs to keep the aggressors at bay. She aimed for Adena, but the woman managed to swerve. As she recovered, the Prime saw an opening, sending another leg for her.

Edric dashed forward, his sword slicing through the demon's flesh. The limb tore clear, blood spraying from the severed joint.

With a searing pain to her back, the Prime was simultaneously attacked from behind. Looking around, a woman slashed at her with her sword. She lashed out, but the attacker grabbed at her leg and vaulted onto her carapace.

Anaya could see how Vixen stabbed at the Prime while Edric released several arrows. Knives were thrown, blades licking out from all angles. The beast's limbs were cut off, one by one. The priestess could sense the immense grief emanating through the demonic aura, its lack of tears seemingly rolling out with the mists. It tore into her heart, watching the scene play out, how the Prime hopelessly struggled on, biting another priest before it finally slumped to the ground.

Adena stepped forward, her glowing sword travelling deep into the creature's head, then everything went silent.

The priests froze where they stood, slowly fading away. Left alone with the massive spider, Anaya walked up to the corpse. She sat down on her heels, placing a hand on its head.

"I don't want to die," the priestess heard within her mind.

"You are already dead," Anaya replied, as she did last.

A tear rolled down from the demon's dead eye. "Will I see him again?"

"You will. He will be waiting for you."

Dark mists flared around them, enveloping the spider. As they settled, the body of a woman had taken its place. It was the same as before, her black hair spread along the stone surface.

Anaya came forward, gently lifting her upper body onto her lap.

Listlessly opening her eyes, the Prime met her gaze. "Place me... with my Consort. Let our spirits travel as one into the afterlife."

Gripping her tightly, the priestess managed to lift her body and carry her over to the far side of the cave. She placed her beside the man, then knelt before them.

"Thank you, *Prophet*," whispered the Black widow Prime. "For granting me... the serenity of *Salvation*."

✶✶

Opening her eyes, the priestess still held firm over Samael's head. He was gazing back at her, his mists wholly gone. She felt his hand touch her face, gently stroking the tears away from her cheek. He rose to embrace her, and she threw herself forward, instantly sobbing against his chest.

"What happened?" he questioned. "You were passive for such a long time, despite my push towards the feral having dispersed."

"They are locked inside you," she said. "Undead beings... It is all their grief and pain, all of them fighting for survival, as the scene of their death repeats itself... They cannot find rest."

"But you managed to heal one?" he asked.

She merely nodded, tears still staining his grey shirt.

With his arms around her, Samael picked her up and placed her on the bed. Sitting down, he clutched her hand. "Tell me what is going on, Anaya."

Inhaling a ragged breath, she attempted to calm herself. "Their violent deaths have caused their spirits to linger within their remains. I believe they found life through your feral state, thus clinging on to what little is left."

"And what did you do now? Did you... help them?"

"It was a Black widow Prime... When she died, I spoke with her. She wanted to be put to rest with her Consort."

"I see," Samael said. "That was probably when she finally released her hold over me."

"I would assume so," Anaya agreed. "But I need to ask you."

"What is that?"

"She... the Prime, she called me a *Prophet*. Why would she do that?"

"A prophet?"

"Yes."

He shrugged. "I am not sure. It might refer to the prophecy about *the Salvation*. Perhaps, the frosted beast is indeed a prophet."

"What is this prophecy? You all mentioned it as I appeared as a white panther on our wedding, but no one has truly explained it yet. I have been attempting to find it amongst the books given to me by your mother, but so far, I have not been successful. Your mother even mentioned it a couple of weeks back, but she is yet to elaborate on the subject."

Samael rose, walking through to the hallway. Entering his wardrobe, he headed straight for a small bookshelf just inside the doorway. "It is because it has to do with demonkind as a whole – or the Spirits, more exactly – not only the panther tribe," he explained, grabbing a single, small tome from the top shelf. He blew the dust off it, then returned to the priestess' side, sitting back down on the bed. Carefully opening the book, he flicked through the thin pages.

"That looks incredibly old," Anaya said.

"It is. Spirits know how many generations have read through it. It was quite a few years ago for myself though, so bear with me." He continued to carefully turn the pages until he finally found the one he sought. "Here it is. I shall read it out since the handwriting is somewhat poor." He forced air through his throat. *"Behold, those who called for righteousness. There shall be strength; there shall be protection, as you are Delivered. Demons shall no longer be forsaken, but the dwellers of Darkness gather within the Light. The Salvation of Demonkind shall spring from the dead of night; a glorious, frosted beast amongst raging flames; a prismatic arc spanning the worlds, it shall rejuvenate the thousand-year divide."*

"My Goddess, that sounds comprehensive if anything," Anaya exclaimed. "Am I meant to achieve peace between humans and demons?"

"I cannot say," Samael admitted. "But what did the Prime tell you?"

"She said I granted her salvation." The priestess felt her tears welling once more. "I am so sorry, Samael. All the suffering we have caused… How could I possibly be the one to offer deliverance to demons? It should be seen as offensive, to even suggest it!"

Putting the book away, the demon placed his hands behind her head. "You need to remember that the path taken by the Priesthood is what unified us, my love. Do not let the road travelled taint the destination. But for those gruesome acts, your resolute beliefs would never have faltered, and I would never have been allowed to become acquainted with yourself. We are both part of prophecies voiced by the Spirits, and as such, we need to trust in them. The same with your Goddess." Pulling her in, he kissed her softly.

Anaya felt her body throb at his touch, moving in to return his affections.

Parting his lips from hers, he gently kissed her forehead. "I am not exactly one to ask for trust in the Spirits, but with recent events, I feel as if it might be wise."

Nodding, the priestess sighed. "You are most likely right. I only wished I knew more, for I feel myself becoming increasingly confused with everything going on." She dabbed the edge of her sleeve over her moist eyes. "As I told Lilith of the Goddess, she said much of the story resembled your own, about your Spirits. What are the Spirits?"

Samael's expression pulled tight. "I am not the best person to answer this question. This is a discussion to be held with one of the Shamans, or at least my mother."

"Just explain it simply," Anaya pressed him. "Anything is better than being left in the dark!"

"Fine, yes. I suppose you are right." He scratched his head. "If I recall correctly, the six Spirits – Earth, Fire, Air, Water, Light, and Darkness – joined to create the world. Earth formed the ground, water made the lakes and the oceans, and so on. They all designed the world's animals and the souls of life within them. The Spirit of Light made humans, whereas the Spirit of Darkness conceived demonkind. They also joined to establish night and day – thus being the founders of time."

"And so, who, or what, is evil?" Anaya asked.

"What do you mean? Why would a Spirit be evil?"

Stumped, the priestess blinked. "For us, the Darkness is evil incarnate. It is the entity that brings damnation and chaos. Is there no such thing?"

Samael shook his head. "Much like what the Shaman explained at the wedding, the Spirits work together, as if in a constant cycle. It is only if a demon is left without the Spirits blessing – ending up in hell – that one is truly lost. But that is not a world ruled by the Spirit of Darkness, it is a world of absolute emptiness."

"Such as when you were lost to the Feral?"

"Exactly," the demon replied, clasping her hand. "But Anaya, I do not see how this will help to remove the taint upon my own spirit. Do you believe the Spirits have forsaken me?"

"Oh, no, not at all!" she exclaimed, holding him tightly. "We will see this through, no matter what happens." Placing her hands on his head once more, she smiled. "Now, let me scan you. I want to make sure the enchantment had the desired effect."

Light bathed the couple where they sat, then sparkled through the air as it dispersed.

"The rift is indeed sealed," Anaya declared. "There are several of them left, but perhaps this new tactic is worth pursuing, as long as you can handle it."

"I can," Samael said. "If that changes, however, I will tell you."

7

THE UNN

Walking across the camp, the young girl avoided eye contact with everyone around her. A man, travelling the path in the opposite direction, brushed against her, and she halted, squeezing her eyes shut. Her body tensed as she expected him to claim her. No matter how many times this occurred in her life, she would not grow accustomed to the idea of acting as someone's source of entertainment. At least not in a – dare she think the words? – carnal manner.

The last thing she wanted was to lay with another mercenary this day, the mere thought making her shiver. Almost every night, someone would take her in, which was enough for her. The favours asked would differ significantly, and even if they were often simple, the risk of a mundane conversation turning into a sexual encounter was not worth it.

As the man's touch faded, she allowed herself to open her eyes. She had been spared, at least for now.

Despite being undecided on her destination, the young woman resumed her trudge through the campsite. She stopped at the far end of the grounds, stumbling upon Gus as he sat alone in front of a fire.

"May I sit with you?" she asked.

Without looking at the girl, he angled away. "Do as you please," he replied.

Placing herself opposite the man, she held her hands up towards the flames. She watched him intently, but he would not meet her gaze. He was a large man, his stature imposing, but oddly enough, his grey eyes would often hint towards a warmer side. His brown hair had a reddish hue to it, and it was always kept reasonably short, but he would neglect his beard. Both showed silver streaks through them, despite the man only being in his mid-thirties. He had been with the band for a long time, over a decade, but originated from somewhere up north, in the snowy mountains. But that was all she knew about him.

Gus came forward, leaning his chin onto the palm of his hand. A golden band gleamed as it reflected the light from the fire, placed on his right ring finger.

The girl had seen it before, making her wonder why he wore it. He had no other trinkets, and he was certainly not the kind of man to want any. "Are you married, Gus?" she inquired.

"None of your business… *Nia*."

The emphasis he had put on her name was not in any way positive. Her posture stooped, the man as aloof as always. Pushing her black hair back, she tied the unruly mop together with a leather strap. The curls caused it to spread out, and it was often in the way.

Sitting close to her tent, she looked across at it. She had been given someone's spare canvas, hung over a piece of string which was suspended between two trees. Whenever there was terrible weather, the rain would seep into it, leaving her cold and wet. Those nights, she would stroll the camp more regularly, waiting for one of the men to take her in. For no matter how much she ached to leave this life behind – and her subsequent nightmarish memories that would always spawn in the wake of the act – it was still better to warm someone's bed than to lay alone and freeze to death.

Spending the last three months with a mercenary band, she had been with most of them. The only ones not to show any interest at all was Bella, their leader's on-and-off girlfriend, and Gus. The girl had lost count, but about twenty of the twenty-six men had all had their share of – what they claimed to be – pleasure.

This had never been Nia's plan as she travelled away from her home country of Kanadesh. She had lived a happy life in the southern deserts, shielded from the miseries of a low caste life by her father's work as a performer and musician at the royal courts.

Unfortunate events had left Nia an orphan before marital age, and eventually – at merely nineteen – she had no family left. She had lived the last year with her uncle, who sadly passed away from illness. Having very little money left, she journeyed north in search of a new living. Being one of few people of colour ever to reach as far as As-Uru, she found herself unwanted, many treating her as if she were a demon. The trade inherited from her father did little to save her from a life of grief.

Arriving in a large city, she had by chance met a woman claiming to offer her a respected line of work. She had brought her to a grand house, within which lived several young women, all nicely dressed, with their own, individual rooms. Nia had been elated to find such accommodation, her room offering a large bed, a dresser and even a desk with a small chair. Little did she know what she had agreed to.

Watching the swirling flames of the fire, Nia visibly shuddered, her memories cruelly resurfacing, as they always did.

"This will be your home, lass," chirped the more than voluptuous lady of the manor, holding the door open for Nia to enter.

Barely enough space left between the doorway and the matron's voluminous dress, the young girl squeezed past, the dirt of her clothing smearing against the door jamb. A breath left her, her mouth agape as she took in the sight of her new, most fashionable abode. It featured furniture from all over the continent – even a Kanadeshian rug, bold colours and edged patterns adorning its surface. Oh, how she had longed for the feel of the luscious frieze under her feet!

Something changed in that very moment. All those months spent on the road, being called every derogatory name under the sun, then left abandoned in the mud alongside a deserted mining town... It all seemingly washed away, standing aside for this new, yet familiar emotion – excitement.

"A bath has been prepared in the next room, to the right along the corridor. Get yourself cleaned up, then dress in one of the garments available in your wardrobe." The matron's many skirts swished as she turned in the doorway. "Make sure you are ready within the hour."

If Nia had only known what the time limit had referred to, then she would have taken the opportunity to escape without delay. Regardless of the cost, she would have left, avoiding the one moment of her life which had stripped her of all her innocence and self-worth.

Blissfully unaware of her upcoming ordeal, Nia wasted not a moment, enjoying a warm bath for the first time in months. Layer upon layer of dirt and grime was rinsed away with soap and water, revealing her unblemished, velvety skin beneath.

Wrapped in a towel, Nia skipped back through the hallway, returning to her new chambers. She started sifting through the generously filled wardrobe, soon pulling out one of the less garish gowns. Every single garment held plenty of colours, stitching, lace and pearls. They were not quite to Nia's taste, but still, she settled on a soft shade of blue, with a deep neckline and layered skirt.

The young woman had barely tightened the garment around her waist as a man suddenly barraged through the door, leaving it swinging on its hinges.

Nia spun to face him, her eyes wide. She opened her mouth to speak but found her tongue affixed as the stranger gained on her.

Stopping before her, he roughly grabbed at her face, his eyes tracing her. "Ha! And I did not believe the matron!"

Nia reared back, pulling herself free from his grip. "What are you doing?" she howled, feathering her now sore cheek. "You don't treat a lady like this! Who are you?"

A vicious grin spread on the man's lips. "Oh, I'm no one important. At least not to you, dear *desher*."

Her fists tightening, Nia frowned at him, offended by the term. To anyone from the areas in and outside of Kanadesh, the word *desher* was incredibly demeaning and insulting. It was only ever used by those who believed people of colour were somehow worth less than those who carried a lighter complexion.

"I've always wanted to try one of you out," he continued, his savage smile growing. "To see if you women are all the same!" He reached for her again, but she moved further back into the room.

Nia felt a coldness shoot through her body, fearing where this might lead. "No!" she asserted. "Don't you *dare!*"

"Dare what, desher?" he challenged. "You are mine for tonight. I paid extra for you." He bolted forward, leaving no chance for her to escape. The young woman screamed in his grip, but he would not yield.

Tears streamed down her face as Nia cried and fought for all what life was worth, unwilling to succumb to his assault. She desperately called for anyone to help her, to save her from this atrocious man. Yet all she heard was how the door shut behind him.

Nia now knew what establishment the matron worked. Sadness and horror flooded the young woman all the same, for there was no aid to be had.

The stranger had been rough, believing Nia to be feigning her surprise at his advances. He had said it was a good show, enhancing his arousal. The young woman remembered how she had bled that night when she lost her virginity, locked up in her room, and left to deal with her misery alone. And thus, her fate was sealed.

Growing up with a strong-willed mother, Nia had been taught to speak her mind and stay true to her beliefs, but everything that had happened since she left Kanadesh, as well as her current situation, was breaking her down, bit by bit. Soon, there would be nothing left of her old self, a woman so proud of her origin and heritage. She would slowly hollow out, submitting to what was now her new living nightmare.

Tears stung her eyes, but Nia hurriedly blinked them away. Looking up, she noticed how Gus, only for the faintest of moments, stared back at her. Had he seen the signs of her distress?

Seemingly forcing himself to focus elsewhere, the swordsman reached for another log, placing it in the fire.

Wringing her wrists, Nia needed a distraction, to lessen her growing anxiety. She quickly chose to return to her previous subject. "I would have liked to get married someday."

"A wedding band is worn on the left," he scoffed, finally meeting her gaze again.

"Yes, but you do not have that finger, hence why I asked. I only wish for some pleasant conversation."

The man grunted but said nothing.

She knew that, even if she pressed, he would not respond. Looking up into the sky, the young woman could see clouds gathering, blocking out what little light there was. "Can I stay with you tonight?" she asked.

His eyebrows raised at the inquiry. "Me?"

"Yes. You… never ask for me."

"Because I don't want you," Gus answered. "Stay in your own tent."

Nia released a whine. "It does not shield me from the rain."

The man rose, towering over her. "Not my problem," he said, then strode away.

The girl watched him leave, holding her hands up towards the fire again. Perhaps, she would nonetheless have to pace the encampment as night fell. The men had shown a lessened interest in herself as time moved on, but some would still regularly take her in. Maybe Landon would be enticed. Even though none of the mercenaries would forcibly take her – in stark contrast to many of the men who had frequented her former matron – he was the softest of them. She was not surprised he was nicknamed *the Gentleman*.

They all had informal titles, most of which referred to their personality or a physical trait. However, their leader, the man named Cyrus, was often called *Dog* or *Black Dog*. She was unsure of where it originated, but it did not exactly give great confidence in his character.

Surveying the camp, Nia could tell they were getting ready for an outing, several men emerging from their tents with weapons strapped to their belts and backs. They all wore black, heavy cloaks with large hoods, with a silver clasp holding them together at the front. On the fastener, there was a simple ring cut out, with nothing within. Cyrus had said it was because that was what they were: *nothing*.

The Unn did not exist.

Gus strode past again, equipped with his weaponry. He wore black clothing, dark leather shoulder guards and high boots, as well as a double belt around his waist. With his longsword sheathed on his back, the front strap to the scabbard was lined with throwing knives.

"Good luck, Gus," Nia said, but the man did not reply.

Grabbing hold of the reins to his new horse, he mounted it, locking his feet into the stirrups.

It was time to leave.

✶ ✶

Leaving Nia behind, the Unn headed off towards their next target. It was a two-hour ride, staying clear of the roads as to travel under the cover of darkness. Nearing the prominent household of Al Cadina, the thunder of hooves was quickly reduced to a low clobber over the soft terrain.

"I wonder who we'll leave behind today," Gus muttered, pulling his hood over his head.

Cyrus laughed. "Get over yourself, Nine-fingers. You know we can't risk failing our assignment for the life of a band member, not even you."

The swordsman hawked and spat on the ground. "Only goes for whoever has a cock in his trousers," he retorted. "I've seen you help out *Angel* more than once."

The leader glanced at Bella, the woman riding a grey mare. "That may very well be true. Even so, the rule applies to the rest of you, so quit yapping. We are nearly there." He held his hand up, motioning for the crew to halt. "We'll move on foot from here. Everyone who hasn't already pulled their hoods up should do so now."

The group dismounted, then headed into the forest, slowly moving through the trees. There was a low wall built around the Al Cadina estate, with guards evenly positioned alongside it.

"*Dead-eye*," Cyrus simply commanded.

Jason stepped forward, readying an arrow, silently eliminating two guards in short succession. The mercenaries stepped out into the open.

Fargo placed himself against the wall, heaving the archer and Bella across. They were to move around to the entrance, opening it from the inside.

Gus remained at the back of the group, acting as the rear guard, which he most often did. He had lagged too far behind on their last mission, fighting deep into the enemy lines, and allowing the rest to escape. The Unn had already gathered the treasure they were sent to collect, so there was little point in risking their lives any further against the opponents.

The fort, where the fortune was kept, had been erected at the edge of the Abyssean sea, big waves crashing against the rocks and cliffs below.

As Gus' last adversary was stabbed, he had grabbed hold of the swordsman's weapon, sending them both crashing down into the murky waters.

"Come on, Nine-fingers," Landon hissed, noticing him slowing behind them. The blond man held a sword in either hand, but his face was barely visible under the hood.

"Mind yourself, Landon," Gus snapped. At a noise behind them, he unsheathed a throwing knife, spinning around. Releasing it, he sent it flying straight into the head of a guard.

Moving along in silence, they neared the front gates. The massive doors creaked open, revealing Bella on the other side.

"Killed three on the way," she reported. "The grounds are littered with sentries."

"Aye," Cyrus said, walking through the opening. Surveying the area, he could see guards further ahead, a few camped outside the main entrance of the Al Cadina mansion.

"You reckon they received word of us?" the woman asked.

"No," he answered. "This is most likely their regular guards. Let's work our way around. Kill on sight. Do it silently. Spread in the regular groups, half inside and half outside the walls. We don't want them to receive reinforcements."

Gus went north along the inside of the wall, together with Landon, Fargo, and another six mercenaries. One was six feet tall, carrying a giant mace and shield.

"You take the rear, *Crusher*," Gus said to the man.

"Aye, captain," he replied, waiting for the rest to pass him by.

Cyrus followed the perimeter south, with Bella and Jason. They, too, were accompanied by several more men.

✱ ✱

Gus slid his sword along the chest of the last guard, cleaning the long blade. It was a double-handed weapon, but the man usually wielded it with only one. Crafted using two types of steel, the different metals had been folded and forge-welded, creating swirling patterns along the blade. It made for a dependable and durable edge, needing minimal sharpening between uses.

Gus' group had merged with the rest of the mercenaries who had followed the inner wall, the surrounding area now clear of guards. Those beyond the wall would join them as soon as they had come full circle.

Walking around a stable building, the crew waited for all to be gathered before proceeding. Cyrus waved at his men, approaching the far end of the mansion. They descended a staircase, leading into what looked to be the servants' quarters.

"Gus and Skrill at the back," Cyrus ordered, keeping his voice low.

The man with the mace nodded, halting with Gus as the rest continued.

There were muffled noises as they moved through the floor. The Unn would not risk leaving any witnesses. Room after room was cleared, until they ascended another flight of stairs, reaching the ground floor.

"You two stay at the door," Cyrus told Gus and Skrill. "We will take care of the rest." Half the group followed their leader up the winding staircase, to the first floor.

Gus knew what it meant, which was one of his reasons for volunteering to keep watch.

Razing a household such as this, meant leaving no one alive. No generation was to be spared, as the Unn's employer otherwise ran the risk of their enemies returning for vengeance when reaching adulthood.

The man clenched his jaw, awaiting the screams of death.

There were noises of a scuffle, someone banging into a wall. A brief clash of swords, then a thud, before the ensuing shrieking. They were loud and high-pitched, clearly female.

"I beg of you, have mercy! Please!"

Another thud, the voices dissipating. Children were suddenly heard, desperately wailing, the distraught sound reverberating throughout the mansion.

Then silence.

A cold chill travelled through Gus' back. He would never get used to it, no matter how many times. The front door suddenly flung open, causing him to instantly point his sword in its direction.

A young man stepped through, pulling his hood back to reveal his face. "The grounds are cleared," he said.

Lowering the weapon, Gus released a breath. "Good work, Davis," he said. "Prepare to head back."

It was early in the morning as the crew arrived back at camp. Luckily, there had been only a little rain during the night. Nia was sleeping in her makeshift tent, but she immediately stirred as the sound of hoofbeats clapped in the distance. She sat up, rubbing her eyes. Throwing her blanket aside, she walked out to the nearby campfire, beginning to revive the flames.

It was one of her assignments – to keep the fires going whenever the band was away. She had also been made to cook and do the washing, especially whenever they had the luxury of camping alongside a stream.

A cloud of dust rose amongst the trees as the Unn neared, the first to arrive being Cyrus on his white stallion. The beast was covered in foam as it was halted at the edge of their encampment. The leader jumped out of the saddle, grabbing the reins.

Bella came up behind him, blood splattered across her face. "Good run," she concluded.

"Aye," he replied. "We are to be paid well, should they deliver what they promised. If not…"

Steering his gelding past the older man, Gus also dismounted. "Then we'll off them too," he filled in.

Cyrus merely nodded, hitching his horse before striding across the camp. As it flooded with his men, more fires were lit.

Nia stayed to one side, avoiding eye contact with all those walking past. She always struggled with what to do, as she wanted a warm place to sleep, but dreaded spreading her legs to suffer at another man's pleasure. An arm flashed out before her, grabbing hold of her linen dress. She flinched with the touch, squeezing her eyes shut.

"Come with me," the man said.

She met his gaze. It was Landon, his blue eyes friendly. She breathed a sigh of relief, offering him a polite smile. The young man led her away towards his tent.

Sitting down at the fire, Gus lifted his scabbard and row of throwing knives over his shoulder, placing them next to him.

"Damn it, Landon," Bella complained as they had gone. "Taking the girl before she prepared a meal."

"Do it yourself then, if you're hungry," Gus grumbled, instantly receiving an unforgiving stare in reply.

Wrapping his arm around the woman's waist, Cyrus grinned. "Oh, I'm hungry, alright," he said. "But not for food." He reached out, cupping her breast.

Bella licked her lips. "I could agree to that," she granted, her hand cradling his groin. Moving in, they began to kiss, their tongues tasting each other in excitement. The blood around her mouth smeared with the contact.

The man pushed his hand inside her trousers, his fingers finding their way into her core. Pulling her in, he pleasured her.

She moaned softly, nibbling at his lip.

"Go to your tent, at least," Gus said, increasingly annoyed.

"Jealous?" the woman asked, looking over at him. "Or… perhaps you'd like to join us?"

"Oh, yes. My Angel here is excellent at pleasuring two men simultaneously." Cyrus chuckled. "So, how about it?"

Gus merely glared at them.

"Never mind you then," Bella said. She grabbed Cyrus by the hand, then led him away towards his tent.

Facing the fire again, Gus flicked a dead leaf at it. "Sometimes I wonder whether or not I'm some sort of practical joke, planned by the Gods for their own entertainment."

Jason sat down beside him, offering him a piece of dried meat. "If so, we're all part of it," he said. "Perhaps, it was their idea with *the Unn*."

"Surely, it's better than *the Unnamed*."

"I tend to agree," the younger man said. "Even though Dog would've rather had us named nothing."

"Which is why we were called the Unnamed, to begin with," Gus stated. "He should've just chosen something."

Jason laughed, then took a bite out of the meat. Some pieces flew from his mouth as he spoke. "In retrospect, yes, but whatever. Not much to do about it now. Besides, we've had the name now, for what, ten years? Long before I ever joined, anyway. Why is it even a discussion?"

Skrill sat down opposite them. "Because we're bored to tears with every subject imaginable," he said. With his hood gone, he revealed his bald head and a pair of hazel eyes. He was older than the other men, having turned forty-two the same winter. "We need to reach a town, and find some entertainment," he continued.

"Aye," Gus agreed. "We'll see in the morning what Dog's got planned for us."

Cyrus shielded his eyes from the sun, watching his men accepting a chest filled with coins. "Pleasure doing business with you," he scornfully said, despite the choice of words.

The messenger bowed, ignoring the belittling tone. "The family of El-Takesha will be forever grateful," he said.

"Until someone hires us to kill you instead. Be careful spreading the word… And telling us your names."

"Yes, sir," the messenger said, slowly backing away. "Goddess' speed!" He turned, scrambling up on the wagon and retrieving the reins. Whipping them onto the horses, he sped off down the road.

There was loud cheering behind the leader, a large group of his band members gathered around a fire. It was noon, most of the tents having been disassembled during the morning.

Cyrus could see two of his men kneeling on either side of a small table. "What the hell are you doing?" he asked, pushing himself through the crowd.

Gus held Fargo's gaze, the larger man already sweating, a pearl running down his hairless head.

"I'll win this time," Fargo hissed through his teeth. The two men had locked hands, attempting to wring the other one's down. A stalemate had ensued as they stared at each other.

Coins were spread across the table, indicating a large number of bets placed by those around them.

"Never!" Gus taunted, leaning into a final push. He heaved the man's arm over, slamming his hand into the wooden surface. The legs of the table snapped, the entire piece of furniture crumbling underneath them.

The crowd roared with excitement, swords and daggers held up high.

"Sard it!" Fargo barked. "What is with you and your skills with arm wrestling?"

"That's exactly it, *Little Giant*. It's all *skill*, not strength."

The man couldn't help but chuckle. "Fine, but it still infuriates me."

"Break it up now, lads," Cyrus said. "We have to get going unless we want to risk another assignment in this hellhole. I would like us to reach Bechua soon." Joining arms with Fargo, he aided him to stand. "Bloody nobles obviously despise each other here. We'll have killed every single one of them, should we stay any longer."

Gus rose, patting dust off his trousers. "What was that other man here about?" He referred to an older gentleman who had arrived early in the morning. The men around the camp had been busy at the time, so none had heard the conversation.

"He wanted us to rid them of a demonic settlement close to their property, but I turned him down, as usual. Makes you wonder though, why these requests are becoming ever more frequent. One said it's rumoured the Priesthood is no more; that demons overrun their village and slaughtered every single one of them."

"Really?"

"Aye. That's what this last geezer said after I referred him to them. Might be worth keeping an ear out, as to the truthfulness of the statement." Cyrus rubbed at his stubble. "For if that is true, we might not be able to avoid encounters with demons for much longer."

8

CONTAGION

Adena recognised her surroundings; the bright, cloudless sky and endless fields. The poppies blanketed the earth as she slowly made her way across the grassy plains. By now, the Senior Priest had seen it several times. The tranquillity of the place only caused her to feel melancholy, as she knew what was to come.

Grabbing hold of a flower, she snapped the stem, pulling it away from the rest. She held it to her face, inhaling deeply, yet there was no scent. Lowering it back down, the petals wilted and turned to ash in the palm of her hand. The wind picked up, whirling the dust away with the wind.

Adena turned to watch it fly away with the breeze, but she immediately froze.

The row of children was already present. They all stared at her, unblinking, their expressions blank and unemotional.

For a moment, all was still. Adena knew it was merely the breath before the plunge.

As darkness fell, droplets began rolling down the children's cheeks. The tears slowly turned crimson, their cries shifting into heart-breaking sobs as the blood trickled down their faces.

Adena shut her eyes, yet it made no difference. She would still see them, within her mind, the children wailing in front of her.

Thunder roared above them, startling the Senior Priest with the noise. The skies opened, a heavy scarlet rain quickly drenching everything around her.

The children gasped for air as they desperately tried to stay afloat in the red and thick liquid.

Adena attempted to aid them, but they would only push her away as if they would rather die than allow her to touch them.

She cried, the blood around her rising fast. Soon neck-deep, she tried to swim, but to no avail. The scarlet enveloped her, the flood depriving her of air. She could see the skies above her through the claret, slowly fading away as she drowned.

It was almost a month since the Scion Prime and his Consort had entered wedlock. The couple occupied Anaya's study, with Samael lying upon the bed. His hair was gathered, the raven strands blanketing his shoulder as he threw a small leather ball into the air above him. Catching it, he flung it once more, continuously repeating the procedure. His mists slowly rolled out along the mattress, cascading over the edges.

The priestess sat at her desk, dipping her quill pen into an ink container. Books were spread out around her, most of which were left open. She scribbled notes on a piece of parchment, then placed the quill back down on the desk. She turned, looking at her husband.

He returned her gaze, clutching hold of the ball without even watching its descent. "What?"

There was a faint bob to her shoulders before she looked over at Aaron's crib, the baby asleep since the previous hour. Standing up, she walked over to Samael, joining him on the bed. She huddled up against him, holding on to his shirt, taking a deep breath. She felt the delightful frisson from his aura and inhaled his rich scent, his essence hinting everything from pepper to cardamom. Her grip curled ever tighter around the fabric of the garment, the young woman throbbing with their contact.

Gently stroking her hair, he smiled. "Are you alright?" he asked, placing a finger under her chin. He guided her up, his eyes soft as he brushed his thumb across her cheek.

"I am," she said. "I only wish we could… enjoy a bit more closeness."

The demon grinned, even though there was a certain sadness to the expression. In truth, he was frightened of what his volatile feral state might lead to, and could thus not allow them the pleasure of making love. "I suppose it is nice to hear I am not the only one longing for it."

"You are certainly not alone," she told him. "Let me scan you and see if this might be a good time for a session. I can tell your mists have increased since this morning." She sat up, straddling him, placing her hands over his head. She felt his hands curve her hips, the grip firm but gallant. A whirl of emotions rippled through her as she focused, allowing her Light to spread out around them. With the demon surrendering to her touch, they were ready to begin.

"It is not as bad as last," she said. "But I believe it is worth doing. It may very well be another Prime."

Samael closed his eyes. "I am ready when you are," he answered.

"Good. I shall begin."

✶ ✶

It was strange, how the priestess' spirit so easily drifted away. The previous time, it felt as if it had been ripped from her body, but now it merely floated through her mortal flesh, whooshing into the rift inside Samael's mind.

Anaya's vision was still blurred as she arrived at the destination of the memory, first unsure of where to look. She could make out movements before her, tiny lights swirling in all directions. The priestess was standing inside what seemed to be another cave, the walls made from compact dirt. There were several smaller rooms attached to it, creating a decent-sized dwelling.

A rangy man traversed the space at speed. "The scent of blood is upon us," he proclaimed. "All able-bodied, come with me. *Now!*"

Men and women came running from the adjacent hollows, hurrying up the path towards the entrance.

The priestess sped past them, her spirit suspended in the air. She saw smoke billowing around the demons, the man at the front now standing tall as a large lynx. He was their Prime.

"I SHALL ATTEMPT TO SPEAK WITH THEM," he said. **"I HAVE NO INTEREST IN ATTACKING. I WILL NOT NEEDLESSLY RISK THE LIVES OF OUR YOUNG."**

One of the other lynxes affectionately pushed her snout into his. "Be careful, my love."

The Prime nodded, then stepped forward, looking across at the gathered priests. A woman at the front seemed to be their leader, gaining his attention. **"WHAT BUSINESS HAVE YOU WITH THE LYNX TRIBE, HUMAN?"** he called, the distorted voice echoing in the forest.

Anaya saw how the priests shuffled at the sound, but also how Adena addressed them.

"Do not despair!" she shouted. "It is only his demonic aura. It cannot affect you if you do not allow it!"

"They will not back down," the Consort whispered.

"I AM AFRAID NOT."

Light flashed around the priests as they charged, the lynxes coming to meet them. The inevitable clash was bloody, and Anaya struggled to make sense of the mayhem. The demons burned themselves within the powerful spells, but the Prime dampened the effects with his spreading aura. They gained ground, despite losing several of their kin.

The priestess could see Eden fighting amongst them, this most likely being the fight where he had been mortally injured. He was pushed back by one of the beasts, rolling with the force.

Having already singled Adena out from the rest, the Prime focused on her. He swerved from an attack, then slashed at her with his paws. As he ruthlessly fought against her, he felt pain to his side. Claret poured from several wounds, arrows protruding from across his flank. He roared, the black mists raging with his agony.

More shouting was heard. Anaya looked past the fighting, noticing another group of priests joining in the battle. Kaedin ran at the front, slamming his shield into the Prime. He slashed into the beast's leg, then avoided a counterattack.

The Prime suddenly shrieked, facing Adena, but she had drifted away from him. At the end of her blade, his Consort laid dead, her blood trickling down the cold steel. Mad grief consumed him as he dashed for the female Senior Priest. A young man came into his path, the beast whipping his paw along the ground, then crashing into him.

Eden had merely been in the way.

Bearing down on him, the Prime bit into the youth, filling him with his black mists.

Arrows rained, digging into the head of the massive lynx. The scorching Light finally forced him to release Eden as he desperately clawed at anything around him. Feeling a sudden heat to his back, flames licked his tanned coat.

Anaya recognised the panicked state within the demon as he shook himself, attempting to extinguish the fire. He ran into Kaedin, then staggered forward.

All was still as the Prime felt his strength slipping, his legs giving way. Lowering himself to the ground, he heaved out a staggering breath.

In a whirl of dust, all the priests were gone.

Anaya soundlessly floated down to the ground, then approached the massive corpse of the lynx.

"Am I dead?" it asked.

"You are."

"Mm. I assumed as much." The voice was quiet for a moment, then resurfaced. "Why did you kill us? We had done nothing."

The priestess swallowed a whimper. How was she to reply to such a question? It was something she had wondered so many times herself. "Because there is evil in this world," she said, her voice tearful. "And we were part of that evil."

"But you are no longer, *Prophet*. I can sense it. You walk *the Path of Salvation*."

Anaya hesitated at his words. "How... how am I to reach it? Even if I never want to be part of evil again, I do not know where to turn."

"Salvation is not a destination," the Prime replied. "You experience redemption as you travel the road of your existence, through your actions, and that of others."

"My journey through life is salvation?"

"It is... if you allow it." Black mists enveloped the lynx' body. When they slowly diminished, his human form was revealed on the ground. "May the *Spirit of Light* guide you."

The world disappeared, the priestess travelling back towards her body. A sense of calm settled over her, knowing this Prime would peacefully reach the afterlife.

A trickle of coldness ran down Anaya's back as she was about to cross through the rift. She attempted to shake it, yet it prompted her to look across her shoulder.

As the crevice closed, the priestess saw something. She was only offered a glimpse of it before it vanished, but the image became seared into her mind. It lied just below the surface, dark and hulking... lurking within the taint.

Lilith sat facing the flames in the open fireplace. She would often watch them, finding herself mesmerised by the dancing shades of red and gold. It fascinated her, how the blaze would continuously change, no matter how long she gazed at it. Seated in her dining room, the Matriarch had pushed her chair away from the table after finishing her noon meal. As soon as the food had been cleared away, she had called for Kaedin.

Arax held the door open for the man, then stepped back outside.

"Welcome, Master Reed," Lilith said. "Come on in."

The officer walked over to the table but remained standing.

"How are you managing the changes within the Priesthood?"

"All is going well, my lady. All those suggested have accepted their positions. Whenever we have a base of operations, the new ranking systems shall be put into effect."

"Good. Any news from your scouts?"

"Only that the Temple village is in ruins, and is still overrun by demons."

Gathering her hair, the Matriarch placed the locks forward across her shoulder. The raven strands merged with her black dress. "Indeed, I have received a similar report," she affirmed. "It is mainly hound demons, is it not?"

"Aye, my lady."

Lilith leaned against the backrest. "From the correspondence with the said tribe, they seem unwilling to retreat due to a grudge with yourselves.

However, I believe our company might entice them into changing their minds."

"I would imagine so," Kaedin stated. "When would you plan such a visit?"

"Whenever my son has recovered."

"Recovered?"

"To keep a long story short," she said, unamused. "Your High Priest's concoction is causing a few issues at present, something which Anaya is working on. Whenever it has been dealt with, he will be dispatched. His presence alone will scatter them, trust me."

"That... wouldn't surprise me, my lady."

An appeased grin spread on the Matriarch's face. "I have already spoken to Mistress Barton about the possibility of meeting with your King. She suggested rebuilding the Priesthood first, which I wholly agree with. We need something to show for, before we make allegiances, so other parties know who they are to be affiliated with."

"Aye. We spoke of it amongst the officers."

Lilith was silent for a moment, twirling a lock of hair between her fingers. "How are the panther scouts treating you, Master Reed?"

He scratched his beard. "Suitably, considering I am... human."

"Do they not follow your orders?" she questioned.

"They do, but not with a great deal of enthusiasm."

The Matriarch's brow lowered. "I have a feeling that is not the entire truth of the matter."

Kaedin remained silent, holding her gaze.

"Anyone who fails to execute orders is liable to corporal punishment due to insubordination. Give me the names, and I shall have it done."

"Let me speak to them again," he said. "I was meant to give them a chance, but it is fast becoming less than ideal. Benjamin is the only one not to question my authority."

"As you wish, Master Reed. You need only to send word, and I shall see to their penalty." She nodded in response to the officer's silent bow. "You are dismissed."

✶ ✶

Leaving the Matriarch's home, Kaedin strode off towards the Priest-hood campsite. He nodded greetings to a few of the priests before entering his tent. He was to change into his armour, readying himself for a round of sparring with Eden. The officer was not about to let him slip, the young man seething with potential. Today, he was meant to teach him weak spots in a suit of armour, until they could find another set for Eden to wear and fight on equal terms.

Eden was both a hard worker and a fast learner. Whenever he wasn't busy with the local blacksmith, crafting tools and weapons, he would ask Kaedin for practice.

It was cumbersome for the male officer to don the gear as this was in truth supposed to be a two-man job. However, through his years as the sole user of plate armour within the Priesthood, he had learned ways to tighten the various straps on his own, but it was time-consuming. He first needed to dress in a layer of thick cotton, then one of chain mail, before the armour plates were strapped on. They included shoulder guards, a chest- and backplate, leg guards, plated gloves, and reinforced high boots. His sword was sheathed on his back, together with his shield, as well as a thick cloak.

Coming back outside, Kaedin held his helmet under his arm.

The weather was fair, only a few clouds in the sky and the temperature was comfortable.

Eden was already dressed, standing ready at their allocated training grounds. He excitedly hefted his spear at Kaedin's approach. "Good day, sir," he said.

"Good day," the former Knight replied. He viewed the fenced-off area, looking at some newly installed target dummies. They were made from leaf-stuffed burlap sacks, enhanced with armour fashioned out of fire-wood. They were certainly not the prettiest of things, but they would serve their purpose.

Adena was swinging her sword at one, hacking away as she clutched the hilt with both hands. She seemed flustered, overly tense, and her fighting style was brutish.

"Adena," Kaedin called, but she did not react. He took a step closer. "Adena!"

She jerked, spinning around to face him. Her expression was severe, and her eyes dark.

"Are you alright?" he asked.

Briefly running her hand down her shirt, she then returned to attacking the target dummy. "I'm fine," she mumbled.

Kaedin stood unmoving for a moment, watching her. He knew she had lied, but he was not sure why. With the number of onlookers, it was not the time to challenge her about it, so he decided to focus on Eden instead. Turning around, he found Edric standing outside the low fence.

"Practice is it?" Edric inquired. He was fully garbed, his quiver loaded with freshly fletched arrows, and he was holding the reins to his horse. A stag was strapped to the rump of the beast, as the man had just returned from a hunt.

Eden nodded. "Yes, sir."

Rubbing his hands together, Kaedin beamed. "The boy is relentless," he acknowledged. "I like it."

Edric laughed. "Good sign. I shall see you all later. I need to prepare this for tenderising."

Gently releasing Aaron's hold over her breast, Anaya cradled him in her arms. He was asleep, taking a deep breath before slowly exhaling it. Behind her, she heard a similar sound, but more low-pitched. She closed her eyes, enjoying the tone and the soothing response it would bring out in her own body.

Samael was asleep, lying on his back on the bed.

The priestess still found it strange, how he would spend most of his time awake, to suddenly fall asleep in such a manner, completely closed off from the world. It would happen when he was genuinely relaxed, most often in her company.

Their son was growing up so fast. He was soon to be seven months old, spending more and more time awake. He would often lie on a soft pelt on the floor, dribbling over various carved wooden toys. He could sit up on his own but would occasionally fall over.

As her husband was most often with them, he would sit with Aaron, the size difference between the two almost remarkable. The baby was large for his age, but his father would always dwarf him where they sat.

Unsure of what expectations she even had before they reunited, Anaya had found Samael to be the most devoted father. Not once had he questioned a request to care for their baby. Instead, he would take on each task with conviction, no matter if it was only that of changing swaddling clothes. His unstable demonic aura seemed to have little effect on Aaron, their son being always content whenever close to Samael.

Carefully placing the baby in the crib, she turned towards the demon.

He was suddenly awake, staring into the ceiling while his mists billowed out around him. "Something just happened," he startlingly announced.

Anaya hurried forward, bending down over him and placing her hands on either side of his face. "It might be what I saw... with the last Prime," she said. "I have only seen lesser demons since, but this is obviously different."

"It is unlike the others," Samael rumbled. He locked his jaw, then stared at the priestess. "**YOU HAVE TO HURRY.**"

With an unyielding expression, the priestess resolutely chanted.

This was it. This was the root of all the fractures within the demon's mind. Sealing this rift would finally heal him.

✶ ✶

The priestess once again found herself floating in the air, her spirit free from the bonds of flesh. The surroundings were lighter this time, and her blurred vision quickly cleared.

A rolling fog expanded along the ground below, but blood was visible in every open area. The noise around Anaya was deafening, forcing her to cover her ears, yet it was fruitless to attempt to shut out the blaring hissing and cracking of trees.

A knot formed in the priestess' stomach as she recognised the ongoing event. It was the Stricker mines, body parts strewn in all directions. Looking across the open space, she gasped. She could see herself lying underneath a tree, battered and bloody. For a second, her beaten body was reaching out, but her hand merely slumped to the ground.

There was a roar behind Anaya's ethereal form, prompting her to turn. A cloud of demonic mist blasted through the trees, a black feline emerging. Leaping forward, it halted before her unconscious body.

The gargantuan iguana Prime stepped forward. "**WHAT IS THIS?**" he challenged.

"**STAY AWAY, TYPHOS**," Samael snarled. Pressing his claws into the dirt, he flashed his fangs.

The lizard's eyes narrowed, his tongue darting from his mouth. "**GET OUT OF MY WAY, PRIME.**"

"**NO**," the panther growled. "**SHE IS *MINE*.**"

The distorted voice of the iguana drummed as he chuckled. "**YOURS? SHE IS A PRIESTESS. NOW, BEGONE WITH YOU.**" Spinning around, the wicked lizard's tail whipped towards Samael, cutting through the black smoke.

The feline barely avoided the attack, the tip of the tail sending hair whirling into the air. Samael roared, jumping onto Typhos' back, then bit down across his neck.

The iguana shrieked, attempting to claw at the panther to remove him. Unable to reach, he vaulted forward, tackling the mountainside. Slamming Samael against the rock, he felt his bite loosening, then a chafing against his flank as he slid down.

With the panther momentarily dazed, the lizard's mouth closed over his back. Samael screamed, his ribs snapping under the terrible pressure from powerful jaws. Wrenching himself free, patches of flesh and fur tore away from his body.

Typhos righted himself, then aimed for Samael's tail, snapping hold of it. With a thrash of his head, he sent the panther hurtling into the rock face again. He watched his opponent slumping to the ground, the stone behind him smeared with crimson.

Blood dripped from Samael as he grunted, yet he spread his paws wide and arduously rose.

"**IS THIS HUMAN REALLY WORTH DYING FOR?**" Typhos questioned. Receiving no answer, he turned, quickly gaining on the priestess.

Samael forced out a sharp breath, then bolted into a sprint. With a violent contact, he charged the lizard down. He ran forward, placing himself over Anaya's body. Baring his canines, a rumble rolled out as he stood firm, his tail flicking from side to side.

The iguana righted himself, peering at the feline. "**ARE YOU SERIOUS WITH THIS, SAMAEL?**" Still offered no reply, he snorted. "**IT MATTERS NOT. MAY THE SPIRITS GREET YOU IN THE AFTERLIFE.**" He spun, his tail subsequently shooting out.

Samael's jaws swiftly closed over the priestess as he swerved, and he barely managed to dodge the attack. Placing her away from the battle, he dashed for Typhos. He slid under another swing, then bit down over his leg. In a feat of immeasurable strength, the panther hauled him aside.

Toppling over, the lizard hissed furiously, scraping at the ground as he attempted to rise. There was a sudden pressure over his neck, and he found himself unable to draw breath.

His teeth sinking through the scales, Samael crunched down over Typhos' windpipe, slowly suffocating him. He used his claws to secure a firm grip over the iguana's body, then clenched his jaw, deepening the bite.

Desperately flailing at the panther, Typhos fought to free himself. With his tail rendered ineffective, he opted for his claws, striking and slashing at the other Prime, but to no avail. He felt his life slipping away, his vision dimming.

Even when his opponent sagged, Samael reaffirmed his grip. Smoke spewed from his mouth, mixing with the gushing claret. He was not to risk the lizard regaining his consciousness. He needed to be rid of him.

Anaya watched from her vantage point, how her lover ended the life of the iguana Prime, the creature's mists immediately receding as his heart finally stopped.

Running back to the priestess' body, Samael picked her up between his jaws once more, then sped off along the mountainside. He headed west, the ground underneath him staining with his blood.

Anaya's ethereal form came down to the ground, soundlessly walking up to Typhos.

"I have been waiting for you, priestess," he said.

"Waiting for me?"

"Yes. For you to release me."

Washing her hands in a bowl of water, Corliss gazed out the open window. The air was fresh, so she enjoyed a deep breath. People were lining the streets below, trading and bartering as they made their living.

She had not worked for a long time, ever since she first fell ill. It had been many years since she first experienced the symptoms. Her husband had still been alive back then, to care for and support her throughout. Her state of health had worsened in the last couple of years, but this winter had thankfully been remarkably good. She was often capable of caring for herself, allowing her nephew additional freedom.

Lee still needed to find employment somewhere, as their funds were running dangerously low. They would soon not afford food and thus be forced to rely solely on the young man to hunt and fish.

"Aunt Corliss."

Turning around, the woman smiled, seeing him. "Lee," she said, holding her arms out to greet him. "Happy sixteenth birthday."

They embraced, then the boy stepped back again. "Thank you," he replied. "I brought a loaf of bread. I received it as payment for delivering some goods for the baker."

Corliss accepted the food. "Did he say if they would need any additional help?"

"Unfortunately, he wasn't looking for any extra hands, at this point in time. But I will keep inquiring, aunt Corliss. I promise."

"I know you will," she said, gently stroking his cheek. She noticed his attention shifting and how his gaze became distant. "What is the matter?"

"Look!" he exclaimed, pointing out the window.

Beyond the Matriarch's grand house, smoke billowed up with the wind.

"What is that?" Corliss asked.

"It has to be the Prime!" Lee answered. He hurried for the door, ripping it open. "I will go investigate."

"Be careful!" she called after him, but the boy was already gone.

Samael growled fervidly, sending Anaya lurching back. His eyes were dark as he threw himself off the bed, heading for the door.

"**I NEED TO GET OUT OF HERE!**" he snarled. "**AWAY FROM AARON!**" He staggered through the opening, out into the glaring sun. The demon made it halfway to the river before his mists exploded out around him, then fell to his knees.

"Samael!" Anaya cried, pursuing him.

"**STAY BACK!**" he demanded.

Priests began gathering at the top of the hill, alerted to the commotion and having noticed the swirling smoke. Kaedin – quick to leave the training grounds – hurried to the front, his sword drawn and shield ready. Edric joined him, still wearing his leather armour, clutching an arrow in his hand. Adena and Eden came into view, following Kaedin's lead, and Leo arrived only moments later.

"Please, let me help you!" Anaya begged her husband.

"**NO!**" Samael roared. "**I AM NOT... PUSHED TOWARDS THE FERAL. THIS IS... SOMETHING ELSE!**"

Another wave of his demonic fog pushed out from underneath him, then formed a vast black pillar, whooshing high into the air.

Anaya squinted, attempting to discern what was happening within.

A long, grotesque tail suddenly flicked amongst the mist, then a leg stepped out onto the ground. Hissing loudly, the mammoth iguana Prime solidified from the surging aura. Its body was lined with black scales, tar oozing out between them. A slim tongue darted from its mouth as it dug curved claws into the undergrowth.

Typhos' massive head flashed a long set of razor-sharp teeth as he screeched. "**I AM FREE!**"

9

RESURRECTION

E dric readied his bow, an arrow swiftly landing on his finger. "What in the world is that?" he exclaimed.

"Whatever it is, we need to subdue it," Kaedin said. He turned towards the priests around him. "Everyone, ready your arms!"

People scattered, hurrying to collect their weaponry from within the tents.

Adena hefted her sword in her hand. She was not wearing armour, but this was no time for donning equipment. "Kaedin, keep that thing busy from the front. Edric and Leo, focus your arrows at the demon's head. Eden and I will attack from the sides. Whatever you do, do *not* get hit by its tail!"

Anaya watched as her comrades raced down the hill toward the black, dragon-like creature. She chanted, Light forming around her. She needed to help them in whatever way she could, then find Samael. She needed to retrieve him from within the mists. *He must be in there somewhere.*

Charging forward, Kaedin bashed his shield sideways into the demon's head, sending teeth and blood spraying from the open mouth. Slicing his sword across its face, he then ducked under a swing, the lizard's knife-like claws flashing above him.

Swerving from the attack, Adena's weapon shot up along the demon's side, Light flashing around the blade. As parts were cut away from the beast, they merely evaporated as they hit the ground.

Typhos screeched as he spun, his tail aimed for the small crew.

Adena ducked, Edric and Leo leaping back. Kaedin barely dodged, the tail rasping against his shield. Eden was far enough away to remove himself out of its path altogether.

Renewing her attack, Adena drove her blade deep into the iguana's flank. The beast lurched with the pain, drawing the weapon free from her hand. She moved to regain it, but the lizard immediately twisted again. The tail came flying back, this time faster than last.

Kaedin saw the inevitable clash, dashing forward to save Adena. He took the full brunt of the force, being thrown back from the hit. He rolled with the added speed, thus managing to get back up on his feet. He spat crimson on the ground, then advanced on the demon.

Anaya knew she could not remain idle, no matter how she was to rescue Samael. The beast had to be thwarted, else all risked succumbing to its powers. She ran up behind Kaedin, healing as many of his injuries as she could while moving, then joined the amassing priests as they focused their Light upon the enemy.

Panthers came over the yonder, the Matriarch appearing at the top. Having both seen and felt the demonic presence, she sent her guard to their aid.

Black mists billowed out with renewed force as Typhos flicked his tail around again. He ploughed through the crowded area, tearing a panther in half, and injuring several priests. The lizard clawed at his foes, more demons perishing, but none would fall back. The priests offered no quarters.

Kaedin whacked his sword against his shield, gaining the Prime's attention, and thus granting the rest a moment to regain their strength. Arrows and spears hissed past, piercing the demon's body.

Light shone through the cracks between the iguana's scales, the black liquid sizzling and sputtering out. He shrieked as the fog further increased. His leg came crashing down on another panther, completely obliterating the creature. Reaching forward, Typhos' jaws then locked over Kaedin.

Chanting, the officer's sword glowed brightly as he stabbed it into the roof of the beast's mouth. The armour held against the pressure of the shutting mandible, and the man soon noticed the grip loosening. Kaedin let out a battle cry, his spell raging with intensity.

Typhos recoiled with the pain, releasing the officer. He whipped his body sideways, hurtling into other assailants.

On the ground behind Typhos, they could see the source of the smoke. It was as if the iguana Prime was siphoning his potency from Samael, the demon's mists swirling into the lizard. Samael was on his hands and knees, struggling to stand.

Within moments, the whole area was covered in smoke again, making it impossible for anyone to see what was going on. A sudden scream rose, unlike anything the iguana had ever brought forth – a gutwrenching primordial roar, causing everyone around them to instantly tremble.

All except Anaya.

She instinctively knew who it was. *Samael.*

"NO ONE TAKES THE POWER FROM A DESCENDANT OF FAHD!" Samael strenuously rose, his feet dragging along the ground. **"I AM THE *SCION*!"**

The mists suddenly turned, like a change in the wind. The darkness began circling Samael, creating a torrent around him. As it withdrew from Typhos, it caused the lizard to slowly come apart before them.

"NO! THIS IS NOT THE END OF ME!" the iguana screamed.

Anaya approached him, holding a hand up to his face. "But it is, Typhos. You need to find peace." Light flared out, the priestess eyes a shimmering white.

He flinched, then stood perfectly still, staring at her. *"Prophet?"* he asked, his voice soft and low pitched.

Engulfed in Anaya's brightness, Typhos appeared out of the fog, in his human form. He looked to be in his forties, tall and slim, but with long greying hair.

Everyone watched as Samael laboriously made his way for him, his returning mists pulling pieces away from Typhos' body.

"Yes," Anaya replied, holding a hand up to halt her husband. "Tell me what you need, Prime."

Heeding the priestess' command, Samael stood silently behind them.

Typhos averted his gaze. "Only to know my family will be safe." His hands and feet turned to dust, whirling up behind them as they joined with the mists.

"I will make sure of it, I promise." She reached out, touching the dead man's face. A tear descended his cheek as he looked at her. "You will see them again, but not now," she said.

He quietly nodded, his hair and head gradually disintegrating.

Anaya cried, watching him, a single witness to the tremendous pain in his expression. "I am so sorry, Typhos. You will not be forgotten."

In a whirl of air, his body crumbled, the remaining particles swirling around her before they finally settled over Samael.

Breathing heavily, the demon threw a glance at the crowds around him. Several lay dead, and many more were wounded, yet his concern lay elsewhere. Coming forward, he embraced Anaya, lifting her away from the ground. "It is over," he whispered.

She nodded as her tears flowed, her arms encircling his neck. "We will do right by them, Samael. The evil ends here."

⁕ ⁕

The Matriarch sat down on her daybed. "He did indeed call you *Prophet*, Anaya," she said.

Servants were running past them, scrambling for bedlinen and mattresses to accommodate the wounded. They were to be given a place to rest in her entrance hall, until such time as all had been healed.

"Yes, my lady," the priestess replied. "And he was not the first."

"Oh?"

Anaya looked at Samael, who merely nodded. "When removing the taint of the Primes, I experienced their moments of death," she explained. "As I attempted to offer them peace and an ability to move through to the afterlife, they have all called me *Prophet*. One even specifically mentioned the Spirit of Light, praying for... Her? Him? To guide me."

Lilith clasped her hands, pressing her thumbs together. "The Spirit of Light, you say?" Her eyes narrowed as the priestess nodded. "I did not want to voice my theories before, as I do not wish to insult your religious beliefs, but suppose the Spirit of Light is connected to the entity you call your Goddess?"

Anaya struggled to respond, as the exact same thought had been on her mind ever since her encounter with the lynx Prime. She felt torn, her most deep-rooted notions challenged in such a rigorous manner. "If... if they are one and the same?"

"Indeed," Lilith replied. "Your Goddess, and our Spirit of Light. It is not far-fetched to think they share a connection, or – beyond that – are the very same entity. This is, of course, not something we have to delve into at this moment in time, but I feel we must allow the subject to be open for discussion."

Stunned to speechlessness, Anaya merely acknowledged her words.

"It is intriguing, I have to admit," Lilith went on. "I am willing to wager all of this is to play a much larger role than we anticipated. And I would suggest you keep an open mind as we move forward, should the Spirits wish to bring further prophecies upon yourself." She silenced, pondering the event. "However, at present, rebuilding the Priesthood is our main concern. Without it, we will not be able to make the most of your form as a frosted beast. Demonkind is more likely to heed our word, should we bring proof of a possible union between humans and demons."

"I agree, my lady," the priestess said.

"Now, I would ask for Samael to oversee that the dead are gathered for a funeral ceremony, ready for when the shaman arrives."

"Yes, mother." He offered a modest bow, after which he left.

"Go ahead and rest, Anaya. You look as if you need it. I shall take care of Aaron until dinner, for which I would like you and Samael to join me."

"We will, thank you." Rubbing at her eyes, Anaya yawned at the mere thought of a bed.

"Good, now go." The Matriarch watched her leave, then looked about the room.

Holding on to his chair, Kaedin cursed. His upper body was stripped of armour, his woollen shirt stained scarlet. He grunted as another piece of his metal gear was removed, blood trickling down his leg.

"You should have said something earlier, Kaedin," Adena chided him. Unfastening more straps, she placed yet another metal plate onto a heap of all those already taken off.

"I'm fine," he said, but his expression did not mirror his speech. "The gear took most of the force."

"Yes, but certainly not all of it. And you risked your life to protect me."

"You would have been smashed to pieces otherwise," he fussed.

Adena expelled a breath. "Yes," she wheezed. She released another part of his leg armour, the man flinching as she lifted it. A large gash was revealed underneath, which she quickly healed.

Lilith approached them, leaning forward to inspect the sealed laceration. "You all did very well," she said. "You have impressed those of the Panther tribe."

"Happy to-" Kaedin snarled as the next part of his gear was lifted, exposing another wound. "Oblige... my lady."

The Matriarch smiled. "And Adena," she continued. "You are all exceptionally fierce warriors. You will make great allies for demonkind."

It was evening as Samael finished clearing the area of the battle, the grounds outside his hut now free from signs of dead and wounded. The shaman had arrived and constructed a large bonfire, administering the last rites further down the waterways.

Walking along the riverbank, the demon looked down at his bloodied shirt. He needed to get changed before his mother would summon them for dinner. Entering their hut, he found Anaya sitting in the middle of their bed. The covers were left untouched, only slightly tousled.

She smiled as the demon walked through the hallway. "I have slept," she informed him. "And Goddess knows I needed it."

"I can imagine," he granted. Fetching a new shirt from his wardrobe, he threw it on the bed, then removed his current one. Placing it over a chair, he joined Anaya, seating himself on the edge of the bed. Worn down, his raven hair spread like a blanket over his back. He felt her hand touch the strands, pushing them aside.

He glanced at her. "What?"

She gently traced his back, examining the skin. "Typhos," she said. "He... bit you."

Samael's brow furrowed. "You said you could not remember what had happened."

"I cannot, but… as I travelled into your mind, I saw the memory play out."

He sighed. "And you have concerns about it?" he asked.

"I was only curious to see… if there were any traces left."

"No. By the time I reached your village, most of it had healed." He turned, placing a leg on the bed. "Was that all you wished to know?"

"Well…" She paused, unsure if she should ask.

His flat voice would not allow for her to stall. "Continue."

She squirmed where she sat. "You… told him I was yours."

"Ah. Indeed, I did."

"May I ask why?"

Samael ran his thumb along his stubble, sitting silently for a moment. "Well, I… I did it in an effort to claim you. A male who asserts possession over a female, especially a Prime, should be left unchallenged. If Typhos had heeded the established practice, then he would have left you alone after that. I suppose, with you being human, he chose to ignore it."

"I see," Anaya said, quieting down, and leaning back onto her arms.

As he went on, he watched her intently with every spoken word. "Either way, my reason for saying the words doesn't matter. You and I both know I already loved you by then."

The priestess blushed, unable to mouth a reply.

"Say, how long was my mother going to care for Aaron?" he continued.

"Until dinner," she said, her voice low and her cheeks further reddening. She felt her heart race in her chest, anticipating his advances.

Coming down over her, Samael restrained her on the bed, leaving her hands pinned above her head by a one-handed grip. Pushing his face into her hair, his other hand felt the increased rising and falling of her chest. He took a deep breath, planting a slow, lustful kiss to her lips. "Say no, if you do not allow me to *take* you."

Anaya's mouth soundlessly fell open, feeling his hand trail her body.

With his long hair spread around them, Samael moved in for another chaste kiss. Their connection quickly intensified as her lips parted, tongues curling around each other. His body instantly trembled, his breaths deepening and joining with the vibrations. It created the resounding rumble which undeniably announced his arousal.

Anaya wanted to shriek as she heard it, to call out his name and

99

demand for his commanding presence to engulf her. She yearned for him, her body melting to his touch as she succumbed to his enthralling presence.

Unravelling the strings at the front of Anaya's dress, Samael flicked her skirt up. Their lips parted as he motioned her to sit, then he freed her from the gown. Revealing her naked body, he stopped, his gaze full of hunger.

Anaya shivered as he caressed, the man guiding her back down onto the mattress. He pressed kisses to her exposed chest, her skin singing with sensation.

Cupping her breasts, the demon's mouth feathered one of the nipples. His fangs grazed her skin, like they most often did.

The priestess twitched underneath him, experiencing a thundering ache for the man. His now dampened aura sent quivers through her, like flames flickering below the surface.

Descending her flawless body, Samael felt her softness under his lips, leaving a cool trail in his wake. Replete with her divine scent, the hair raised on the back of his neck. The demon knew he was going to need her help as they unified, but at least he enjoyed his mind being solely his own. He was not to restrain himself, even if her intoxicating essence would drive him towards the feral. With a firm grip over the priestess' knees, he spread her legs. Her silky centre was already wet to the touch, his fingers dipping into her. Her maddening fragrance caused his muscles to seize, the anticipation of breaching her painfully halting his exploration of her. Samael snarled, forcing his way down, and finally allowing for his mouth to settle at the junction of her thighs.

Anaya's voice feverishly left her, the gratifying moans brought forth as she felt his dancing tongue. Her fingers clawed into the bedding, her elbows pressing down into the mattress. Samael's fondling was startlingly arousing, taking her by surprise despite repeatedly having experienced it before. The priestess pushed out her hips, subtly imploring him to continue. She shuddered, throwing her arms over her head, and grabbing at her pillow. Her exhilaration quickly gave rise to her oncoming climax.

Releasing the priestess, the demon towered over her. He grinned, flashing his set of pearly white canines. Angling across her, he instantly pressed his lips against hers, parting them and claiming her mouth, tongues slipping and sliding against one another. Reaching down, Samael untied his trousers, pushing them down. He craved to enter her, and he needed it now.

Anaya playfully dragged her teeth along his lower lip, the two momentarily parting. She delighted in the sight of his naked body, his imposing athletic build, and deft movements. Readying a hold over him, she laced her fingers into his hair, then initiated her hymn. Light crackled around them, but his mind was crystal clear, the golden bands connecting them rapidly pulsing. Closing her eyes, she focused on the enchantment. Her head fell back on the pillows as she felt him sink into her, his length satisfyingly filling her. As the first rift began to form, she instantly closed it, then met his gaze.

Samael chuckled, impressed at her ability to stay composed. With a firm grasp over her hips, he pushed against her, over and over in seamless motion. A brazen groan left him, and his raving need for her only grew as he lavished in her saturated entrance. Unhampered, he could watch her euphoria, only adding to his own hunger. Tightening his grip on her, he burrowed deep, his breath sawing with the effort of not roaring out his pleasure.

It bordered on surreal, their ability to share such ecstasy together. Anaya savoured every second of their intimacy, desperate for more. His thrusting moves were commanding yet touching at the same time. His hands would delicately caress her, then suddenly compel her to meet him. She moistened her lips, releasing her subdued sighs with the bliss of their lovemaking.

Leaning forward, the demon greedily traced every rise and fall of her luscious body. He could not get enough of her smooth skin, her lustful eyes, and the sweet, captivating scent. Baring his fangs, he growled, pressing the sharp teeth against the soft muscle above her shoulder. He was careful not to break the skin, unwilling to cause her distress. There was just something about showing his supremacy which greatly provoked him.

It was contradictory, how he could lavish in the thought of dominating her, for in no way would he ever consider her a lesser being. She was his whole world, raised above all else, yet his attraction to her being caused him to crave subjugating her.

The very same allure once brought him back to her, time and time again. No matter his approach, no matter his hunger, *she would not back down*. He was wholly entranced by her inexhaustible fearlessness.

Rocking against her, Samael's fingers curled behind her neck. He pulled her in, his canines further forcing against her velvet skin.

Anaya tilted her head, whispering into his ear. "Just do it."

The demon's deep rumble rolled out as his fangs sunk into her, the release of tension sweeping across his body. The bond stung him as her blood trickled onto the bed linen, but he ignored it all. Yet again, she had daringly permitted his indulgence.

The priestess' overwhelming lust outweighed any pain caused by her husband's primal needs, and her soft voice changed into a cry. Her height of bliss was undeniable, and she gasped for air, releasing an elated laugh as she moaned, her state almost dreamlike.

A final shift in Samael's grasp saw his release of her shoulder. He pushed himself up, recognising the fire of his climax, clenching his jaw as the sensation flooded him. Moving above the priestess, again and again, the inferno spread through his limbs. The demon's overwhelming ecstasy roared into life, thrust by thrust, and he unleashed a deep growl. He pulsated within her, after which he finally slowed. He breathed heavily, cradling her head as he remained inside her.

Anaya silently healed the four puncture wounds left by his fangs, then brushed his hair over his shoulders. "You will just have to get used to that now, I think."

"The... purring?"

She giggled. "You said it."

Samael glared at her. "Fine. Damned nonsense, if you ask me."

"As I said, I like it. You may do it whenever you want... or don't want."

He was silent for a moment, then gently kissed her. "Whatever you say, priestess."

It was a warm day despite the gathering clouds. Now February, the mood amongst the priests had begun to sour with the lengthy outdoor living. Adena walked across the encampment, alongside Kaedin and Leo. They were on their way to attend another meeting with the Matriarch.

Inside the grand mansion, Edric waited by the door to Lilith's dining room, together with Arax.

"Welcome," the manservant said. "I shall announce your arrival." Walking ahead of them, he entered the room to address the Matriarch.

She readily acknowledged them, and the party was led inside, all sitting down at the table before her.

"A decision has been made," Lilith guilelessly stated.

Some looks were exchanged amongst the officers, but they remained quiet.

"We are to reclaim your village, on behalf of the Panther tribe."

"On *your* behalf?" Adena questioned.

"Yes. The grounds on which your village is located originally belonged to us. As such, we shall seize it by force from those currently occupying it, thus reinstating it as ours. I intend to lease the land to the Priesthood, an agreement for which has already been written up."

Arax brought out a lengthy parchment, placing it on the table.

"You are all free to read it before you make your final decision," Lilith added.

Silence fell over the room as the parchment was passed around.

"You intend to make use of your old settlement, my lady?" Kaedin asked.

"Indeed. I am currently undecided as to what extent it will be used, but I am inclined to have a base of operations there. To be divided by the eastern forest is not to our benefit. However, as the settlement is situated above your village, it should make no difference to yourselves."

"And the road leading up the city is to be renewed?" Adena inquired.

"Yes. For us to travel quickly between our respective headquarters, something more suitable than a flight of stairs might be wise."

"Then, correct me if I am wrong, my lady," Kaedin cautiously said. "You will retake the village, allow us to live there undisturbed much like before, all in exchange for… *what* exactly?"

"I was wondering the same, being as there is no clause for reimbursement from our side, your Highness," Edric pointed out.

"No, because I do not intend for you to pay with coinage." She leaned forward, placing her elbows on the table. "I have seen your strength and mean to make use of it. You shall protect the Panther tribe."

She eyed each of the officers. *"Forever* as we go forward. You shall swear allegiance to us, and as such, in a time of need... stand to *pay with your lives."*

The courtyard was brimming with life. The Priesthood wasted no time, prepared for the trip back to the Temple village already by the next day. Rows of wagons had been loaded with gear, and all the officers were already mounted on horses. Most of the priests would travel by foot, so they expected a cumbersome journey despite the clear and dry ground.

A black gelding emerged from a nearby building, surrounded by panthers. Lilith sat perched in a side-saddle upon it, with the train of her dress cascading across the beast's rump.

One of the panthers was bigger than the rest, keeping to her right-hand side. "Are you sure about joining us, my lady?" the feline asked.

"Yes, Arax. Now, stop pestering me on the subject."

He immediately lowered his head. "My apologies, my lady."

The Matriarch motioned her horse forward, joining the gathered Senior Priests in her courtyard. "Are you all ready to depart?" she inquired.

"We are, your Highness," Adena swiftly answered, but then awkwardly shifted in her saddle. Her expression changed as her eyes flitted between Lilith and her horse.

"Speak up, Mistress Barton," the Matriarch responded, having clearly noted the Senior Priest's confusion.

"You... you are riding?" Her words came out more like a question rather than a statement.

"Yes? So?"

"Well, we... or at least I, did not think demons used horses, consider-ing... your auras."

Lilith snorted. "Don't flatter yourself. You are not the only ones with the expertise to train and hold horses able to withstand a demonic pres-ence. Sure, it does take meticulous breeding, but our horses are of the highest quality." Uninterested in any further discussions on all things equestrian, she looked about, seemingly scrutinising each of the humans present. "Where is Anaya?"

"Ah, yes. We are still waiting for her," Adena said. "She said Samael was missing."

"Missing?"

"Yes. She left their son with Lenda to go find him."

The young healer sat in a carriage with Vixen, both wrapped up in thick blankets. Eden was in the front seat, holding the reins of two draft horses.

Lilith heaved out a breath. "Unusual for him not to be on time. We shall give them a minute before I send someone for them. The sun is rising, so we need to be leaving."

✶ ✶

Anaya rounded the hut, pushing the door open. Walking inside, she found the demon seated on their bed. "Samael, we need to depart," she said. Traversing the room, she halted, puzzled as he peered at her, his expression strange. He looked to be anxious. "What is the matter?" she asked.

His leg shifted, increasingly bouncing on the spot. He leaned forward, attempting to suppress the movement. "It is ridiculous," he mumbled.

Coming forward, the priestess knelt before him. "What is?"

He briefly opened his mouth, seemingly reluctant to speak. "I… need to change," he finally said.

Eyeing him, Anaya wrinkled her nose, confused. "You look fine," she said.

"No, not my clothing," he snarled. "My… *anatomy*."

No less perplexed, she cocked her head. "Yes, but why is that an issue?" she asked.

"Why do you think?" he snapped. "I was bloody *feral* last time I assumed the form!"

Ignoring his upheaval, she smiled at him, gently caressing his knee. "You have since healed, Samael. You have nothing to fear."

"That may be so, but I can't say I am very excited about it."

Anaya rose, grabbing his hand. "We will manage."

He returned her grasp, his features lightening. "What would you suggest I do? I am not in a state of great confidence at this point."

"Let us walk outside," she said, motioning him to stand.

Leaving the hut, Samael's black cloak fluttered, caught by the winter breeze.

Anaya spun, locking eyes with him. "I shall focus my Light upon you as you go through your metamorphosis."

He tensed. "Are you sure? It is not... the prettiest of sights."

"May I remind you; I have gone through it myself? I am not to be deterred."

Kneeling before her, Samael did as she asked. "Very well," he said. Taking a deep breath, he invoked his demonic powers. They instantly raged within him, yet not in the manner which he had feared. His dark mists burst out, whirling up around the couple.

The priestess held firm, Light shining from her hands while she chanted. As his soft pelt pushed against the palms of her hands, she sensed no feral tendencies. With her eyes closed, she felt as his head widened, the bones fracturing as they reshaped and expanded. His inner self was complete, the demon in control of his ferocious form, and their bond drummed to the beat of his unyielding heart.

Opening her eyes, she saw the colossal panther standing before her in all his magnificence and deference. Black smoke pushed out underneath him, and, picked up by the wind, it rose high above them.

Anaya grinned. "See? I knew you would be fine."

Samael affectionately pressed his head against her chest, releasing the now characteristic rumble of contentment. "**AS ALWAYS, YOU ARE RIGHT.**"

With her hands on either side of his muzzle, she angled forward, planting a kiss to his damp nose. "Happy to hear you have accepted your fate."

There was a roll to his snarl, as if he attempted to strangle a laugh, but he did not reply.

With the massive demon soundlessly following her, Anaya came around the corner of the Matriarch's home. Samael's mists flared out over the courtyard from behind her, causing the gathered crowds to rear back from his shrilling aura.

"Finally," Lilith expelled. "Are you ready now?"

Allowing the priestess to mount him, Samael rose. "**I AM.**"

The small army of priests and demons set up camp along their journey across the Midya plains, reaching their destination just before noon the following day.

Lilith halted her horse as the front gates of the Temple village appeared in the distance.

Stopping beside her, Samael's fog rippled amongst the tall grass.

"Go and assert our ownership, my son," she commanded. "We shall wait here."

"**YES, MOTHER.**" Samael briefly knelt forward, and Anaya slid down to the ground. He felt her hand caress his face, then a kiss to his forehead.

Adena joined the Matriarch's side. "Are you sure he can do it on his own, my lady?" she asked.

As her son sped off, Lilith merely glared at the Senior Priest but said nothing.

There was a roar in the distance, mists billowing up amongst the trees.

Looking at her hands, the Matriarch tended to her nails. "It should only take a few minutes. We might add to our collection of enemies this day, but we had warned them, long ahead of time. Any who remained, had it coming."

Scores of demons funnelled through the main entrance of the village, others climbing over the walls. They fled in every direction, fearing the wrath of the merciless intruder.

Samael re-emerged, his jaws locking over a hound demon, then flinging the mutilated corpse aside. "**I CLAIM THIS LAND FOR THE PANTHER TRIBE!**" he thundered, his anamorphic voice echoing across the grasslands.

Lilith flicked the reins, walking her horse forward. "It is ready for us to enter."

✶✶

Demonic mists surged from Samael. He walked ahead of the rest, not to scare the horses while he attempted to allay his aura. Anaya sat just behind his withers, her fingers buried within the raven fur. Nearing the village, she held her breath. She was not sure what to expect, struggling to even take in the sight of the charred outer perimeter.

It was hauntingly quiet as they came through the open gates. Fresh demon corpses littered the road, bearing proof of Samael's recent onslaught, yet everything was perfectly still. The stables were left untouched, but they were empty of any creature. Peering through the trees, Anaya could tell the eastern living quarters had survived, with only some of the vegetation singed by the inferno.

As the crowds reached the square, any lingering hope of the village surviving the attack was all but eradicated.

The area was empty, the scorched buildings having crumbled around the open space. In the centre stood the ancient oak, dead and blackened. Further west, the Park of Serenity was no more, the area flat and dark.

Looking up towards the Temple, the priestess felt the urge to avert her eyes. The exterior walls were covered in soot, and the roof had collapsed from the fires. All the windows had been shattered, the charred statue of the Goddess visible through the gaping holes.

People soon scattered, most attempting to locate the remnants of their comrades and homes. Much of the boundary wall had broken apart, with the whole western part of the village burnt down. Everything from the Proving grounds to the centre square was in ruins, including the High Priest's mansion and all which was kept within.

Adena walked full circle, soon rejoining the other officers in the square. "There are no survivors," she sadly told them.

"I figured as much," Kaedin said. "There was nothing more we could have done."

The woman nodded but could say no more, her eyes welling with tears.

Embracing her, Kaedin motionlessly held her. "Do not let this break you, Adena. We will pay respects to all the fallen, offer them a proper burial, after which we shall rebuild."

"Yes," she whimpered.

Walking along the road, Anaya returned after inspecting her old home. It had been ransacked, but the furniture and books remained, and it was luckily enough spared from the fires. Lenda and Eden's cottage had received the same treatment, and the couple were still setting straight whatever was left.

Samael leaned against the dead oak, his cold stare trailing the priestess as she approached. He stood silently, his mists still seeping out after his battle with the demons.

Edric and Leo joined them after a quick visit at the eastern quarters. Vixen was still at home, taking inventory of their belongings.

Lilith placed herself in their midst. "Since all the officers have gathered," she began but did not finish the sentence. She turned towards one of the panthers, motioning it forward.

In a whirl of smoke, it transitioned into human form, the old shaman rising from the mist. Leather straps rippled along his legs, bones and feathers hanging from the ends.

Looking at the humans before him, he reached into a pouch and brought forth a light-coloured powder. "You may see us as creatures of Darkness," he said. "But we are much more than that." He walked up to the oak, ushering Samael to step aside. Placing a hand on the stem, a green light flickered around the shaman's hand. He spoke words in an ancient language, spreading the fine dust around his feet, causing the entire tree to become engulfed in emerald flames. As they settled, the blackened shell around the oak fractured and fell, revealing a layer of healthy bark underneath. Leaves sprouted on the branches, instantly canopying above them.

The priests were speechless, in awe at what had just transpired. They briefly looked at Anaya, but she was just as taken aback as the rest.

"Before you ask, then no," the shaman continued. "It does not work on living creatures, for our spirit has already left us as we passed away. Trees and plants are different. They gain their spirit through the water in the ground and from the rays of the sun, in a continuous cycle of life."

Blank stares and open mouths had spread amongst the onlookers, the disbelief unrelenting.

"I believe we have your attention now," the Matriarch interrupted, breaking the awed silence. "Make sure you immediately begin to work on removing the taint from these grounds. The shaman shall help you put the dead to rest and revive that which can be brought back. This village needs great healing."

"Thank you, my lady," Kaedin said, his words most heartfelt. "We will be forever grateful."

"You have already agreed to my terms, so it makes little difference,

even if I do cherish the gratitude. Now, I shall go up into the mountains...
as I wish to see our old settlement."

✶✶

It was less than a mile walk from the Temple village to the Panther
tribe's previous habitat. Following the stairs running up past the burial
site, the trail continued into the mountains. Soon arriving before a wall
formed from natural rock, Lilith, Samael and Anaya stood looking through
a grand opening leading into the abandoned town. The head of a panther
was carved into the mountainside, old metal braziers still lining the main
street.

In silence, the three of them strode through the empty settlement,
underneath an alameda of ancient oaks.

The buildings had taken a hard beating in the years since Forcas' death.
Most had disintegrated entirely, with thick vegetation shooting up through
the rubble and into the cobbled streets.

Furthest up, on a raised plateau, the grand main household was still
present. It stood tall amongst the rest, majestic in its sheer size. This was
the estate erected by the late Patriarch, still holding up against the passing
of time.

Tears instantly flowed down Lilith's cheeks as she stared at the structure. Her jumbled emotions were overwhelming; elation, wistfulness,
sorrow, love, regret, and yearning, feelings roiling within her heart, and
pounding in her chest.

The man relentlessly made himself known inside the Matriarch's mind,
her lips moving as she mouthed his name: *Forcas*.

She attempted to wipe her tears, but they only kept coming. The memories of his horrifying death were as though embedded into her soul, never
to release their unyielding grip.

How Forcas had burst through the door to their entrance hall; how he
had staggered the length of the room.

. . .

The front door jolted open, slamming against the wall as mists swirled into the entrance. A boot-clad foot cumbersomely shuffled across the threshold, and white fingers clamped over the door jamb.

Seated atop an elaborately carved oak chair, Lilith gasped at the sight of her husband. His brown hair tumbled across his slumped shoulders, a ragged breath leaving the man as he took another step forward. With a hand to his chest, he coughed, blood sent splattering over the floor.

"Lilith..." he wheezed, a trickle of claret spilling down the corner of his mouth. Looking up, his hazel eyes met her wide-eyed, shocked stare. He stumbled further into the room, and his trail of mist ominously dampened with each foot he cleared.

Lilith sat frozen, her total disbelief delaying her call to action. Guards bolted in every direction around them, some leaving the mansion, others scrambling for anything that might be of use.

A full breath finally found its way into the Matriarch's lungs, and she cried out in response. "Forcas!" Leaving her seat, she ran for him, only just reaching him as he collapsed. She clawed at his shirt, desperately attempting to aid him, to lessen the impact of his fall. The smell of blood and seared flesh stung her nose as she wrapped her arms around his neck and shoulders, her dress smearing with scarlet.

Unable to move any longer, Forcas could only feel the slick wetness of his blood as it pooled around him. His breathing rasped and gurgled as he tenderly gazed at Lilith, his kind eyes raw with exhaustion. "I... I love you, L-Lilith... Tell Samael... I love..."

Reaching for the Matriarch, Anaya lightly tapped her arm. The soft touch startled Lilith back to the present. She shuddered, the emotional effects of her reverie most unexpected.

"My lady," Anaya said softly, moved by the Matriarch's heartfelt reaction. She had seldom seen her in such a state, let alone upset in this manner. Perhaps a question to focus on would help her regain her composure? "With the grounds reclaimed as your own, why not relocate?"

Lilith gently dabbed the fabric of her sleeve against her damp eyes, then joylessly looked at Anaya. Her cheeks flushed in embarrassment, but the excuse provided by Anaya was enticing, and she accepted it without pause. "Move back here?"

"Yes. You said yourself that you would perhaps create a base of operations here, but why not re-establish this as *the City of Fahd*? As it once was."

With her eyes fixed on the large manor again, Lilith smiled. "Yes. Perhaps... it is time."

10

SLAVE

Tiny blue flowers sprouted alongside the dirt roads of Bechua. It was the month of March, and spring had arrived. The Unn erected a new camp, settling down in an area outside the modest town of Orua.

Gus was already finished as he strode across to the tethered mounts. He and a few of the other band members were to ride into town for some leisure. Dressed in black clothing, he had his leather belt strapped around his waist and a dagger attached to it. They were to avoid being heavily armed, as it would raise suspicion.

Donning his cloak, he vaulted astride his gelding.

Jason sat on the horse next to him, inhaling a deep breath. "Smell that?" he asked. "That's the scent of freedom, that is."

Gus glared at him. "Idiot." Touching heels to his mount, he took off down the road.

"Hey! Nine-fingers, hold up!" Jason's mare reared, and he struggled to calm the beast. As it finally settled, he chased after the swordsman. It took almost the entire journey into Orua before he caught up with him. "Damn it, Gus! I thought we were meant to go out for some fun."

"Piss off already. I'll find you later if I intend to gamble." Gus dismounted, then strode down a side street. Finding the others later would be little trouble. He would only have to make an appearance at the closest tavern.

Striding further down the road, Gus entered a large establishment. Its name contained the word *inn*, but he knew that was not the entirety of their business. Walking up to the counter, he read a sign showing several offered services, including food, accommodations, and baths, as well as something referred to as *Specials*.

A bath was highest on Gus' priority list. The Gods knew he needed a good clean.

"Can I help you, sir?" a woman asked as she approached him. She was older but nicely dressed in a form-fitted gown.

"I need a bath," he replied.

"Very good, sir," she said. "For an extra three copper, I'll throw in a *Special*."

Reaching into his pouch, Gus left her the coinage. "Sure," he said.

"Excellent. It is on the first floor, second door to the right. She will be with you, momentarily." The woman accepted the reimbursement, then disappeared into a back room.

The man followed her directions, entering a decent sized room upstairs. There was indeed a bath situated within, with buckets of fresh water placed before a roaring fire. It seemed to be ordinarily kept as sleeping quarters, with a large bed set at one end.

He began removing his clothing, throwing his belt over a nearby chair. Pulling his shirt free, he heard a knock at the door. "Come in," he said.

A young woman walked inside, wearing a simple linen dress. She had long dark hair and brown eyes, her body petite. Remaining silent, she merely began filling the bathtub. Retrieving a soap, she frothed it in her hands, mixing it with the water.

Kicking his boots off, Gus opened his trousers. He removed them, placing them with the rest of his gear, then stepped into the bath. Sitting down, his knees were drawn up in the cramped space, and his arms rested on the raised sides.

The woman began running the soap along his upper body, cleaning his chest and arms. He was littered with scars, some still fresh, the skin red and raw.

Walking around to stand behind him, she momentarily stopped. The top of his back showed bold black lines. She could not tell what they depicted, but she knew it was what was referred to as a tattoo. They were uncommon in Bechua and the Midlands, so she knew he had to be from somewhere further north.

Pouring water over his head, the maid proceeded to wash his hair and gently remove dirt from his face. She trailed along his shoulder, then down to his hand. Massaging his fingers, she noticed his ring, carefully turning it.

Gus instantly flinched, retracting his hand.

"I apologise, sir," she swiftly said. She rounded the bath, moving on to clean his left arm. Again, she kneaded his fingers, feeling the stump of his ring finger.

"It's fine."

She smiled apologetically. "I should not have touched your belongings." Moving down, she guided his leg onto the edge of the tub. It wasn't long until she was satisfied with leaving the skin free from dirt, so she headed back to his right side. Using the last of her soap, she rubbed him down, then washed him with another pot of water. Finished, she placed a soft hand on his thigh. Tracing his wet skin, she submerged her hand below the foam-covered surface.

Gus felt her caress him, the sensation causing him to exhale.

"I am yours for the evening, sir," she said.

"I assumed as much." He locked eyes with her, the young woman surprisingly resolute in her expression. "However, I won't force it upon you."

"Treat me right, sir, and we shall both enjoy it." She rose, pushing her dress over her shoulders. It immediately gathered around her feet, revealing her naked body.

Coming out of the bath, Gus collected her in his arms. He lowered her onto the bed, placing himself above her. Water dripped onto her as he outlined her body, his hand settling over her centre. Feeling the soft hair, his fingers nestled between her inner lips. He gently pushed them inside, slowly working her, the surfaces soon slick against him.

The woman remained silent, yet he could see her mixed reaction of enjoyment and confusion. His handling was probably rare in her profession. Gus angled down, his tongue swirling around one of her nipples. She instantly tensed, her back lifting away from the mattress. A soft moan soon left her, and he grinned. He heightened his fervour over her sex, the woman increasingly animated. He rubbed at her, his fingers following the inside of her velvet sheath. He felt her move with him, crying out as she shuddered, then finally relaxing on the bed.

Releasing his grip on her, Gus waited for her to calm.

Her breathing slowed as she looked at him. "What about you, sir?"

Gus did not reply. He merely spread her legs, then seized hold of her hips. A single thrust saw him embedded inside her. It had been a long time since he last rutted with a woman, the sensation as gratifying as ever. It was always better once his bedmate had been pleasured, the entrance saturated and soft. Closing his eyes, he was silent as he moved over her. Still wet from his bath, tiny droplets trickled down upon the maid's chest, tapping across her pale skin.

She reached up, caressing his cheek to gain his attention, but he would not look at her. A sudden rise in the strength of his movements forced her to raise her arms above her head and hold firm against the bedframe.

Gus' mouth cracked open, releasing a deep sigh, after which he immediately slowed. He had no interest in prolonging it, only wishing for the satisfaction of a climax. Sliding from her, he said nothing as he traversed the room.

With his back revealed, the young woman saw the entirety of his adorned skin. The bold outline of a bear covered the best part of his upper back, trailing down into patterns and, to her, unknown symbols. She watched as he quickly dressed, and she pulled a blanket around her, sitting up.

Delving into his pouch, Gus retrieved a silver coin amongst the contents. He pinged it across to her, the maid catching it in the air.

"S-sir… this… I can't accept this," she said tentatively.

He fastened his belt. "You can. Just take it."

"But it's a month's wages!"

"I have no use for it. Treat yourself to something nice. Some time away from this, perhaps." Grabbing his cloak, he moved for the door.

The young woman came forward, her hand landing on his arm. "What is your name, sir?"

Gus pushed the door handle down. "Don't waste your time, girl. You won't see me again."

✶✶

The sun was setting as the swordsman returned to the Unn's campsite. The rest of the men who had made the trip into town were still to return. Coming off his mount, Gus loosened the girth on the saddle, then proceeded to walk through the encampment.

"Gus!" Cyrus called as the man moved past. "Come, join us."

Gus halted but remained still.

"Get over here already," the older man snapped. "I have some things I wish to discuss with you."

Obeying his orders, Gus sat down opposite. Bella was present, as well as Fargo and Skrill.

"Have you been to the barber's?" Cyrus questioned.

"Is that what you wanted to talk about? My personal grooming?"

"You just look very… clean."

"Yes," Gus flashed. "I went to the barber's! Now, get on with whatever you were about to say."

"Fine. My contact in the Capital of the Midlands has sent a reply as to my inquiry on the Priesthood. He confirms that they were raided by demons, and that the High Priest had allegedly gone mad."

"Mad?"

"Aye. He sent his priests to certain death, then left the rest as easy pickings in their own town."

Gus' brow lifted. "I have to admit, I didn't expect that."

"Neither did I," Cyrus confessed. "But something obviously happened out of public view. Not even my contact knew what had transpired, despite visiting the Priesthood on a number of occasions. However, he did relay that there had been strange activity in the Temple village lately, only that he couldn't say if it were caused by demons or humans. Either way, the King seems reluctant to approach the area."

"I hope you still intend for us to stay clear of demons," Gus emphasised. A moment's silence saw his features harden. "Cyrus, don't tell me…"

"Ah, nothing to worry about. It's a strange assignment, and I've already turned it down more than once, yet each time they reappear the payment has increased. I'm therefore in some discussions, as it's currently a vast amount of coin for little to no effort, but we shall see."

"That's what they all claim," Gus grimly stated.

"Yes, but this time, it rings true."

"And that's what you always say."

Cyrus cursed. "Shut up, Gus. You will just have to trust me on this."

The swordsman crossed his arms. "What are we even using the money for? We all have more than we could ever spend on the road."

"We won't be on the road forever, Nine-fingers," Bella said. "With a mission such as this, anyone who wishes it could retire afterwards."

"*Retire*? And do what? Bore ourselves to death? None of the crew would ever do that."

Cyrus shrugged. "Every man for himself, at the end of the day. You can always leave if you want."

Gus instantly met his gaze. "You know I wouldn't."

The older man laughed. "Indeed, I do." He reached for a hunk of dried meat, cutting a piece off with his knife. Handing it to Gus, he smiled. "Now, eat. We need to finish off our old stock within the next few days, so we can replenish before moving on."

✷ ✷

Eating in silence, Gus flicked a piece of sinew at the fire, then looked across at Nia's tent. She was lying beneath the worn-out canvas, wrapped up in blankets. She shivered, the cloth physically shifting over her body. "What are we going to do with her?" the swordsman wondered.

"Who?" Cyrus asked.

"Nia."

He seemed surprised. "What about her?"

"Just look at her!" Gus rumbled. "She's clearly ill."

"Nothing to worry about. No one is going to force themselves on the girl when she's sick."

"But we're just about to leave her like that?"

Cyrus made an unconvincing gesture in response, the palms of his hands held forward. "She's reimbursed for her... *services*. She'll be fine."

Gus glared at him. "That's laughable. You and I both know she's not paid."

Their leader choked on a breath. "May I remind you, she cost quite the sum! I paid very handsomely for the girl."

"Which only proves my point!" Gus admonished. "You essentially bought her from that brothel. She's not received a copper of it."

"Yes, but I offer her an honest living!" Cyrus countered. "She performs her womanly duties, and we supply her with everything she needs. A home, clothing, food – you name it! Even spending money, whenever she visits a town."

"Which she so far never has."

"Fine, but I intend to, should she be given the opportunity."

"And what the hell do you mean by 'home'? She lives under a ragged piece of cloth, unable to even hold water."

Cyrus' eyes narrowed. "What are you getting at, Gus? Why this show of conscience from your side?"

"You and I both know this is fast getting ridiculous, her living the way she is," the swordsman said. "At least give her a decent tent. Other than that, I couldn't care less what you do with her."

The older man looked at him intently. "If you say so."

Gus leaned back, stacking his legs. "It ain't any better than what *the Shadows* did to that boy back in the day."

"That girl isn't a child, Gus," Cyrus said earnestly. "Not even I would stoop that low."

"What boy?" Bella asked.

"You don't remember Raven's boy slave?"

"Oh, you mean *him*. What was his name? Blond boy, right?"

"Aye, that's the one," Cyrus said. "*Pretty little...* what was it again? Eric?"

"*Edric*," Gus corrected him.

"Yes! But close enough. Anyway, no children in camp here, as far as the eye can see."

"Mm, full of honest men," Gus muttered.

Fargo brought a jug of mead to his lips. "Good we didn't stick around with them for long," he said.

Cyrus nodded. "Raven was always the eccentric kind of guy."

"That's a nice way of putting it," Gus scoffed. "I'd have called him insane."

The older man laughed. "Indeed. I still remember when you beat him up that last time we saw them. What was all that about again?"

Gus looked away. "Can't remember."

As if ignoring the reply, Cyrus went on. "And what kind of name was *the Haunted Shadows* anyway? What a bad choice for a thieves' band. Besides, I knew that whole plot about the nobles outside of Tinta was a sham. It reeked of a setup from miles away. He was greedy to a fault, that Raven guy."

"And still we worked with them several times," Gus pointed out.

"Well. I am greedy also."

"But for some reasons, have higher standards?"

"You are free to take the girl in for the night, Nine-fingers," Bella said, an impish smile spreading on her cheeks. "Show how compassionate you are, with your... *higher standards.*"

"Shut up." Gus rose, then strode off towards his tent.

✶ ✶

It was midnight as Gus emerged from his canvas shelter. The camp was empty, as most of the band members had already gone to bed after the strenuous day. The air was warm, with no breeze and the sky clear. Stars littered the dark heavens, the moon high and bright.

Walking up to Nia's dwelling, the man leaned into the opening. "Girl," he said.

The young woman tiredly looked at him, offering a bleak smile.

"I'm not to do anything to you, just come with me." He reached out to Nia, who accepted his hand as he helped her rise. He held on to her as they silently moved to his tent. "I've prepared the bed for you. Go and rest."

Nia nodded, then walked inside.

"If I notice anything gone missing, I'll kill you," he threatened, then strode off.

Seating herself, she waited, believing he would return. As minutes passed, she carefully lifted the front piece of fabric of the shelter and peered outside.

Gus was sitting at a nearby tree, leaning against the stem.

Was he to leave her alone for the night? Nia was unsure of what to think, the development unlike any other she had experienced. Here was a man, bringing her to his home, yet not for his own sake, but for hers. Laying down, the woman felt the soft pelt underneath her. It was warm and comfortable, instantly returning her body heat and allowing her to finally stop trembling. Her eyelids heavy, she drifted off into a deep slumber.

Nia jerked, sitting up. She was initially confused by her unfamiliar surroundings, then remembered the previous night. Daylight was evident through the fabric of the tent as she looked around Gus' home. She rubbed at her eyes, then held her hands up in front of her. She was no longer aching, feeling better than she had for days. Smiling, she was relieved at her return to health. Throwing the covers aside, she headed out into the morning sun.

Jason was seated at a campfire, watching her amble past. "Ey!" he called. The young woman was wearing only a simple dress, and her feet were bare. "Ol' Mister Nine-fingers couldn't keep his remaining fingers off ya then?" His eyes traced her, but she did not reply.

Coming up to her tent, Nia halted. It was missing, replaced by one similar to the rest erected around the camp. It was small but looked new, the fabric dry and clean. She leaned forward, noticing her belongings placed inside. Straightening herself, she looked around, as if to see if anyone knew what was going on.

"You must have pleased him beyond belief," Jason went on. "Him supplying you all that."

Nia blushed at his words. "Where… where is he now?"

"Don't know, don't care. His horse is gone. But he'll come back. He always does."

11

TIME HEALS

ime. Time heals. Time corrects. With it, one might be able to move forward and find a new path through life.

As spring came, all that had been burnt, flourished once again. The Summer Solstice had marked the revival of the Priesthood, with their village completely cleared of evidence from the inferno.

It had taken almost two months alone to repair and restore the Temple. The amphitheatre, cut out from the bedrock below, was the only western structure left untouched. It had allowed for the now General Priest Edric Ramsey, head of recruitment, to immediately begin training new disciples.

He worked alongside three Lieutenant Priests, the rank below his own, all of whom had their individual areas of tutoring: Eli Nash, one-handed combat; Rick Charlton, double-handed arms; and Perry Lindsay, ranged weaponry.

General Priest Kaedin Reed had gathered a substantial crew of scouts, a mix of both demons and humans. They worked surprisingly well together, not seldom collaborating on missions. As responsible for intelligence and strategy, Kaedin often found himself buried in correspondence, spending many hours at his desk.

Anaya had also gained the title of General Priest, but she mainly focused on her education towards becoming a Matriarch. She was thought to assume the role in late August, and Lilith planned to announce it as the Master Primes of the Panther Tribe would gather that very same month.

The Temple village was alive with its inhabitants, the centre square shadowed by the leaves of the ancient oak. Tables were spread out underneath, many sitting down for their meals. The pantry was stocked, a new chef employed, and the infirmary had been reopened, although only daytime for now, as they still lacked healers. Managing the entire village was General Priest Leo Blythe, acting as the one with the highest level of responsibility. He would delegate work around the settlement, including everything from organising supplies to caring for their horses.

Cardinal Adena Barton continued their preachings, albeit slightly different from what the late High Priest once did. She focused on their will to do good and retain peace amongst the people, no matter if they were demon or human. The daily prayers had been reduced to weekly, held every Sunday morning. This was done because of the intense workload on everyone left within the Priesthood. The bells would nonetheless chime at the same hour every morning, marking the start of the day's work.

As the height of summer had passed, the Panther tribe was also moving into their new home.

The work on the City of Fahd had long since begun. The Matriarch's manor had already been renovated, and the lady herself moved in. She lived there together with her son's family and their servants, to stay close to the Priesthood.

Slowly, more and more panthers settled into the town, hut after hut being rebuilt, and shops opening along the central streets. Taverns played music at night, and the populace was in good spirits.

Samael and Anaya only temporarily stayed with Lilith, as they were still to finish their own home. It was designed and erected close to the cliffs overlooking the Temple village. Anaya was keen to stay as close to the priests as she possibly could. The house was therefore placed at the edge of the Panther settlement, but within the perimeter, so it had been approved.

Soon, all the tradesmen would have moved from their old village in the eastern forest, and the city would be officially opened for travellers and guests.

It was time for the Priesthood to hold their meeting with the King of the Midlands, and his castle stood ready for their arrival at the Capital.

Lilith strolled through the Temple village, several of her guards fanning out around her. Arax was walking some ways behind but kept a close eye on her and her surroundings. It was the second of August, and her home was currently being prepared for her grandson's first birthday. It was to be held the same evening, only for friends and family. Leviathan and Lyra were to arrive with their respective families, as well as Anaya's closest friends.

It was a hot day, the sun high in the sky and only a minor breeze hinting of more comfortable temperatures. Despite this, the Matriarch was still wearing a long black dress, the skirt trailing behind her.

Ambling past the street reserved for the Priesthood's officers, she arrived at the last area to be completed. The old buildings were already demolished, and new housing was currently being erected. Closest to the road, Kaedin was working together with a few of his men. They had all undressed in the blistering heat, wearing only trousers folded up to their knees.

Heaving a sledgehammer over his head, the officer slammed it onto a wooden peg, securing another log to an exterior wall of the soon-to-be cottage. He stood back, wiping sweat from his forehead, and leaning against the tool.

"Looking good," Lilith declared.

Spinning around, Kaedin's mouth opened, but he did not utter a sound.

She looked him over, her eyes tracing his half-naked body. Her lips curled in the mere hint of a smile, the man's powerful build hard to ignore. Almost six feet tall, his muscle-bound chest and arms were tanned gold from the relentless summer sun. The light hair on his chest tapered down into a fine line across his defined abdominal muscles, pointing like an arrow to his loins.

The former Knight's sturdy build was unsurprising, especially considering the strain of heavy plate armour. There were plenty of visible scars on his body, proof of his early military career. "The cottage," Lilith added, nodding towards the wall behind him.

"Ah," he said, chuckling. "Of course, my lady."

She laughed. "At ease, Master Reed. I am only here to check on your progress, not to give construction advice. I shall see you in Congress tomorrow."

"Aye, my lady."

Moving on, Lilith surveyed the park centred in the village. Most of the plant life had been revived, leaving very little evidence from the fires. Priests sat within, most reading or meditating. As she arrived at the proving grounds, she stopped at the edge to the amphitheatre. Edric stood in the arena, together with the three Lieutenants responsible for training their newest recruits. They were welcoming the group, a meagre crew of fifteen.

Satisfied with her round of the Temple village, the Matriarch decided to return home, to wrap more gifts for little Aaron.

Edric arrived at the door to his and Vixen's new home. It was larger than their previous one, as were all the officer's accommodations. Constructed over one floor, the houses included three spacious rooms. One served as a bedroom, one for receiving guests and office work, and the third for general storage, which held several wardrobes, as well as shelves and benches.

The Ramsey family's home was no different. Entering the house, Edric saw Vixen in their front room but proceeded to fetch a fresh shirt from the back.

"Edric, is that you?" she softly called.

"Yes. I'll be with you in a second." Holding the new top in his hand, he stepped into the reception room.

Vixen was seated in an armchair, holding their child. Born at the beginning of March, the baby was now almost six months of age. She was sleeping soundly, enjoying her new life at the Temple village. Their previous stay at the Matriarch's mansion had been a life of luxury, yet it was still a greater comfort to have a place to call their own. Edric often couldn't believe how his life had turned out, and the love he felt for his daughter was unlike anything he had ever experienced. She was so innocent and beautiful, and he treasured her to no end.

"I shall be quiet," he said, keeping his voice low.

"It is alright," Vixen told him. "It is about time for her to wake, as she needs to be fed before we head off to the birthday party." Gently touching the baby's round face, she cherished the plump cheeks, and the short blond hair ruffled on her head. Becoming a mother had been a massive leap in Vixen's life, yet it had felt as natural as sleeping after a long day of hard work. Every day spent in bed, every pain she had suffered, had been worth it – ten times over. And Vixen's relationship with Edric had only strengthened from this new connection. Looking up, she suddenly frowned, noticing her husband's bloodied shirt. "What have you been up to?"

"I went hunting this morning, remember?"

"Yes, but have you not been with the recruits all day?"

"I have, but I never had a chance to get changed in between." He scratched his head. "I must have scared the life out of them arriving like this. A bit hypocritical as well, preaching the importance of managing the violence needed in our prospective line of work, and I look as if I've just killed a man."

Vixen giggled. "I would imagine so." She was silent for a moment, her pleasant smile growing. "I remember when I first saw you with a stag."

He smirked. "I still cannot believe you did not find me repulsive."

"You know I am just as obnoxious as yourself. I cannot find fault in traits I keep as my own. That would be duplicitous if anything."

Edric chuckled. "I suppose you are right." Coming forward, he sat down on the floor, placing a hand on her knee. "How is Kiera?" he inquired.

"Good. Whatever she suffered from during the night, seem to have gone now. But we shall see later, I suppose."

"I am sure we will, but tell me if you need rest, and I shall stay with her."

Vixen caressed his face, looking into his deep blue eyes. "It is fine, love. I have never been happier."

Grabbing her hand, Edric gently kissed it. "Happy maybe, but tired, nonetheless. We all need sleep, no matter how cheerful we are."

"I know, but she is worth every second of my time." Vixen gazed once more at the sleeping baby, unable to release her smile. When awake, Kiera possessed the brightest of azure eyes. She was most often content but had lately suffered from restless nights due to some unknown discomfort.

A soft crow came from the baby, her arms stretching out as she yawned.

"Ah, I will feed and change her then, so we can head off," Vixen said.

"I'll fetch Grey, so you needn't walk."

"It is only a mile, Edric. We will be fine."

Standing up, the man leaned in, allowing for their lips to softly connect. "Then let me at least be the one to change her."

The mansion built by the late Patriarch Forcas Fahd of the Panther Tribe had been constructed with a grandiose entrance hall, but with Lilith soon to retire, she had asked for it to be redesigned and split into two. Most of it had been retained as a spacious hallway, open through to the first-floor ceiling above, and housing a generous staircase. The rest of the space had been added to an adjacent sitting room, with windows facing the front of the building. It was the same room which had been prepared for the day's celebrations.

"Nana!" Aaron called, seeing Lilith enter the room. The boy's raven hair reached down to his shoulders, and his dark eyes instantly locked with hers.

Sitting down on her heels, she held her arms out as he ran into her embrace.

Samael and Anaya were seated on a wide sofa by the empty fireplace, both smiling at the exchange.

"He learned that quick," the demon said.

"With his intelligence, that's no surprise," Lilith pointed out. "And besides, we are the best of friends."

The priestess laughed. "Indeed, you are." She referred to the room, adorned with pendants and glittering tinsel. In the corner closest to them, there was a large heap of wrapped gifts, taller than the boy himself.

Aaron had grown big, and began walking just before the Summer Solstice. He spoke few words, often remaining silent, but would call for his parents. The boy always stayed close to his caregivers, happy with whatever entertainment they would offer. He had yet to bear a demonic aura, but Lilith had said he would probably do so within the coming year. If he were as much like his father as he so far seemed to be, then it would occur around the age of one and a half.

Standing up, the Matriarch traversed the room, but the child clutched on to her skirt.

Throwing himself forward over the layers of fabric, the boy giggled as he was pulled across the floor.

Lilith sat down on another generous sofa, opposite Samael and Anaya. "No wonder my dresses only last for so long. Poor Benjamin is up to his eyeballs in repairs."

Flicking his hair across the backrest, Samael reclined in his seat. "Why do you think Anaya does not wear trains?" he questioned.

"Oh, but I couldn't do that, son. He loves it."

Pushing himself up, Aaron swiftly rounded his parents' sofa.

Within moments, Samael flinched. His body immediately tensed as his fingers curled around the armrest.

"What is the matter?" Anaya asked. Receiving no answer, she leaned over the backrest to investigate. "Ah."

Aaron was behind them, attempting to climb up his father's hair.

"Aaron, let go," she said. She walked around to gather him, but he squirmed in her arms.

"Dada! Dada!" he cried.

"Yes, yes. Here then," Samael conceded, accepting the toddler. Instantly content, the boy snuggled up against his chest.

There was a light knock on the door, and Arax gracefully stepped inside. "Master Prime Leviathan Sia has arrived, as well as Protector Prime Lyra Sia, and their respective families."

"Excellent," Lilith said. "Show them inside."

"Yes, my lady." He bowed, then left to fetch the guests.

As the room began filling up with people, Arax re-emerged. "General Priest Edric Ramsey with family, and Sergeant Priest Eden Huxley and his wife, have arrived."

Anaya instantly smiled, watching them enter through the open door.

Edric carried a small box, presenting it to the birthday boy. "This is for you, little guy. Happy birthday."

Aaron initially gave the officer a suspect look, but grabbed the gift, leaving it unopened as he examined it.

Vixen sat down next to Anaya, holding baby Kiera. "How are you all doing?" she asked.

"Very well, thank you," the priestess replied. "And you?"

"Good! I am tired from being up all night, but other than that, we are doing well."

"I know what you mean. Samael was spared from most of it, but Aaron still has his moments."

The Prime glared at her but remained silent.

"It is only the truth," she affirmed. "You were not there for his first few months, which, by far, were the worst." She watched as Aaron attempted to climb up on his shoulder, using his thick hair as a rope. "Sleep wise... I mean," she measly added.

"Sure," Samael said flatly. "Aaron, let go now." He lowered him onto his lap again, then grabbed the box he had been given. "Let's take a look at what you have in here instead." Opening it, he pulled out a carved wooden toy. It was hollow, with a small bell inside.

Aaron shook it wildly, laughing as he repeatedly bashed it onto his father's leg.

Samael glowered at his wife. "Yes, I sure as hell got away lightly," he coldly stated. "I am only to be beaten to death by a toddler."

"Mm, it does look harrowing," she agreed, giving him a flat look.

"I might need healing."

Pinching hold of his chin, she pulled him into a soft kiss. "I'll tend to you later," she whispered.

He smiled, then returned to entertaining their son with his new toy.

At the other end of the room, Leviathan stood with his two sisters. "I must say, you have done tremendously well reviving the city. It is truly marvellous to walk along the ancient streets."

"It was a hard decision to make, leaving this place," Lilith said. "But it was much easier concluding we should return. With the development between our tribe and the Priesthood, it felt like the right move."

"Indeed. Only somewhat further for us to travel when we come to visit, but we shall manage."

"You will have to, as I intend for us to stay here now. Although I am to retire soon."

"Do you have any date set for it?"

"No, not as of yet. Anaya is more than ready, probably knowing more about demons than demons themselves, but we are currently focusing on establishing our settlement here, after which we shall deal with the matter."

Leviathan nodded. "A sound plan, sister." He looked across at his nephew, the demon laughing with his son and holding him high into the air. "I must admit, I never thought I would see the day."

The Matriarch instantly became emotional with the subject. "Neither did I," she said, her eyes glossy. "But now he is genuinely content, in a way he never was before. It was always as if he could never truly enjoy his time in this life... until he met her."

The priestess sat with a hand resting on Samael's leg, but she was still speaking with Vixen.

"Traits from his father have most certainly come through with this change," Lilith continued. "I used to think Samael only inherited Forcas' looks, but with this... He can joke and laugh and do little things I remember his father doing back when we met. Things he cannot possibly have learned, having been so young at the time of Forcas' passing. So, his inherited charm is there, only deeply connected to his own family."

"Forcas would have been proud," Lyra said, allowing her arms to curl around her sister.

Gently caressing Lyra's hands, Lilith smiled. "He most certainly would. Even if the Spirits would only allow for this offspring, then he shall be cherished beyond imagination."

Leviathan leaned in, keeping his voice low. "Have you heard the rumours?"

The Matriarch's expression grew severe. "I have."

"Who do you think would stand to question his legitimacy?"

"Probably one of the lower houses. Suspicious meetings have been held, but no confirmed names have been brought forward. They will receive just punishment as soon as I have them. Even if I am to retire, I shall not rest until I have their heads."

"I suppose they are right by definition, but are they truly so disloyal to the House of Fahd, that they would dare bring it forward?"

"As I said, I will find out who they are and what they are planning."

"Have you told Samael?" Leviathan enquired.

Lilith gave him a sharp glare. "No."

"And you don't intend to?"

"I do, but we need to focus on our prospective meeting with the King. I cannot cause additional distractions. You know the effects of his aura and what happens when he is agitated. And trust me, this kind of news will not allow him to retain his composure."

Lyra lowered her voice. "You believe the rumours to be of malicious nature?"

Lilith allowed her gaze to settle on her precious grandson once again. "I remain cautious, that is all."

✶ ✶

Samael assisted little Aaron with his gifts. The boy was given a multitude of items, including a rocking horse, several pieces of clothing, soft toys and stuffed animals, as well as more wooden figurines and tools. He instantly loved a hammer he was meant to use on small pegs inserted into a solid block of oak.

After the cake was served and eaten, most left the celebrations. Leviathan and Lyra had left for the Sia village, and Lilith took Aaron for his afternoon nap.

Samael kissed Anaya goodbye, before leaving to oversee the day's progress on their new house.

Lenda released a sigh of relief as she sat down opposite the priestess. "Aaron is so energetic!"

"Indeed, he is," she replied. "Samael most often has his hands full."

"I can imagine, but he seems a very comfortable father."

"He is," Anaya granted. "I think he's surprised not only me but himself also."

"I would say *everyone*," Eden said, joining his wife, and placing an arm around her on the backrest. "I am not to pretend I know the man, but he feels somewhat out of character whenever he is around you and your son."

"I know," Anaya said. "But there is so much more to him than most will ever see."

Edric leaned forward. "So… when are we to call you 'your Highness'?"

A redness crept across her cheeks. "I... don't know," she said. "It is up to the Matriarch to decide, and she is yet to give word."

"I see," he said. "Well, I shall be delighted whenever given the opportunity. If anyone, you have what it takes."

"Thank you, brother, but you will not have to use such titles whenever we are in private."

Edric smirked. "You say that now, but we both know you will love being a *Queen*."

Snatching one of Aaron's toys, she flung it at him, but he grabbed it in the air.

"Nice try," he taunted.

Anaya pressed her lips flat as a staring match ensued.

"Another subject," Lenda said, snapping them out of their stalemate.

"What is that?" the priestess asked.

"How is your relationship now... with Adena?"

Silence fell over the group, as all were curious for the answer.

Taking a deep breath, Anaya sighed. "I am not to pretend it is all as well as it ever has been. It is indeed strained after what happened with Ekelon, but in all honesty, I have a feeling she is giving herself more grief than I ever could."

"You have forgiven her then?" Edric asked.

"Long ago. Her manner of conducting herself that day was to be expected, considering her beliefs."

"Yes, but we all knew he was out of his mind," he maintained. "She should have known it was a horrible notion."

"Perhaps, but we must remember her complete trust in Ekelon and his teachings. She must have thought he could somehow 'bring me back to my senses'. Even you hesitated when you saw Samael presented as my saviour."

"With that aura of his, who wouldn't?" he countered.

"Well, there you go. Adena had seen us together. We kissed that evening, so no wonder she was in shambles. No, I do not hold her actions against her. And to be honest, it is not worth dwelling on. We are where we are *because* of these events, not *despite* them."

"But so many died," Lenda said dejectedly.

"That is true, but not because Adena told the High Priest of my dealings with Samael. They need to be kept separate, for he would have attempted to achieve his vengeance regardless. We all know his family was murdered by panthers."

"What about that then?" the young girl questioned. "Why did demons do that?"

Anaya held her open palms out as if she was unsure herself. "I initially believed it was due to the attackers being young and newly gone through their first metamorphosis. Commonly, youths struggle with their demonic nature, becoming much too caught up in their animalistic instincts." She settled her hands on her lap, looking at each of her friends. "However, the Matriarch recently gave me access to criminal records from proceedings all those years ago. I told her I was curious of the attack on Midya, not only due to the relationship I had with Ekelon but also because I believe it is the one event that set in motion all that later became the Priesthood."

There was another moment of stillness as she paused, not a single one present daring to interrupt her.

"It was indeed a group of youngsters who had attacked Midya that night when Ekelon's family was murdered. With the recent expansion of the town, its inhabiting humans had roamed the forest more often, and the young panthers had encountered them on several occasions, even been hunted on some." Anaya's brow drew tightly together, the subject upsetting despite the many decades passed since its occurrence. "On the evening of the attack, one of the youths had apparently fallen into a camouflaged hole. He died instantly, impaling himself on several spears lining the bottom. It was obviously a trap, that had presumably been dug by humans, according to the testimony. This was believed since there was another such pitfall only about thirty yards south of the first. Unfinished as the trap was, it was still worked upon by humans. And that's when it all began. In a quest for vengeance, the panthers entered what can only be called a blood-thirsty rage, slaughtering everything in their path. Some of the humans made it back to their mounts, but the demons pursued them all the way to Midya, and the rest is history."

"What happened to the panthers afterwards then? Did the records say?" Edric wondered.

"Indeed, they did," Anaya told him. "The panthers that survived Ekelon's retaliation actually returned to the City of Fahd by choice, apparently to warn the tribe of the humans' presumably new powers. Neverthe-less, it was not enough to serve as a mitigating factor, and they were all subsequently sentenced to death. The death penalty has always been the lawful punishment for assaulting human settlements, and thus, said attacks have never been sanctioned by ruling demons. Instead, it seems such acts have always been perpetrated by individual demons, or groups of demons, independently of their tribes."

"You are right, no doubt," Lenda granted. "Yet, I still worry, sister."

"I know, Lenda. We have all been indoctrinated with demons being inherently evil, so it is hard to shake, but we need to make an effort... and go the extra mile."

"Have you spoken with Adena lately?" Vixen asked her, returning the focus on their Cardinal.

"Only briefly. I know she is busy with the changes within the Priest-hood, so I did not wish to bother her further, but surely, she knows I am not to hold a grudge?"

"Not you, maybe, but what about Samael?" Edric enquired.

The priestess sneered at him. "He is more likely to hold one against you, for shooting him in the chest."

All the colour drained from the officer's face as he developed an empty stare.

"Oh, do not concern yourself," she cackled. "I am merely jesting. He allows your presence, which is more than with most people. You have nothing to fear, brother."

Black mists billowed around Samael as he halted before the innermost gates of the royal castle. Anaya sat perched behind his withers, holding on to his raven fur. The guards lining the entrance steps were shaking, unable to lift their gazes from the stone underneath their feet. A knave had been sent to fetch the King's guests, but he, too, was cowering in fear.

A rumble erupted from Samael's feline form, his low growl sending shivers through everyone around him. He laid down, allowing the priestess to dismount.

Riding up behind them, the Matriarch was joined by Arax and several of her guard. Within moments, the officers of the Priesthood stopped around them, and Adena motioned her mount forward.

"We are here to meet with the King," she proclaimed.

The knave attempted to raise his hand, but unable to keep it steady, he immediately retracted it.

"Assume human form, Samael," Anaya said. "Otherwise, this is clearly not going to work."

"**I KNOW.**" He snarled as mists whirled across his body, completely enveloping him. The uncomfortable noise from snapping bones reverberated in the courtyard, then there was silence. Samael's cloak fluttered as he rose, the towering Prime visible through the dispersing smoke.

With all her guards assuming their human forms, the Matriarch was assisted down from her horse by Arax. He offered her a hand, supporting her as she stepped down from the saddle.

"Show us to your King," she ordered the knave.

The young man was finally able to stand. "Y-yes, my lady," he stuttered as he strenuously bowed.

Lilith was first to follow him, with Samael and Anaya close behind, then the officers of the Priesthood.

The entire building was made out of stone, and the outer walls were fashioned with a turret in each corner. The inner courtyard was empty of people, with the centre grounds cobbled and clean. Along the sides were the gardens, towering trees and bushes perfectly cut, the grass short and green despite the winter chill.

The main part of the castle had large double doors at the front, requiring two people to open them.

The Matriarch's guards were asked to wait outside the Great Hall, after which the group was escorted by the King's Royal Knights.

Entering the hall, they saw the King seated at the far end, in a large armchair with a high backrest. The room was expansive, both long and wide, with tall windows on either side and seats placed along the walls. It was reminiscent of a cathedral; panes of stained-glass sending swirls of colour to the floor.

Long rugs were spread out, creating a path on which the visitors could silently traverse.

"Welcome," he said as they approached. "I am Kenneth Erchenwine,

King of the Midlands and all of its provinces." He was an imposing man in his mid-fifties, with short grey hair. On his head rested a golden band, engraved with intricate patterns and embellished with diamonds. His clothing was remarkably simple, but impeccably made, every hem decorated with gold stitches. He had an open expression, his blue eyes viewing the crowd. "A table is to be prepared momentarily, but feel free to introduce yourselves."

Each name was spoken, and the officers of the Priesthood were about to begin as the King's eyes locked on Kaedin. "Sir Kaedin Reed!" he exclaimed, a full grin instantly spreading. "My Goddess, are you yet to return to your service here amongst my Knights?"

Kaedin chuckled. "No, my liege. I am quite busy still with the Priesthood."

Lilith blanched. "Are you only temporarily given leave?" she questioned.

"Depends who you ask, my lady," he replied.

"Indeed, for if it were up to me, then I would say yes," the King said. "But I did allow Sir Reed free reins with this project, and I do not intend on going back on my word now, even though I have regretted it ever since. It is most unfortunate that it was all put into writing."

A servant came forward, whispering into the King's ear.

"Ah, well. We should go and be seated, then the rest can present themselves."

✲✲

The conference was held over three hours, with a short break for luncheon. The new structure and concept of the Priesthood were explained, as well as the thought behind the collaboration between humans and demons. It was still somewhat of a utopia, considering it only included the Panther tribe thus far, but with the King's blessing, more tribes would be invited.

"I am indeed intrigued by all this, I must admit," he said. "And you will offer your support in return for my approval of this?"

"Yes," the Matriarch said. "In a time of need, the Panther tribe, and all others who join us, will stand by you against any opposition."

Kenneth's expression sobered. "Very interesting, indeed, for I might require your support sooner than one might think."

Looks were shared amongst those seated, and one of the King's advisors motioned as if urging him for silence.

"No, they deserve to know," Kenneth candidly argued. "For this agreement to be on equal terms, it should be given with equal knowledge."

Lilith tilted her head, her lips thinning. "Do continue."

"The war against Tilea was short-lived, no doubt, but it seems the quarrel has stirred another one of our neighbours." Gesturing another servant to come forward, a map was rolled out over the table. "We first noticed a faltering communication with countries to the south already through spring. However, our… mutual understandings have since further deteriorated, and the situation now affects several trade routes, rendering them useless. None of the rulers south of the Midlands has openly declared themselves an enemy, but they are manoeuvring us out of our trade agreements, little by little. I have a feeling it will not stop there."

"No," Lilith agreed. "That will only be the beginning."

"My thoughts exactly," the King said, leaning forward with his elbows on the table. "They are pressing ever closer to the border of Bechua and Engiann. No soldiers have been sighted so far, but additional scouts have been dispatched to keep an eye on any growing activity. We will have to see if it is indeed Abyssa conspiring against us, or someone else." He silenced for a moment, looking down at the supposed contract between himself, the Priesthood, and the demons. "That being said, I will have to ask you: are you still willing to uphold your end of the bargain? In a time of war, you will come to our aid?"

"Yes," the Matriarch answered, instant and indubitably. "As long as we would receive the same support from you, should we be met with an enemy.

"Of course." Kenneth licked his lips. "Considering the years of fighting against demons, we have seen much of your strength, as well as the effects of your auras. I would be highly curious as to the usefulness of this on the battlefield." He glanced at Samael. "Your son is a mighty demon, is he not?"

"He is."

"May I inspect him?"

Samael's brow lowered. "What is that supposed to mean?"

The King smiled, stacking his hands. "You see, if you are to aid me in a time of need, then I would like to see what you are offering."

"I am to become the next Patriarch," the demon hissed. "Not some kind of soldier."

"Perhaps," Kenneth said. "But you are still far stronger than the rest of you."

"I am, but I will not flaunt my demonic powers on a whim. I have nothing to prove to you."

Kenneth laughed. "Very well, I shall not push it. I may be King, but I know when to stop. I shall walk you out later. Maybe then I can catch a glimpse."

Samael scoffed, looking elsewhere.

"You will have to excuse my son," Lilith said. "He is strong-willed. However, he is right in not following your orders, since it is unwise to use the form indoors."

"Very well."

"As to the next part of the agreement." The Matriarch made use of the map already available, pointing to the spot where the City of Fahd was located. "We all know you have long disregarded demonkind. As such, we require equal rights, protection by law, as well as true ownership of our land. In the eyes of humans, we need to be seen as citizens of equal worth. We do not wish to be questioned as we roam our forests."

"Indeed," the King said. "I believe your list of requirements to be of great importance for equality, and we cannot expect tribes to join if they are given nothing concrete in return. Were they to be offered legal ownership of land, they might very well be more inclined to agree. As such, I give you my permission." He cleared his throat. "All land will be open to everyone, human and demon alike, as long as it is not private property. However, the territories given to a human or demon settlement are not allowed to be worked upon, or hunted within, by a third party. I shall have a map drawn up over the area you suggest being awarded to the Panther tribe. It will include the lower parts of the Leve mountains, the majority of the Eastern Forests, as well as the area of the Temple village. Because the Priesthood has already agreed to this, yes?"

"We have, my liege," Adena confirmed.

"Good. My Head Counsellor will draw up the agreement and have it sent to you for approval. He will also draw up the law changes, to incorporate both sides with equal punishment, no matter if the crime is committed against humans or demons."

"Excellent. We shall do the same," Lilith said.

With the King rising, all those seated around the table stood. "You all have my blessing in this new endeavour," he declared. "I pray we shall never need each other in war, and instead benefit from one another through mutual affluence. Now, go in peace."

12

THE CONGRESS

Adena released an agonising groan. The scarlet fields were becoming increasingly reoccurring, sometimes as often as several times a week.

Walking through what she knew was only a meadow of illusion, she reached out and grabbed one of the vibrant poppies, but the petals instantly blackened and withered in her hand. Her dress was now ebony in colour, with long sleeves and a high neckline, as if she had dressed for a funeral. She was already crying, in anticipation of what was to come, but these were no regular tears. The warm liquid was thick and red, smearing on her hands as she attempted to wipe them away.

No longer did she want to turn around and watch the children as they disintegrated before her. Instead, she strode on, holding her gaze high as she looked up into the blue heavens.

There was thunder in the distance, dark clouds quickly gathering above.

Adena grabbed at her skirt, and started to run. She needed to get away from there – to escape the horrors of death. The Cardinal suddenly stumbled, falling forward into the tall grass. As she pushed herself up from the ground, she could see eyes peering at her through the blades of grass. She immediately reared back, scrambling to break away. Turning around, the nightmarish sight greeted her yet again; the children stood quietly in a long row.

All movement seized as an ominous silence settled.

The rain of blood ensued, drenching the field.

A small boy stepped forward from the line of children. His long hair was heavy and wet with claret. "The light of great deeds cannot overshadow the darkness of sins. Demonkind shall never forget. There is no forgiveness."

Adena could not reply, as if a weight pressed against her constricted chest. There was no air to inhale, her conscience strangling her. She could no longer deny from where she recognised the children. Every single one of the boys and girls had died by her hand, either through her orders or by her own disgraceful sword.

And again they stood there in defiance, choosing to rather die than allow her to aid them.

A whirlwind formed around the children, tearing into them, whipping the crimson drops against their skin like razor-sharp pebbles. Mutilated corpses fell one by one, and soon the children were gone, their screams slowly fading away.

The door creaked as it opened. Adena had not been into Ekelon's cellar since his burnt mansion was cleared, but it was time to descend the dark staircase again. The space contained what little was left of his work: a few books only singed in the fires, and letters of correspondence that had been hidden away in his cave. Everything was boxed up and left in a small room, furthest down a narrow hallway.

She knew the cellar had been mainly used for storage of less valuable items, so the walls were dilapidated, and the doors no longer functioned. Either they would not open, or they refused to close once they did. Some hung at an angle, and others had gaping holes through them.

The corridor was long but straight. It led into ten separate storage rooms, of which five were more significant in size.

Using her powers of the Light, Adena created plenty of spheres to guide her way. Reaching the far end of the hallway, she entered the last room. Ekelon's belongings were placed along the wall, in dark wooden crates.

She walked up to the one with letters, proceeding to empty the contents on the floor. Before it was all disposed of, she was to see if there was anything she might have missed. She sat down, bringing the first parchment up. She only skimmed it, as it was bearing the signature of the King's counsellor. It was nothing of importance now. The next outlined the threat of bear demons within Rover. A third paper was a report given by Kaedin's scouts on the Panther tribe, dated just before Ekelon had planned the attack on them.

Considering how much of the High Priest's work was still half done as they left, he must have been confident he was to return. In no way could he have contemplated the risk of dying as he used his rage potion.

Making individual piles, Adena saved letters from those having brought forth genuine issues with demon tribes. Even if it was a long time ago now, they could still be valuable.

There were only a few parchments left as Adena read a short note. It did not offer much information, stating only one word: *Secured*, then signed by the initials *C. B.* She squinted as she scrutinised the writing. She could not recognise it, so she folded the letter up and whipped it across the room, aiming for her trash pile.

She suddenly jerked as the door opened.

"I apologise. Did I catch you off guard?" Kaedin asked.

Adena huffed. "Indeed, you did," she granted. "I must have spent more time with this than I estimated. Is it already noon?"

"Nearly," he said. "Found anything of worth?" He took a step forward to join her, planting his foot on the letter she had thrown. As the edges folded together, the remnants of the wax seal lined up.

"Not really," Adena said. "I have a separate pile with what little is worth keeping." She looked up at him, noticing him staring at his feet. "What is the matter?"

Bending down, Kaedin brought the letter into the light of one of her spheres. "Does that not... look like our old seal?"

There was not enough of it to complete the symbol, but the wax showed what looked to be two circles of different size, with a larger accommodating a smaller within.

Adena joined his side, leaning closer to examine it. "It does," she agreed, then pointed to some dots on the right. "But with some added detail to one side."

"Aye, but it is very similar." He unfolded the letter, reading the contents. "Doesn't give much away though."

"No, which is why I was about to discard it. I never noticed the wax."

"Who is C. B.? Have we ever had an officer with those initials? I only remember Lia and Alexander from the time I first came here."

Adena wore a tight expression. "No. Before us, there were only Ekelon, Daniella, Henry, and…" She stalled, her voice dying away.

"Jaxon," Kaedin grimly filled in.

She quietly nodded, a shudder shooting through her. The mere mention of his name – the very first of Ekelon's disciples – brought a flood of mixed emotions to the surface. "And there isn't even a way for us to check. All the records of past members were burnt in the fires."

Kaedin ran a finger along his neck. "It could obviously be a different faction, but it makes me believe it is sent from one of us. The only problem is why it is still here? And if it was meant for Ekelon, why would he have been sent a letter from within our own village?"

"You think he might have had a separate agenda with certain people within the Priesthood?"

"If so, they either left before our attack on the panthers… or they are dead. With no date stated, it is impossible to tell when it was sent. If this was done at any point during his more comprehensive experiments, any such letters could have very well been from one of his test subjects. Goddess knows what he was up to in that cave." Kaedin felt shivers even considering it. "Keep an eye out for any additional letters with the same seal though."

"I will," Adena said. "Are you to inspect the rooms now?"

"Aye. Hopefully, with a bit of renovation, they will function as decent holding cells. I need only to manage opening the doors first."

The sun shone brightly over the amphitheatre as Edric concluded a training session with the new recruits. From now on, the three lieutenants would take over, as he had finished assessing the disciples. Sheathing his cleaned blade, he sat down on the lowest stone step, watching as the students were still practising against each other.

"You are such a lazy bastard, Edric," was heard from behind him.

Without turning around, the man smiled. "Indeed, I am, my love."

Coming down the steps, Vixen placed herself before him. With baby Kiera cradled onto her hip, she was wearing her full set of armour. A satisfactory grin bloomed across her face. "It fits!" she proclaimed. "Finally!"

"You look amazing, as always," Edric complimented.

Motioning another priest to join them, Vixen kissed her daughter's forehead, then handed her over to him. "Here, you hold her." The recruit fumbled, taken off guard, but the baby seemed content with his presence.

Drawing her sword, Vixen pointed it at Edric. "I am in dire need of practice, so let's have at it."

Edric grinned as he rose, the man already wearing his fighting equipment. "Alright then," he said, pulling his weapon clear.

Stepping back, Vixen held his gaze, her expression suddenly resolute.

Disciples around them halted, recognising the ensuing battle, then moved away to allow them space.

Lancing forward, Vixen's initial attack flashed past Edric as he swerved. He spun around, with his sword crashing down on her. She parried, grabbing hold of her hilt with both hands. Rolling under another swing, she lunged, piercing his shirt with the tip of her blade.

Edric cursed, his brow furrowing. Taking a step back, he reaffirmed his grip on his sword, then charged.

Deflecting the blow, Vixen sidestepped, sending a reverse cut up along his side. Crimson instantly sprayed with the motion.

Groaning, the man grabbed at the open wound.

"You drop your shoulder in your swing," she explained.

Edric chanted, closing the gash. "So?"

"You do it for added strength, correct?"

"Yes."

Vixen's sword licked out, but she was unable to land her surprise attack. "You need not do it against an opponent such as myself. I am inferior in strength, so you should avoid it for the benefit of extra speed."

Their blades clashed, creating sparks with the contact. Edric and

Vixen's eyes locked, a drop of sweat trickling down the man's face. "I thought this was for *your* practice, not mine," he hissed.

She laughed, then twisted their blades around. "Why not combine the best of both worlds? Me winning against you, while teaching you a lesson!" She slashed upwards, cutting into his flesh, just below his shoulder guard.

Edric grunted as he allowed her to gain ground. "Blasted woman!" he snapped.

There were sudden cheers from the crowd as the battle intensified. The blades continuously met, none showing any sign of slowing their assault.

Breathing heavily, Vixen stepped back. "I will not allow you a win!"

"I am not backing down!" Edric forcefully challenged, throwing himself forward. Slamming his shoulder into her, he sent her flying backwards.

Rolling with the momentum, she vaulted herself up into the air, landing on her feet again. She barely managed to bring her weapon back up to parry another attack.

Edric kicked out, tripping her as he pushed against her. He came over her as she slammed down on her back, then jabbed his sword into the ground beside her. "Ten to nine!"

With the woman squirming underneath him, he grabbed hold of her hands to pin her down.

Vixen swore, snarling to his face. "Fine!"

There were additional cheers behind them, then clapping. The recruit holding Kiera stepped forward. "Who is this, your Excellency?" he asked Edric.

"My wife," Edric said as he rose, and the crowd instantly fell silent. He reached out to Vixen, but she slapped his hand away.

"I can get up on my own," she muttered.

Healing his wounds, Edric then reached for Kiera, immediately gathering her in his arms. He pressed a kiss to her cheek, then looked at Vixen. She was busy tending to her own injuries, her frown as fierce as ever.

Staring at one another, they attempted to keep a straight face, yet within mere moments they couldn't help but smile. Vixen came forward, huddling up inside Edric's extended arm. The family gathered in a loving embrace, with the two of them exchanging a soft kiss.

The weather was surprisingly good, considering it was the second week of August. There had been plenty of rain in the last few days, but today Anaya was keen on making the most of the sunshine. Lilith was tending to Aaron, in her newly established royal gardens, allowing the priestess to leave for a walk.

Anaya came down the widened path towards the Temple village, then followed the road past the square, all the way down to the stables. The building had been extended, adding enough space for plenty more mounts.

Waving at the stable hands, the priestess continued along the small trail leading to the stream. Soon standing atop the stone bridge, she closed her eyes for a moment. It still felt surreal, being in the exact same place as where she first saw Samael. All that had transpired since was astounding. Opening her eyes, she viewed the waterfall and the stone upon which he had stood. The notion made her tremble and caused a flutter in her stomach. Anaya always felt that way while they were apart, and she looked forward to their reunion.

Moving across the bridge, the priestess followed the road outlining the edge of the forest. She watched the nearby grasslands, but her thoughts still centred on her husband. She wondered if there was a way to call for him, should she need him? She knew he would come if she were injured, but what if she merely wished it?

An unexpected coldness travelled through her, and the hair on her neck stood up.

A demonic aura was clearly present, but it was none Anaya recognised. Spinning around, she saw swirling mists as a large panther dashed for her. It leapt into the air, extending its claws as it pounced.

The priestess instantly brought her hands up, sending a blinding Light out in front of her. The beast whooshed through it unhindered, slamming into her. She flew back with the hit, her flesh ripping along one of her arms. Tumbling backwards, Anaya found herself face to face with a young boy. She had managed to push his demonic powers away with her spell, leaving him in his human form.

He instantly scurried away from her. "I-I-I am so-sorry, my lady!" he cried. "I'm dead. I am so *dead!*" His eyes welled with tears as he covered his face with his hands.

The priestess rose, healing her arm before stepping forward. She was about to reach for him as she noticed smoke in the distance. Hearing a beastly roar, a shiver rippled through her.

Samael was coming.

Looking down, Anaya recognised the boy. It was the same as the one Samael had beaten for killing a horse outside of Midya.

The youth threw himself forward on the ground, with his arms held out in front of him. "Please, I beg you, spare my life!"

She was about to reply as Samael arrived. His mists swirled around him as he transformed, the man still on the move. He ran forward through the fog, his hand flashing out and grabbing the youngster by the neck. Lifting him away from the ground, Samael squeezed over his windpipe. **"THIS IS YOUR THIRD STRIKE, BOY!"**

The teenager writhed as the grip tightened.

"Samael, wait!"

The Prime instantly looked at Anaya, his eyes dark, but he said nothing.

"Don't kill him," she urged him. "There is something amiss here! Allow me to speak with him."

The boy was released, and he instantly collapsed on the ground.

"He *attacked* you!" Samael snapped. "That alone is reason enough for him to be put to death!"

Anaya's unwavering eye contact bore into him. "Must I remind you that you have also made yourself guilty of crimes in the past?"

"Don't even get me started, priestess. I did all that for you!"

Crossing her arms over her chest, she looked at the youngster. "Perhaps there was an idea behind this?" she suggested. "Would his prospective outcome justify the means?"

"Oh, so let's hear it then. This better be good." Samael turned to the youth. "What *brilliant* plan had you concocted, coming out this evening after my Consort?"

He gulped a breath. "I... had no plan."

Samael let out a grim chuckle, sending chills down the youth's spine.

147

"There we are then. Only as well-conceived a scheme as ever." He snatched at the boy's shirt, hauling him in.

"Hold on, my love," Anaya said, putting a hand on her husband's arm.

His mouth cracked open, his fangs showing through.

"I shall take him on as my manservant!" she blurted.

Stunned at the proclamation, Samael dropped the boy. "You *what*?"

"To be fair, I believe it is an excellent idea. He attacked me, but I easily fended him off myself. Should he not best be left alive for others to hear of this? And besides, I still need to choose a manservant." Anaya walked up to the youth, extending a hand.

Not accepting her help, he merely looked away.

"You are to take this ignorant whelp as your servant?" Samael's mists resurfaced. "Have you fallen and hit your head?"

"He clearly has heart. I believe he will step up to the challenge if given a chance." She once again looked at the boy. "Tell me the truth now. Why did you attack me?"

His gaze dropped. "I… I was not supposed to, your Highness. I lost it… I… I am struggling with my demonic form."

"Struggling with your demonic form?" Samael retorted. "You are of lesser birth. You should have no such issues. Where is your father to guide you?"

"Dead. I live with my aunt."

"No other living relatives?"

"No. And my aunt is unwell. I heard of your Consort's background with healing, so I figured I could ask her, should she ever leave on her own. But I… turned, as I tried to catch up with her… and pounced. I am sorry."

Pulling him back on his feet, Samael growled. "You'd better be sorry, or I shall wring your neck."

Tears rolled down the boy's cheeks. "I am, your Highness. I wish only to help my aunt, then I shall leave the City of Fahd."

"No need," Anaya said softly. "Release him, my love." As her husband obeyed, she came forward. "My offer still stands. Become my attendant, serve me well, and you will be rewarded accordingly. The Scion Prime shall see to your training, and teach you how to suppress your feral urges while transformed."

Samael shifted where he stood, but he refrained from protesting.

"Now, what is your answer?" the priestess asked.

"I... I accept, my lady."

She smiled wide. "Excellent!" she said. "Pray, what is your name?"

Straightening himself, he cleared his throat. "Lee Victor, my lady."

"Lee, I shall have you come to the Matriarch's mansion later this evening, as the sun sets, then I will visit with your aunt tomorrow. However, I can make no guarantees concerning her recovery."

✶ ✶

With Lee out of sight, Samael clutched around Anaya's arm. The sleeve of her dress was torn entirely, only attached at a single seam. "What was all that about?" he upbraided. "Are you insane?"

Pulling free of him, her face reddened. "Do not grab me like that, Samael! And no, I most certainly am not!"

The demon's features softened. "I am sorry," he quickly said. "I did not mean to hurt you." He stepped in, embracing her. "My heart is still racing from when I felt your pain. It... scared me."

"Do not concern yourself. I am fine," Anaya promised. "But there is something with the boy."

Releasing her, Samael's hands settled on her hips. "What about him?"

"You claim he is of lesser birth," she said. "But he certainly did not look it."

"What do you mean?" he questioned.

"He was quite large, and he... produced mists."

His eyebrows raised, Samael blinked. "Really?"

"Yes. I was perplexed when I saw the boy's face as I removed his demonic form... since I recognised him."

Samael moved a hand across his head. "That is, indeed, strange. He should be of higher birth or more to have any mists, other than during his metamorphosis. Unless that was what you saw?"

"No, he had already changed as he attacked me. And as I said, his size makes me wonder..."

"I suppose that would explain his troubles, but not why he would carry such power, originating from a lesser household."

"Perhaps, it is something we can research later," Anaya said. "I only wish to know if you accept?"

Leaning in, Samael lovingly kissed her. "I would do anything for you, and you know it."

She smiled. "Yes, but I would not want to force it upon you."

"It is fine. I shall manage. And if he turns out more powerful, as you suspect, it is only to our benefit, since a manservant needs to be able to defend the Consort." The demon paused momentarily. "Otherwise, he would have both age and strength against him."

Anaya clasped his hand in both of hers. "You are right, but I would like for him to be given a chance. That is why I would prefer to meet with him as soon as I have attended Congress this evening."

Samael nodded, gently caressing her cheek. "As you wish, priestess."

The first official Congress after the King's approval was to be held. Anaya walked along the centre aisle in the Temple, gazing up at the ivory statue of the Goddess. She was as beautiful and mighty as she had ever been.

Two of the large conference rooms at the rear of the Temple had been joined together, creating a vast space. It contained a sizable table in the centre, around which stood plenty of chairs. Most were empty as the evening Congress commenced, but they were all to eventually be filled, as more tribes joined.

Coming through the open doorway, Anaya sat down beside Edric. Lilith was seated at one end of the table, with Adena on her right and Kaedin to her left. Leo was also present, as well as a representative of the King. It was his Head Counsellor, who had arrived to hand out all the paperwork from their previous meeting. The gathering had been going on for some time, until it was his turn to speak.

"It is merely a summary of all which was said and agreed upon. There are three copies, all of which are signed by the King. They need to also be signed by Cardinal Adena Barton, and Matriarch Lilith Fahd of the Panther Tribe. Those are the empty lines down the bottom. There is one copy each for you to keep, and the third to be brought back with me as I leave in the morning."

"Very good," Lilith said. "We shall only read through it first."

The vast amount of writing took some time to study, but as they finished, they quickly signed them off.

"I also saw that he did indeed release Commander Anna Ramsey from her military service."

Edric couldn't help but smile as he heard it.

"Indeed, he did. The terms of their agreement will be similar to those of Sir Kaedin Reed's. She shall be free to go for as long as she wants, but will be offered her position back, should she ever want it. I will leave separate paperwork for that."

"Excellent. She should be given a high-ranking position within the Priesthood, effective immediately. Her knowledge would be best put to use in the field; thus I would suggest her area of responsibility to include such."

Adena nodded. "I agree, my lady."

The rest of the officers also consented.

"It is decided then, should she agree to it herself, of course."

The Cardinal brought her parchment back up. "The next subject of the evening pertains to the Fox tribe."

"Aye," Kaedin said. "I have received word they are interested in a meeting. The scouts are a bit hesitant, saying it may very well be a trap, but we need to give it a chance."

"Indeed, it might be," Lilith agreed. "Since you are responsible for killing one of their local Master Primes."

Silence fell over the gathering, as it most often did when the issue arose.

"Be that as it may, I will send a representative with you as you meet with them," the Matriarch went on. "Perhaps, even Anaya and Samael might be able to go. My son's presence will most likely halt any plans of an ambush."

The priestess acknowledged her words. "Yes, we are willing to go, as long as it does not interfere with any other commitment."

"If so, I will send someone else of high power, perhaps even my manservant."

"Have we heard from any other tribe, as of yet?" Adena asked, sharing a look with Kaedin.

"Not yet," he said. "But we only just sent out word after the meeting with the King, so it is to be expected. I am hoping to hear from a Bear tribe south of the capital, as well as the Lynx tribe close to Midya." The man brought out a map, spreading it on the table. "I believe it would be best to focus on Ovena for the time being, considering we have the best potential of a close relationship with them, and therefore gain trust within the demon community. That in itself might entice outsiders to join."

"Are you yet to decide whether you will accept demons amongst your ranks?" Lilith asked.

"It is the next part of today's agenda," Adena said. "And yes, we believe it might be best to work together side by side, and not only offer a place for demon representatives in our Congress. I would like to experiment with demons and their ability to use the Light. I have a feeling it might clash somewhat, but at least we'll know for sure then."

"Indeed, I believe we might not be very proficient," the Matriarch admitted. "But demons and their demonic form are very useful nonetheless, both as scouts and warriors. The joint strength of priests and demons would create a force to be reckoned with."

"The panther scouts have been invaluable," Kaedin vouched. "I would love for them to stay under my management."

"Certainly, Master Reed. Those willing to stay will be offered the position."

"Should we move on to the next subject?" Adena asked.

"Yes," the Matriarch replied.

The meeting went on for another hour, and the sun had set as they went their separate ways for the evening.

✶ ✶

Arriving back at the Matriarch's home, Lilith and Anaya noticed someone sitting on the front porch. As they came closer, the priestess saw it was Lee. He quickly knelt down, pressing his forehead against the wooden floorboards.

"Good. You came," the priestess said.

"I was about to ask what this was about, but you clearly know, so I shall leave you to it," Lilith said. "However, once you are done, meet me in the drawing-room, for I need to speak with you and Samael."

"Yes, my lady."

Lee had yet to lift his head as the older woman walked past.

"You can stand now, Lee," Anaya told him.

Dusting his trousers off, the boy rose, but he would not meet her gaze.

"Goodness, if you are to be my manservant, you need to face me. You will be my closest confidant, not someone who shines my shoes."

"Yes, my lady," he said, finally looking up. His long, dark-brown hair was gathered, and his green eyes were soft. His short stature and thin build were worrisome, evidence of lengthy malnourishment, but Anaya attempted to mask her concern.

She gave a warm smile. "Have you considered the offer?"

"I have, my lady. And I really do want to accept it, not only for my aunt, but for my own sake also."

"I see. I would ask you to gather all your belongings and come live with us from next week onward. That gives us a bit of time to prepare a room for you, as well as for my husband, to schedule training with yourself."

"Is he truly to do it?" Lee asked, hope apparent in his voice.

Reaching out, Anaya placed a hand on the boy's shoulder. "He is. He has promised me such, so do not worry." She could see his eyes water at the news. "Just keep your head low until then. Do not, under any circumstance, take on your demonic form."

"No, I won't, my lady," he assured her. "You have my word."

"Good. Now, head back home, and I shall see you in a few days."

"Yes, my lady." Lee bowed, then hurried off down the road.

Watching him leave, Anaya then walked inside, finding Samael in the hallway. "Did you overhear?" she asked.

"I did," he replied.

She paused for a moment. "And?"

Samael shrugged. "You spoke the truth. We have agreed. And the timing is good."

"Thank you," Anaya said. "We only need to see your mother now."

"I know. I met her as I came down the stairs."

The couple walked along one of the ground floor corridors, entering the Matriarch's drawing-room. It was a spacious area with a fireplace and several bookshelves, as well as a desk and two armchairs, upon one of which she was seated.

"Come in," she said. "We have an important matter to discuss."

Seeing her stern expression, Anaya felt anxious. "What is this about, my lady?" she asked.

"There has been... an unconfirmed rumour, amongst some of the houses within the Panther tribe."

"Rumour?" Samael questioned.

"Yes. I have heard it from several sources now, which make me believe there is truthfulness to it." Lilith leaned forward, heaving out a breath. "We speculate there is an uproar forming against you as Patriarch, Samael."

13

ATTENDANT

"An uproar?" Samael repeated.

"Yes," Lilith confirmed. "Not against you personally, but because you technically still have no legitimate heir."

Anaya's eyebrows raised. "What about Aaron then?"

"In essence, he is a bastard child, no matter if you have married or not. Most of the houses are choosing to look the other way since it is only formality, but there seem to be those of the opposite opinion."

Samael cursed. "I should have expected this."

The priestess turned to him. "But surely, with Aaron being of the Fahd lineage-"

"If there is a question to his legitimacy, then there are those who will stop at nothing to overthrow us." Samael locked eyes with his mother. "Let me guess. It includes Ziva and Caera?"

The Matriarch nodded. "Even Knox, and perhaps as high up as Onyx."

"Really?"

"Unfortunately, so," she replied. "And I do not know their intentions. Nevertheless, I am planning for you to take over the Patriarchy after the yearly meeting with the Master Primes."

"You have decided then?" Anaya asked.

"Yes. I believe it to be a good time. I shall bring the news of my abdication on the day, then you will assume the role within the coming weeks after that. I would suggest you be extra cautious until then."

The demon tightened his fists. "You believe them capable of dethroning me?"

"I cannot say. With enough of them, I assume they would feel confident about it, yes. But would they succeed against you? No, most likely not. I speculate them coming after the prospective heir."

"They would attempt to assassinate Aaron?" he growled.

"It would be the fastest and, by far, easiest way."

"But..." the priestess intervened. "Don't think me foolish for saying this, but nothing is stopping us from having more children, all of which would be legitimate. Why would they believe ending Aaron's life to be a sure way to overthrow Samael?"

"Out of all the generations since the Patriarch Fahd, merely a handful have had more than one offspring. In the last five, there has only been a single child. Thus, your son being illegitimate, makes them certain Samael shall never sire one in wedlock."

"Then... what are we to do?" Anaya feebly inquired.

"Keep out of sight for the time being. Do not walk outside of Fahd territory. I shall have the outer perimeter guarded by those who know to give word, should they spot inhabitants from the other houses."

Gritting his teeth, Samael snarled. "Should they so much as lay a hand on-"

"Yes, son," Lilith said. "They shall all be severely punished, but we cannot persecute them on mere rumours. No spy has been confirmed to actually listen in on a first-hand conversation. We need to either attain such news or keep a low profile until they make a move."

It was early morning as Anaya dressed. Samael was still asleep in their bed, with Aaron snuggling up against him. The priestess was about to go and see Lee's aunt, praying there was something she could do for the woman.

She had a last look at the slumbering demon. Their son held his father's hair in a tight grip, lying halfway across his chest. It didn't look particularly comfortable, but at least none of them had stirred.

Leaving the room, Anaya silently moved down the corridor, then descended the stairs.

"Good morning, my lady," Arax said as he saw her.

"Morning, Arax," she replied. "I am off on a quick errand, only here in town."

"Do you wish for an escort?" he enquired.

She shook her head. "No, thank you. It is not meant to be far."

"Very well, I shall see you later, my lady." He bowed as the priestess walked past.

Coming outside, Anaya saw Lee standing on the other side of the courtyard.

He showed reverence as she approached, then decided to hold her gaze. "I have been waiting for you, your Highness. Are you perhaps on your way to visit with my aunt?"

"I am," she declared. "Take me to her."

* *

As the Panther tribe relocated from the eastern forest, Lee had claimed a ground hut in the west, along the outskirts of the city. He had attempted to repair it to the best of his abilities, but the structure was decrepit. The roof was clearly leaking, puddles and buckets spread across the floor, and the floorboards creaked, many of them needing to be replaced. The window shutters had been nailed closed, and the door was only attached to one of its hinges.

"It is not much," the boy said. "But at least now, aunt Corliss can walk outside whenever she feels better. We used to live high up in a tree, so she would only ever catch a bit of fresh air from the window."

"You have done well," Anaya praised him as she traversed the room.

There was a narrow bed at the other end, a figure laying upon it. The covers were pulled high across the shoulder.

Coming closer, Anaya could see it was a female, the woman facing the far wall. Her skin was pale, and her dark hair was pulled back in a ponytail. Placing a hand on her, the priestess felt her shiver.

Slowly turning around, Corliss looked at Anaya with dull eyes. "Who is there?" she asked.

Anaya's voice was soft, barely louder than a whisper. "None of importance, dear Corliss. I am merely here to examine you."

Nodding, the woman turned back, closing her eyes.

Light enveloped them as Anaya quietly chanted, running her hands over Corliss' body. The priestess held her breath as she saw the extent of her illness: large swellings present on almost every organ. She had seen the dense tumours before, the cancerous growths nigh on impossible to cure. They were different from a regular disease, as they were part of the body. The tumours were thus hard to treat, most often spreading before they could be removed. In this instance, it was much too late.

Turning around, Anaya faced the young boy. "I need to speak with you outside," she said. The two of them exited the small hut, after which she grabbed his hand. "I am so sorry, Lee, but your aunt is dying."

He quietly nodded. "I figured as much," he said. "But is there anything you can do? At least to relieve her of the pains."

"Indeed, I can," Anaya assured him. "And I shall. I will treat her as best I can now, then send for a healer to tend to her, for as long as she requires it."

Lee's eyes watered. "How can I ever repay you?" he asked.

"Do not concern yourself with that," she urged. "Focus instead on your new assignment and spend what time you can with your aunt."

"I will. Thank you, my lady."

Lenda had been visiting daily with Corliss, using pain-relieving spells on her, as well as caring for her in her bed. One of Anaya's servants was assisting throughout the day, and another during the night.

The hut was being repaired, with Eden stopping by whenever he had a minute to spare. The roof had already been finished, as well as the door and window, so he was currently working on the inside floor. Lee would assist at whatever time he wasn't with Anaya and preparing for his new position as a manservant.

The day had finally come when he was meant to move in with his new Mistress.

Clutching a small bag in his hand, he left Corliss' hut, leaving her with Lenda and Eden. His heart was pounding in his chest, the nervousness overwhelming. What if they would not have him? If they had changed their minds? Or if he would fail at his duties, and be dismissed and left to his own devices again?

Lee clenched his fists. He would not let this opportunity slip. He would do this, not only for himself but also for his aunt and his late mother, allowing them to rest in peace as Corliss would join her in the afterlife.

Coming up to the courtyard, Anaya was standing on the front steps of the mansion. "Welcome, Lee," she said as he placed himself before her. "A room has been prepared in the servant's quarters. The Matriarch's manservant will show you there. He is inside."

"Thank you, my lady."

"After you have unpacked, the Scion Prime is awaiting you east of the city, along the Leve plateau."

"Yes, my lady. I shall make haste." Bowing deeply, Lee hurried through the door.

"This way, Master Victor," Arax said, leading him down a corridor on the ground floor. His room was small, but neatly furnished with a comfortable bed, a thick rug and a desk and a chair. It had a small fireplace and a single window facing the rear of the property, with a view of the Matriarch's gardens.

"Place your belongings in the wardrobe, then head off to meet with the Prime. He does not like to be kept waiting."

"Yes, sir!" Lee opened his backpack, his hands diving into it. He only had a few items of clothing and a couple of trinkets, so it took him mere minutes to finish unpacking. As he strode back through the hallway, he was already coming into a sprint. Pushing the front door open, he slammed into something, then instantly found himself covered in fabrics.

"Oh, goodness me," he heard a voice.

Lee was fighting against the heavy draperies, scrambling to get out from under what seemed to be clothing. Coming to his feet, he looked across the heap of garments, meeting the blue eyes of a young man. "I am terribly sorry!" the boy exclaimed. "I was rushing and wasn't thinking."

"Do not worry," the man said. "But do help me gather everything. I will need to go through it to make sure nothing ripped. These are all the Matriarch's gowns I just finished repairing."

Lee's face went pale as he stood there, seemingly frozen in place.

"Heavens, she won't have you executed for it," the man laughed. "My name is Benjamin. Benjamin Elton. I am her tailor."

"I-I-I am…"

The clothier rolled his hand, motioning Lee to continue.

"I am the n-new…"

Benjamin remained silent, placing his hands on his hips as he smiled at the boy.

"Damn it!" Lee snapped. "I am terrible at this. The Scion Prime Consort is employing me as her manservant."

"Really?" the man asked. "You look mighty young for such a position."

"I am sixteen, sir," he argued.

"Mm, still pretty young, I'd say, but who am I to judge? I am merely a clothier."

Lee blushed. "I am, I know, but I intend to do my utmost to live up to their expectations."

"I am sure you will," Benjamin said, offering him another warm smile. "Now, would you be so kind as to help me with the dresses?"

"Yes!" he blurted. "Of course, I am so sorry."

The young man grabbed Lee's hand, attempting to calm him down. "I know you are, so you need not apologise any further."

The two men gathered the gowns, then carried them upstairs to a designated bedroom. They placed them upon the bed.

Pinching hold of a skirt, Benjamin scrutinised the garment. "I will look everything over before bringing them to the Matriarch. If anything needs additional repairs, I will just take them back with me."

Lee wrung his wrists. "Again, I'm-"

"I know," Benjamin said. "You are free to go, as long as you tell me your name."

"Lee Victor, sir."

"Good name," the man said. "I shall see you around, Master Victor."

✶ ✶

Lee's face was damp with sweat as he ran towards the Leve plateau. Situated east of the city, it was a long stretch of flat land, often covered in tall grass. At the far end, there was a stream running through it, the same one to supply the waterfalls outside the Temple village.

Walking through the eastern gates, Lee could see the Prime standing only a short distance north along the perimeter wall. He slowly approached, anxious for his reaction to him being late.

Turning around, Samael swiped his cloak aside. "Where have you been?"

Lee instantly threw himself on the ground. "My most humble apologies, your Highness. I had an incident on the way."

"Get up on your feet," he rumbled. "There is no way I can help you, if you are nailed to the dirt."

The boy scrambled to get up, but his low gaze lingered.

"I asked you to come out here, to reduce the risk of you doing something foolish while in your demonic form."

Lee swallowed. "Yes, your Highness."

"How many times have you turned?" Samael inquired.

"Only… three, not counting my *evolution*."

"Three?"

Lee audibly sighed. "Yes, and each time I have royally screwed up, so I am not exactly excited about this."

Samael pursed his lips. "Well, the worst thing that can happen is that you go feral and I kill you, which should have already happened anyway. So, essentially, it can only go up from here."

The boy inhaled sharply as all the colour drained from his face.

"Oh, come now. I am attempting to humour you." Samael dragged a hand across his head. "Which is a career I should obviously stay clear of." He stepped forward, grabbing hold of the boy. Feeling his upper arm, he then patted him on the back. "You are one scrawny little guy, but you are still young, correct?"

"I am sixteen, your Highness."

"Mm. You may very well continue to grow for a few years. What about your clothing; is that the best you have?" Samael referred to the boy's trousers, having been repaired several times. The shirt was in one piece, but very thin from extensive use.

"I... I have more, but they all look more or less the same."

"Ah," Samael acknowledged. "After we finish today, I shall have you sent to the tailor's for a new wardrobe. You will not receive anything extravagant, but at least something more presentable than that."

Excitement rose in Lee's belly. "Th-thank you, your Highness!"

Samael expelled a breath. "'Your Highness' is fast getting old. You need not use it when it is only the two of us."

"Yes, I am sorry."

"Nothing to apologise for. You are merely correct. I am the one not to exactly follow tradition." The Prime cleared his throat. "Be that as it may, are you ready to have a go?"

There was a pause before Lee responded. "And... turn?"

"What else?" Samael challenged, more forcefully than intended. He clenched his jaw, trying not to become agitated. "What have you been told of the transformation?"

"Nothing, sir. I... I turned earlier than expected, and my aunt was already ill by then. I hurried out into the forest so it wouldn't happen around people... then as I endured it again, I couldn't control it and ended up killing cattle outside of Midya."

"Right, well..." Samael was silent for a moment, unsure of what to say. "I could thank you for that, at some point. But for now, we might want to leave that story untold."

Lee blinked, his eyebrows shooting upwards.

"Ignore what I just said," Samael huffed. "We should focus on you now. You will need to concentrate through the actual change. Otherwise, you will run this risk of the form taking over. Anaya said you did not appear feral, but in somewhat of a state in between."

"I suppose that is right," Lee admitted. "It is as if I get these urges I can't... ignore."

"A good start is to remain resolute in your mind as you transform," Samael explained. "The body will change nonetheless, so it is the mind you must retain."

"Yes, sir."

"Then go ahead," Samael allowed. "I am ready when you are."

Lee took a deep breath, mists instantly enveloping him as he exhaled.

Samael shuffled back, not expecting his aura to be so strong. Within seconds, he heard a low growl through the fog.

The boy cursed, finding himself drifting as he always did. He felt a sudden tug to his clothing, and the Prime came forward.

"Concentrate!"

Lee nodded. He needed to manage it, to prove to the Scion Prime that he was worthy of becoming his Consort's manservant. As the smoke swirled around the boy, he fell to his hands and knees but then felt himself lifting off the ground.

"Lee! This is it; you need to *focus*. Open your eyes!"

Looking in front of him, he saw Samael through the torrent. Holding his hands up, Lee noted the fur spreading across his body. With a roar, his mists exploded out, and he found himself low to the ground. He was standing on all fours, but they were now wide paws, with long sharp claws digging into the soil.

With a sudden movement before him, he instantly pounced.

"Damn it, Lee!" Samael bashed him aside, then grabbed hold of his scruff and lifted him up.

The panther hung motionless in his grip. "I am sorry, your Highness."

Samael scrutinised the young boy. He was indeed more massive than the average member of their tribe, and his mists continuously flowed from him. The strength of his aura was at least that of a high born, if not more, considering his age. "It is fine, you only ripped my sleeve." There was a trickle of blood running down the Prime's arm, dripping through the torn fabric. "How do you feel now? Are you in control?"

"I... think so." Being lowered to the ground, the boy took a few tentative steps. "Yes, I feel like myself now. How strange. I have never experienced this."

"I believe we might want to work on the metamorphosis, being your initial hurdle. Once that is overcome, we will move on to other things that stand to trigger the feral, such as hunting, fighting, and maintaining the demonic form for a lengthy period." Samael stood back. "You may return to your human form."

In another flow of mists, Lee rose from the ground, then straightened his clothing.

"I should also warn you, should you enter a relationship, that sexual intercourse is another trigger."

The boy's face immediately reddened, his eyes flitting around.

"Trust me, I understand it is not a subject you wish to hold with someone such as myself, but I need to warn you."

Lee nodded, but he said nothing.

"Good, then we are finished for today. If the weather is good tomorrow, we shall have a more rigorous session. We will meet here, at the same time. And remember visiting with the tailor."

"I will," Lee promised. "Thank you, your Highness."

"Do not thank me," Samael told him. "Thank my wife."

Kaedin folded his paperwork away, replacing the quill pen on the desk. He was to meet with the Matriarch, so he was forced to leave the rest for later. Pushing his chair out, he stood. He needed to get changed, as he was only wearing a woollen shirt and pair of trousers. They were dyed black, which he often wore, but they were very informal. He had no obligation dressing up for a conference with her, but it did not feel proper to arrive in this manner.

Pulling a fresh shirt from his wardrobe, it was a light grey, with silver stitching along the hem. It would have to do, paired with his black trousers.

The walk to the mansion was becoming easier with time, the man now less out of breath as he reached the Matriarch's home. The regular strolls up the hill must have had a positive effect on his overall fitness. He had always been a burly man, building muscle mass quickly, but he personally found his stamina to be lacking.

Opening the front door, he was greeted by Arax.

"The Matriarch awaits you in the drawing-room," the manservant said.

Moving down the corridor, Kaedin knocked on the door.

"Come in," Lilith said, prompting him to enter. "Have a seat, Master Reed."

The officer sat down opposite her, resting his arms along the cushioned sides.

"I would like to start with the most pressing matter. That of my son and the allegations against him. Have you received any additional news on the subject?"

"None that you do not already know, my lady," Kaedin replied. "But they are all originating from the northern houses, it seems. My latest report was given yesterday, from the Caera village."

"I see." She pondered his words. "But it did not state who in the family was involved?"

"No, your Highness."

"I can, of course, speculate, but that gets us nowhere," Lilith said. "If you hear anything else, I will need to know immediately. It is getting dangerously close to when Samael and Anaya are to take over the Patriarchy, so if their enemies are ever to become desperate and make a move, it is very soon."

"Certainly, my lady," Kaedin concurred. "Would you like to have additional protection arranged for them?"

"No, as I do not want to raise suspicion. No one has ever managed to maintain this level of secrecy within the tribe before, except for myself." Lilith leaned back, holding her chin in thought. "And as long as Samael stays close to Anaya, they would not dare attack."

"As you wish," Kaedin said.

"My next question," Lilith continued. "Have you noticed anything strange with your influx of correspondence?"

Kaedin moistened his lips, unwilling to word the answer. He had wished it to be a false interpretation on his part, but with her query, it was clearly not. "I have. Especially from southern tribes. Some have even stopped replying. I am not quite sure why."

"Mm. I thought it strange," Lilith stated. "A trade route was recently set up for a newly established Lynx settlement, but as we were finalising our agreement, I received no word. Would you mind investigating?"

"I have already sent scouts, my lady."

She grinned. "Of course, you have."

He shrugged. "Had it not been for the disturbance originating within the Midlands, I might have given it more time, considering what the King told us about the border to Abyssa. But this seems highly strange."

"I agree with your judgment," Lilith told him. "Another matter. Has Commander Anna Ramsey accepted the offer of becoming General Priest?"

"She has," Kaedin confirmed. "She was promoted this last Sunday."

"Very good. I am sure it brings peace to Master Ramsey's mind, knowing she is relieved of her duties in the army."

"Aye, he is very satisfied with the King's decision."

"Speaking of which," Lilith went on, coming forward again. "Tell me something, Master Reed."

"Yes, my lady?"

"Your agreement with the said King... Do you truly intend to stay with the Priesthood?"

Kaedin features grew severe. "Have I done anything to make you doubt my devotion to the cause?"

"You have not," she granted. "But it is a valid question, with the contract comprised as it is. For obvious reasons, I need to know you are here to stay."

His jaw tightened. "With all due respect, your Highness, it is offensive to be questioned in this manner. I have been a part of the Priesthood for twenty-three years. I stayed despite the High Priest's ensuing insanity, as did I throughout the rebuilding and reconstruction of the Temple village and our organisation, much of which I did with my own two hands. I have done everything you have ever asked for, as well as all that of the Priest-hood, and as such, I am *insulted* at the mere suggestion that my loyalty might lie elsewhere."

Lilith grinned, clasping her hands. "Excellent, Master Reed. That is all I needed to know. You are dismissed."

Kaedin clenched his fists, rising, then left without another word.

14

PROVISIONS

The Unn had travelled further north, setting up camp outside the township of Monua, along the Bechuan border.

The grounds were thick with mud after several days of heavy rain. Nia was lying in her tent, having read since noon. She had been allowed spending money last time they visited a town, so she had bought new clothes and several books.

And how she had missed a good book on art and poetry! Growing up, her mother had kept quite the collection, especially from her years bedridden due to disease. With no other source of entertainment as Nia and her father performed at the royal court, she was often left on her own for many hours of the night.

Running her hand across the leatherbound tome on her bed, Nia smiled to herself. It reminded her of her mother's words; to stay strong in times of need, for life was a curious thing, a treasure hunt of sorts. It was only a matter of finding the gems.

And Nia was set on acquiring the treasure of her existence. For there was more to sentience than merely survival, of that, she was sure.

The last few months had only served to strengthen Nia's buoyancy. It was strange, but her situation had drastically changed since Gus had – at least momentarily – taken her under his wing. It was as if his interest in her, or what others believed to be such, had somehow halted everyone else's advances on herself. Nia had been lovingly nicknamed *the Maid*, assuming the role of caretaker of their camp. She was also given a second tent, but with an open front, in which she could cook and serve food. This, she had already erected beside the Unn's main campfire. She provided breakfast, luncheon and dinner for the band, then spent the time in between clearing up and washing clothing. If they were stationed near a town, she would also be sent on simple errands.

There were still times when men would approach her, asking for sexual favours. But as she had begun to decline, she was left alone.

Gus never did show her any affection, even if he seemed to care for her. Or perhaps he only pitied her, a young girl trapped in a brothel against her will, then sold to the highest bidder, who happened to be part of a ruthless mercenary band. But it was hard to tell Gus' intentions, with the man most often keeping to himself. Whenever around the other mercenaries, he acted as if he was part of the group, but then he would withdraw, sometimes being gone for several days at a time. This was one of those occasions, his tent having been empty for almost four days.

Nia wanted to know more about Gus, for something other than his charity drew her to him, like an innate penchant beyond her control. However, the reasons behind it were yet lost on her.

The rain had let up, with only a light drizzle gently peppering the roof of Nia's tent. Closing her book, she popped her head outside. It was time to make dinner. She grabbed a thick robe and pulled it over her head, then left her shelter. Ever since it had been given to her, she had been dry and warm at night, and her quality of life was much improved. She was increasingly cheerful as she took on her chores, now feeling as if she had found meaning to her existence once more. Her situation did in no way compare to her life in Kanadesh, and the luxuries she had been brought up with, but it was a start, and certainly much better than offering her body in return for a roof over her head.

Making a fire, she placed a pot of water over the flames. She added potatoes, meat and vegetables. It was going to be a hearty stew tonight, making the men fall asleep within minutes. It worked like a charm.

After adding in the spices, the aroma quickly spread throughout the camp. It didn't take long before members of the band started gathering, waiting for her to declare their dinner as ready. She smiled at the thought: that this group of full-grown men would stand there and pause, no longer grab her and do with her what they will. She felt a kind of power with the sensation, despite only being a servant to them. Perhaps, in time, she would yet find herself equal to them and thus have some of her lost dignity restored.

Placing bowls and spoons on a table, she brought out a few loaves of bread. She cut them into portions, then carefully toasted the slices over the flames. With a separate bowl of freshly churned butter, she declared the evening meal as commenced.

As men flocked around her, she served them their food. Some came for seconds, others satisfied with the rations given.

Cyrus sat down on a log next to the fire, throwing his feet up against its warmth. "Damn wet that never goes away."

Bella placed herself beside him, cradling her bowl. "It's getting old, I have to admit."

A horse whinnied in the distance, and there was the sound of a single set of hoofbeats.

Turning around, Cyrus stood as he saw who it was. "Nine-fingers!" he called.

Gus pulled on the reins, his black gelding coming to a halt next to the other horses. Tethering it, he strode across the campsite, merely passing the group of men.

"Oy!" Cyrus shouted, hurling his spoon after the man. "Get back here!"

Gus stopped, glaring at him over his shoulder. "What?"

"Come chat with us at least. I believe we deserve a small portion of your presence."

"Give me a minute," the swordsman replied, then continued to his tent. Coming through the opening, he froze. It was not as he had left it. Nothing seemed to be missing, but all his items had been taken off the ground, placed across makeshift wooden stands. Everything felt dry and clean, and his bedding was newly washed, a scent of citrus left within the textiles.

Removing his cloak and weaponry, Gus came back out, then stopped at the corner of the meal tent. He remained silent, unwilling to look at the young woman standing within.

Nia stepped closer, only the fabric of the tent separating them, but she, too, kept quiet. She could see his shadow moving, the man kicking at the ground.

"Thank... thank you, Nia."

"Don't give it another thought, Gus. Have something to eat." She saw him nodding, so she immediately retrieved a bowl and came out of the tent, quickly handing it to him. She was determined not to give him a chance to change his mind.

The man moved away from her, sitting down opposite Cyrus.

"Nice to see you back," the older man said, but received no reply. "Where have you been?"

"On a few errands," Gus answered. "Nothing interesting."

"Nothing interesting?" Cyrus echoed. "You have been gone for *days*."

"Leave it, Dog."

Cyrus shrugged, then watched him eat in silence.

Nia came forward, handing Gus a jug of mead and slice of buttered bread, which he accepted.

Their leader let his eyes settle on her behind as she headed back to the meal tent. "A shame that ain't for free anymore."

There was a shiver shooting down Nia's spine with his words, the notion of returning to warming someone's bed bringing on a cold sweat. But she still refused to dignify Cyrus' comment with a response, hoping it would go unnoticed.

Jason sniggered, unfortunately having heard the statement. "No wonder, when she's at ol' Nine-fingers beck and call. Or was it the other way around?"

"Shut up, dimwit," Gus replied, then took another bite out of his toast. "You should be happy with the time it lasted; no woman to ever give themselves willingly to you."

The young man's laugh intensified. "Oh, so those are your words of wisdom, are they? Because you enjoy so much banging, it just has to be true."

Cyrus placed a hand on Jason's shoulder. "At ease now, men," he said. "Take it out on the battlefield, not amongst yourselves."

Unwilling to cause an argument, Gus silently finished his meal.

"I know a fun game!" Jason proclaimed. He flung his bowl aside, angling towards Gus again. "How about a round of *Rock, Paper, Scissors* for who takes her to bed tonight?"

"Are you seriously that stupid?" the large man replied. "You must be the biggest idiot I've ever met."

"Come on!"

Dropping his bowl, Gus found himself at his wit's end. He swore, making a fist as he rose.

Jason stood to meet him but held his extended hand forward. "Aha! I went for paper, so you lose. Paper beats rock!"

Hammering his fist into the man's face, Gus sent him sprawling to the ground. "It's not a rock – it's a fist, you bonehead. Fist beats face every time!" Spitting on the youngster, he stepped over him as he headed for his tent.

✶✶

Plenty of drinks were poured throughout the evening, but Gus remained absent. Nia was up long into the night clearing up after the Unn. With the last plates dried and cleaned, she left the meal tent. The rain swiftly became heavier, so she grabbed a bowl and held it over her head as she ran across to her home. The mud made it slippery, her shoes sliding on the surface. She stumbled as she dived for the opening in her tent, but landed safely on the edge of her bedding.

Rolling over on her back, Nia giggled. She kicked her shoes off, then cleaned her feet with a towel. Her life was so different from the one she had led back in Kanadesh, the change felt almost surreal. Sometimes she wondered if she was to wake up, and find herself back there with her parents, almost as if her current existence was merely a dream.

If so, the dream had thankfully changed in character.

Climbing up on her bed, Nia reached for her book.

The front panel of her tent suddenly flared open, a man coming through. He grabbed at her ankle, forcedly pulling her down.

✶✶

Gus jerked, waking to the sharp sound of a scream rippling across the camp. He sat up, straining for his eyes to become accustomed to his roused state. It was still dark outside, so he couldn't have slept for long. The man gathered a knife, sliding it into the shaft of his right boot before donning it. Coming out into the night, there was heavy rain, water splashing as he strode towards Nia's tent. It was the only valid source for the sound, with the shriek being clearly female and Bella highly unlikely to give one such out.

Reaching Nia's home, he moved the front fabric aside, seeing the back of a man pinning the young woman down. Clutching hold of the assailant's shirt, Gus hurled him out into the rain.

It was Jason, who immediately came back to his feet. "Get out of here, Gus! You know I won," he hissed.

The two men were quickly drenched in the downpour.

"I don't give a shit, Jason. Go sard yourself!"

The younger man pulled out a double-edged dagger, then charged him.

Gus sidestepped, bashing Jason's arm aside and sending the blade flying out of his hand. Tackling him to the ground, he whacked his fist against his chin.

Jason attempted to defend himself, throwing punches and kicking the man above him, but to no avail. He felt another smash, then warmth across his cheek as blood poured from his nose.

Pushing Jason sideways, Gus buried his face in the mud. He held him down, watching his climbing desperation as he was deprived of air.

"Gus!" Nia called as she hurried from her tent. "Please, don't kill him!"

"Why do you care? He attempted to rape you, for what? The tenth time?"

"Just let him go, Gus!"

Slamming Jason into the dirt a final time, Gus rose. He kicked the young man, then spat on his back. "Worthless piece of shit, get out of here before I finish you off!"

Clawing for stable ground, Jason stumbled as he attempted to rise. He ended up crawling several paces before finally managing to get up on his feet, after which he scurried away.

"He has never raped me," Nia told her saviour. Awaiting a reply, she stood in silence. Her dress was soon utterly soaked as the rain continued to increase. She grazed Gus' hand, but he pulled away.

"Don't... don't waste your time," he said.

They shared subdued eye contact. "I have a feeling you have said that more than once."

His jaw tightened as he began walking away. "Get back in your tent, else you want to become ill."

The night had been long and dark, thick clouds looming above the camp. By morning, Nia had enjoyed very little sleep. She soon stood in the meal tent, slicing a final loaf, then placing the dish of butter on the table. The porridge was already prepared, so she needed only to start dividing the block of cheese, then breakfast would be served. Most of the men had gathered with the rising sun, but neither Gus nor Jason were amongst them.

Cyrus and the main crew sat closest to the fire, as they most often did, holding loud discussions. The subjects would range from everything between heaven and earth, and Nia had learned to just phase it out. It was simply not worth listening to, as much of what was said only proved the members' prejudice and ignorance.

As the band parted, the young woman grabbed two pieces of bread. Toasting them above some smouldering coals, she buttered a side each, before placing some cheese between them. She strolled across the camp, careful not to step in the deep mud. She would stay to one side, taking a detour as she attempted to reach Gus' tent.

"Gus," she said, keeping her voice low. She heard the sound of metal on metal coming from the shelter but received no reply. "Gus," she repeated.

"What?"

"May I come in?"

The tip of his blade came through the opening, pushing the front piece of fabric aside. The man was holding a whetstone in his other hand. "What do you want?" he asked.

"I brought you breakfast," Nia said, offering him the sandwich.

"I'm not hungry, which is why I didn't show."

"Well," she began, temporarily leaning in to place the food upon his bedding. "I will leave it with you nonetheless."

"Fine," he said, releasing the canvas and closing the tent.

Nia felt herself tense, pressing her arms against her body. The man was infuriatingly hard to please, or at least he would never show any appreciation. But why would he still come to her aid? Ever since she asked for his help and was refused, she had never done it again. Their interactions played on her mind constantly. She was not going to allow him to slip away as he managed with everyone else. She was determined to become acquainted with the man, no matter if he liked it or not.

Arriving back at the meal tent, Nia saw Jason helping himself to the last of the porridge. He turned away as he saw her, his face badly bruised.

The fear he had instilled in her the previous night was all but gone. The sight of his hunched form only spawned a sense of commiseration within Nia. Did he perhaps regret his actions?

Walking past him, she grabbed some bread which she buttered, then approached him. "Here," she said. He would barely lift his chin as he accepted it, but she could clearly tell one of his eyes was swollen shut.

"Thanks," he mumbled.

The young man ate in silence as Nia cleared away all the plates and the last of the food. She would spend the next hour cleaning, as the members of the band were not the most considerate. They would leave everything where they stood, sometimes even throw plates or cutlery aside, so she would be forced to search for them.

Satisfied she had gathered everything, she placed most of it in a basket, ready to be brought down to the nearby stream for washing. Balancing the remaining items on her arm, she carefully headed for the waterways.

✷ ✷

Gus returned the whetstone to one of his bags, then pulled a piece of cloth along the blade. Sheathing the sword, he leaned it against the back of his tent. He glanced at his sandwich, suddenly feeling hungry as he could smell the melted butter and cheese. Grabbing it, he proceeded to devour the light meal. He must have been more famished than he thought, yet he had no wish to be outside with the others. Nia had done him a favour, her attentive services becoming a rapidly increasing recurrence lately.

The man cursed. He wondered why he had even come to care for her to begin with. She had never taken his interest as Cyrus had bought her, but it was something about her that compelled him to be protective.

Still, Gus would only feel shame. He was ashamed that it had taken him so long to act on his empathy. It was as if the emotion had been all but eradicated through his years with the Unn. These days, he was merely a seasoned warrior, with no prospects for his own future. He wished to die on the battlefield and leave all the pain behind. He only hoped it would be sooner rather than later.

So, why would he feel any concern for the young woman? Or anything else for that matter? If he only longed for his own bereavement, then why would he pay attention to someone with so little impact on himself?

Gus knew he had been cursed to this life. He would live by the sword and die by the sword. He was merely a ghost; a whisper in the wind. He was a man alive, only because he was not yet dead.

Despite this, he had not once contemplated taking his own life. The act was for the weak; for those who truly had nothing left in this world. Gus felt different, for he, at least, had the Unn. His career within the band had only been much longer than anticipated. He had seen many members come and go, the majority of which had moved on to the afterlife.

Falling off that cliff, he had closed his eyes and relaxed, for he believed it to have been his time. Plunging into the dark waters, his body had suddenly fought for survival, thrashing desperately in the crashing waves. Coming onto shore, he had pulled himself onto a rock, breathlessly laying there with a racing heart. Had the experience changed him?

Four members of the Unn mounted their horses, ready to depart. The mission would take them on a journey of stealth, not violence. It was the reason for the meagre crew, as Cyrus had explained it.

"I thought I'd get the day off," Bella said, seated on her grey mare.

"With Jason missing, there isn't much we can do," Cyrus explained, then glanced at Gus. "Or perhaps you know where to find him?"

The swordsman merely looked away, saying nothing.

Their leader snorted. "Either way, nothing to dwell over." He pushed his heels into his stallion, fast coming into a sprint. With the others joining him, they travelled at high speed through the darkness.

"Did you say the reimbursement was increased since the previous outings?" Bella asked.

"Aye. Since the King's sudden collaboration with demons, and the change of heart from the Priesthood, our customer's... calling has become a passionate affair of theirs."

"The Priesthood is up and running again then?" Gus asked.

"Indeed, they are, but with a wider purpose," Cyrus elucidated. "Apparently, they are supposed to enforce laws, both on demons *and* humans."

"We better watch out then," Gus jeered. "So we don't get hunted down by the dress-wearers."

Cyrus released an amused chuckle. "The Priesthood, hunting us down? And do what? Kill us? Ridiculous. There is no way they could take down *the Unn*."

Landon leaned forward on his mount, gaining the older man's attention. "*The Unn* now, is it? Is the name about to stick perhaps?"

"Shut up, lest you want that pretty face smashed up."

✶✶

Bella's features could not avoid admitting her distaste. "Why do I have to do this part?"

Cyrus placed a soft hand on her shoulder. "You and I both know you are the best at pressure points, after Jason. And any of us are much too large to sneak up on the guy." With his touch travelling down her back, he motioned her on with a gentle push. "Now, get on with it."

"No celebratory shagging for you," she hissed, then walked across to a wagon on the other side of the road.

It was loaded with various merchandise, the boxes covered with a large canvas. Nimbly clearing the edge, the woman sat down behind the front seat, hiding in the shadows. Wearing black, she was nearly invisible as she pulled her hood forward.

A man emerged from a nearby building, out to make his last delivery for the day. Climbing up on the wagon, he reached for the reins. As he grabbed them, Bella slowly rose behind him. A precise hit on a point just above the man's right temple, and he instantly sagged.

The men from the Unn immediately sprinted forth, Gus and Landon pulling the fabric aside to reveal the cargo.

Cyrus pulled a cloth over his face, looking at the others. "Step back," he told them. He opened a small pouch, proceeding to dust the wares with a yellow powder. As he finished, he retied the leather container. "Replace the tarp."

Grabbing a corner each, Gus and Landon pulled it across, then fastened it on either side of the wagon.

"Landon, take Bella's horse," Cyrus said, then looked at the woman. "Ride for as long as you dare, then leave before he stirs. Just make sure he goes through with the delivery."

"I know," she said. "You can stay here. He won't be unconscious for long." Retrieving the reins, she whipped them over the horses' backs.

Gus returned to his mount. "We should leave unless we want to risk being seen."

Cyrus followed the swordsman. "Easy money," he said.

"We ain't paid yet," Gus muttered.

"Fine, but we will be, just like last… only more, this time." Cyrus grinned. "Unless our employer has a death wish, that is. He knows who he's dealing with."

"If you say so."

The leader angled for him. "Aye, I say so. What is up with you, Gus? You have been unusually testy lately. The same with whatever happened between you and Jason. I know you've never particularly cared for the man, but to beat him up? Over that wench, as well."

The swordsman averted his gaze, saying nothing.

"Is there something I can do for you?" Cyrus asked, sincerity in his voice.

Gus released a breath. "No."

"Then tell me if that changes," Cyrus said. "But please, don't go around beating my men up. I need them."

"I'll do my best."

✶ ✶

Plenty of fires were burning as the modest group arrived back at camp. They dismounted, hitching their horses before moving across the grounds.

With his hood forward, Gus's cloak fluttered as he strode past the meal tent.

Nia had prepared a light snack for everyone, something she often did after missions. Usually, she would only serve three meals, but this would be a special occasion, with plenty of mead for refreshment. She hurried around the corner of her tent, attempting to catch up with the aloof swordsman.

"Gus!" she called, immediately halting him.

He turned. "What?"

Sucking in a breath, she steeled herself. "Stay."

"*Stay*?" He scowled at her. "What do you think I am? A *dog*?"

"No! No, I just… please, stay." She stepped forward, holding his gaze.

The coarseness of his features lessened. "Allow me to remove my weapons, and I'll come out."

Nia smiled. "Of course. I shall prepare a plate for you." She darted back across the encampment, not giving him a chance to go back on his word.

Gus watched her, shaking his head. She was a strange woman, relentless to the core.

It took only minutes for the man to unequip his gear, emerging dressed in his black garbs and high boots. He pushed a hand through his greying hair, then stopped at the campfire where the rest of the evening's crew were seated.

Cyrus seemed surprised. "Are you here by your own free will, or is someone standing behind you with a knife?"

"If someone were, that person would be dead," Gus flatly stated, then sat down.

Nia hurried forward, offering him some food and a pint of mead. As she righted herself, she felt his hand trace her arm, his fingers wrapping around hers. She instantly froze, ending up standing over his shoulder. "I'm… I'm sorry, sir. If I did something wrong," she said.

"No, nothing like that."

The conversation and laughter around them seemingly faded away in the moment. Nia found herself holding her breath, the firm but gentle touch sending shivers through her.

"Thank you," he said, offering a last brush against her skin before releasing her hand.

"No... no problem, sir," she said as she retreated.

Cyrus leaned forward. "What was all that about?" he asked.

Gus stared at him. "What?"

The older man smiled. "Oh, nothing."

15

ADRIFT

The cobbled streets were still wet from the early morning rain, but as the sun broke through the clouds, some areas began to dry with the rising temperatures. It created a wispy fog, spreading low over the City of Fahd.

Lee was on his way to try on his new clothing and, hopefully, to pick any and all of the garments up, should they fit. Knocking on the door to the tailor's shop, he stepped back.

It swung open, Benjamin already smiling as he stood on the other side. "Come in, Lee," he welcomed.

The smell of dye stung the boy's sensitive nose, but he entered the small building.

Noticing his struggles, the tailor laughed. "You should see your face. Priceless."

Instantly reddening, Lee averted his gaze.

"Ah, no use becoming timid now, young man," Benjamin said. "You have been blessed with a handsome face, so continue to make use of it." Not awaiting the boy's reply, he walked through to the rear of his shop, retrieving a large pile of clothing. "I am very confident in my abilities, so I have already made you what you need. Feel free to try them on, but I am sure they will fit."

Lee looked down at himself, his shirt threadbare. "I wouldn't mind putting some of the new items on."

"Of course! No problem." Benjamin placed the items on the sewing table, grabbing one of the shirts and a pair of trousers. They were both made from fine linen and dyed black. "Black will stay clean longer. They are double stitched, so they should hold. No embellishments, but you will look presentable enough to appear as a servant of the court."

"Thank you very much," Lee said. "But how am I meant to pay you?"

"Do not concern yourself, Master Victor. The Scion Prime has already sent reimbursement."

Lee gawked. "Th-the… Scion Prime?"

"Yes. He paid me as he placed the order." Benjamin handed Lee the garments. "Go ahead and change."

Accepting the items of clothing, the boy placed them over a chair, then pulled his shirt over his head.

The tailor felt a knot in his stomach as he watched him but attempted to mask his concern. Lee was emaciated, all of his bones protruding under the skin. Taking his measurements, Benjamin obviously knew about his condition, but to see him naked was a whole different experience.

Stepping into the trousers, Lee tied them at the front. They were surprisingly soft for linen, and the black colour was rich. It was unlike any quality he had ever felt before. The shirt was perfect in length, the sleeves reaching down just below his wrists. "I love them," he said, facing the tailor.

"Great!" Benjamin cheered. "I told you they would fit."

"Indeed, you did." Lee ran another hand down his shirt. "You are excellent at your craft, sir."

"I have worked as a tailor since childhood, so I may be young, but I already have an extensive career."

The boy cocked his head. "How old are you? If I may ask, sir."

"Of course, you may." Benjamin smirked. "I turned twenty this year but have been a clothier since the age of twelve. Before that, I was an assistant since I was five."

"I know you have had the shop for a long time," Lee said. "But you are often away, so I have never had the chance to ask you for work."

"I am often away on business since I need more extravagant fabrics for the Matriarch."

"I see." The boy clutched his old clothing in his hands. "Thank you very much, sir."

"My pleasure. You look very fine." Benjamin gifted him another cheerful expression. "I would only wish for you to… take care of yourself."

Lee smiled tepidly. "I know, but it has been… hard lately."

The tailor stepped forward, running a hand along the boy's arm. "Things are about to change for you, from here on out. Trust that the Scion Prime and his Consort will treat you well. They are good people."

"Thank you again, sir. I feel hopeful… for the first time in my life."

"Blasted recruits," grumbled the lieutenant of the panther guard, hurrying down the broad oak stairs of the barracks. "And at a time like this!" His black hair barely touched his shoulders with the speed, as he skipped steps for a faster descent.

Another sentry followed in his tracks, sweat pearling across his forehead. "Sir, I am sure it is nothing," he appealed. "They are most likely just held up for some reason!"

"Held up? In the forest?" The lieutenant snorted. "I think not! The night shift should have returned long ago." Pushing the front door open, he ran out onto the barracks courtyard. In a cloud of smoke, he shifted into his feline form, a black panther sprinting off towards the west – and closest – entrance to the city.

The sentry struggled to keep up, his demonic frame not quite as strong and fast as that of his superior. He dug his claws deep, building speed as best he could. Swearing under his breath, he growled. His lieutenant was always so excessively strict and punctual; it was all but taking on ridiculous proportions. This was positively another one of his overblown assessments.

The narrow game trail twisted and turned through the forest as the two panthers dashed along the path. Leaves and needles whirled behind them as they headed for the northernmost watchtower. It was uphill, and the young guard became badly winded within minutes of leaving the city.

"M-must we... be in... such a hurry?" he questioned, the taste of blood building on his tongue.

The lieutenant ignored his complaints outright, unwilling to compromise on his sense of urgency.

Passing over a hillock, the demons came to an abrupt halt. Before them, on the path, laid a man and a woman in human form. Facedown onto the packed dirt, the man looked to have been rolled over, his body covered in dust and leaves. The woman, however, lay as if she had suddenly fallen, her upper body twisted and her legs awkwardly crossed. Their bodies were completely still, no sounds leaving them as the lieutenant neared.

Shifting into his human form, he bent down to examine them. They were indeed the sentries about to have been relieved from their night shift.

The young guard stood back, his jaw slackening.

"Their necks are broken," the lieutenant determined. He assessed their skin for colour and temperature. "They have not been dead for long. We need to find the other guards."

In another cloud of black mist, the lieutenant transformed, taking off running again in his feline form. He could hear the young guard behind him keeping up as they ascended another hill, then up a rocky mountainside to reach the lookout they were initially heading for.

Situated high up in a tree, the small structure was abandoned. No sentries, but neither were there any corpses. What had gone wrong?

"No strange scent," the lieutenant concluded, his broad paws padding across the floor of the watchtower. "Or..."

"What?" the guard expectantly asked.

"Panther."

The young sentry jerked his head back. "Panther? Why wouldn't-" He stopped himself, not finishing the sentence.

"Exactly," the lieutenant said. "We need to hurry back!"

Samael viewed the Leve plateau, the grass tall and green. He still had vague memories of himself playing there as a child, spending days outside with his mother and father. He watched Anaya as she strolled along the plains, holding Aaron's hand. They were heading for the stream, to go and see if they could spot any fish.

There was a noise, prompting the demon to turn. He was met by Lee, who seemed ready for his fourth session with him. "You look good in your new outfit," Samael commended. "Did the tailor treat you well?"

"Indeed, he did, your Highness." Lee's cheeks flushed. "He is a very pleasant man."

"Good," Samael said. "Now, do not let yourself become too caught up in the formalities again, boy."

"No... sir."

"Have you eaten this morning?" the Prime questioned.

"I have," Lee confirmed.

Samael smiled. "Excellent. You will need the energy for these sessions, so never skip a meal. Today, I planned for us to advance your training to the next level. Since you can now change without the demonic form acting out, I would like us to provoke it." He stepped aside, revealing a small cage behind his cloak. Inside sat a hare, its ears facing forward and the tiny nose fluttering.

Lee's eyes darted between the Prime and the critter. "P-provoke it?"

"Yes. We will allow it to stay in the cage as you change, then have you approach it. Should you manage, I will release it, and you will have to resist the urge to hunt it down and kill it."

The boy nervously scratched at his arm. It was going to be a challenge, as he still had to concentrate severely only while changing.

"Feel free to transform whenever you are ready," Samael went on.

Taking a deep breath, Lee slowly exhaled as he closed his eyes. He desperately wanted to pass this test, since he felt as if he were enough of a disappointment as it was. His heart was racing, and he felt himself tremble. There was a sudden weight to his shoulder, causing him to open his eyes.

Samael had placed a hand on him. "I am with you, every step of the way," he said.

✶✶

Walking along the edge of the water, Anaya looked up towards her husband. Lee had arrived, and they were talking. She smiled, satisfied that Samael had taken the boy under his wing. He had reported the training to be going well so far, and he saw plenty of potential in the young man. Perhaps he would make a sterling manservant and protector one day.

There was smoke billowing around them, the boy most likely going through his metamorphosis.

"Mama!"

The priestess looked at her son, the child holding his arms up towards her. Picking him up, she felt a tug to her hair. His fingers had instantly wrapped around her chestnut braid. Sitting down, she kept him on her lap, pointing to the fish in the stream. He showed little interest, mainly wanting to be close to her instead.

Lowering him on the grass, she grabbed his hand, then followed the stream north. Tall mountains rose before them, and a thick forest spread to the east. The sun felt warm on her face, the late summer's day incredible.

She suddenly heard shouting, in the direction of Samael and Lee. She saw her husband sprint after the boy's demonic form. They were soon out of sight, disappearing towards the forests to the north. Perhaps, the lesson didn't quite pan out.

Anaya felt an involuntary tremor, the sensation unusually strong. She had often felt it as she got to know Samael, but it had since dampened as she got used to his aura. However, this was different. It was not her husband, but someone of similar origin – a *Prime*.

With a tight grip on her son, she turned. A giant panther growled at her, baring its fangs.

"YOUR BASTARD HALF-BREED OF A SON IS UNWORTHY TO EVEN DRAW BREATH!"

It was close to noon as Kaedin arrived at the Matriarch's home, back from a short trip to neighbouring Pella. He handed the reins to his horse to a servant in the courtyard, then entered the house. Arax greeted him as always, after which he was allowed to join Lilith in her drawing-room. The officer stood motionless at the door.

"Take a seat, Master Reed," she said. "Or would you perhaps prefer to stand?"

His expression was that of stone. "I am fine here, my lady."

"Very well." The Matriarch leaned back in her seat. "What do you have to report?"

"The scouts stationed around the main settlement of the Fox tribe claims there seems to be no ill will with their agreeing to a meeting with us."

"And you trust their assessment?" Lilith inquired.

"Aye," Kaedin answered. "The Patriarch has been overheard arguing with other highly-ranked within his tribe, defending the decision. However, their Patriarch is not the only one able to orchestrate a trap."

"Indeed." The Matriarch steepled her hands. "We will still need to send members strong enough to fend off a possible attack."

"I intend to go myself, my lady."

Lilith raised an eyebrow. "Really?"

"It is the only viable option," Kaedin explained. "With the new recruits, I am the only one available. I cannot send someone else in my stead, with the risk of an ambush."

"As you wish," she said. "We will obviously send a representative, as I previously stated. It is a bit unfortunate in time, however, considering the ongoing troubles within my own tribe."

"I am assuming you meant to send Samael with us?"

"Yes. The problem lies in the fact we are still unsure of some... tribe members' intentions. As such, I am less inclined to offer his protection."

Kaedin traced his jaw with his thumb. "I was to bring the subject up at Congress for discussion. Perhaps we will make a decision then."

"Certainly," Lilith agreed, then fell silent as she watched him.

The man's eyes narrowed, as if suspicious to her thoughts.

"Are you cross with me, Master Reed?"

Kaedin flinched at the words. "No, your Highness. I am not. Why would you ask that?"

"You refuse to sit with me, and you have a shortness to your tone. Considering our last meeting, it would be unsurprising, should you house negative sentiments towards myself."

"My lady, I am not one to hold a grudge. You ask what you will, and I shall answer it. I am not to pretend it did not vex me greatly to be challenged in such a manner, but you most likely have your reasons. I have not reflected upon it since."

The Matriarch laughed. "And here I was preparing an apology speech," she said. "Nevertheless, I was about to say that it is merely a habit of mine to delve into such affairs with conviction, no matter if they are justified or not. See it as a… hobby of sorts. Through my years as a ruler, I have always had to be stern with my subjects, and, as such, it comes naturally."

"I understand, my lady."

"Yes, yes," she urged, circling her hand. "It still does not stand as a reason for what I said, so I… apologise."

Kaedin smirked. "Apology well received, your Highness."

"Good. Now, please, sit. It is acceptable if you do not appreciate myself, as not everyone can have good taste, but I would still like for you to join me."

The officer refrained from showing his amusement. He was about to move forward as the door suddenly flung open.

"Your Highness; your Excellency!" a young man called, throwing himself on the floor. He wore the signature outfit of the local guard. "I am terribly sorry, but I bring urgent news."

"Out with it then!" Lilith snapped.

"We believe panthers not native to the City of Fahd have breached our border. Lieutenant Erano is gathering troops as we speak. They seem to have split up, and from the group I stalked, I only just managed to identify one of the intruders."

"Who?"

"*Protector Prime Gaeric Onyx.*"

The Matriarch jolted out of her seat. "We need to find Anaya and Aaron this *instant*. Arax!"

Her manservant rushed through the door. "Yes, my lady?"

"Hurry and find Samael! He was meant to meet with Anaya's prospective attendant, somewhere outside the city. I have no clue as to Anaya's and Aaron's whereabouts, but they are most likely in the same area. We need to warn them!"

Without a word, Arax disappeared out of the room, with Kaedin hurrying after him.

16

HUNT

"Lee!" Samael shouted, but the boy was too far gone, his feline form whistling away amongst the trees. The hare had most certainly caught his attention – and his underlying instincts – in a tight grip. Coming to a halt, Samael dragged a hand across his face. He knew he risked this outcome with this particular exercise, but it was disappointing nonetheless. Perhaps they would have to revisit some of the earlier training sessions to further enforce Lee's ability to counteract his demonic impulses.

But for now, he merely needed to find him.

Loping through the forest, tracking the youngster was no trouble, but Samael was yet to see any trace of him actually catching the hare. There was no blood or fur visible in the undergrowth. Was he indeed that inept at hunting that he could not even run down critters? If so, this feat would also need to be planned for future outings.

The Scion Prime suddenly stopped, a strange smell hitting his nose.

He instantly recognised it as belonging to a panther. Or many? But not Lee.

He swivelled in the spot, his stance lowering. "Who is there?" he challenged.

No answer came, at least not by words. Rumbles and snarls sounded all around him, then the first panther took to the air.

Samael swerved, backhanding the assailant into a tree, but a second one instantly charged him, then a third. Crushing the skull of one, he growled as he felt a set of canines sink into his neck, and claws lodging into his back. More panthers ran for him – too many to count. Thoughts raced through his mind; what could he possibly do, other than transform? There were too many of them.

Ripping the panther away from his back, Samael felt its fangs tearing through the flesh of his neck, blood gushing from the wounds. "**YOU DARE STRIKE AGAINST ME?**" he thundered, greeting another panther by grabbing it by the snout and catapulting it into another assailant.

Black mists exploded out, bringing the demons into complete darkness. Samael viciously roared amongst the settling smoke, his tail whipping out as he bore down on the first of his opponents. A single bite ended the panther's life before the Prime turned on the next. He slashed and clawed, leaving a trail of blood and gore behind him along the disturbed forest floor. Out of patience, there was no mercy left in him. He tore a panther's leg away, then flattened its head against the ground. Soon losing count on how many he had slaughtered, Samael looked around, assessing the unexpected circumstances of his surroundings.

The panthers kept on coming. Why were there so many of them? And seemingly so willing to throw their lives away for nothing?

A searing pain suddenly ripped through Samael's stomach and his front legs buckled. He barely managed to heave himself up before a demon vaulted onto his back, then another. Teeth and claws dug into his flesh, claret oozing from the lacerations.

The bond of a Prime drummed within him, wrenching at his insides, and screaming for him to run – to find the priestess. The air around him seemingly surged with an invisible pull, back towards the Leve plateau, in her direction.

He needed to hurry. *Anaya was in danger.*

The foreign Prime attacked in absolute silence, with only a low growl rolling out as he pounced. He was not as large as Samael, but most certainly very powerful, his terrifying mists flowing out from his dark form.

Anaya had no time to consider his menacing presence. With an arm around Aaron, she threw herself out of the panther's path, landing heavily with her son safe in her embrace. Rising, she hastily moved him in behind her, taking a wide stance to ready herself for another attack. Aaron whimpered, clutching hold of her dress. Chanting forcefully, the priestess enveloped them in a barrier of Light.

Turning on the spot, the Prime charged again, but the strength of her spell slowed him down, reducing the weight of his impact. He reached out, the fur on his paw sizzling as it came down over her leg. Knife-like claws ripped through the fabric of her skirt and tore into her flesh, blood immediately flowing from the gashes.

Powering through her protective spell, the Prime's jaws opened.

Anaya's eyes flickered as her open palm whacked across the demon's head. Swerving, she spun with him, Light crackling out like lightning across his body.

The demon tumbled forward, landing on the grass behind Anaya. He groaned, rising, then held his hands out in front of him. He had involuntarily been reverted back into human form. "What the hell!" he snarled. His long black hair flicked as he turned towards the priestess.

Anaya could sense more demons. Grabbing onto Aaron's clothing, she ushered him away, and they sidestepped a few paces along the field. She grunted, unable to ignore the pain in her leg. Her green dress stained further red with every limping step.

Another two panthers arrived. They, too, were large, but not Primes. One of them immediately made a move to attack, leaping forward with its claws extended.

A flash of Light rippled out, engulfing the demon. Anaya stumbled aside, barely avoiding being hit despite her attack. Reinforcing the protective barrier around Aaron, she steeled herself. This was no time to wait for her husband to heed the call of their bond. She needed to thwart these on her own, if only to save her son.

Surging with the powers of the Goddess, Anaya conjured a towering wave, hurling it in the demons' direction. The Prime moved out of its path fast enough to avoid it altogether, but the third demon screamed as it ran through him.

"Where are the others?" the Prime grumbled, cursing.

Anaya retreated further, ushering little Aaron behind her. She was unsure how long her spell would hold an effect on the Prime, and she was unwilling to fight him single-handedly. She needed help.

The two smaller panthers, both badly burnt, whined as the Prime yet again ordered for them to attack. "Why are you just standing there?" he shouted. "Get them now!"

One of them jerked as to move, but halted at a sudden roar in the distance. In the north, a plume of demonic mists burst out, telling of who was coming.

"You all better stand down, should any of you wish to live," Anaya threatened. With a sturdy grip on her son, she backed further away from the three assailants. She continuously held a hand towards the panthers, her fingers sparkling with Light.

With little time left, one of the demons dug its claws into the ground, then leapt for Anaya.

Light flashed out, further searing the beast's coat and skin. It writhed and shrieked, slamming down next to her.

The priestess' eyes narrowed as she scrutinised her opponents, the Prime now united with the last panther. Anaya knew she needed only to stall them for a few more moments. She already felt the exhilarating thrill of Samael's aura as he gained on them.

The Prime visibly swallowed at the sight of the oncoming Scion. He knew he had no choice. Enveloping himself in mists, he came into a sprint, and the two panther Primes clashed in the middle of the field.

With no time to waste, Kaedin had signalled for all available priests to be summoned atop the cliffs outside the City of Fahd. Many came by foot, others were mounted, as they set off through the forest in pursuit of any hostile demons. Knowing there was a Prime in their midst, the priests had to tread carefully, albeit with haste, as they also searched for Samael, Anaya and Aaron.

Having split up with Arax and his group of guards, who opted for rounding the city in the opposite direction, the members of the Priesthood soon came across a most ghastly sight.

Dead and wounded panthers; some were torn from limb to limb, others crushed or slashed wide open.

Kaedin halted his mount, his chestnut gelding snorting at the stench of the recent slaughter. Priests fanned out around them, Edric and Eden amongst them. The former Knight motioned Edric forward.

A single arrow arched over the area, its Light flashing out like a tide across the landscape. The number of demon tracks that flashed in its wake was staggering. Growls sounded from the trees above and from the nearby vegetation. They were not far away.

"Remember we are here to *capture* the demons, not kill them!" Kaedin cautioned, jumping down from his horse. He unsheathed his blade, rolling it in his hand. "Ready yourselves!"

A dozen panthers, of varying strength and sizes, all made themselves known to the priests. At a numeric disadvantage of almost two to one, Kaedin was surprised at their boldness. There could only be one reason for it, and that was that the panthers had nothing to lose. Were they captured, they would all face the death penalty nonetheless.

Light spread amongst the many priests, forming long shimmering bands between them. Standing in a broad line, they created a barrier as they charged the demons.

Panthers snarled and yelped as the Light hit them, twisting and turning as it wrapped itself around their dark bodies. One demon pounced before the glowing net reached it, extending its claws as it headed for Kaedin.

With a chant of fortification, a wall of Light appeared before the General Priest. The panther slammed into it, the coat sizzling as it fell to the ground. Kaedin quickly conjured a single net, encasing the demon within.

More attacked, Eden being one to defend himself against the massive beasts. His spear lodged itself sideways inside one's mouth, barely keeping it far enough away not to allow its teeth to sink into his chest. He let out a cry, his weapon flashing as he spun it around, then brought it down to pierce through the panther's snout. Aided by Edric, they subdued the creature, leaving yet another encased within bonds of Light.

Kaedin blocked a paw swipe, his weapon slicing through claws. Dark demonic blood splattered his unarmoured body, and he swerved from a powerful bite. His magic of the Light rolled out across the beast's back, then quickly slammed down, pinning it against the undergrowth.

One by one, the demons were successfully captured, and the priests had suffered only minor injuries. The panthers left had not been of high strength, and certainly not anywhere near a Prime, so Kaedin knew this would not be the entirety of the intruders. He turned to Edric.

"You and another three priests stay here and make sure the demons are kept confined," he ordered. "Follow-" He was interrupted by the sight of another panther cowering behind a tree further into the forest. "Come forth, intruder!" he demanded.

"I am not an intruder!" the demon yelped, his body dragging along the ground as he crawled forward. "It is I – Lee! Lady Anaya's manservant!" Dark mists enveloped his shivering frame, only to reveal the young boy equally shaking as he laid flat before the General Priest.

"Lee? What in the Goddess' name are you doing here?"

"I-I was out... training with the Scion Prime... here in the forest," he explained, still not lifting his gaze from the leaves and dirt underneath him. "I failed... miserably... but as I returned to reunite with the Scion, I hid as I saw... all these panthers."

"You stay here with Edric, boy," Kaedin decided. Returning to his gelding, he swiftly vaulted astride. "I will continue with the rest and secure the perimeter."

"What about Anaya? And Aaron?" the younger man questioned.

"We need to hurry if we are to aid them. I pray Arax was more successful in locating them."

It was unlike anything Anaya had ever seen, the distorted roars cutting through her and the two panthers despite the distance. The Primes slashed at each other, blood spraying as flesh and fur were torn away. Samael's teeth lodged, mangling muscle and skin with violent jolts to the head. The lesser Prime fought desperately to defend himself against the Scion's raging onslaught.

It was quickly becoming hard to discern what was going on through the billowing smoke. A low gnarl caused Anaya to view the last panther. She eyed him up and down. "Do not even think about it, demon," she challenged. "May I remind you I fought against the feral Scion and won?"

The scorched beast laying beside her released a soft whine, opening its eyes.

The priestess stood tall, looking down at it. "I will kill you if you make a move."

Meeting her gaze, the panther merely crawled back to his comrade, slumping to the ground again.

With a chant, Anaya healed her wounds, her leg showing through the torn fabric of her skirt.

Aaron was surprisingly silent, the young boy's expression resolute as he held on to his mother.

There was a sudden whirl inside the Primes' demonic mists, with the lesser one sent flying through and landing just short of the other demons. He was breathing heavily, bleeding profusely from a multitude of deep lacerations.

Samael was in close pursuit, coming through the mists and bearing down on him again. Locking his jaws around his throat, the Scion Prime squeezed the windpipe shut as his enraged eyes glared at the other panthers. With his opponent's vigour trickling away, Samael bit down, then ripped the flesh clear. In oozing crimson, he ended the Prime's life.

Snapping bones sounded, the demonic mists flaring out around Samael. His black cloak fluttered in the breeze, then settled around his human form. **"WHERE ARE THE REST OF YOU?"** he demanded, pointing to the demon still on his feet. The panther crouched, visibly shaking.

A group of panthers bolted out from the trees, spearheaded by one which Samael instantly recognised.

"We have caught a group of the intruders to the south," Arax explained, stopping on the opposite side of the stream. "The Priesthood is hunting down more of the traitors north of the city."

Samael scoffed. "If there are any left of them still alive." He rumbled with his seething emotions, facing the two demons again. "Turn back to human form, or I will kill you this instant!"

The two demons soon stood in their human forms before him, both badly burnt from Anaya's magic.

Grabbing the throat of one, Samael lifted him away from the ground. "Both of you better tell us *everything* we need to know. Otherwise, we shall cull every single generation of your house."

✶ ✶

Lilith lurched from her daybed. "You *killed* Gaeric?"

Anaya felt herself longing for additional space between her and the Matriarch. Her foot dragged back, creating swirls in the black mists whooshing from the two demons.

Samael menacingly growled. "Yes!"

"He was most likely the instigator of all this!" Lilith cried. "How are we meant to find those involved with the leader no longer available for questioning?"

"**I DO NOT CARE!** He attempted to *murder* my family! I will kill every single member of that house, if I so have to, in order to identify all those entangled in this act of *treason*!" Samael felt a touch to his arm as Anaya neared him. He let out a breath, his aura dampening. "Were it not for our son's presence, I would have killed them all."

Lilith sighed. "I can recognise your standpoint, Samael, but it would have still been in our interest to keep him alive. Be that as it may, we must now make do with what we have. I shall personally see to Lente and Alune Ziva and their interrogations."

"Both the younger brothers of their Master Prime?" Anaya inquired.

"Indeed. I would prefer to know if he was also involved. It would be devastating to their lineage."

"They would all have to be executed then?"

"Yes."

"What about the House of Onyx?" Anaya asked. "With your sister married to one of them."

"Since she is a Prime, they took the name of Sia. Unless her Consort is personally involved, he and his family will not be punished."

Samael cursed. "Depending on how many are involved, we stand to cull a good portion of our Prime lineages."

195

"Undoubtedly," Lilith wistfully agreed. "Those merely aware of the fact will be executed. The inhabitants of their respective villages will be relocated, and the settlements destroyed. There is not much else to do."

Anaya briefly covered her face with her hands. "I have been very naive, Samael," she said.

"In what way?" he questioned.

"I believed- or, I *hoped*, that Aaron being a demon, there would be no such language spoken around him."

"What do you mean?"

"I knew there could be issues with him being born outside of wedlock, but the Prime, Gaeric, he called him… a *half-breed*."

Samael bared his fangs. "Were he not already dead, I would kill him for his insolence!"

"I can understand their concern," the Matriarch acknowledged. "With this union being the first of its kind, it is hard to predict the future. Aaron does indeed carry a demon's scent, but until he grows older, there is no telling what power he holds." She looked at the priestess. "You know how we choose partners for our Primes, and the effort placed into making a suitable combination of lineages. With you being human, we cannot know whether he shall harness a lesser, equal or higher strength to that of his father."

Anaya had indeed read a lot on the subject. The heredity of demons and their abilities was much more complicated than what she had ever thought, where they would mix and match very carefully as to not run the risk of the offspring's *Evolution* turning feral. It had to do with the combined power of the lineages, as well as the rate of Primes amongst the descendants.

"Higher strength? You believe it possible?" Samael asked.

"As I said, there is no telling, as this has never previously occurred. You are of superior power than your father, and he was in no way a weak demon."

"I know," he said. "I am certainly not looking forward to Aaron's *Evolution*."

Lilith stepped forward, placing a hand on Samael's arm. "Aaron will have something you did not: a *father* to guide him. Along with Anaya's magic, I feel safe to say that you shall manage, even if he were to house greater potential than yourself."

"You are right, but… he is my son. I cannot bear the thought of something happening to him."

The Matriarch grinned. "The joys of parenthood. I have had my fair share."

Samael glared at her but said nothing.

"Now then. While Arax and Kaedin round up all the captives, I shall tend to the Ziva brothers. You two can relax, for I believe this feat will scare away any remaining doubters. Anaya's ability to thwart Primes single-handedly is surely to be to your benefit."

"I am not sure I would have beaten him, even in his human form," the priestess admitted, meeting her husband's gaze. "We fought once… and I know you held back. You could have easily fended me off. I may have been able to stand my ground momentarily, but I would have run out of spiritual powers very quickly."

"That may very well be true," Lilith granted. "But that is not something anyone has to know."

"I understand that, but it begs the question of whether the Priesthood should know."

"How so?" Lilith wondered.

"We were ignorant before, but no longer," Anaya said. "The priests are bound to run into demons in human form much more often than their demonic counterpart. It is therefore important not to become complacent, such as believing demons are somehow weak as humans."

The Matriarch stood in thought for a moment. "It is true. Our strength in human form is correspondent with our demonic powers, which is why Primes would be perceived as unnaturally strong amongst your kind. Perhaps a demonstration for your recruits would prove a point. We cannot risk them dying because they believe a demon to be rendered defenceless merely due to the chosen form."

"My point exactly," Anaya concurred. "It is what the Priesthood had always believed. I even taught it myself, as I held classes in demonology."

"We shall ponder a solution to the problem, but for now, let us focus on the issue at hand. The Panther tribe faces a comprehensive reformation."

17

EFFICIENCY

U nwilling to waste time, Kaedin had left for the Fox tribe in the days after the assassination attempt. As their main settlement was local, the round trip was less than a week.

The investigation into the revolt of the panthers was rigorously led by the Matriarch, but her prisoners had yet to reveal the names of all those involved. The treacherous members, along with their implicated families, were held in a dungeon beneath the City of Fahd, guarded by both demons and members of the Priesthood.

On the day of the Harvest Festival, the yearly gathering of the Master Primes was held. Except for those to stand trial, all had responded to the calls of summon. It was breaking dawn as they sat at a table in one of the Matriarch's reception rooms.

Lilith stood at the far end, together with Samael, Anaya and little Aaron. The boy was beside his father, half-hidden behind the heavy royal cloak.

"We can sense the uneasiness in the room, as some of our Master Primes are unable to attend," the Matriarch began. "I am not to pretend this does not affect me also. I am deeply disappointed in my subjects and their actions. I would have wished for a different outcome, but everything points to their lineages being eradicated within the coming month."

Looks were shared amongst those gathered.

One of the Primes raised a hand. His thick hair was cropped short, and his brown eyes were harsh. "I mean no disrespect, your Highness, but many of us are concerned. We have in no way been involved in this uproar against the House of Fahd, yet we are still worried we might be implied by those captured. What safety can we be offered against their untruthful words, if any of those are shared?"

"I am sure the prisoners will try any tactic to reduce their sentences, no matter how it might affect those implied," Lilith agreed. "However, I will see to this investigation personally, and it shall be done justly."

"What guarantee is there that this will also be upheld by the Scion Prime Consort?" another Prime questioned. "I agree, I mean no disrespect, but we stand before a precipice with a human assuming the role of Matriarch. Can we truly place trust in her abilities to judge fairly? To bring unity to our tribe?"

Anaya felt her heart rate increase, and she swallowed a breath. Samael shifted his weight, agitated, but said nothing.

"As Matriarch, I can never be lenient, but neither am I to make thoughtless decisions as to the tribe's future," Lilith made clear.

"We understand that, your Highness," the first Prime replied. "But would it not be wise to at least wait until everything has settled? Perhaps the Scion Prime Consort can remain a Consort? And not take on the role as Matriarch?"

Listening to the insulting suggestion, Samael could no longer remain idle, his rumbling voice sharp. "Such insolence! I should have you-"

"No, Samael," Lilith interjected, her voice unyielding. "To vent concerns is not to commit treason. They have the right to raise the subject. I stand firm in my decision as to the mate of my son and rightful heir of the throne. With that said, I am hereby to abdicate, effective immediately. Today will be my last day as Matriarch of the Panther Tribe. From tomorrow onward, you will refer to Scion Prime Samael Fahd as Patriarch and his Consort as Matriarch."

The suddenness of the declaration sent the Primes into silence. Some merely peered at each other, others showing expressions of disbelief.

"I shall instead focus wholeheartedly on the investigation of treason," Lilith went on. "After which, I shall live out my days in peace."

Undeterred by those doubting the Scion Prime and his Consort, Leviathan nodded. "Well deserved, your Highness."

Another Prime agreed. "Very much so, my lady."

They all rose, bowing deeply.

A man at the other end of the table spoke. "On behalf of the House of Bao, we salute your years of service, your Highness. You have done something truly remarkable leading the tribe after the unfortunate passing of Patriarch Forcas Fahd. He is sorely missed, but you have left no stone unturned. We look forward to a new generation to take hold where you left off."

Lilith felt tears sting her eyes as she listened, the turn of tone amongst the Primes unexpected. "Very good," she mouthed, attempting to shake the emotion. "I shall obviously stay as a supporting mother-in-law to Matriarch Anaya Fahd, but it shall be pleasant to finally take a day off now and again."

The Master Prime of the House of Brint smiled at her. "And enjoy your grandson," she said. "He does, indeed, look precious." She peeped around the back of the chairs at the young boy.

Leviathan requested his turn to voice his thoughts. "I believe I speak for everyone here when I say we all swear allegiance to the continued rule under the House of Fahd. I can appreciate the opinions voiced today, and we may very well face struggles in the near future, but they shall be overcome."

Walking along the exterior wall of Samael and Anaya's Royal mansion, Lenda could not help but stare, her eyes ceaselessly darting. She felt as if she had shrunk with the size of the building. All the doorways were abnormally large and the ceilings high. The structure dwarfed the young healer as she continued in a hurry, heading for the rear gardens. Anaya had invited her to inspect her choice of flowers and greenery.

Rounding the last corner, Lenda saw the priestess standing amongst some bushes. Her chestnut hair was braided across her shoulder, and she was wearing a flowing verdant gown.

"Anaya!" the girl called.

Turning around, the priestess extended her arms. "Oh, Lenda," she exhaled as they embraced. "Thank you so much for coming. I need your advice. I was unsure of to what extent I should grow certain plants."

The healer drew a sharp breath as she looked around. "Goddess, you have gathered quite a collection! There are several that do not normally grow around here."

"Indeed, but I had them planted in movable pots, so they can be brought inside during winter. I am hoping they will survive that way."

"Genius! I love it," Lenda exclaimed. She shared an excited look with the priestess. "Can I...?"

"Of course," Anaya allowed. "The plants will be for everyone to use, as long as they are not damaged through harvesting. They would be no good if they were to perish due to mistreatment."

"Certainly, I shall be most careful," Lenda promised.

"Come, let us take a walkabout. There are many for you to choose from." Strolling along a narrow path paved with stone slabs, Anaya pointed to several as she spoke. "They will need to take root first. Some have only been planted a few days ago."

"I see," Lenda said. "I am very impressed by the collection."

"I will have more arriving in the coming weeks, as not all were initially shipped to us," Anaya explained. "The ongoing disturbances along the border to Abyssa affected our orders, but Samael has spared no expense when it comes to my indulgence. He says he does not wish for me to stop living my life, merely because I am to lead the tribe. I am not entirely sure how I am meant to combine the two, but this is hopefully one way to do so."

"He is most generous," Lenda granted. "And caring for yourself."

Anaya smiled. "He is. Although I feel bad about it myself. I have never spent more than a few coppers on a dress, and then to receive all this... I do not dare consider the cost."

"I would feel the same way," the healer admitted. "We have all been taught that material things are unnecessary, but you deserve them, sister. Especially if we all get use out of-" She stopped herself, noticing an odd plant with pinnately compound leaves. Tiny hairs grew across the green surface, creating a soft look. There were several of them, some even in bloom, with flowers of rich purple. "Astragalus!"

"Yes," the priestess said. "I had them delivered from Kanadesh. I am surprised so many of them survived the journey. Perhaps, you will have use for them with Lee's aunt?"

Lenda smiled bleakly. "It might offer some relief, but no more."

"That is what I feared. I only wish for her a peaceful passing."

Exhaling, the healer's arms fell to her sides. "I am doing what I can. She is currently not in pain, as I offer her enchantments, but I feel she might have as little as weeks left."

Anaya nodded. "I must admit, I am surprised she has survived as long as she has."

"It might be the demons' ability to heal," Lenda said. "According to Lee, she has been ill for years."

"You may very well be right," Anaya agreed. "We will need to look into differences between the humans and demons, all of which to be recorded if we are to teach new healers to treat both. Because even if demons have certain rates of self-healing, they might still need our aid." Anaya paused for a moment. "Speaking of which, I would like to hear your opinion on something other than the herbs."

"What could that be then?" Lenda asked.

Anaya's voice lowered. "Turning demons back into their human form."

The young girl stared at her. "I heard you did it again as you were attacked. Did something happen?"

"Indeed, I did, and no. I am only inquiring if you should wish to learn the feat."

Moistening her lips, Lenda hesitated. "You... would teach me the spell?"

"Well..." Anaya said. "I am not entirely sure how to, but as the situation between humans and demons is still very much infected, I would not want to teach just anyone. I know I can trust you."

"Sure, but I am not very good with the Light in that manner."

"It is not an offensive spell," Anaya told her. "It is based on healing and has a defensive nature, which is why I believe you might become proficient, should I manage to pass it down."

Lenda's brow furrowed. "Healing?"

"Yes. I know it sounds strange, but you will know what I mean when you see it. I will look into how we are to proceed. I only wanted your confirmation on my suggestion."

"I am willing to try, yes," Lenda declared.

"Thank you, sister," Anaya said. "It gladdens me."

Bending over a low plant, the young healer touched an amber flower. Water trickled down its petals as it swung. "Are you to become Matriarch now?"

"Yes." Anaya clutched at her wrists, wringing them. "Officially from tomorrow onward." Her eyes dropped, and her eyebrows drew together.

Lenda looked at her, immediately recognising a state in her friend seldom seen. "Are you nervous? I understand it is a massive undertaking, but this is not like you. What is the matter?"

"I…" The priestess sighed. "I am not so sure the Panther tribe will follow me."

"Nonsense!" Lenda exclaimed. "The Matriarch would never allow that."

"No, she would not, yet it gives me little comfort at this point in time. I am lucky my mother-in-law is to stay close by, so I can look to her for advice, but I do feel that a seed of doubt has been planted amongst our… subjects. Oh, how wrong it feels to call people that."

Lenda's features softened as she gave her a supportive smile. "I am most positive you will be able to deal with this, sister. You have not once given up on anything in your life. This will be no different."

Returning the smile, Anaya embraced her life-long friend.

"How does Samael feel about it?" Lenda asked.

Anaya contemplated the question. "About the other Primes? He is vexed, to say the least. But with taking over the tribe, he is fine, I suppose. Even though he once told me that he never wanted the position… until he met me."

"Is that why his mother is still the leader?"

"Correct. I have obviously read extensively about the House of Fahd since our marriage and considering his father died so many years back, he is over ten years late to take over as Patriarch. Although he is only about five years behind to produce an heir, so I suppose that counts for something."

Lenda scratched her chin. "Does it normally take long for demons to conceive?"

"It seems to depend on the type of demon, but with panthers, yes," Anaya replied. "They have issues with fertility, struggling to retain the population. The Fahd lineage, specifically, has seldom had more than one heir. In retrospect, I can understand why Samael was shocked at the fact I had birthed a child in the year we spent apart."

Lenda laughed. "It was amazing, no matter if you were both human or not. But are you not expecting to have any more children then?"

"Historically speaking, no. Unless there is something nearly magical in our combination, we should only stand to have one child, perhaps two, if the Goddess is with us. However, I am yet to see my cycle returning, so I could not become pregnant now, even if I wanted it."

The young girl smiled as she made eye contact with the priestess. "So, you would want another?"

Blushing, Anaya averted her gaze. "I... I am not going to lie. I would, yes, not only for myself but for Samael. He is an attentive father, and I feel he would appreciate it. And, from an objective standpoint, it would be very beneficial for the bloodline. It is something that would truly make me feel as if I made a difference."

"Then I shall pray for it," Lenda chirped. "I am yet to decide a good time for a first child, so I am in no rush."

"I can see Eden nagging you about it more than the other way around, sister."

"Indeed, he already is, in his own way. And to be honest, we might not be quite as careful as we used to be, but I am not to actively try for one. Perhaps, in the new year, depending on how the Priesthood develops. We will need more healers."

"You are too good for us, Lenda," Anaya said, grabbing her hand. "I am ecstatic that we can live so close still, despite my new... position."

The girl squeezed her friend's hand. "So am I."

The priestess motioned for them to resume their walk. "I would like for us to continue the tour. I have many more plants I want your opinion on."

"Of course," Lenda said. "It is nice to spend time, even if it is short. I will need to leave within the hour to prepare for the celebrations. I am only hoping they can retrieve enough truffles until then."

"Truffles?" Anaya questioned.

"Yes. We lack them, as always. And with our pigs long gone, we have been largely unsuccessful locating them. You still hold the record for the most found while searching by hand."

Anaya attempted to disguise a redness sweeping across her cheeks.

"What is the matter?" Lenda asked.

"I, eh… Nothing." The priestess cleared her throat. "I shall see if I can manage to find some. When do you need them by?"

"Oh, would you? Any point before dinner service is fine. They can be added at the end if nothing else."

Despite the early morning, Kaedin had already made a round of report with the General Priests. His final meeting was meant to be held at the Temple with Adena, but she was nowhere to be found.

Deciding to try her home instead, the officer soon knocked at her door.

There was a noise from within, then the door creaked open. Adena's face came into view in the small spring. "What do you want, Kaedin?"

"To take report from you," he said. "May I come in?"

The woman's hand dragged along the door jamb. "Yes, of course. My apologies." Allowing him entry, she stood dressed in a simple linen gown. Her face was lined, and there were dark rings under her eyes.

"My Goddess, you cannot have slept for weeks," he blurted.

"I have not, no," she admitted, then turned and walked inside. Leading the man through to her front room, they sat down before the empty fireplace.

"You need to tell me if there is something I can do for you," Kaedin said. "Is it due to your position as Cardinal?"

"No, not at all," she said. "It is… personal."

"Very well. I shall not trouble you further on the subject," he promised. "Is there anything you would wish to report?"

"The representative of the Fox tribe is doing well," she said. "However, he has moved in with the panthers. I suppose, no one would want to be the first demon to live amongst us."

Kaedin chuckled. "That may very well be true. With enough of them, however, I could see that turning around."

Adena agreed. "Have there been any further tribes interested in meeting with us?"

A grin spread on Keadin's lips. "I am to leave and visit with the Matriarch of the Wasp tribe, most likely to depart tomorrow, after Congress. Apparently, they live deep in the forest, south of Greer."

"In Rover?"

"Aye."

"Who will you bring with you?" Adena asked.

"The Panther tribe will send representatives," he told her. "Then I shall have Eden come with me. We do not want to bring an entire brigade unless we wish to risk them believing we are amassing an attack."

Adena rubbed at her temple. "Are you sure that is our best option?"

"I am," he asserted. "We cannot bring additional priests only because the Panther tribe is unable to spare us a Prime. And to be honest, the Scion Prime has taken on more than enough duties to do with the Priesthood, despite having no obligation to do so."

"Indeed, he has, to my astonishment."

"Anaya has her ways," Kaedin said. "Now, I would like to go through our economy."

Adena's eyebrows drew tightly together. "About that," she said. "Leo provided me with the books yesterday. He voiced concern about the lack of funds left by Ekelon. Since the paperwork was destroyed in the fires, we initially believed the treasury to be divided, but we have yet to find the bulk of the money."

"Perhaps, he spent much more coinage on his experiments than we initially believed," Kaedin suggested.

"Most likely," she said. "Or it was indeed divided, and the demons who overrun the village found the other stash."

"Either is possible," he agreed. "If that is the case, it could explain the silence from the hound demons."

"Let me fetch the books. They are in my bedroom... since I was unable to sleep anyway." As Adena stood, the male officer grabbed her arm.

"You would tell me if there was anything I could provide for you, would you not?" he asked.

She gave him a weary smile. "No matter the potion, my dreams still haunt me, Kaedin. Trust me when I say, there is nothing you can do."

"Your dreams? What of?"

"I... I do not wish to speak of them. Please, question me no further."

Releasing her, the man briefly nodded. "As you wish."

✶✶

The renovation of Ekelon's old cellar was nearing completion. Descending the stairs into the stone structure, Kaedin was to inspect the work on his way home. New heavy doors had been installed, and the floors refurbished. Each cell featured a set of simple bedding, as well as shackles attached to the walls. Situated below ground level, there were no windows, making escape less probable. The inner walls had also been reinforced, and sacred runes carved outside each cell, should they house demons within. Guards would be stationed both inside the building and beyond the entrance.

Satisfied with the results, Kaedin left. There was no rest to be had, only the next assignment to assume.

Samael bent a branch aside, then ducked under another. "Why the hurry, Anaya?" he asked. He stepped close behind her, his hand caught in her unrelenting grip. "Has something happened?"

"No, just come with me," she replied. She turned right, rounding a few oak trees before arriving at a clearing. "This is it." Releasing him, she grabbed her basket with both hands.

The demon blinked. "What are we meant to do here? Are you to collect herbs?"

"No! No, I... I need you to..." Anaya's voice seemingly gave out as she attempted to word it. "Locate truffles for me."

Samael angled towards her. "You brought me here to find *truffles*?"

With his face inches from hers, she stood firm. "Yes," she said. "Lenda needs them for the Harvest Festival. And I... I need some much-needed distraction."

"We are to take over the Panther tribe tomorrow, and you want us to go hunting for fungi?"

"Yes!" she reaffirmed. "Stop questioning me about it. Get on with it instead."

There was a rumble to the demon, but he knew there was little point arguing his case. He pushed his cloak aside as he turned, then began moving through the terrain.

Anaya felt an excitement building with the event, remembering how he had helped her in the exact same way, only two years prior. She silently stalked him, holding her basket at the ready. As they walked through the eastern forest, she found herself relaxing at the subdued leisure. The surrounding nature of late summer was a delight to the senses, offering continuous music of rustling leaves and bird song.

The sun reached deep into the forest, dappling the undergrowth with its warm rays. Taking a deep breath, the priestess closed her eyes. She tilted her head back, enjoying the wondrous moment.

There was a grunt, and she found herself bending across Samael's back. Grabbing onto his black cloak, she had accidentally walked into the demon, who sat on his heels before her.

"Watch where you're going!" he flashed. Returning his attention to the ground, he carefully dug through the soil. It wasn't long until he unearthed a truffle of good size. He held it up, brushing dirt away from the top before giving it to the priestess.

Accepting the truffle, she placed it in her basket. They shared a glance, the woman's features no less determined. She demanded more.

Samael rose to his full height, throwing her a sinister glare, but said nothing. He continued along his chosen path, soon stopping below a wide oak. He delivered another two truffles.

Arranging them in the hamper, Anaya pressed her lips flat. She was not to word her expectations, so instead, she ushered the demon on. She needed more.

Moving south, they followed the outline of a crevice.

As number four, five and six touched down on the bottom of the basket, Samael was increasingly unamused.

"Just one more, please," she said.

"Fine."

Anaya grinned, her complete satisfaction only further aggravating the demon.

The edge was soft along the fissure, so the couple stayed at a safe distance. Anaya knew too well the experience of plunging into the darkness, as to not repeat it. Samael stopped, his eyes flitting as he determined the direction of their upcoming find. He took a few steps closer to the ledge, coming down to his knees before beginning to uncover the fungi.

"You have no idea how grateful I am, Samael," Anaya said. "You are much more efficient than any pig I have ever had."

He instantly rose. "Did you just compare me to-" There was a muted rumble as he slipped into silence.

Anaya's face flushed. She was about to speak when he slammed his hand against her chest. She wheezed as she fell back, struggling to draw breath. Momentarily dazed, she looked across herself, only to find the demon gone.

18

COUNTRYWIDE CELEBRATIONS

Anaya gripped at a nearby root as she hurried to rise. "Samael!" she called. Looking to where he had been standing, the ground had given way. He must have pushed her to prevent her from falling with him. "Samael!" she repeated, louder this time.

"I am fine," he replied. The sound of his voice echoed within the crevice. "I tend to land on my feet."

The priestess released a sigh of relief. "Thank Goddess," she said. "Will you be able to climb up on your own?"

Samael's face came into view to her left. "Yes," he said. Clearing the edge, he quickly moved away from it.

Anaya immediately ran into his embrace.

"Although," he continued. "When you managed the same feat, I lacked enough arms to carry you myself, hence the rope."

She blushed. "I would have thought so. I remember the soil being much too soft anyway."

"Indeed, it was." Samael reached for her hand, granting it a tender grip. "Did I hurt you?"

She rubbed at her chest. "For a moment, I thought you pushed me in anger. But it is only a bit sore."

"I am sorry. You know I never mean to hurt you," the demon stressed.

He paused before expelling a chuckle. "Nostalgic day, to say the least. However, I might have some consolation to offer this time." Kneeling before her, he reached behind his back, presenting a giant truffle. "For my Queen."

The Harvest Festival was extraordinary this year. Not because of the music played, or the food and drink served, but because of those attending. A year ago, this event would have been unfathomable. None could have foreseen a guest list including humans and demons alike; the grounds were alive with members of the Panther tribe.

The Matriarch never intended to hold any celebrations of her own this year, with the move of the city so recent. Instead, she was satisfied with spending the evening in the company of her new allies, leaving those against the idea to be sullen elsewhere.

Anaya was seated along one of the tables, currently in conversation with Edric, Vixen, Lenda and Eden. She had given her basket of truffles to the young healer, unsure of whether or not she should tell her the truth behind her excellent harvesting abilities. In the end, the priestess decided to be quiet about it, as it would make for a good story at a later date. She cradled her drink, slowly sipping it as they spoke of all things, big and small. It was a welcome distraction to her since she felt increasingly nervous on her last day being merely a Consort of the Scion Prime. Yet she couldn't help but experience a tingle of excitement. The pleasant emotion warred against her nervousness, helping Anaya ready herself for her new position as Matriarch. She had prepared rigorously for the best part of eight months, so she could do no more.

Samael stood behind her, leaning against the ancient oak centred in the square. Unless referred to, he would still not speak with her friends, but he would continue to allow their presence.

She knew she could not expect much more than that, so she was content with the situation.

Lilith traversed the festival grounds, watching scores of people as they danced. She had enjoyed the performance while young, but since she had taken on the role of the supreme leader of the Panther tribe, there had been little time for it. The same went for any type of recreation, the woman rarely enjoying herself. She had longed for her upcoming retirement, now counting down the hours. She had already planned to expand her gardens, adding multitudes of plants and flowers to tend to.

Coming past a set of tables, a chair was pushed out in front of her. She swerved but stumbled on the skirt of her dress. She braced herself for the impact but suddenly halted mid-air. A heavily muscled arm was curled around her, clutching a firm hold of her waist. Looking up, she was met by Kaedin's face.

"Careful there, your Highness," he told her.

Arax hurried forward as he saw the impertinent embrace. "Release the Matriarch!" he demanded.

"Stand down, Arax," Lilith ordered, then felt the officer pull away. She thanked him, watching him bow before he removed himself. Smiling gleefully, the woman found the event oddly contrasting with the harmless drama. It was a welcome change to the severe reality she normally presided over.

Perhaps, she would go the extra mile this day, enjoying a glass of red wine in celebrations of her upcoming freedom.

The rain had ceased only hours earlier, leaving the air cool and crisp. There was a light breeze, but the temperature was comfortable.

"Come on, Gus, don't be such a downer," Cyrus said, pulling the front panel aside to the man's tent.

The swordsman sheathed his oiled blade, rising. "Shut up, Dog. Leave me alone."

"The local Harvest Festival seems *really* pleasant," Cyrus insisted. "You of all people could do with some joyful moments."

Grabbing hold of the canvas, Gus pulled the opening shut. "Go away."

The leader snorted. "Fine! You sit there and rot; see if I care." Striding away, he joined the rest of his band, all mounted on horses. "Let's go, men."

Bella shot him a fierce glance.

"And woman."

She grinned wide, blowing him a kiss.

As the thunder of hooves faded away, Nia emerged from her tent. She so longed for a social gathering, as she had been very active in arranging and attending them back in her homeland. The young woman loved to dance and play instruments, music being one of her great pleasures in life. There was only one issue: she had no means of transporting herself there unless she was to walk the entire distance. It would be her last option, but she was to pursue a different one first.

Walking across the camp, she approached Gus' tent. She took a deep breath, bracing herself for his dismissal. She cleared her throat. "Gus."

As always, she was met by silence. Folding her arms across her chest, she decided to wait. A minute passed, but it felt like a lifetime.

"What?"

"Can you take me into town?" she inquired. "I would like to go to the Harvest Festival."

"No."

Nia shut her eye, exhaling. "Please? I will have to walk otherwise. I am intent upon going." She heard him curse, then shuffling.

The man opened the front of his tent and came outside. He was dressed in his usual black outfit but remained unarmed. "Fine," he said. "But I'm not staying all night."

"Yes!" she cheered. "That is perfectly adequate, just allow me to get changed."

"Fine," he repeated, not any less irked despite her chirping. "I'll saddle my horse."

Nia hurried, fearing he might change his mind if she didn't. She knew exactly what she wanted to wear: a gown she had bought last time she was in town. The young woman usually only wore plain linen dresses, with their natural beige colour. This new one, however, was a lush green, the tone soft against her brown skin. It was nicely fitted around the waist, with long sleeves and a plunging neckline. It had no embellishments, but it was all she could afford at the time.

Exiting her tent, she halted, finding Gus standing outside. Holding the reins to his gelding, he stared at her, his intense focus on herself causing her cheeks to warm. "Do... you like it?" she asked.

The swordsman found himself struggling for words. "It... it is presentable." He inwardly scolded his choice of compliment, tightening his grip on the reins.

Nia smiled courteously, then came forward. "We should get going then."

Mounting the gelding, Gus pulled her up behind him, then felt her arms hug around his waist. He touched heels to the horse, heading towards the town of Monua.

✶✶

The celebrations were already ongoing as the two of them arrived at the festival grounds, halting along a slightly raised part of the field. The road ended there, the gravel replaced by a long row of hitching posts and water troughs. Gus dismounted before aiding Nia by lowering her to the soft grass.

"Thank you," she said. "I will be fine from here." She strode away, heading towards a large gathering of women.

Satisfied his horse was securely tethered, the man paused for a moment, viewing the area from his vantage point. The grounds were vast, an expansive piece of land designated for dancing, with a live band playing music adjacent to it. Further down were tables, with endless barrels of mead and various beverages stacked alongside them. Food was continuously being prepared by several chefs. All the way down the other end was a mill, powered by the nearby waterways. There was a pond next to it, and some people were seated along the edge.

He soon identified Cyrus sitting with Fargo and Bella at a table.

"Nine-fingers!" the woman exclaimed as she saw him. "That's a sight for sore eyes. Are you feeling good this evening? No fever or nothing?"

Gus sunk down on a chair. "Hilarious," he muttered.

Cyrus laughed. "It's true though. We didn't expect you here." He pushed a jug of mead to the man. "Have a drink. You might as well enjoy yourself since you're here."

Accepting it, Gus drank greedily. "That's actually quite nice."

"I know, right? We were only just discussing the subject." The older man sipped his drink. "We heard they could throw a party here, but we didn't expect it to be anything quite like this, considering the size of the town."

"Agreed," Gus said. He leaned back in his seat, finishing the last of his mead.

"I'll fetch more," Fargo offered, gathering the empty jugs.

* *

Nia joined the other young women with a smile. She presented herself, telling them she was travelling with a mercenary band. It worked like a charm, the other girls flocking around her for stories and a chance to meet with any of the men. Nia would point to several of them, telling them their names and what weapons they would use. She thoroughly enjoyed herself, drinking and dancing with the women. They laughed and chatted all night, eventually settling down at a table not far from Cyrus and the others.

"I wish I knew how to play an instrument," one of the girls said. She longingly gazed at the live band, resting her chin on the palm of her hand.

"I can play several," Nia said.

"Really?" she blithely enquired.

"Yes, every instrument I have ever come across. I see it as a personal challenge, to learn each one."

The girl laughed. "I shall attempt to find you something new!" She ran off, heading for the musicians. She soon returned, holding a small stringed instrument the shape of a stubby violin, paired with a short horsehair bow. There were keys visible under the strings, and the wood was intricately adorned with runes. "I have never before seen one of these! I challenge you to play it."

Nia's lips parted, but she made no sound. A mere whisper left her, her throat thick with emotion. She fought back the building tears in her eyes, blinked, then smiled at the other woman. All she could think of was her father, and how he had gifted her the exact same type of instrument on her fifteenth birthday, not long before her whole world came crashing down… in more ways than one.

"It looks terribly complicated. Can you use it?"

Directed at Nia, the comment returned her to the present. Accepting the instrument, she placed it in her lap. She held the bow in one hand, allowing her other to softly feather the keys. Angling the instrument to grant additional room for her fingers, she took a calming breath. Within moments, the young woman began playing, sending light and sweet notes into the night air. She let the bow gently caress the strings, her music rippling across the seating area, gaining the attention of all those around her.

"Impossible!" one of the girls exclaimed.

Looking across at the Unn's table, Nia locked eyes with Gus. He held her gaze but showed no expression to suggest his thoughts. She suddenly twitched, feeling a nudge to her side. It momentarily soured her pitch, but she quickly recovered as she continued to play.

"Who is he?" the first girl asked.

"Gus," she said.

"One of the mercenaries?"

"Yes."

"He has been watching you all night," the girl said. "At least, I have a feeling it isn't the rest of us that have caught his attention."

With her eyes settling on the instrument, Nia felt her cheeks flush again.

"What is the matter? Are you surprised?"

"Indeed, I am," she admitted. "He is such a miserable man."

The girls around her laughed.

"Perhaps, he only needs a bit of love and care," one of the women suggested.

"Perhaps," Nia allowed. She was about to finish the music piece as she noticed the swordsman gaining on her. Her hand dropped, separating the bow from the tightened strings.

"Have you played that before?" Gus asked.

"Indeed, I have," she replied. "My father once imported one. It is a nickel harp."

"*Nyckelharpa*," he corrected her.

"Yes! That's the word. I cannot pronounce it to save my life. A keyed harp, one might call it."

He smiled, straightening the collar of his shirt. "Aye," he agreed.

Noticing the group of women's eyes upon him, he shuffled a step back. Without another word, he turned and stalked away.

Nia was left feeling somewhat shocked at his approach. She cradled the instrument, then looked at the others. "Who wants to dance?" she suggested. She was met by cheering and giggling, then they all left the table. Sauntering along the allocated walkways, a man stepped into Nia's path.

"Well, hello there, beautiful," he said. "Don't see your kind here very often. Where are you from?"

She curtsied. "Thank you, sir," she answered. "I am from the country of Kanadesh."

"I see. Not sure where that is, but I am sure it is a wonderful place if they house pretty ladies like yourself." He flashed her a dazzling smile, the young man's features soft, yet attractive.

"I appreciate the compliments, sir."

"Oh, they are well-deserved," he affirmed. "May I ask your name?"

"Nia Adisa," she said. "And you?"

"Alton Chester. But call me Alton. Would you, perhaps, allow me the next dance?"

Nia glanced over her shoulder. Gus was still watching her, so she nodded. "Sure."

✶ ✶

It was midnight as Nia retired from dancing, heading back towards the tables to sit down. Her feet were weary, and her head spun. She had not drunk alcohol for over a year, causing the small amount she had now ingested to seemingly go straight to her head. She felt a touch to her arm, prompting her to turn.

Alton stood behind her, smiling politely. "Come," he said. "I can tell you need some rest. Let's go sit at the watermill."

Gus had yet to leave, the man seated with Cyrus and the others, so Nia agreed. He would come to find her, should he wish to depart.

The young couple shared some pleasant conversation as they strolled along the grass, with Alton curious of her travels. She was about to ask him the same as they reached the mill. Leading Nia to the entrance, Alton suddenly yanked at her arm, pulling her inside. He pushed her across the floor, sending her tumbling backwards. A flick of his fingers pinged a copper coin in her direction, then he smirked. "A simple journey of exploration, you say?" He snorted, making fun of her blatant white lie. "I know you're a prostitute. It didn't take much talking to your 'band members' to attain the information, so get undressed."

Not again! Nia's mind screamed within her, fear instantly washing over her. She could not – would not – allow this to happen again. Furious determination pushed her dread away, and Nia's expression was bold as she rose. "No!" she shouted.

The man stepped forward, squeezing her arm in a tight grip. "You will do as I say, *whore.*"

She squirmed with the pain, attempting to wriggle out of his grasp. "Let go of me!" she cried.

He tugged at her dress, the fabric ripping across her shoulder. "We're getting there now," he exulted, grabbing her hair, and forcing her lips onto his.

Refusing to surrender to yet another man, Nia drew on all the power she could muster. *He will not have me! By the Gods, he will not!*

Pulling her knee up, she slammed it into his groin, causing him to instantly double over. She shoved him aside, heading for the door, but then found herself unexpectedly stopped.

"A bit hot-headed, are you?" Alton hissed, hauling her back by her dress. Throwing her over his shoulder, he carried her outside. "Perhaps, you need cooling off in the water?" He heaved her over the edge of the pond, cracking up at the sight of her flailing arms.

Nia cried out for help, frantically attempting to keep herself afloat. She was terrified of water, despair flooding her as she felt it splash against her face and mouth.

She sunk, watching as the night sky blurred above her. Bubbles whirled as she tried to scream, the water quickly choking her. As her lungs emptied of air, the world around her plunged into darkness.

✶ ✶

His fist bloodied, Gus pummelled the young man a final time before hurling him aside. *"Förbannade döling!"* he swore in his native tongue, then looked back across the water. A coldness hissed through him.

Nia was gone.

Gus ran in the direction he last saw her, diving into the murky depths. Reaching the bottom, he searched with his hands, unable to see in the absence of light. The swordsman touched something warm, instantly clutching hold of it as he pushed himself up. Breaking the surface, he held the young woman against his chest, swimming on his side towards the shore.

Hauling her over the ledge, Gus climbed up and placed himself beside her. He bent down, listening for her breathing, but could hear nothing. Her chest was not moving.

He swore, grabbing hold of her head. Pinching her nose shut, he pressed his lips against hers, then forced air into her lungs.

There was nothing.

Repeating the procedure twice more, there was still no response. "Come on, girl!" Gus wheezed through his teeth. Leaning in again, she suddenly twitched, then coughed. He quickly turned her on her side.

Nia hurled, water and stomach contents spewing out of her mouth before she finally gasped for air.

With his arms around her, Gus pulled her onto his lap.

The young woman's breathing was coarse, and her eyes wide as she stared at him. She felt his hand push her wet hair away from her face.

"Are you alright?" he asked.

She coughed again, straining to speak.

"Just nod if you are."

Nia nodded, then threw her arms around his neck. She felt him embrace her, the man holding her close to his chest. They sat still for a moment, and her breathing soon calmed. She began to shiver, despite the heat radiating from him.

"We need to get you into some dry clothes," Gus said, moving his leg back underneath her. He grunted as he rose but retained her in his arms. Carrying her around the outskirts of the festival area, the swordsman lifted her onto his gelding. He mounted up behind her, then motioned the horse into a gallop. Holding the reins with one hand, he used the other to keep her steady. He felt her trace his arm, her fingers soon intertwining with his.

Nia looked down as she ran her thumb over his, gently caressing. In spite of her building cold shivers, she felt warm inside. There was a flutter in her belly as he responded to her invitation, the man reaffirming his grip on her.

Did he… perhaps care for her after all?

Arriving back at the encampment, they found it empty of people. They were the first to return. Gus jumped down first, then assisted Nia, holding her hand. Allowing her to maintain her grip on him, they walked across the campsite. "You should get changed," he said. "I will make a fire. Bring a blanket out."

As she disappeared into her tent, Gus tugged at his shirt. He was soaking wet, but with a fire, he would dry quickly.

The flames soon roared, and the young woman re-emerged, dressed in one of her simple linen gowns. She sat down, throwing a cover over her shoulders, then held her hands out towards the blaze. "Thank you, Gus."

"Don't worry about it," he replied, seating himself next to her. "I only wish I'd realised sooner." He held his hand forward, the knuckles still bleeding.

"That I can't swim?" she asked.

"Aye. I wouldn't have spent as much time with the lad then."

She smiled feebly. "I am alive. That is all that matters."

"True."

Nia sat quietly for a moment, her fingers feathering her mouth. "You… you breathed for me."

Gus clawed at the back of his head, unsure of what to say. "I… suppose I did."

Looking up at the man, she found him focused on the fire. "Gus," she said, but he remained firm in his gaze. "Gus, I want you to face me."

The man shut his eyes for a moment before he finally looked at her. "What?"

Reaching up, the blanket soundlessly slid away from Nia's shoulders. She circled his neck, gently pulling him in. She felt his beard rub against her chin, then how his lips reached hers.

They kissed, the motion slow and restrained. Gus made no attempt to further advance on her. Instead, he merely enjoyed their unexpected closeness, with not a single thought to his previous distance to her. Their affection was pure and unconditional, their age difference not even crossing their minds.

Nia was no longer cold, a heat flickering inside her. She felt pleasure pulsing through her limbs as she touched his cheek, then ran her fingers into his hair.

Her move prompted Gus to trail her sides, one of his hands settling on her lower back, and the other worshipping every inch of her body through its descend.

Their kiss immediately intensified, tongues shamelessly brushing against each other.

It felt so right, so different from any of Nia's previous encounters with men. But why this attraction? What was Gus hiding? Had he suffered like she had? Or worse?

The sound of hoofbeats echoed in the distance, sending Gus rearing backwards. He instantly came to his feet, placing distance between them. He left Nia without so much as a word, walking away at a high pace.

Nia's whole body throbbed as she sat there, the sensation new to the woman. Her breathing had increased, leaving her mouth half-open. She felt her lips, the soft skin damp after the exchange. Sitting in silence, she was unsure what had transpired, the event nigh on incredible.

A single broom was dragged across the centre square of the Temple village. It was afternoon, the day after the Harvest Festival, and the area had been cleared of evidence from the previous night.

Anaya was walking along the road leading into the settlement, heading for the Temple. It was time for another meeting with the Congress, but now for the first time as ruling Matriarch of the Panther tribe. Reaching the conference hall, the rest of the Congress members had already gathered, and Anaya sat down in her usual spot. But there was another factor adding change to this occasion. For the first time, her new manservant was attending. He was standing behind her, neatly dressed in his black linen clothing and his hair worn up in a tight ponytail.

As nurses had been employed for the Priesthood, one had been set to care for Kiera, allowing both Edric and Vixen to attend the meetings undisturbed.

"I announce the Congress as commenced," Adena declared. "I would like to start by hearing the news from the Fox tribe."

"An agreement was struck," Kaedin said. "The tribe will obtain ownership of their land in exchange for their allegiance to the King and the Priesthood. They will send a representative within a few weeks."

"Very good," the Cardinal said, smiling. "Fantastic, to finally have an ally."

Lilith huffed, folding her arms across her chest. She had retained her position along the far end of the table, acting as the representative of the Panther tribe since Anaya was also a General Priest within the Priesthood.

"After yourself, of course, my lady," Adena quickly added. "And, while the Panther tribe is on the subject, I would like to offer congratulations on your retirement."

"Yes, well... were it not for the current climate within the tribe, I would be much more positive about it. But thank you."

Adena lowered her head briefly, then straightened a parchment on the table. "Our next subject for today is-"

The door suddenly bashed into the wall as it turned full swing on its hinges. A young man rushed through, with two panther demons behind him.

"The Lynx village!" he cried. "They are all dead!"

19

BIRDS

At first, there was complete silence in the conference room. The members of Congress merely stared at the scout.

"All of them must have died unexpectedly. We found the inhabitants slumped over their food or still in their beds," the young man continued. "Even the Master Prime had perished, in his own sitting room."

"*All?*" Lilith asked. "Every single Lynx settler?"

"Yes!" he asserted, then grabbed at his mouth. "I am so sorry, my lady. I have completely lost my manners."

"Forget it," she reassured him.

"The dead," Kaedin intervened. "Were there any signs of injuries?"

"No, your Excellency. Not a single one. Even with the ongoing decomposition, nothing pointed towards an attack. Every man, woman and child has expired."

Anaya rose, her eyes wide as she leaned across the table. "Disease," she exclaimed. "It might be a disease! You need to be quarantined this instant!"

✶ ✶

A small cottage was prepared along the outskirts of the Temple village. The three scouts were led around the outer perimeter, then allowed entry before locking the door behind them. They were to be guarded, not due to them being untrustworthy, but because no one knew how a potential disease might affect them.

Despite a long break in their meeting, the members of Congress were still gathered in the conference hall.

Vixen turned to Anaya. "Do you really believe it to be an illness?"

"For all to die in such a manner, as described by the scouts, makes it highly suspicious," she explained. "However, I doubt it is infectious since all of them seem to have perished simultaneously. But one cannot be too careful."

"I agree with the Matriarch," Lilith said. "This will need to be examined thoroughly. As I am yet to finish certain… affairs within our tribe, then I would suggest the Priesthood taking charge. It matters not whether the Lynx tribe intends to join us, as this needs to be looked into regardless." She turned to Kaedin. "Will you oversee the investigation, Master Reed?"

"Aye, my lady," His expression was grim as he rubbed at his beard. "The whole settlement will have to be searched for a possible source. The scouts did right to run as soon as they realised the severity of the situation."

"Are you to send more scouts?" Anaya asked.

"Without more intelligence, we will be unable to draw conclusions. I shall go myself, as to not risk the lives of innocent people."

"Allow me to go with you," Edric said. "You will need another set of eyes."

The priestess rose. "What if I am wrong? Are we to risk losing the two of you?"

"Without risk, there is no reward, my lady," Kaedin said. "I cannot send others in my stead if I intend to keep a clear conscience. We will have to place ourselves under quarantine as we return."

"Take Benjamin," Lilith urged them.

"Are you sure, my lady?"

"I am. Allow him to circle the settlement and search for any distinct scent. Anything he picks up can be used as evidence at a later date. Neither you nor Edric have the ability."

"As you wish." Kaedin looked at Edric. "Would you be ready to depart tonight?"

"Yes." Edric met Vixen's gaze, her concern evident, but they both knew it was their best option.

In the week that followed, more reports trickled in from Kaedin's scouts. With the man unavailable to collect them, they were all referred to Lilith. They told similar stories, of settlements entirely decimated by an unknown source. The outriders were then placed in cottages with the rest of the scouts. The Congress had decided on a three-week quarantine, calculated from the time communication had seized from the individual villages to the approximate time they had perished.

For the Panther tribe, things had developed quickly. Samael and Anaya had moved into their new home, with the rear of the property offering a stunning view over the Ovena province. The paintings depicting generations of the Fahd lineage now hung in their dining room, a fresh one placed amongst them. Samael stood on the right, Anaya on the left, and little Aaron in front of them.

Assuming their new roles as leaders of the Panther Tribe, a celebration had been held, inviting all the inhabitants in the City of Fahd. The weather had been fair, offering warm temperatures, and allowing the festivities to take place outside their entrance hall. They had a spacious courtyard, with an outer wall along the perimeter. They also housed their own stable and stable hands, with the building part of the surrounding boundary line.

Lee had been allocated a room across the hall to the couple's chambers, thus staying near to the new Matriarch. He received daily lessons with Arax, who had been pleasantly surprised at the fact that the young boy already knew how to read and write. Samael still most often stayed by the priestess' side, until such time as Lee was fully trained.

As the Priesthood had searched for nurses, one had been employed full-time for Aaron as part of Samael and Anaya's servants. Despite the heir's young age, the woman's position included not only general care-taking but also tutoring. Anything beneficial for his future education was to be present in his daily life.

★ ★

Samael stretched in his bed. He had a busy day ahead of him, as he was about to meet with Lee for another session, then see the Captain of the Royal Guard. They were meant to allocate the available sentries to the new Matriarch, as well as retain sufficient protection for his mother, the now *Peeress* Lilith Fahd.

He felt his feet reach down below the end of the bed. No matter how large the piece of furniture, he would always manage the performance. Sitting up, he rubbed at his eyes. He had slept for very few hours, but it would have to do. Taking a deep breath, he felt a tingle go through him. There was a scent he recognised, yet he was unable to determine the origin. He sniffed the air, the fragrance definitely emanating from the priestess. She was lying naked beside him, the covers blanketing her from the waist down.

Leaning in, Samael pressed his face into her hair. Baring his fangs, he snarled, inhaling the marvellous essence of her being. Removing the covers, he placed himself over her.

The priestess stirred, feeling the cool air against her skin. She rolled to her back as she opened her eyes. Finding the demon standing over her, she jerked. "Goddess, you frighten the life out of me sometimes!"

"Bad habit," he teased, smirking, then clutched hold of Anaya's wrists. "I want you."

Running her tongue along her bottom lip, the invitation was sent.

★ ★

Seated at their dining room table, the Patriarch and his Consort silently looked at each other. Aaron was still asleep in the nursery upstairs, leaving them alone.

Anaya's face had barely recovered from their intimacy the same morning, a slight sheen visible on her skin. The demon's returned stare was intimidating, his eyes smouldering with intensity. Finished with her meal, she replaced the fork on the table. "What is the matter, Samael?"

"I do not know," he coldly stated. "But I *yearn* for you."

The priestess' lips parted, but there was no sound. Lost for words, her whole face reddened.

Leaving his cloak hanging over his chair, Samael stood, then rounded the table. He pulled Anaya out of her seat, swiping his arm over the wooden top and sending everything crashing to the floor.

Covering her mouth, the priestess attempted to muffle a squeal as he perched her on the elevated surface. No matter how welcome, his repeated advances took her by surprise. She felt his hands travel inside her skirt, promptly ripping her undergarments clear.

There was a sudden knock on the door, followed by a servant calling from the other side. "Do you need assistance, your Highness?"

Samael growled, annoyed at the interruption. "No!" he rumbled. "Have the servants sent to their quarters!"

The closed door muffled the sound of the attendant's reply. "Yes, your Highness!"

As footsteps faded beyond the dining room entrance, Samael returned his attention to Anaya. His lips brushed over her silken skin, travelling across her tantalising shoulder and neck. They kissed as he touched her, caressing the inside of her thigh. His fingers soon explored her core, the sheath still wet from their previous union. The sensation brought forth his rumbling snarls, his cravings sizzling just below the surface.

Samael's urges were more significant than ever, now unhindered with Anaya's last enchantment. He felt like a hypocrite, attempting to teach young Lee the importance of self-control and the ability to manage the feral, to then fail so miserably at it himself any time he answered to his sexual desires for his wife.

Images flashed within the demon's mind. It was something with Anaya's scent, frustratingly challenging to place. It was as if he had lived this before, the moment playing out as a memory in his head. Pushing her skirt up, he knelt before her. The couple shared a moments glance before he clutched around her buttocks, pulling her in.

Supporting herself on her arms, Anaya leaned back, surrendering to the whisper of his tongue. Her recently increased lust for her mate was a pleasant surprise, considering he seemed to share the sentiment. She thought it perhaps was due to their duties becoming more routine, allowing for additional diversions. She had slept better lately, able to enjoy herself with the few hours of free time that she had.

With a racing heart, Samael unleashed a growl, relishing in her being. Her essence only further intoxicated him, the mere thought of having her again physically aching inside him. He tensed, fighting against the impulse for every second he pleasured her.

Weaving her fingers into his hair, Anaya gripped at the black strands. She searched for a means of surrendering to her rushing excitement, unable to contain his effect on herself. If he were to continue, the priestess would peak for the second time already this day. She moved with him, reclining back onto the table. With her legs folding over his shoulders, she brought him closer.

Clutching her thighs, Samael noticed her movements becoming increasingly vivid, her breaths more and more filled with a throbbing lust. Her climax was undeniable, the man's satisfaction sweeping across his body like a cool breeze.

Samael rose, wasting no time in opening his trousers. With a firm hold on her hips, he breached her, the euphoria immediately flooding him. The divine aura of her presence was inconceivably provoking, causing the hair on his neck to stand up. It was as if he felt fear as well as exhilaration, the emotion hard to determine.

Thrusting into her, again and again, memories appeared in his mind's eye. He envisioned his claws as they frantically tore into her bodice.

Leaning across her flawless form, Samael kissed each part of exposed skin on Anaya's neck and collarbone, cupping her breasts over the fabric of her dress.

Guiding him up, the priestess allowed their lips to meet. Her mouth cracked open, inviting him in. Her tongue grazed one of his elongated canines, causing him to smirk.

A chuckle escaped him, after which he pressed his fangs against her neck. He would not repeat his act of supremacy, yet he allowed his teeth to graze the soft skin.

The priestess inhaled sharply as he merely reaffirmed his grip on her hips to deepen their intercourse. She finally let go of her need to suppress her enjoyment, her covetous voice carried with every breath.

Visions rippled into the demon's mind as he continued to delve into her, over and over again.

Mountains.

Forests.

The chill of early winter.

As they first made love.

How their worlds collided with the solidification of their bond.

It offered the very same scent, creating an almost mystical air around her.

Samael traced her perfect body, his hand stopping over her leg as he felt her velvet skin. He aggressively buried himself inside her, her titillating softness sharply contrasting his raw cravings. He planted a final kiss on her shoulder before he snarled, the sound similar to distant thunder.

Their bond.

Pulsing, vibrating, flashing.

It lavished in their connection; in their moment of becoming one.

Anaya cried out underneath him, shuddering to his thrilling command. Waves of pleasure swept over her, and she pulled him down, locking her fingers into his hair again. She chanted through her cries of passion, sending her Light shimmering into the room. She could see it so clearly with his untainted state; his unimpeded spirit, the glowing bands transmitting like lightning as they unified.

How could she affect them? How could she control his summons?

Watching his Consort's flawless features, Samael bared his fangs, knowing he was about to finalise his indulgence. He had thought the repeated event would lessen the satisfaction, but it made no difference. He rocked against her, again and again, unleashing a rumble of his scorching arousal.

Sounding out her pleasure, Anaya felt a change in his movements as their fiery bond flashed within her mind. There was a pulsating sensation before the demon finally stopped.

The temptation was too great, Anaya's curiosity peaked with the intense reaction of their primordial bridge. Her spirit reached into the depth of his being, achieving a tight hold of the embodiment of their bond.

Samael instantly looked at her, his eyes dark with seething emotions. With a grip over her hips, he forcefully growled to his rising anger. Dark mists flared out, cascading over the edges of the table with his activated aura. His demonic powers were unhinged, unexpectedly boiling to the surface with a raging fury. "**STOP!**" he demanded.

Anaya released him, her arms dropping back on the table.

With a hand to his temple, Samael shook his head. "What did you do?" he asked.

"I… I wanted to call for you."

His brow furrowed. "I am here, in case you missed it."

She pushed herself up onto her elbows. "I mean, I would like to invent a way to call for you, despite being uninjured."

"And you thought of doing it *now*, of all times?"

"Yes, because you were still under the effects of my previous spell," she explained. "I was not attempting to push you towards the feral."

"I assumed as much," he said. "No, I believe what you were about to achieve was a state of rage, but that is no more fun in a tight space such as this. I would have turned, should you have continued."

Anaya sat up at the words. "So, it worked?"

Samael stepped back to retie his trousers. "Indeed, it did, but how is that meant to help if you need to be so close to me? Just ask, and I shall turn." Folding his arms, he leaned against the table, watching the priestess as she seated herself beside him.

She thought for a moment. "Mm. It was not quite what I wanted to accomplish. I hoped for the physical pull, more than anything."

"I see," he said. "You may have to work on that in the future then. Just tell me beforehand."

"Yes, of course. I am sorry."

Leaning in, he kissed her. "It is fine. With days such as these, I might finally come to enjoy breakfast."

✶ ✶

The Patriarch was nearly coming into a run as he crossed the city, knowing he was already late leaving home. Coming up to the last stretch of road, he saw the young man standing at the eastern gates. He stopped before him, hastily gathering his hair before fastening it with a strap. "I am terribly sorry for the delay. I, eh… had some urgent matters to attend."

"Certainly of no concern for myself, your Highness," Lee chirped. "I have practised turning on my own this morning."

Samael leaned in close. "Really?"

"I have, indeed, and it has gone very well. I am beginning to feel some confidence in my abilities now."

"I actually feel glad to hear it," Samael said, seemingly surprising himself. "And I am not even faking the sentiment." Walking past the boy, he motioned him to follow. "I am inclined to go on a live hunt today."

Lee hurried after him, attempting to keep up with his long strides. "But, your Highness, I failed miserably with the rabbit. And then all that followed-"

"It was a hare," Samael corrected. "And yes, you did, but all other trials have worked out so far. And since I have no live subject to test you with today, then we shall have to acquire one. It will also be interesting to see how you react around my aura."

The boy swallowed a breath. "Last time, I was terrified enough by merely finding the traitors you had killed. I struggled, despite having been way too caught up with the... hare."

"Yes, but that was an extraordinary situation, so I would not put too much weight on the results."

Lee squirmed a little as he pondered it. "Did... did you *rage*?" he asked. "If that is what it's called."

"It is, indeed, if by *rage* you mean the controlled state of feral."

The boy nodded. "Did you rage as you fought those panthers?"

"Yes," Samael answered, rounding a large boulder in the field. The tall grass brushed against his leather-covered legs. "My bond to Anaya is exceptionally strong, meaning any harm to her risks placing me in said state. Should she be mortally wounded, it will transition into the feral, so I suggest you do your utmost to protect her."

"I swear on my life, your Majesty!" Lee pledged.

"Good. I assume you remember what happened when I was forced into that... condition."

"Yes. I promise to do everything in my power for it to never happen again."

Satisfied with the answers, Samael stopped to face him. "Tell me, Lee. What do you know of your lineage?"

"Nothing, really," he replied. "My mother was a low-born. She had me when she was seventeen but never spoke of my father. She only said he had died when I was very young. As my mother passed, I moved in with my aunt."

"And your aunt does not know anything more on the subject?"

"Not that she has told me, no," Lee said. "Why? I know a Matriarch should choose someone of higher birth, but I promise I will not disappoint."

Samael smiled as he listened to the boy's conviction. "I only wonder, because you do not seem to be of low birth. You are both larger and boast a stronger aura, hence why I ask. I am beginning to believe your father might have originated elsewhere. Perhaps even as far up as being a Peer."

"A *P-Peer?*"

"Yes. But with your weakened state, as well as young age, it is hard to tell. With time, we will most likely know whether you are of High birth or even a Peer yourself. It would explain the difficulties you are suffering from, with your demonic form."

There was blank look to the boy as he blinked.

Ignoring his reaction, Samael patted him on the shoulder. "Now," he said. "Enough chatter. Let us begin today's session."

It was late in the day, the sun slowly setting in the east. Kaedin, Edric and Benjamin had ridden hard to reach the Lynx settlement ahead of time, arriving half a day early.

"Birds," Kaedin said, pointing into the sky. "They are circling the area." The man had his sword strapped to his back but was wearing no heavy armour. They were not expecting any resistance, but to leave unarmed was out of the question.

Edric sat on his dapple stallion, releasing his bow from the saddle. "We should walk from here. It will lessen our presence as we approach."

Nodding, the former Knight leapt off his mount. He drew his blade, his fingers tapping the hilt. "One can never be too sure, I suppose."

Benjamin tethered his horse, placing himself between the two humans. "I will meet you back here later."

"Yes," Edric said. "Do not engage either humans or demons if you locate any." Coming down to the ground, he watched the scout leave, then nocked an arrow.

Following a nearby stretch of road, Kaedin and Edric headed for the forest. The path narrowed as they came through the first row of trees, but it was easily traversed. They walked for some time, deep into the woods.

"We must be close," Edric said. "Although I have to say it is well hidden."

"Indeed, it is. This is not something done by random." Kaedin halted, the malodor of death stinging his nose. "We are most certainly in the right place."

"Yes, but where are the dwellings?"

Looking around himself, Kaedin noticed a slight curvature to the landscape. "Below us," he said. "They are probably in the surrounding mounds." Resuming the walk, he continued along the path past some thick brambles. Rounding them, he stopped once more. There were several corpses spread out in the area.

Edric approached the one closest, kneeling beside it. It was a young man, the eye sockets hollow and his skin torn from the scavenging birds above. "It will fast become hard to tell, but I can see no signs of struggle."

Having moved further away, Kaedin examined another dead man. "Not on this one either," he replied. "Let's go down the entrance westward. It looks the largest."

The oak door leading into the den was already open. Creating a small orb of Light, the two officers descended into the residence. Several more demons lay dead, some along the corridors, but most in their beds. In the largest room, a man was slumped below an elaborate chair.

"Most likely the Prime," Kaedin concluded, circling him. "No signs of injuries here either."

Edric emerged from an adjacent room. "It is strange. They seem to have plenty of supplies, and obviously, nothing that points towards an attack. If it is a disease as Anaya said, then where from?"

Kaedin surveyed the room a final time. "Keep it in mind as we move along. We need to find the source."

Not a single demon had survived, two small children huddled up in bed together in the last housing they searched. Pulling the cover over their bodies, Edric had a heavy heart as he rejoined his colleague. "Everyone has suffered a sudden death. There are no funeral pyres or evidence of anyone being tended to as if ill."

"I second the opinion. It is much too suspicious. I believe Anaya right in her initial assessment."

"Why would someone target a small settlement such as this?" Edric inquired. "It is not even ten dwellings."

"Newly established," Kaedin suggested. "Perhaps, they were encroaching on someone's land. They were most likely known of in the area, thus an easier target."

"Mm. Worth looking into."

"Aye. We should head back. There is not much more for us to see here. We can discuss the case-" Kaedin seized to move, his eye's narrowing as he looked at Edric. He received a silent acknowledgement before they proceeded to move in the direction of the path.

"Here to check out your work, Priesthood?" a demon hissed from a tree above them. "To make sure it was done correctly?"

"We are investigating the suspicious deaths of those who presided here," Kaedin calmly stated. "Who are you?"

"No one," the demon answered. "I would prefer to stay that way unless I wish to be your next victim."

Edric gritted his teeth but said nothing. Retaliating would serve no purpose for the Priesthood.

"Do you know what happened here?" Kaedin questioned.

"Why would I tell you anything? You already know since you arranged it all. Interesting plan, attempting to not get your hands dirty. But then to show up at the scene of the crime, pretending to be the hero of the hour... Laughable, that is what it is."

Kaedin ignored the insults, intrigued by the accusations. "You saw it as it happened then?"

"I have said enough, human. Do not think that you will all get away with this. Trust that you will be caught. With time, everyone becomes complacent."

Back on the Leve plateau, Samael patted some dirt from his trousers. There was blood on his shirt, evidence of their successful hunt. Straightening himself, he looked down at the boy. "You did well, Lee. Much more so, than expected."

"Thank you very much, sir. Frankly, I am satisfied enough with being able to remain levelheaded in your presence."

"You were, which proves my point about your origin. With higher strength, there is more resistance to the aura. You are of no low birth, as we initially thought."

"As long as I receive your guidance, I am happy to be whatever," Lee said.

Samael smirked. "I have no intentions of going back on this now. I see potential in you, which is enough for me." Determining the positioning of the sun, he released a breath. "I apologise, but I need to leave. I have another engagement to see to."

"But… were we not to have lunch?"

"I will have to skip it."

Lee peered at him. "I have learned not to downplay the importance of a nutritious meal, your Highness."

Samael snarled, sending the boy jolting backwards. He angled away at the response, knowing his reaction was unnecessary. "I am sorry. You are right, yet there is no time. I shall have a more substantial meal for dinner. You go and continue your training with Arax. Good day to you."

The meeting with the Royal Guard was cut short. Recruitment would be needed, and Samael ordered for the Captain to oversee applications, then send a list of suggested trainees to him. He had no interest in prolonging the conference, as he found his mind focused elsewhere.

With Anaya's scent still lingering on himself, Samael soon strode across their courtyard. He entered the manor, viewing the entrance hall. She was not present. There were a few seated at the front, most likely awaiting her arrival.

They turned as they heard him, throwing themselves on the floor as he walked past.

Ignoring them, he sniffed the air, concluding she was on the first floor. Ascending the stairs in but a few steps, he laid eyes on her.

Finished tending to Aaron, the priestess had just managed to lull him to sleep. Strolling along the hallway, she halted as her husband came into view. She felt a knot in her stomach as he gained on her, his countenance severe. Her eyes widened as she saw the blood on his shirt. "What in the world happened?" she asked.

Saying nothing, Samael ducked into her at an angle. Rising, he grabbed her legs as he laid her across his shoulder, then continued down the corridor. Arriving at their bedroom, he slammed the door shut behind them, then approached the bed. Heaving her down, he clutched hold of her dress.

Anaya felt her heart pounding wildly in her chest, her whole body flushing hot with his forceful advances.

Extending his claws, the demon made quick work of her gown, pulling it clear. Unclasping his cloak, he left it to fall to the floor, then came down over her on the bed. "Nothing happened," he said. "But I need you. *Now.*"

20

TIME WELL SPENT

T he rays of the sun were barely reaching above the horizon as the Unn prepared to leave. It had been an extended stay outside of Monua, but the men were pleased, which was the reason for them lingering.

Nia loaded up the last of her belongings and utensils on a wagon, then climbed up on the front seat. She looked at the men around her, all mounted on horses. Furthest in the back, alongside Fargo, was the black gelding.

Gus had been gone once again, but this time only for a couple of days. He had arrived back in time to join the others for the next move, but he had yet to speak with her. It was as if he ignored her very existence, not even looking at her as he retrieved his breakfast in the morning.

Her heart ached as she watched him, unsure of what had happened between them, or how she should act around him.

"Ready?"

She jerked, Landon seating himself next to her. She rubbed at her eyes. "Yes, sorry. I am merely tired."

He offered her a friendly smile. "Tell us if you want to kip in the back, and I shall halt the wagon."

"Thank you, but I think I will manage."

Urging the mounts on, Landon flicked the reins, causing them to lean into the harness. Travelling to Seba in the west, they had received another mission from the same employer. They were heading for Crera, one of the larger towns, an ancient site alongside a river with the same name. It had become a trading hub in recent years, their economy flourishing.

The local Duke was no other than the younger brother of the King, Brett Erchenwine. He was an ambitious man, noticeable by his ability to manage the land to the greatest of its potential.

As they neared their destination, the crew reached a wooded area apace with the river.

Cyrus halted the long caravan of riders. "We shall make camp here," he declared. "All dismount!"

Fargo proceeded to chop down several smaller trees, creating a makeshift hitching fence, as he always did. The rest had already started erecting their tents, often creating a similar layout to their last camp. Creatures of habit, they found themselves with the same neighbours.

Gus finished just before dinner, emerging as the sun was setting.

The meal tent was prepared, and Nia was standing within as she hurried to finish. Focusing on supplying the others with food, she had yet to make her own shelter for the night. The young woman had merely left all her belongings in a pile, where she intended for her home to be placed. It was a clear sky, so she was in no rush, with little risk of rain this evening.

Nia had soon completed one of her more common stews, this time with plenty of root vegetables as they were coming into season. Being early September, fresh potatoes were becoming commonly available. As she announced the food as ready, it was not long until all had been served.

Last in line was Gus. He scratched the back of his head as he stood before her, coming across as indecisive despite his robust build. Being handed a bowl, he accepted it but made no remark.

Despite Nia offering a warm smile, he merely turned and walked away. With her grin fading, she did not feel surprised.

When all had finished, she was left alone to clean up. Grabbing the basket full of dishes, she headed for the river. She sat down at the edge of the water, watching the calmness of its surface. It gently moved along, in a southwestern direction. She was to make use of the last daylight as she cleaned the pots and pans, so she would have to attempt finishing her tent in the dark.

Nia was sure she would be fine, having done it so many times by now. She knew the knots and strings like the back of her hand.

Satisfied with the dishes being ready for use in the morning, she strolled back the short distance to the encampment. Placing the items on the table in the meal tent, she then left to assemble her own shelter. Finding the pile of sticks, ropes and fabric gone, she halted.

There was her tent, already erected, her belongings visible through the open front.

Confused, she looked around herself. She was alone. A few men were sitting by a fire further down the camp, but they were not likely to have been involved.

With tight fists, Nia strode towards Gus' tent. Without asking, she whipped the front panel aside.

The man instantly stood, coming forward to meet her. "What the hell do you think you're doing?" he snarled.

"Requesting to speak with you," she replied. She turned on her heel, heading for the river again. She refused to look behind her, instead furiously praying he would follow. Reaching the edge of the camp, she heard footsteps. She soon stopped at the water, facing the man.

"What do you want?" he asked.

"I need to know what is going on, Gus," she said.

He scowled at her. "Going on?"

"Yes!" she exclaimed. "Have you forgotten?"

"I was drunk!"

Nia folded her arms across her chest. "You were not *that* drunk. I have known you for the best part of a year now. Would you perhaps care to tell me-"

"Know me?" he retorted. "You know *nothing*! You have no clue as to all the things I've done."

Was that his secret? Did he worry about how she would feel regarding all his years as a criminal? Could it be so simple? "It matters not to me, what you have done in the past." Nia reached for him, but he pulled away.

"I didn't want you then, and I don't want you now!" Gus turned to leave, but she clutched hold of his hand. Glaring at her across his shoulder, he wrenched himself free. "You asked me once, and yes, I'm married, so stop wasting your damned time!"

The next evening, Cyrus had gathered the regular crew, ready to depart for another assignment. It was similar to the prior missions: an unidentified powder to be spread amongst a shipment of wares. Their employer had so far claimed all to have been successful, but in what way, the Unn was left unaware of.

It was by choice that the mercenaries would know as little as possible, only asking the essential questions. Very few in the band would actually know who the employer was. They neither needed nor wanted to understand why they were doing a mission, as long as they could execute it, and would be paid for their services.

For most, the Unn's lack of questions was the sole reason for choosing them in the first place. The mercenaries would never interrogate those to commission them, thus allowing the employers to remain completely confidential. The services were expensive, but the clients were all the richer.

The sun had already set as they departed. They stopped along a winding road, with no buildings in line of sight.

"I thought you said we were about to repeat our last mission," Gus said. "How are we going to do that in the middle of nowhere?"

Cyrus held forward the pouch containing the yellow powder. "Apparently, this dust spoils rather quickly once you expose it to the air, so we need to apply it somewhere along here."

"That's why, last time, we couldn't just use it on the cargo, other than when the merchant was about to leave," Bella explained.

"Fine," the swordsman replied. "But weren't you having the evening off?"

"Yes, but Jason still didn't want to work with you. We heard you threatened him again."

Gus huffed. "Only because he's an idiot."

"That may be so," Cyrus acknowledged. "But you all have your own issues to deal with, so give the boy some slack."

"Whatever."

Their leader pulled on his reins, causing his horse to lift its front legs from the ground. "Honest to the Gods – or whatever it is that you believe in – I'm getting sick of your shit, Gus. One minute you're the one and only man of conscience, and the next you have nothing of the sorts. Make up your mind, at least."

Averting his gaze, the swordsman looked sullen.

"Besides," Bella said, pulling her cloak away. "You needed a damsel in distress." She wore a long flowing gown underneath, light blue with an embroidered sash. Dismounting, she walked out into the road.

"At least, in the dim light, you can't tell her age," Gus muttered.

The woman glowered at him. "I heard that!" Reaching the other side, she folded her arms across her chest. "At least my hair isn't greying, you old coot!"

"Shut your trap, the both of you!" Cyrus snarled. "The shipment will arrive any minute, so get ready." He motioned the others to ride further into the trees, out of sight.

It felt like hours as they stood there, the men on foot, hiding behind some thick bushes. They watched Bella as she righted her dress for what seemed like the fiftieth time, clearly uncomfortable in the constraints of the female clothing.

She suddenly perked up, spotting something in the distance. It was the shipment they were waiting for, the woman stepping out into the road as he approached. "Sir! Please, sir, I need your help!"

The man driving the wagon pulled on the reins, halting the horses. "What is a lady like yourself doing out here in the middle of nowhere?" he asked.

"Oh, I merely went for a walk, good sir. And silly me, to not properly estimate how long the return trip would be."

"I see," he responded thoughtfully, pausing for a moment. "Would you like a ride, miss?"

"Most gratefully, I accept your aid," she answered, climbing up on the seat. As the man went to urge the mounts on, she placed a hand on his. "How will I ever be able to repay you, sir?"

He eyed her up and down, the woman's dress hugging her body tightly. "Well," he said. "Depends on what you have to offer."

Clasping his hand, she motioned him to follow behind her as she hopped back down to the ground. She grinned, bobbing her head towards the nearby trees. "Let us go into the forest, and I will show you, sir."

Cyrus and his men watched as Bella led the delivery man away from the wagon and into the woods. Under the cover of darkness, the Unn sprung forward, hurrying to remove the tarp and taint the goods. Their leader was quickly finished, swiftly moving away, soon followed by Landon.

Gus cursed, as the corner strap on his side had come loose from the canvas. He saw Bella emerging from amongst the trees, with the driver close behind her. Ducking behind the wagon, the swordsman attempted to fasten it again, threading the leather string back through the loop.

Bella seated herself, noticing Gus' presence. She stretched, leaning back to cover him, lifting her arms above her head.

The driver climbed aboard, making himself comfortable beside her. "I am only to deliver this some ways down the road, then I am heading back to Crera. Will that be fine, miss?"

"Indeed, it will," she said, forcing a smile, then flashed a glance over her shoulder. Gus was gone.

✶ ✶

The three men from the Unn rode ahead to Crera, awaiting Bella's arrival. As she joined them, she spat on the ground. "At least he was pleased enough with me performing oral… favours. But don't ask me to do that again, Cyrus. I'm not a wench."

Their leader scratched his chin. "I'm unsure of how we would've otherwise solved this. I wouldn't want to raise suspicion about tampered cargo. If we were to actually assault the driver, we risked the shipment not making it to its intended destination."

"Which is where?" she questioned.

"I don't know. I only know where and at what time there is one for an assignment. You know I don't ask for specifics."

"Fine, but we need to solve it some other way next time."

"If there is one," Cyrus said. "At this rate, whoever it is paying us, will be running out of funds. No one can be rich enough for these amounts to be given out regularly."

"You don't even know who it is?" Gus asked.

"Well," Cyrus said. "I kind of do, but not officially. And I certainly will not share it with anyone, not even yourself."

The swordsman stared at him. "I don't care."

"I thought not. Now, let's head back to camp. We'll make it our home for a few more days, then move on again."

✶✶

The usual late-night meal was already prepared as the group arrived back at the encampment. Nia had made fish soup, rich with leek, fresh herbs, and spices. She sliced a lemon, squeezing the juice over the pot as she stirred it a final time, then placed it away from the fire.

"Smells lush, dear maid," Cyrus said as he came up to her. Grabbing a bowl, he helped himself to a generous portion.

Nia smiled, curtsying.

The rest stopped behind their leader, waiting for their turn – all except Gus, who strode past.

Taking a deep breath, the young woman felt herself wanting to call out to him, her determination to befriend him stronger than ever. She hurried after him, catching up with the man as he was about to enter his tent. "Wait," she said.

Facing her, Gus opened his mouth as if to speak.

Nia held her hand up, hushing him. "Just listen. I want to be your friend. And before you start nagging me about that precious time of mine, let me tell you; I have nothing else *but* time. I have much more so than I can spend, so I do with it as I please. You do as you like when it comes to any sentiments you perhaps harbour for me, because it matters not at the end of the day. If you say it was all a mistake, then I shall accept it, but don't come telling me how to live my life." Not awaiting his reply, she turned on her heel and walked away.

Back at the meal tent, Cyrus approached her.

"Nia," he said.

243

She felt a trickle of nervousness within her, with the man seldom calling her by her name. "What is the matter, sir?" she asked.

Instead of answering her directly, he turned to the gathered members of the Unn. "It's a night worthy of celebration, for I believe we shall soon see ourselves rich with the payment of our latest outing. I, therefore, believe we deserve more than just soup and mead." He made a quick round trip to his tent, re-joining Nia with something in his hands. "I suggest a bit of music." Holding the item up, everyone around him could see it was the same keyed harp as the one she had played at the Harvest Festival.

Nia's eyes widened with excitement.

"Here, dear maid," he said, handing it to her. "I'll make it look as if you're being given it due to your hard work amongst my crew, but let's be honest – it's because I want to hear you play it."

She smiled bashfully. "Thank you, sir."

"I've obviously acquired it most lawfully, so use it in good health."

"I most certainly will." Seating herself with the others, Nia tapped her fingers on the strings, then tightened some as she tuned it. Satisfied it was ready for use, she held the bow with a gentle grip.

Within moments, the sound of her music flooded the space. It was rich and pleasant, with the rhythm neither too fast nor too slow. The notes created intricate patterns, luscious and euphonious, but hinting a build-up of tension in the story of the piece.

Inhaling the refreshing autumn air, Nia broke out in song. The lyrics were in her native tongue, but no one cared. The members of the Unn cheered, Cyrus clapping intensely at her show of talent.

Nia's mellow voice was pleasing to the ear, enjoyable even by those who had no interest in this type of entertainment. Beginning a second piece, she noticed a shadow to her left.

Gus silently passed her, sitting down on the log opposite. He held her gaze across the flickering fire as she ceaselessly played the instrument.

The chorus was intricate, bringing her pitch high and mighty to then drop and relieve the heightened growth of the song. She had not performed in so long, she was initially anxious her voice would not hold, but it was solid throughout. Not one pitch soured; not one word erroneously sounded. It was like she had never stopped; as if her travels from Kanadesh had only happened the previous night.

Nia always had the habit of closing her eyes as she played or sung. She would be wholly engrossed in the world of the song so that nothing around her could bring her down. But today, she could not refrain from watching the man on the other side. His unwavering eye contact bore into Nia, reaching inside her soul. The softness of his features was oddly opposing his ardent gaze.

Her music continuously resonated amongst the camp, but her thoughts were still focused on the one man to ever draw her attention.

Why did he come? If he wanted nothing to do with her, then why would he return? This was not the end of their story.

I will know you, Gus. One day.

21

WIDOW

L ee entered his aunt's house after being summoned due to a sudden turn in her state of health. Anaya followed him, placing herself behind him as they joined her bedside.

Corliss was lying on her back, her arms resting on the covers. She smiled as she noticed her nephew. "Oh, sister," she sighed, grabbing his hand. "Please, tell me you have turned down working for that horrid man."

Looking around at the Matriarch, Lee was unsure of what to say.

"She might be delirious as she nears the end," Anaya suggested.

"Aunt Corliss, it is I, Lee. Not your sister. My mother is not here."

"Rubbish, Katelyn. I can see you clear as day." Corliss clasped his hand tightly. "And never did the House of Bao take care of you." Reaching up, she gently caressed his cheek. "Never."

"I-I do not understand what you mean, aunt Corliss."

"He may have said he loved you, but he never did! All lies, sister. See where it got you. Back here with-" She coughed painfully, drawing a coarse breath as it finally settled. "Only to live out your days here with me. Why not find someone else?"

"She is not making any sense," Lee said. "Of whom do you speak, aunt Corliss?"

"The Peer, of course! Forget about him. Never shall he settle for someone like yourself, an underprivileged girl of low birth." She cleared her throat, her voice low and strained. "Katelyn... find happiness. You are young and beautiful. Do not let this trial beat you."

With tears slowly trickling down his face, the boy sunk to his knees. "Thank you for everything, aunt Corliss."

She suddenly blinked, as if realising who he was. "Worry not, young Lee. I would have taken you in regardless of your mother's situation. I only wished she had... been able to heal."

"Heal?"

"Yes... Her..." The woman's eyes were slowly closing, her grip on his hand loosening. "Broken..." A ragged wheeze left her body, then she lay perfectly still.

Anaya stepped forward, kneeling down next to the young man. "I am so sorry, Lee," she whispered, soothingly hushing him. She silently embraced him, allowing the boy to sob against her chest.

"I have nothing," he cried, tears flowing freely across his cheeks. "I am truly alone."

Releasing him, Anaya planted her hands on either side of his face. "That is not true," she told him. "You have us now. We shall be your family from now on."

Edric sent the stable hands away as he arrived back at the Temple village together with Kaedin and Benjamin. They knew they would most likely have to be quarantined with the scouts, so he wished for them to be alone as they stowed their horses.

As the group had travelled away from towns and the general populace, the trip back had taken over a week. With his sword still strapped to his back, Kaedin removed the last of his gear from his mount. It was a sturdy warhorse, with a broad chest and strong legs. The coat was a bright chestnut colour, but it transitioned into white with the feathering at the fetlock. The beast was an older gelding, and he had been the former Knight's trusted companion for almost fifteen years.

Snorting, the horse shook its head, sending the mane whipping across its neck.

"In retrospect, I am happy I lent the horse out," Kaedin said.

"You mean before the demons attacked our village?" Edric asked.

"Aye. He would have been dead otherwise. You end up bonding with them, you know."

"I know what you mean." The young man brushed along his stallion's head when the beast suddenly pulled its ears back.

Kaedin smiled, stopping just short of its reach. "As friendly as always, your Grey."

Edric swore softly. "Damned horse. I pray he shall never sire foals."

"Better keep him locked up then. We will have additional mares arriving in the new year."

Edric shut the door to Grey's box, sliding the bar across. "Shouldn't be an issue. He has never liked another horse in his life."

"You know your steed best," Kaedin acknowledged. "Are you ready to report to Congress?"

"I am, but should we walk in as if nothing has happened?"

"We will approach the Temple, but we shall see as we arrive."

✶✶

With the Temple cleared, the members of Congress stood below the statue of the Goddess, and Edric, Kaedin and Benjamin were positioned at the other end of the great hall. The only one missing was Leo.

"Report your findings," Adena said, her voice echoing within the room.

"We second the opinion of the scouts," Kaedin declared. "We find no evidence of a struggle, or anything pointing to a staggered decline of health amongst the inhabitants. There were no burials or burnt corpses, or anyone being tended to as if ill. They must have all died around the same time."

"They had plenty of supplies and good standards of living," Edric added. "And they were more than hidden away from society. There is no way someone would have happened upon them and done this."

"No, most certainly not," Lilith agreed. "We have received reports of multiple villages suffering the same fate during your time away."

Kaedin took a step forward. "More?"

"Yes. Another four, so far. All correspondence has been placed inside your home, so feel free to look it over as you are placed in isolation."

The former Knight looked flustered. "There is worse," he said.

"Worse?" Adena asked. "In what manner?"

"We believe the Priesthood is to be blamed for it."

"How so?"

"A demon," Kaedin stated. "He was there as we were about to leave, and he had a few things to say about us."

"From what tribe did he originate?" Lilith inquired.

"Hound, my lady," Benjamin said. "As I circled the settlement, it was the only recent scent, except for Lynx and Panther."

"This shouldn't come as a surprise," Adena sighed. "We belong at the top of the list of suspects, considering our past. We need to be vigilant as we investigate this because we stand a good chance of being retaliated against, despite having done nothing wrong."

"Indeed," Kaedin said. "I will have to interview each of my scouts before I agree to quarantine. It will allow me to continue my work." He paused momentarily, looking at the members of Congress. "Where is Leo?"

"Visiting with the Wasp tribe," Lilith told him. "I had him sent in your stead, together with Sergeant Priest Eden Huxley and several of my guard. Due to the recent developments, we cannot waste time."

"Agreed, my lady. How long are we to be isolated?"

"For another week," Anaya said. "Your home has been prepared for the two of you. Benjamin will be placed with the other scouts."

★ ★

A separate bed had already been brought into Kaedin's home, as he would now share the house with Edric. Vixen had been less than pleased with her inability to meet with her husband, but she knew it had to be done. They spoke from afar after the congress meeting, the young man blowing kisses to his daughter as Vixen held her in her arms. It was all they could do for now.

One week. They would manage.

Before locking the door behind them, Kaedin had performed extensive hearings with his scouts. He was determined to see it through, accumulating information about every vital aspect. Ready to take on the investigation, he prepared his reception room. The space had already been dressed as an office, with a wide desk at the far end. The walls held several tall bookshelves, packed with various tomes and scrolls. There were a single armchair and a decent sized table before the fireplace, but the rest of the room was simply furnished with no decorations.

Unfolding a map on the table, Kaedin began marking out all the affected villages. In no way could this be connected to land issues, now being so many. It had to be something else, but what?

It didn't make any sense. If it was a natural plague, then why would there be unaffected settlements situated amongst those perished? A native disease would move in a more predictable pattern, even if there were a slight tendency to this having spread first north, then west.

"Edric," Kaedin said. "Could a criminal band orchestrate something such as this?"

Traversing the room, Edric sat down in the armchair. "A band?"

"Aye. Such as the one you were once part of."

"I suppose," Edric shrugged. "If they were paid enough. Most human gangs, at least back when I was active, would stay away from demons though. Working under the cover of darkness sort of gets lost when fighting against Darkness itself."

Kaedin chuckled. "Indeed, it does. It begs the question if someone would have fallen for a hefty amount. And if so, who would they be and, more importantly, who is their employer?"

"Either the band is relatively new," Edric suggested. "Or they are well-established. Purely due to the secretiveness of this, I would wager on the latter."

"I believe you right." Kaedin walked over to his desk, sifting through a heap of letters. "I have an idea."

"What is that?"

It took some time, but the older man eventually found what he was looking for. Re-joining Edric at the table, he made further notes on the map. "I know who travels these lands. There is a pattern to be had, and I shall find it. Ask for your wife to be summoned again, for I need her to run an errand."

Benjamin sat on his bed, looking out a small gap between the window shutters. The sun was setting, but it made little difference. Nearly a week had passed, and he had yet to leave the confines of the cottage. He shared it with another three scouts, all sleeping in the same room, with the adjoining space used for eating and leisure. He currently found himself alone, the others still gathered after dinner.

"Benjamin."

The sound originated from outside the window.

"Yes?" he replied.

"Oh, good. You are there."

Benjamin's expression tightened. "Is that you, Lee?"

There was a brief silence before he spoke. "Yes."

"Are you alright?"

Lee's breath caught. "No."

Noticing the boy was upset – his voice breaking and sniffling with each word – Benjamin asked, "What is going on?"

"My... my aunt."

Benjamin exhaled. "Has she passed?"

"Yes."

A heaviness spread within Benjamin's chest. "My most heartfelt condolences, Master Victor. I understand she meant a lot to you."

"She did."

Holding a hand up against the shutters, Benjamin's heart ached for the young boy. "I would console you if I could, my friend. I hate to hear you upset in this manner."

There was a muffled sob, but no answer.

"I meant to tell you," Benjamin continued. "I have prepared fabrics for additional clothing for yourself. They are to be of higher quality in their design, for special occasions. Obviously, this precarious situation I have gotten myself into has not allowed me to finish the garments."

"Th-thank you. It... is fine."

"Of course, I would not expect any other answer from yourself," Benjamin said. "But I intend to get out of here and finish the clothing ahead of your aunt's funeral. I shall have you look immaculate on the day."

Lee released a laugh. "I am sure you will."

"You can bet on it. Now, dry your tears. Your aunt would not wish to see you unhappy as she travels to the afterlife. You need to celebrate her life, not mourn her passing."

"I-I shall try."

"I know you will." Benjamin hugged his knees as he leaned forward. "I am sorry I could not tell you of my real profession."

"You need not apologise," Lee said, his voice clearing up. "It was not for you to reveal."

"No, it was not," Benjamin concurred. "But I feel as if I have deceived you."

"But you are a tailor as well," Lee argued. "So it is not a lie."

The man chuckled. "No, I suppose not. At least you know now, as we will most likely see each other plenty of times going forward. I am a source of information to both General Priest Kaedin Reed and the new Matriarch."

"I see."

"And I will send word for you, as soon as I resume my tailoring."

"Thank you," Lee said. "I am sorry if I disturbed you, I just did not know who to turn to."

Benjamin smiled. "You will always be welcome in my home, Master Victor. Come whenever you want."

"I really appreciate it." Lee rose outside the window. "I should head back; otherwise, the Matriarch will start searching for me."

"You do that. I shall see you soon."

Lilith had not met with Kaedin for over three weeks, but the man had finally been released from quarantine. Leo had arrived earlier in the day, so she was most likely to hear of the progress with the Wasp tribe. She was excited to listen to the news, as the wasps had initially been unwilling to deal with the Priesthood. After the Fox tribe had joined, they sent word of their possible change of heart. It only confirmed her beliefs that the more tribes joined in, the more likely it was for additional ones to swear allegiance.

The real trials would be faced when they were to seek out the stronger tribes, such as the nomadic wolves, and the hard-hearted bears of Rover.

The Peeress had little hope for the Iguana tribe to the north. After the murder of Typhos, they would prove hard to entice. The Priesthood had believed the lizards to be of southern origin, but the main part of them lived further north than Ovena, most of their settlements spread out in Tilea. They would prove a great ally, but it was highly unlikely they would even reply to their request of an audience. It had been over a month since that was issued, and the Priesthood was yet to hear from them.

There was a knock at the door. "Come in," Lilith said.

Her manservant stepped through, followed by Kaedin. "General Priest Kaedin Reed, my lady."

"Very good. You may leave, Arax."

The attendant bowed, then exited the room.

"Come forward, Master Reed."

He joined her, seating himself in the armchair opposite.

"Tell me about your progress. I have prayed for good news."

The officer smiled. "Indeed, I have those to offer, my lady."

She grinned wide in response. "Excellent. I take it, they accepted."

"Aye, and sent a representative with Leo on the way back. She has been given accommodation and intends to sit in during Congress tomorrow."

"Even better!" Lilith exclaimed. "Who did they send?"

"Peeress Ninne Eldra."

Her eyes widened. "Really?"

"Aye," he upheld. "Did I understand it correctly, that she is the youngest sister of their Matriarch?"

"The very one," Lilith beamed. "I am more than surprised, and honoured, of course."

"Indeed. I feel that we perhaps will have to offer her finer housing in the future, but for now, she is in one of the officer's buildings."

"We will have to discuss it further," Lilith said. "I shall voice the subject in Congress."

Kaedin sat in silence for a moment. "May I ask something, with the risk of sounding uneducated."

Clasping her hands, the Peeress gained an inquisitive look. "Go ahead, Master Reed. I shall answer as well as I can."

"Why is it different between tribes, with some having only a Patriarch or Matriarch, whereas others, like the panthers, have both?"

Her expression softened. "It is either due to the lineages of Primes, or merely tradition. Wasp Primes are only ever female; Lions only ever male. Panthers come with both female and male counterparts, thus our inclination to having both titles, and with equal power. Similar differences can be found in how Primes bond with their consorts, and how strong their connections become. Depending on the type of demon, they might bond with many, such as with lions; or they might bond with none, for instance with bears."

"I see." Kaedin's gaze momentarily turned distant. "That gives plenty to consider. Thank you, my lady."

"It is a steep learning curve, consolidating humans and demons," Lilith granted. "Do not ever hesitate to ask."

"No, my lady," he replied.

"Good. What is your progress on the investigation of the dead villages?"

"I have several scouts working in the area," Kaedin told her. "Some are meant to return tonight or tomorrow, so I hope for more news then. You need only to call if you receive any before me."

"I most certainly shall, but for now…" Lilith paused, slowly inhaling as she closed her eyes. "I will enjoy an evening of recreation, with a glass of fine wine."

A recently formed thieves' band was located just west of the Capital. Vixen stood with her choice of soldiers: ten priests and seven demons strong. Eden was amongst them, leading five of his own.

Most of the members of *the Soulless* were young, some only teenagers. The leader was a man in his early thirties, having lived his whole life as a criminal. He had never been particularly good at it, which was why the Priesthood had been able to find the band so quickly. As many as possible were to be captured alive, but should they resist, they were to be put down.

The gang was camped deep in the woods, in a small clearing along a shallow stream.

Vixen stood amongst the trees, overlooking the enemy encampment.

With over thirty members, the Soulless would seemingly have the upper hand against the Commander's crew, but she knew numbers were merely that – numbers. The Priesthood had the cover of darkness, as well as the element of surprise. Additionally, they had experience and the added strength of powerful panther demons. The beasts were all of high birth, able to down a man in a single blow.

Using hand signals, Vixen motioned her soldiers forward, split into three separate groups. They were to aim for the leader since his capture, or death, would most likely cause the rest to scatter. She felt a thrilling sensation inside, the guerrilla tactics being the most exciting in ways of war.

Reaching the first tents, they could hear snoring from within. Vixen held her blade to one side, then silently entered the first shelter. Swiftly eliminating its inhabitant, she re-emerged. She flicked blood from the weapon, then slipped into the next tent.

There was a sudden scream, the man in front of her instantly rousing. He scrambled to reach his sword, but the woman drove her own into his chest. Retracting it, she hurried outside, ignoring the man as he slumped behind her.

The thieves chaotically rushed around, struggling to make sense of the sudden ambush.

Eden deflected a blow with his spear, swinging the weapon out in response. It dug deep into his opponent, blood instantly gushing out. Kicking the thug off the tip of his spear, Eden sent him crashing to the ground, then spun, driving the weapon through the back of Vixen's latest challenger.

A panther dashed between the tents, leaping onto one of the bandits. Its teeth sunk into the man's neck, ripping the flesh. Blood sprayed, the demon wasting no time before bearing down on another. Dark mists flooded the space, creating ever-increasing mayhem.

With only a few criminals left, the demons retreated, allowing the scene to come under control. Several men laid down willingly, holding their hands over their heads in surrender. Only Vixen remained standing at a far corner, her blade pointed towards their leader. Poised to attack, he stood with his legs wide as he anticipated her approach.

"Give up," she said. "And we shall let you live."

"Don't make me laugh," he challenged. "I'll be tried and found guilty, sentenced to death by hanging. Don't play dumb, you harlot."

A roguish smile spread on the Commander's face. "It was worth a try." She charged the next instant, swinging her sword down on him. She advanced like a tempest, the man struggling to parry her attacks as she gained ground. She blocked a sword thrust, then swerved as he attempted it again. Ducking under another slash, she buried her weapon in his groin. Yanking it clear, claret pumped from the wound, the femoral artery having been severed.

The man staggered backwards, feebly dropping his sword, watching in disbelief as it clanged onto the ground. His eyes flitted at Vixen, but he said nothing, a mere whimper escaping his lips.

"We can heal you if you wish, then perhaps you will have a chance of gaining leniency with the King. If not, I shall finish you off."

The leader's eyes were wild as he desperately attempted to put pressure over the deep cut. "H-heal… heal!"

Holding the tip of her blade against his neck, Vixen motioned a priest forward.

With the wound sealed, the man slumped back. He snarled as he slammed his head into the ground. "I shouldn't have done that," he huffed.

"True," Vixen said. "But I am satisfied with paying you back, even if it is merely a taste of the dread people experienced as you were about to end their lives."

The sun had set by the time Kaedin got to settle at his desk. He had still not caught up on all his paperwork, since leaving for the Lynx settlement. He let his hand travel over his head, stopping at the nape as he stretched. He could hear his spine crack with the movement before he relaxed again.

Organising the piles of various parchments, he placed his quill pen with the ink container. He would have to continue in the morning, for he was exhausted. Leaning forward, he blew the candle out, then rose.

There was a sudden knock on his door.

Kaedin was initially unsure if he had only imagined it. He stood unmoving for a moment, then the sound was repeated. Walking up to the entrance, he found Arax present outside.

"Peeress Lilith Fahd summons you, General," he said.

"Now?"

"Yes, your Excellency."

Kaedin felt an immediate concern but attempted to mask it. He nodded, pushing his feet into his boots before following the attendant. They walked in silence, the officer deep in thought as to what could be amiss. He considered news from the scouts being part of it, and if so, they would be grim.

Coming inside the Peeress' grand house, Arax stopped before the officer in the hallway. "She is in her chambers," he said, pointing to the stairs. "Last door on the left."

At first, Kaedin was perplexed at the statement, glancing at the manservant as if double-checking its validity.

Arax' features displayed nothing but calm composure in return. Not even as Kaedin raised an eyebrow to further show his scepticism would the manservant's expression soften.

With a shrug, the officer decided to humour him, accepting the peculiar directions.

The lateness of the hour alone was reason enough for the odd choice of venue. Ascending the stairs, he strode down the corridor as instructed. He knocked, and was immediately invited into the bedroom, then stopped just past the threshold.

The room was spacious, featuring a large bed at one end. It had tall bedposts supporting several layers of canopied fabrics. On the walls hung paintings depicting diverse landscapes – anything from steppe lands to grassy plains and deep forests – the skies radiant with the colours of dawn.

Lilith was seated on the other end of the room, in a large armchair beside the fireplace. Her legs were crossed neatly at the ankle as she silently watched the flames. She was wearing a simple black gown made from silk, the fabric glistening in the dim light.

"You called on me, my lady," Kaedin said.

She turned to look at him. "Indeed, I did, Master Reed."

The man had arrived as he was, since he had believed the matter to be urgent. He stood at attention, his legs wide and his hands behind his back. He was wearing a black linen shirt and a pair of grey trousers.

Leaning back in her seat, Lilith allowed her eyes to scrutinise him. "How old are you?" she inquired.

Kaedin paused before replying. "I will be forty-three in a couple of months, my lady. Why?"

"I see." She clasped her hands on her knee. "Come, take a seat. Be at ease, if you will."

The officer did as she asked.

The Peeress' eyes never failed to trace him. "I am a widow, as you know," she went on.

"I am aware, your Highness."

Lilith smiled. "I am royalty no longer. You need not refer to me as such."

"As you wish," he granted. "Why did you summon me?"

"I have been alone for a very long time, Master Reed," she said. "I wish to be so, no longer."

The man raised an eyebrow. "And you want me to solve this how?"

There was a moment of silence as she watched him. "Bed me."

Kaedin jerked in his seat. "Bed you? My lady, I am a high-ranking officer within the Priesthood. It would be unbecoming of me to participate in illicit practice."

"You do not find me attractive?" she asked, her eyes piercing him.

He smirked. "You are indeed beautiful, as I am sure you are already aware."

"Master Reed, I have been alone now for most of my adult life. I have lived purely for the sake of my tribe, devoting myself to it wholly, and sacrificing all of which was mine. As formally retired, I am now to live out my days enjoying what time I have left." The woman moved forward in her seat, her arms resting over her legs. "As such, I would want the intimacy of a man."

The officer remained silent, holding her gaze. She was indeed serious with her intentions.

"I know you are a military man. This would not be your first time."

258

He chuckled. "No, it would not."

"Then, do you accept?" Rising smoothly from her seat, Lilith stepped forward, placing herself between his legs.

Kaedin's throat turned dry, his inherent reaction unexpectedly foreign. It was long since he felt as though his nerves were just below the surface of his skin, and the effect readily gained on him. She shattered every imaginable defence he had built through the years, with her dark, intense eyes focused solely on himself.

Reaching behind her neck, the Peeress pulled at the strings of her dress. It instantly slid over her shoulders, gathering around her bare feet.

Kaedin found himself unable to avert his eyes from her curvaceous body. He knew she was thirteen years his senior, but in no way was she appearing her age. She had a slim build with a narrow waistline but was wide at the hips. Her round breasts were perfectly formed, the nipples raised as she stood naked before him.

It was over twenty years since he had last laid with a woman. He was still in the army then, where such acts were less frowned upon. Finding himself devoted to the Goddess, under the guidance of the late High Priest, he had lived the life of a bachelor. It never bothered him, for that was the fate of those truly committed to the cause.

Lilith bent down, deftly unbuttoning Kaedin's shirt, curious to see how he would react. With the clothing opened, she gently caressed his broad chest, feeling the soft hair centred on his sternum. Grabbing his belt buckle, she slid the leather through, leaving the strap unfastened.

The man had still not moved or said a word, his arms motionless on the armrests.

Undoing the buttons on his trousers, she left them closed. Instead, she rested her hand atop the fabric, delicately cradling his groin. She leaned forward, elegantly circling his neck and pulling him in. Assuring their lips would meet, she felt the roughness of his beard on her skin.

Kaedin's heart raced in his chest as he gritted his teeth. He knew it was wrong, yet the temptation was too great. Her striking beauty was uncommonly arousing, her face alone enough to melt the heart of any man.

Lilith felt how his lips parted, the officer coming forward to meet her. She smiled with content, the excitement instantly building. Their kiss deepened, yet remained slow and sultry, further weakening his resistance. She knew she had him.

Running her fingers through his dark blond hair, the short strands ruffled under her touch. He was so different from those of the Panther tribe, so human with his looks and preconceptions. He was everything she would never have wanted, but she found herself infuriatingly provoked at the mere thought of having him. It was the entirety of the man that caused her to yearn for him. His chiselled body, powerfully built and exuding authority; his rugged looks, battle-hardened and scarred.

Pushing Kaedin's shirt over his shoulders, Lilith disengaged from him, her eyes slitted with lust. She grabbed at the sleeves, guiding his arms upwards as she pulled him free of the garment. She flung it aside, straddling him. With her legs spread over his, she guided his hand to one of her breasts, then returned to wantonly kissing him.

Kaedin planted a hand behind her neck, intensifying their contact. Their tongues circled each other, her hot breath laced with wine. He inhaled the enticing scent of her hair, the perfume rich and heady. He felt her hands trailing down his body, and he shivered with arousal. There was nothing he could do, his body responding to her sensual touch regardless of his attempts to thwart it.

Slipping her hand beneath the waistline fabric of his trousers, Lilith attempted to mask her grin. She saw how he clenched his jaw as she fondled him, and she relished in her power over him. Feeling his shaft swell in her hand, the longing for him was all the more profound. Ever since she first envisaged bedding him, she had craved this moment.

Caressing her body, her skin felt smooth as silk. Kaedin couldn't stay away, reaching in between her legs, and gently massaging her inner lips. She was warm, feeling slick and saturated on his fingers. His mouth cracked open, an audible exhale leaving him through a short pause in their vivid kissing. The officer unexpectedly found himself longing for her to sheathe him, for the two of them to become one. He watched her expression, the woman sighing softly with his touch.

They tantalised each other, to the point of becoming unable to return each other's kisses. Yet neither of them would back down, so engrossed in their quest to satisfy the other. But Lilith was not about to let the opportunity slip. She wanted more of him – all of him. She wanted to enjoy him inside her.

With a hold on his beard, she locked eyes with the man. They both remained silent as she simply opened his trousers. With the generous armchair allowing for her to slide her knees down the side of his legs, she instantly enveloped his erection.

Kaedin released a groan with the sensation, holding on to her hips as she moved over him. Her lush centre was like a burning flame in the cold night, a sense of relief overcoming him as he relaxed. The thought of their union caused him to ache with trepidation, enabling him to leave all his morals and beliefs behind.

Lilith's voiced breaths quickened as she clung to his shoulders, rising and falling over his satisfying shaft. She undulated against him, again and again, whipping her hair back over her shoulder. Her fingers dug into his skin, pressing against his solid muscles. She pulled at him, demanding more without wording it.

Lifting himself, Kaedin matched her, joining the rhythm as he breached her. With a hand forcing her down against him, he used the other to fondle one of her supple breasts, his thumb outlining the nipple. He found himself utterly lost in the waves of gratification, fighting against his soaring need for release. The woman offered something he had thought was part of his past, yet which now so blatantly weakened his resolve.

Lilith swirled over him, her soft moans escaping with every movement as she rubbed herself against him. Sweat was pearling on her skin, transferring onto the man. Lavishing in his body, she craved it all. She wanted to watch him move, feel his muscles, listen to his coarse, hushed voice. Every last thing brought her all the more pleasure, in the moment of their blissful union.

Kaedin pressed kisses to her chest and neck, building his pace plunging into her, again and again. As the passionate twosome intertwined with one another, he increasingly took charge. It was above and beyond Lilith's expectations that he would so easily ignore her social status. At that moment, they were equal, and he treated her as a real woman.

Both of them seemingly lost control, drowning in ecstasy as they thrust against each other, wholly immersed in the purest of lust.

The Peeress cried out, shuddering, his roughened treatment of her enhancing her elation. She dared not hold back, riding out her climax without a single thought to who might listen in on their union. Lilith cared not, for she had received all that she wanted; or even *more* than she desired. Kaedin had shown her unwavering courage, unleashing his carnal urges despite who she was.

The last vestiges of her peak still sang in her veins as the man continued to thrust into her. A riveting groan burst from his chest as he most heatedly spent himself inside her.

Licking her lips, Lilith leaned back, meeting his gaze yet again. His eyes looked feverish, and his jaw was slack as he attempted to catch his breath.

Grinning wide, her triumph over the man was complete. "I take that as a yes... Master Reed."

22

CORRUPTION

I t was dawn. Placed in the centre of Samael and Anaya's courtyard, the funeral pyre quickly consumed Corliss' body of flesh. The flames roared as they reached for the skies, bright and churning. The new Patriarch and Matriarch stood together with Lee, silently watching the Elder Shaman of Fahd. He was performing the last rites, chanting with his staff held high.

The young man was silently crying in the priestess' embrace.

"You will always have a place with us," she gently consoled him. "No matter if you were to discontinue your position amongst our servants, we shall be your family from now on. Trust us when we say this."

Lee nodded but glanced at the Patriarch.

"What she says is true, boy," Samael said. "You are not to walk alone."

The flames flickered, twisting into a roll, like a giant wave continuously travelling towards the shore. The shaman stepped back, looking around at the others.

There was a whisper echoing through the courtyard, the voice slow and soft. *"Prophet."*

Releasing Lee, Anaya approached the flames. She could see the outlines of a face within the blaze, the features feminine. "Yes, Spirit?"

"Great perils await in the Darkness, amongst reverberating hate and nefarious

echoes. Free yourselves from the bonds of dualism; abate the taint from the champions of Light, for the Rift is to distend as you advance amongst the unknown."

With a flash, the flames spread out, then gathered once more as they returned to their normal state.

Samael growled. "Damned Spirits and their riddles! Is that how you are to attain your prophecies now? Through the dead?"

Anaya looked bewildered, facing him. "I do not know, but it is a possibility. I only ever wonder when my life is to play out without predictions." She walked back to Lee, the young man still in tears. "I am so sorry. This overshadowed the importance of your aunt's journey to the afterlife."

"It is alright, my lady," he said. "I am amazed, more than anything."

"What about?"

"That she spoke to us… That the prophecy was given by no other than *the Spirit of Corliss.*"

Despite the rainy season, it looked to be a sunny day. Lilith was walking the distance to the new Royal mansion, about to join Anaya for an additional conference with the Master Primes. Samael was not going to be present, having already left for the House of Ziva.

Arax walked behind her, as well as three of her guard. She had decided to lessen the amount of protection since her current occupation was less hazardous than that of a Matriarch.

Lilith had not once been challenged since she assumed the role, only sixteen years old at the time, yet she had never taken her safety for granted. As the sole ruler, she had always strived for being attentive, but at the same time, she had to be strict and uncompromising. As such, there had not been a single man who had ever neared her, perhaps in fear of her just punishment for insubordination.

Shivers coursed through her body as she thought of the previous night. Kaedin's actions after their union had been immaculate. He had merely redressed, then showed reverence before excusing himself. There had been no signs of the man being uncomfortable. Instead, he acted as though he had attended a regular meeting with herself. His reaction was above and beyond what she had imagined, much pleasing to her.

Walking through the entrance hall, she was welcomed by Anaya and the Master Primes, all ready to begin another meeting. The Matriarch sat on an elaborate chair, with Lee standing behind her.

Placing herself beside Anaya, Lilith looked at each of the Master Primes, the men and women silently sitting in rows before them. There was a palpable nervousness about them, but the Peeress attempted to ignore it.

"Welcome," she said, sitting down beside Anaya, in an equally intricate, albeit larger, chair. "I will start by saying this will not be a gathering equal to any we have held before. First, we shall hold a discussion to – frankly – clear the air as to the doubts raised by some of those here today. And second, I am to present the evidence against those imprisoned for treason."

Not unlike during their last meet, many of the Primes looked even more uncomfortable at the mere mention of the traitors.

"This is your opportunity to voice your concerns, Primes," Lilith stressed. "Speak freely; I cannot possibly do it for you."

"At what risk, though?" asked the Master Prime of Exely, dragging a hand through his short hair. "Surely, you realise what is on the line for each of us, should we speak out of term. An attack of words may not be cause for grace."

"Most often not, Pero," Lilith granted. "Yet, today is that day. For our tribe to move forward, there needs to be transparency amongst us. There is no room for scabbling amongst ourselves when bigger obstacles are at hand."

Pero forced saliva down his parched throat. "I shall start there then," he cryptically began, shooting glances at the two Primes seated on either side of him. "Everyone has heard the rumours. How do we know the Priesthood is not behind decimating all those demon settlements?"

Anaya blinked, her mouth agape at the accusation. "You think the Priesthood is to blame? That they would execute such a scheme?" she questioned.

"Can you deny it?" Pero challenged, his firm words contradicting the sweat now pearling on his forehead. "One looks to another's past conduct in order to predict their future behaviour. The same goes for you, Matriarch or not. You are a human – a priestess. You have killed demons your entire life; *slaughtered* us, whenever given a chance. How are we to ever truly trust your intentions? You might as well have planned your rise to power, as a means of gaining control over a mighty demonic tribe, merely as some sort of distasteful experiment. If that were the case, you would have been very successful, indeed."

A hum, mixed responses of ayes and nays, sounded amongst the Primes. Had they held this discussion before?

Stumped – not only at Pero's words but also by the others' unexpected reactions – the priestess felt her hands go damp, her heart thumping wildly in her chest. "I would never! Samael-"

"Prime Samael would never admit to any suspicion," interjected the demon seated on Pero's right. As the leader of the House of Grey, she sat defiantly tall, a fierce scowl framing her eyes. Her long hair worn up, she looked briefly at Lilith, who allowed her to elucidate. "He is bound to you; forever loyal to you, should you so conspire to kill him yourself. We cannot possibly trust his judgment."

Lilith's eyes narrowed, suspicious of where this argument would lead.

"My previous life as a priestess is no secret," Anaya desperately argued. Tears stung her eyes, but she fought against them, unwilling to succumb to her emotions. She could not show weakness, not in a time like this. Such a display would only be cause for more doubt in the Primes. "I am not proud of my actions, and neither is the rest of the Priesthood! I beg forgiveness for my sins, to the Goddess and the Spirits alike."

"To the Goddess, you say?" Pero echoed, throwing his arms out. "You hold her higher than any of our Spirits! And your position as an officer amongst your Priesthood only makes it clear you have no intention to fully engross yourself in our tribe."

"I am not to abandon anyone, human or demon," Anaya told him, her expression growing severe. "All of you know I have prioritised the Panther tribe. In no way have I forsaken you; I would never allow it for you to stand unaided! And neither would Samael!"

Another set of whispers took hold, but none of the Primes offered a direct response to her statement. Did her pleas fall on deaf ears?

"Speaking of Samael," another Prime chimed in, now the one seated on Pero's left. He shared gazes with plenty of those gathered. "How do we know he is restored from the feral? We believed it once, and it turned out to be false. But now, we are meant to trust him yet again?"

"I cleared the taint caused by the late High Priest," Anaya quickly replied, praying they would believe her. She slammed her foot down on the floor, the wooden floorboards creaking. Would everything she offered only be met by resistance? Were their minds already set? "I swear, you have nothing to fear as to his mental stability, Beren."

"As long as you do not cause him to enter a feral state on purpose," scoffed the Master Prime of the House of Grey.

And there it was, Lilith thought to herself. "That's enough, Kelli!" she rumbled in disapproval, mists flowing out from under the hem of her skirt. "It is one thing to bring up issues you have with the Matriarch's background, but a whole other to accuse her of treasonous plans of her own!"

Kelli reddened, but her countenance would not shed its severity. "We lack faith in her," she hissed through clenched teeth. "And I cannot be ruled by someone I do not trust!" Balling her fists, she came to her feet, Pero and Beren moving with her. Mist swirled around them, whooshing out into the room.

Lee bolted forward, and Anaya instantly rose to meet them, Light sparkling around her fingers. They all came to a halt mere feet from one another, leaving the entire group of gathered Primes shuffling out of their seats. Mists whooshed out, and each and every face present betrayed agitation, eyes bulging and brows screwed up. Had they expected this from Anaya? From a human?

A snort left Kelli, the Prime folding her arms across her chest. "See?" she said, nodding towards the priestess. "She would not hesitate to use her powers against us!"

"There was an attempt on my life, as well as that of my son's, not long ago!" Anaya cried in defence.

Lilith stood, joining the priestess' side. "Trust – as well as respect – must be earned," she said, then pointed at each of the defiant Primes. "You three have not only proved your lack of such in the new Matriarch, but have also lost that of ours."

"Very well," Pero allowed, his chin lifting in defiance as his stare bore into Lilith. "Perhaps, it is best to go our separate ways."

A collective gasp sounded inside the room. The remaining Primes – yet to openly join the discussion – sat dumbfounded. This, they had not expected, judging by their reaction. *By the Spirits, what could Pero possibly mean?*

Pero stood firm, his knuckles white as he tightened his fists. "I cannot accept the leadership of a human – let alone a priestess, part of an organisation which very well may still be out to eradicate demonkind. Unless you allow someone else to assume leadership of our tribe, then we shall stand without charge."

"Then leaderless you shall be," Lilith grimly concluded.

Leviathan took a step closer to the three rebelling Primes. "You cannot be serious, Pero!" he exclaimed, his burly frame heaving out a breath. "Have you no loyalty towards the House of Fahd anymore?"

"I am not as blind as yourself," Pero snarled in response, then looked at the priestess. "Tell us," he continued, more composed this time. "What of those who rose against you? What will become of them? *How are you to treat your subjects?*" His last question was deliberately articulated, laced with animosity.

Anaya licked her lips, choosing her words with care. "They shall have their... just punishment."

"They all confessed to their crimes," Lilith simply stated. "All those responsible are in custody. It is only a matter of convicting them accordingly."

"Which houses stand to be culled, my lady?" Leviathan enquired.

"Ziva, Caera, Knox and Onyx."

"To what extent?"

Lilith locked eyes with Anaya. "What is your verdict, your Highness?"

This was it. Repeatedly finding her suitability and integrity questioned, the priestess had dreaded this day, unsure of which way the pendulum of trust would swing. Either this would prove her worth – and, subsequently, band together their tribe – or this would be the death knell.

Unable to stall her answer any longer, Anaya sought the words, yet her mind only supplied more forboding questions. Would she indeed be the one to shatter the Panther tribe? To ruin everything Samael and Lilith had fought so diligently to reclaim? Would she ever be accepted, or her son ever recognised as heir? Was it already too late?

The young woman viewed those around her, clutching her hands before her to dampen the tremors. She took a deep breath, sending a silent prayer to the Goddess. Or perhaps to each of the Spirits?

A warmth came over her, and she suddenly felt surprisingly calm in the moment, allowing her a steady voice. "Onyx is to be eradicated. I have already spoken to Lyra. She will take over as their Master Prime, since her Consort is of the lineage, thus allowing for the name – and the house – to remain. The settlement will, therefore, be left largely unaffected." She paused, but everyone remained quiet, Pero staring at her in anticipation. "Even after extensive interrogation, there are no signs of the Master Primes in either the house of Caera or Knox actually having been aware of the uprising amongst their subjects. They are to be left alive but under tight control. The House of Ziva will be eradicated, every generation executed, and the inhabitants of their towns relocated. They will most likely move here, to the City of Fahd, since we now rule over a vast area."

One of the Master Primes in the far back cleared her throat before speaking, noticeably uncomfortable with the subject. "And when... when is this to be carried out?"

"The Patriarch has already been dispatched."

Pero swore, spittle flying in the priestess' direction. "Bah! I won't listen to another word of this!" He turned to leave but halted as Anaya called out.

"Wait! Please, you must understand-"

"Understand what exactly?" he hissed, his voice seething with anger as he faced her yet again. "How you have been Matriarch for not yet a month but have already utterly destroyed our tribe? Hundreds of years built, sundered in an instant!"

Anaya stepped forth, her dress flaring out over the floor. "You may think this is an attempt at dividing the tribe, yet it is the exact opposite! It matters not where I come from, for I shall rule according to the laws passed down by your ancestors. We will not tolerate disobedience, much less *treason* against the House of Fahd. We have respectfully heeded tradition."

Pero shook his head, his snarl showing elongated fangs. "I do not condone an assassination attempt on a mother and child, but their punishment is mere vengeance! If you truly wanted the tribe to prosper, never would you eliminate an entire Prime lineage!"

Letting out a breath, the priestess allowed herself a moment of pause.

She knew Pero's position was sound, and she too had attempted to find options for a lessened punishment, but none were to be found. Instead, she had lost; lost in the eyes of her subjects, and in her own set of morals. No matter her choice, fault would undoubtedly be found. "It may feel cruel to end the life of several youngsters, only due to the foolishness of their progenitors, but I am not to begin my rule by changing the foundations on which you have built your society for hundreds of years. Those part of Ziva knew all along what they stood to lose, should they be unsuccessful in their attempts to thwart us."

Despite the tension in the room, Lilith grinned, proud of the young woman and her conviction. Pero, on the other hand, remained unconvinced.

"I am not going to risk the life of my Consort and children running this fool's errand," he told the priestess. "If power cannot be gained by force, it shall be acquired otherwise. You will see, *Matriarch* – in time, the House of Fahd shall stand alone, and the rest of the tribe will prosper in your absence." Turning away from her, he headed for the door, Beren and Kelli stalking behind him. More Primes shifted their positions, but none dared to follow.

Clenching her fists, Anaya refused to surrender, but her body shook with trepidation. How would she ever forgive herself, were she to give up on the tribe? "We shall prove you wrong!" she shouted. "We will gain your respect, regardless of your sentiment towards us!"

Pero stood in the door for a moment, glowering back at her across his shoulder. "I highly doubt it," he said, then left before she could utter another word.

As the door firmly shut, outrage erupted amongst the Primes still present, swirling mists and undampened auras abounding.

"We should all leave!" one cried.

"Are we all to lose our lives?" another howled. "Think of our children!"

"Are you all insane?" dared a female at the back. "This is the House of Fahd! *Fahd*! Remind yourselves of whom you speak!"

"But she is a priestess! She cannot possibly be trusted!" several echoed in agreement.

The words tore into Anaya, giving way to surfacing emotions of sorrow and dismay as her thoughts centred on Samael, and how she had undeniably failed him. Tears welled, fright trickling down her spine with the unleashed demonic auras around her. In her mind's eye, she could see how the House of Fahd violently crumbled, the fragments of which now callously slipped between her fingers.

How could she ever amend this?

Many nights had been spent as Samael and Anaya had attempted to find a loophole in the law, unwilling to spill unnecessary blood. With the increasing number of demonic settlements dying from an unknown disease, it would only be a matter of time until the Panther tribe found itself affected.

Samael knew it had all been a lost cause. No matter if the two sons under the House of Ziva were both of age, it did not please him that he would have to end their lives. Present in the courtyard of the Master Prime's grand house, he searched the faces of each family member. They all stood shackled, ready for the punishment to be delivered.

The Master Prime spat on the ground. "Lucky your father is dead, so he could not watch you bring such disgrace on the House of Fahd! I hope your mongrel of a son dies a horrible death. Should he live to see his *evolution*, then let him fall to the feral and reach only the darkest depths of hell!"

Holding his gaze, Samael offered a sly smile. "Does it make you feel better at this moment, knowing you are about to die, if you offer insults to me? Perhaps, you attempt to ignore the fact that I am about to rip the hearts out of your own sons, all of which could have been prevented, had you not been so ill-advised." He watched as the other man's expression slowly changed, his anger fading as it transitioned into dismay. "My father would have been pleased to see the bloodline continued. Which is something that cannot be said for yourself, Kamden Ziva, considering your household is about to be eradicated."

"Please, your Highness!" the Consort cried. "Have mercy on my children!"

Dark mists flared out around the Patriarch as he locked eyes with her. "Your Master Prime had no intentions on having mercy on my own child. Instead, he was out to murder him, no matter the cost. I am lenient in offering you a funeral ceremony, allowing for your souls to join with the Spirits. Your deaths will be swift."

"Your despicable whore of a human wife will bring our tribe to ruin," the older son hissed. "Perhaps then, the rest of the houses will see what we saw. It is only a matter of time! Turning her into some iridescent beast may fool them, but not us!"

Samael licked his lips, dampening his aura despite his agitation. "Or perhaps the Spirits were right all along, and she shall be *the Salvation* for us all." Stepping forward, he grabbed the boy by the neck and lifted him. "May the Spirits rest your soul." Extending his claws, the Patriarch promptly burrowed his hand into his chest, clutching hold of his beating heart. Mists spewed into the torso and out through the wound before he ripped it clear.

The body slumped to the ground, the youngster's vacant eyes wide as they stared into the distance.

Dropping the bloodied heart on the ground, Samael walked over to the younger of the two brothers. He was only fourteen, yet to go through his *evolution*.

The mother wailed beside them, being held back by the guards as she attempted to reach her perished offspring.

"I am truly sorry, young man," Samael said.

"I know, your Highness," the boy sighed, smiling miserably. "Perhaps... this can be a turning point for the tribe. To unify, rather than sunder us."

Kamden cursed. "Shut up, Hayden!" he snarled.

Ignoring him, Samael held the boy's gaze. "You are wise beyond your years," he acknowledged, then grabbed around his neck. "May the Spirits bless you as you travel into the afterlife." Repeating the procedure, he ripped the boy's heart clear from his chest. Allowing for his body to drop, Samael then walked over to the Master Prime.

"You will go down in history as the man who brought the Panther tribe to *ruin*!"

Samael grinned. "At least I shall be remembered," he spat out, then his hand flashed forward.

The Unn had returned from another assignment, the regular group of four soon joined by the rest of their band. Most of them were standing as they would not fit around the small campfire. Gus sat opposite Cyrus, with Fargo and Skrill on either side. Landon, Jason and Bella sat alongside their leader, all enjoying the evening meal.

Nia had prepared meat over the fire and boiled potatoes, as well as poured plenty of mead. She found herself repeatedly glancing at Gus, but the man ignored her. A week had passed since he told her of his marriage, but he had yet to elaborate on the subject. She wondered how he could possibly have such relations being part of the Unn, as she had seen no signs of a wife during her year with them. *But why would he otherwise wear the ring?*

"Lads, we've got to talk," Cyrus stated, his expression suddenly severe.

"Sounds serious," Bella stated, her facial appearance mirroring his.

"Aye. Or at least, it could be, unless we aren't careful."

"We're always careful, boss," Jason said.

"Sure," Cyrus agreed. "But this is different. It might be nothing, but we still need to keep it in mind." He paused for a moment, flicking a bone into the fire. "The Priesthood is out hunting for thieves, and not just those acting alone, but entire gangs."

"We are officially a mercenary band though," Landon pointed out.

"Aye, but let us speak frankly; we're commissioned to break laws. As such, we are no better, despite the high-end clientele. News has reached me that *the Soulless* were slaughtered by said priests."

"Slaughtered?" Gus questioned. "By doing what? Healing them to death? I would've thought them unable to spill human blood."

"It did surprise me, I have to admit," Cyrus granted. "According to a rumour in town, they even had demons fighting alongside them. Only those surrendering were left alive, but they are to be taken to court and tried for their crimes."

"And hung, I'm assuming," Bella said.

"There's no other outcome," Cyrus concurred. "My point telling you all this is to further demonstrate why we need to be secretive, as to what we're doing, and to stay on the move. Trust me when I say, we cannot be too careful. The Priesthood is working under direct orders of the King himself, so unless we would be paid to assassinate the man, then we stand little chance if we were arrested."

"But why would they even be after criminals?" Jason asked. "Don't they have lawbreakers and the likes amongst themselves?"

"Indeed, they do. One is even an officer, as far as I've heard."

"Isn't he only meant to be some kind of petty thief?" Gus questioned.

"Mm, he is nothing like us," Cyrus said. "The Priesthood does not offer refuge to just anyone. The bandit officer is merely false advertisement."

Bella nudged the man. "Because otherwise, you'd have asked to join, right?"

He laughed. "Of course. I would *love* to wear dresses more often. Anyway, just keep it in mind. We're not to stay here for long, so don't get too comfortable. We have another outing coming up, but then I suggest we move on, as soon as we receive payment."

✷ ✷

With the meal finished, most men began to scatter, while others remained. Cyrus and his selected few had a lengthy discussion on the upcoming assignment, which was to be carried out the next evening.

Nia walked around the makeshift seating area, gathering the bowls.

Leaning forward, Gus placed a few of them on top of each other, then handed her the stack.

Surprised at the act, Nia was tentative as she reached for them. "Th-thank you," she said, her speech low. Due to the size of the man's hands, the young woman had to overlap them as she grabbed the pile. She flinched, noticing his intense gaze. In the moment, his features softened at their lingering touch, his thumbs gently brushing across her silky skin.

"It'll be nice to move on," Cyrus said, causing Gus to withdraw.

"Aye," the swordsman replied. "Are we to expect payment directly after tomorrow?"

"No, but most likely in the days to come," Cyrus answered. "Everything will need to be prepared by then, so we can travel. I would see us going further west. This particular employer has already expressed their wish for such a direction."

Bella came forward, her posture hunched. "Should we not stay clear of settlements, with the increased activity from the Priesthood?"

"Indeed, and I shall plan a route accordingly."

"Then, how will the employer even find us?" she wondered.

"No matter how far we travel, or where, I have a feeling they will. And they have promised riches beyond compare." Cyrus paused, tracing his jawline with his thumb. "We'll most likely see lots of forests ahead," he concluded. "Wet and cold, we shall be."

EPILOGUE

The wind howled, shuddering the panes of leaded glass that shielded the room from the harsh weather. The downpour was relentless, spanning several days. Fire churned in the open fireplace, but the flames incessantly fought against the whipping rain shooting down the chimney.

"We cannot remain idle," a man said. He was not of any significant stature, yet his hulking appearance was more than intimidating as he sat slumped in his chair. He drove a hand through his sable hair, the locks short and curved. "They believe in having us pinned, but we shall show them."

"Your Highness, would it not be wise to hear the other tribes?" another man said, seated below him. He, too, was of lesser height, but much slimmer than the first. "We should not stand alone against them."

"Such deals are out of the question. It mattered not when we last required aid."

"Perhaps now they will see! We have proof of their treachery."

The bulky man slapped his flattened hand on the armrest. "The tribes are too occupied with the promise of land and joint riches! Never shall they listen to reason, should it so fall directly on their heads!"

His eyes dropping to the floor, the other man was quick to show reverence. "My utmost apologies, your Highness."

"It matters not, Kryger. Summon the Master Primes. We must prepare for war."

His eyes wide, Kryger came forward in his seat. "W-war? B-but the panthers," he whined. "How are we to-"

The man interrupted his speech. "I assume you mean The Patriarch of the Panther tribe. I know he stands as their guardian, with his despicable wife a priestess." He shivered as he imagined it. "And their half-cast son; Spirits have mercy on us demons for such a union." He paused, steepling his hands on his lap. "But without his precious wife, the Prime is no more. The Priesthood cannot possibly stand against the entirety of our tribe. We will not forgive them the sins of the past or present. We have reached the end of the line."

ABOUT THE AUTHOR

Catrin Russell is a Fantasy author from northern Sweden. Her books are all written in English and are mainly part of the Epic and High Fantasy Genre. However, she does use influences from Dark Fantasy, and a touch of Fantasy Romance.

With a background in digital design and holding a degree as a registered nurse, she writes novels in medieval settings, with plenty of action and romance. She often brings moral struggles, or issues in society, into her writing. Another subject that is often highlighted is mental health.

Catrin also creates concept art, bringing her characters to life on paper, much of which can be seen on her social media pages!

Catrin's Website: http://catrinrussell.com/
Amazon Page: https://www.amazon.com/Catrin-Russell
Catrin's Blog: https://blog.catrinrussell.com/

BOOKS BY CATRIN RUSSELL

The Light of Darkness

The Power of Conviction
The Path of Salvation
The Resurgence of Light
Nefarious Echos - July 2021
Book 5 - September 2021
Book 6 - November 2021

* * *

The Light of Darkness Prequels

Righteous Dawn
The Redeemed

Made in United States
Orlando, FL
16 March 2023

31067329R10171